ANN M. MARTIN

BABY-SITTERS
LITTLE *SISTER*®

KAREN'S WITCH

A GRAPHIC NOVEL BY

KATY FARINA

WITH COLOR BY BRADEN LAMB

graphix

An Imprint of
SCHOLASTIC

For Laura Elizabeth, the newest Perkins
A. M. M.

For Maddie, my own little sister
K. F.

Text copyright © 2020 by Ann M. Martin
Art copyright © 2020 by Katy Farina

All rights reserved. Published by Graphix, an imprint of
Scholastic Inc., *Publishers since 1920.* SCHOLASTIC, GRAPHIX,
BABY-SITTERS LITTLE SISTER, and associated logos are trademarks
and/or registered trademarks of Scholastic Inc.

Library of Congress Control Number: 2019933276

ISBN 978-1-338-35611-3 (hardcover)
ISBN 978-1-338-31519-6 (paperback)

10 9 8 7 6 5 4 3 2 1   20 21 22 23 24

Printed in Malaysia   108
First edition, January 2020

Edited by Cassandra Pelham Fulton and David Levithan
Book design by Phil Falco and Shivana Sookdeo
Publisher: David Saylor

CHAPTER 1

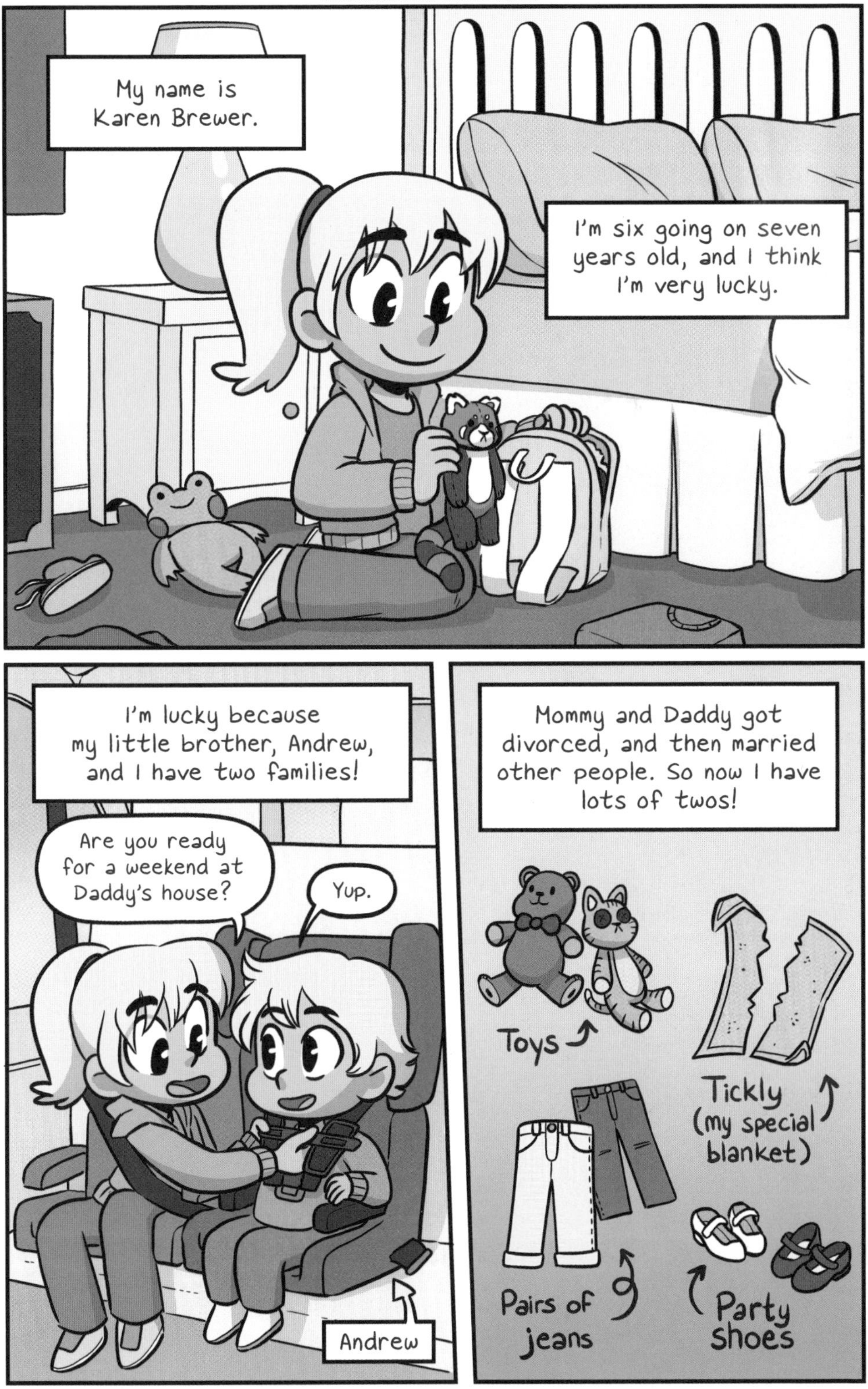

My name is Karen Brewer.
I'm six going on seven years old, and I think I'm very lucky.
I'm lucky because my little brother, Andrew, and I have two families!
Are you ready for a weekend at Daddy's house?
Yup.
Andrew
Mommy and Daddy got divorced, and then married other people. So now I have lots of twos!
Toys
Tickly (my special blanket)
Pairs of jeans
Party shoes

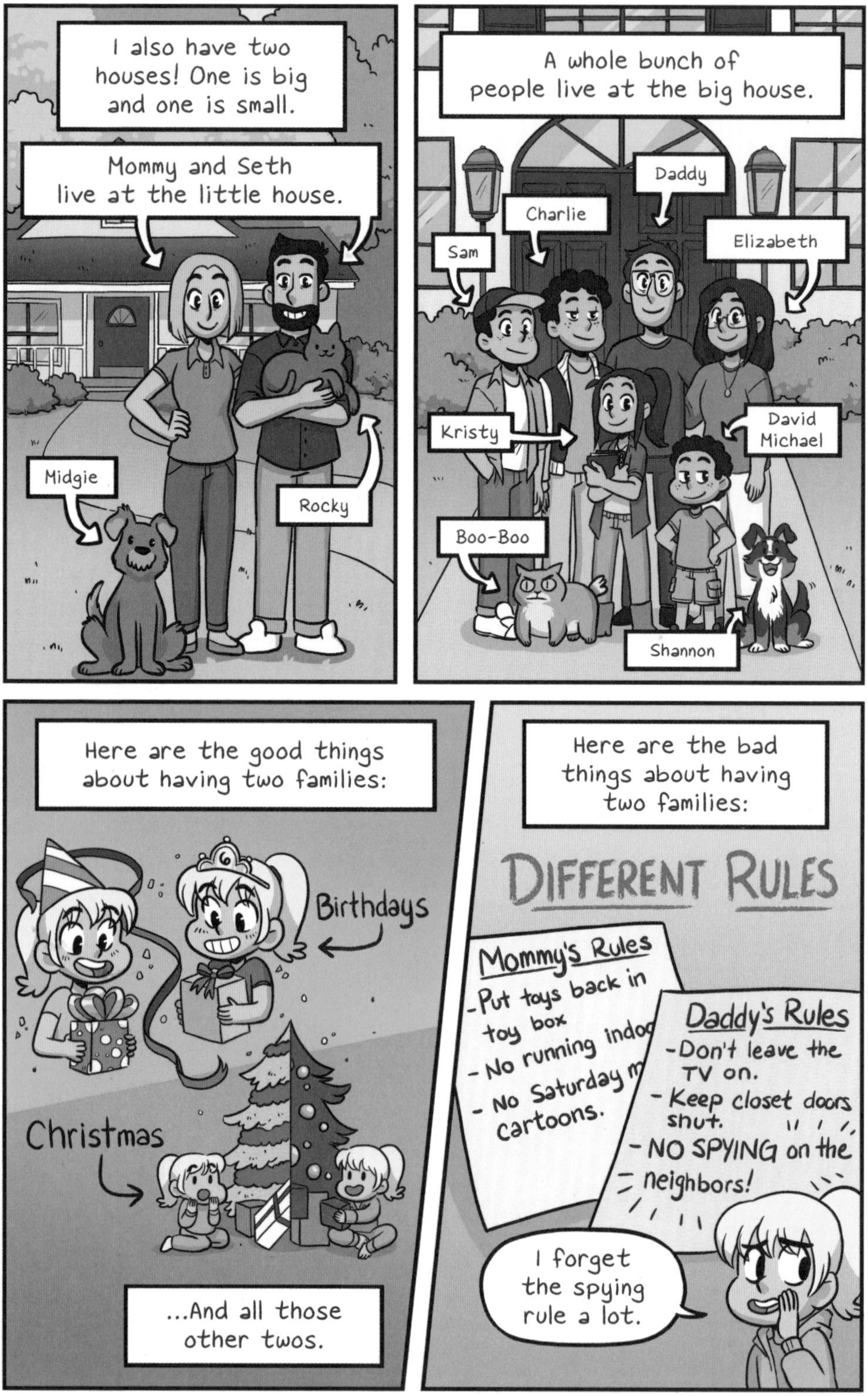

I also have two houses! One is big and one is small.
Mommy and Seth live at the little house.
Midgie
Rocky
A whole bunch of people live at the big house.
Daddy
Charlie
Sam
Elizabeth
Kristy
David Michael
Boo-Boo
Shannon
Here are the good things about having two families:
Birthdays
Christmas
...And all those other twos.
Here are the bad things about having two families:
DIFFERENT RULES
Mommy's Rules
- Put toys back in toy box
- No running indoo
- No Saturday m
cartoons.
Daddy's Rules
- Don't leave the TV on.
- Keep closet doors shut.
- NO SPYING on the neighbors!
I forget the spying rule a lot.

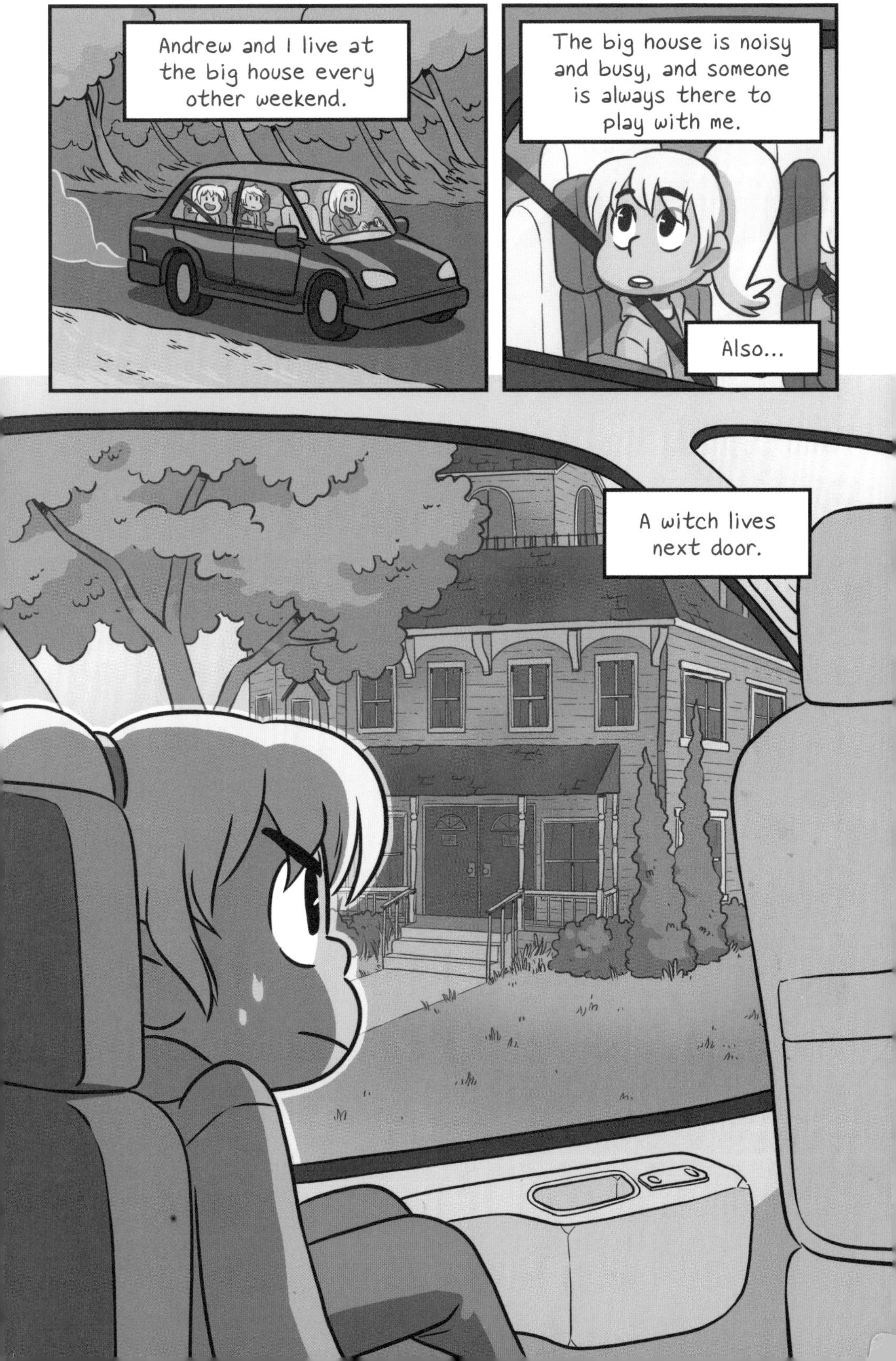
Andrew and I live at the big house every other weekend.
The big house is noisy and busy, and someone is always there to play with me.
Also...
A witch lives next door.

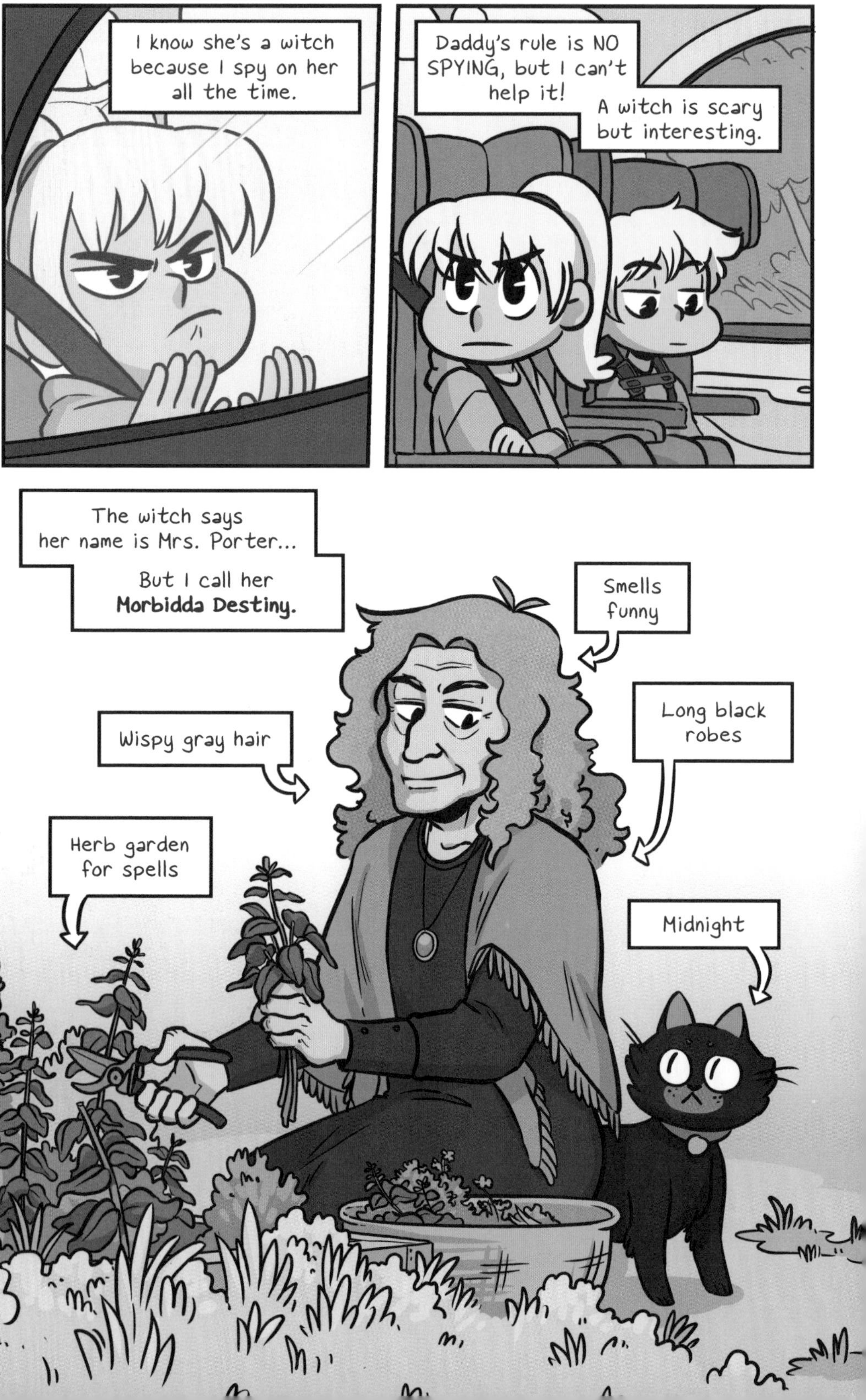

I know she's a witch because I spy on her all the time.
Daddy's rule is NO SPYING, but I can't help it!
A witch is scary but interesting.
The witch says her name is Mrs. Porter...
But I call her **Morbidda Destiny.**
Smells funny
Wispy gray hair
Long black robes
Herb garden for spells
Midnight

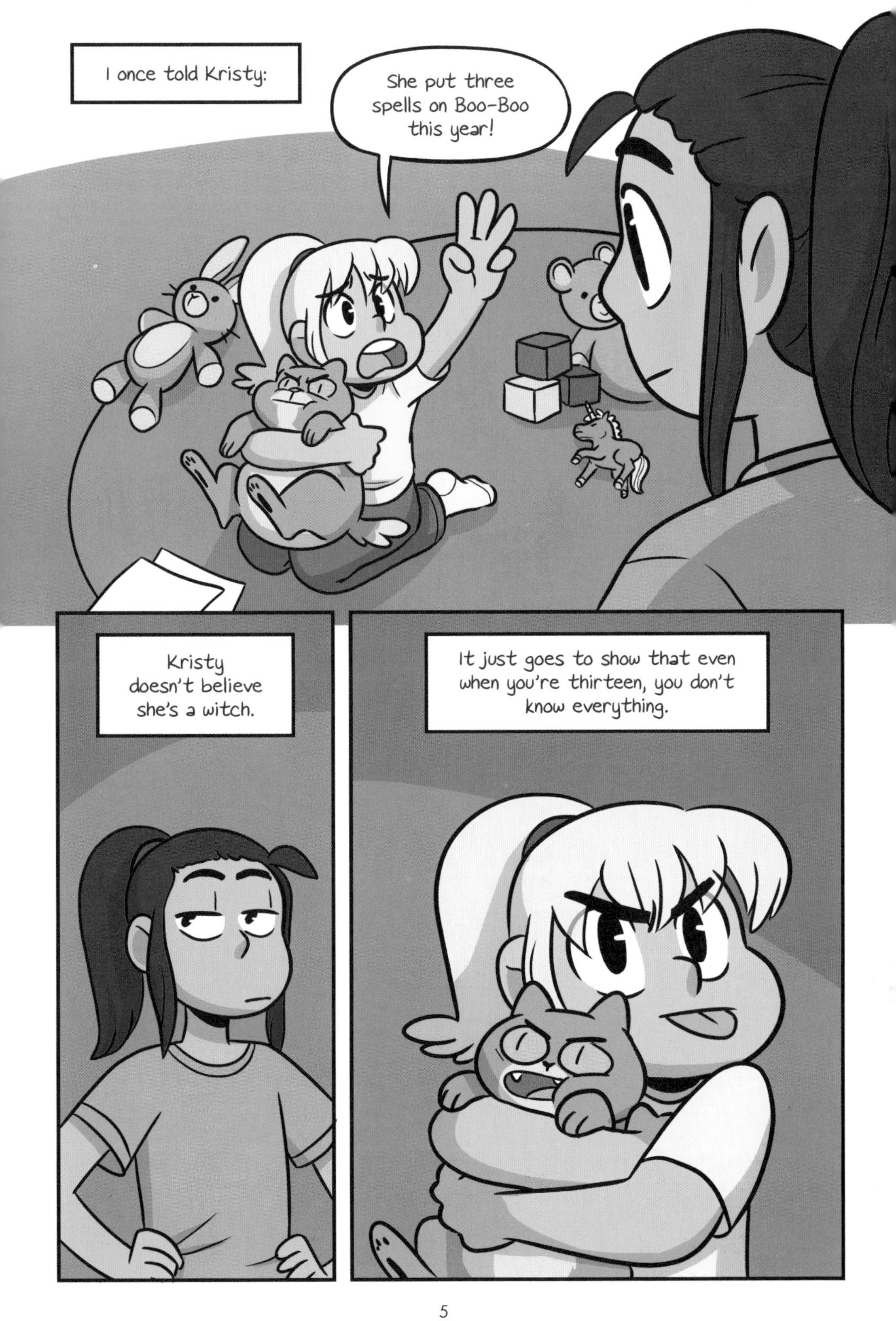
I once told Kristy:
She put three spells on Boo-Boo this year!
Kristy doesn't believe she's a witch.
It just goes to show that even when you're thirteen, you don't know everything.

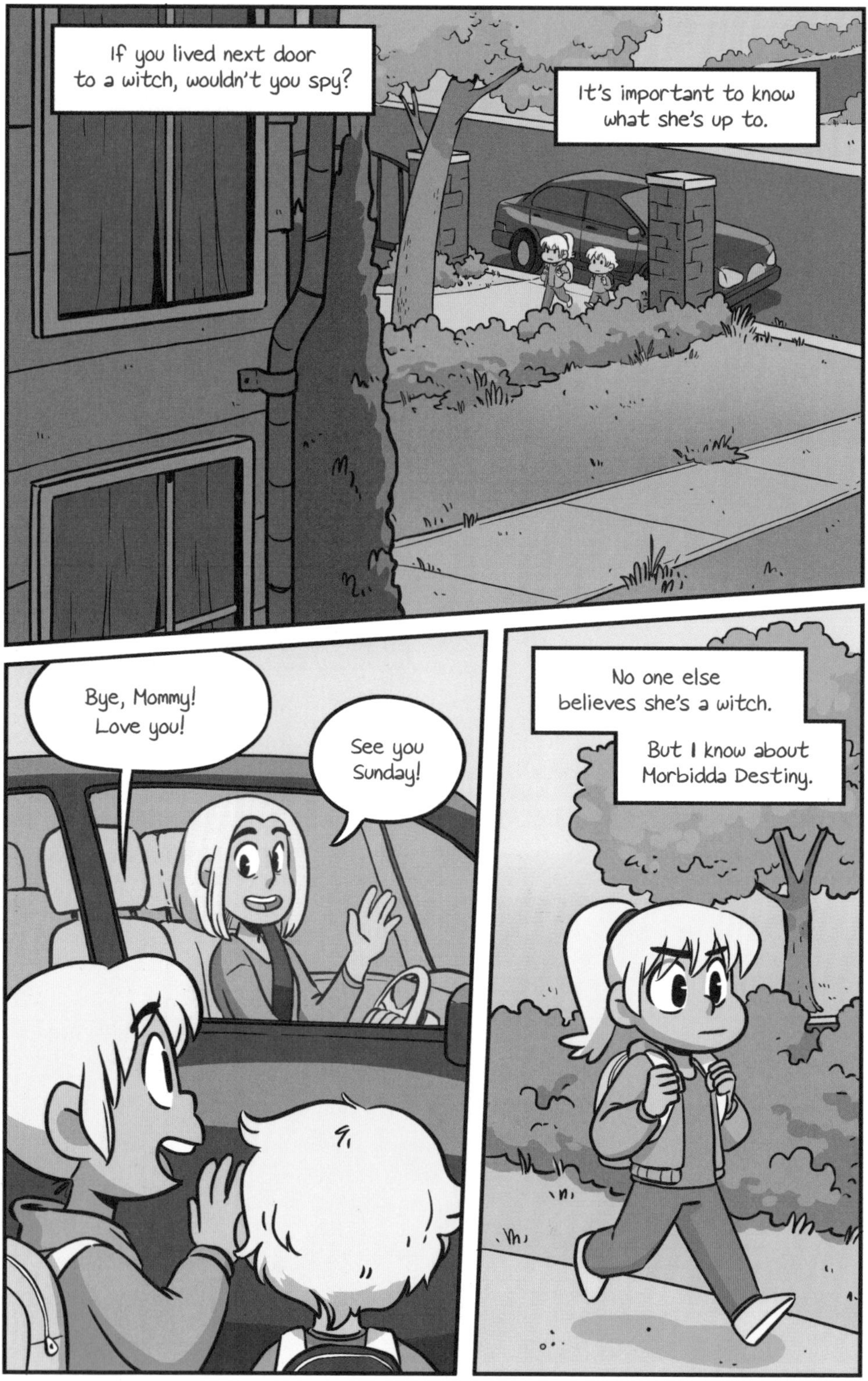
If you lived next door to a witch, wouldn't you spy?
It's important to know what she's up to.
Bye, Mommy! Love you!
See you Sunday!
No one else believes she's a witch.
But I know about Morbidda Destiny.

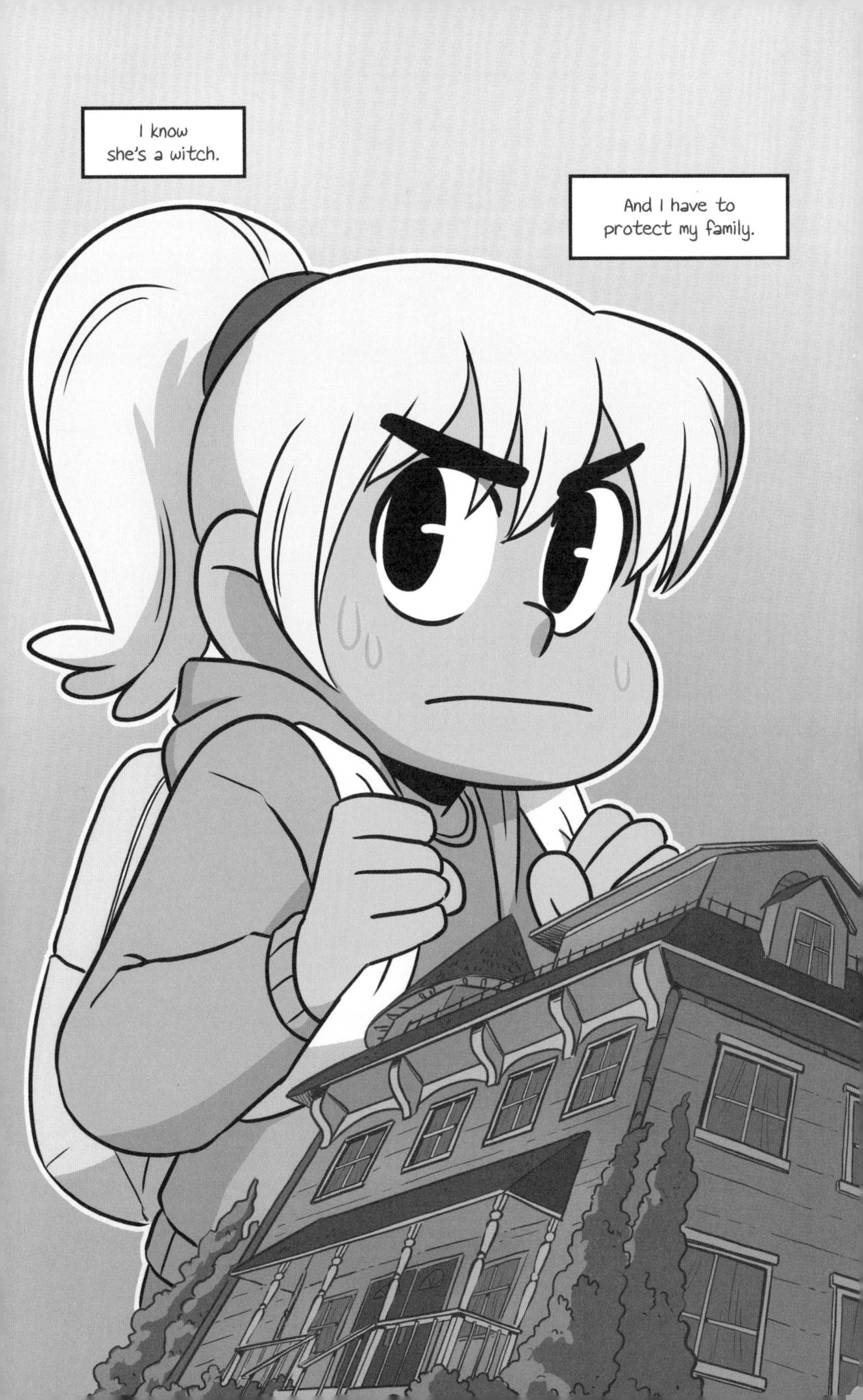
I know she's a witch.
And I have to protect my family.

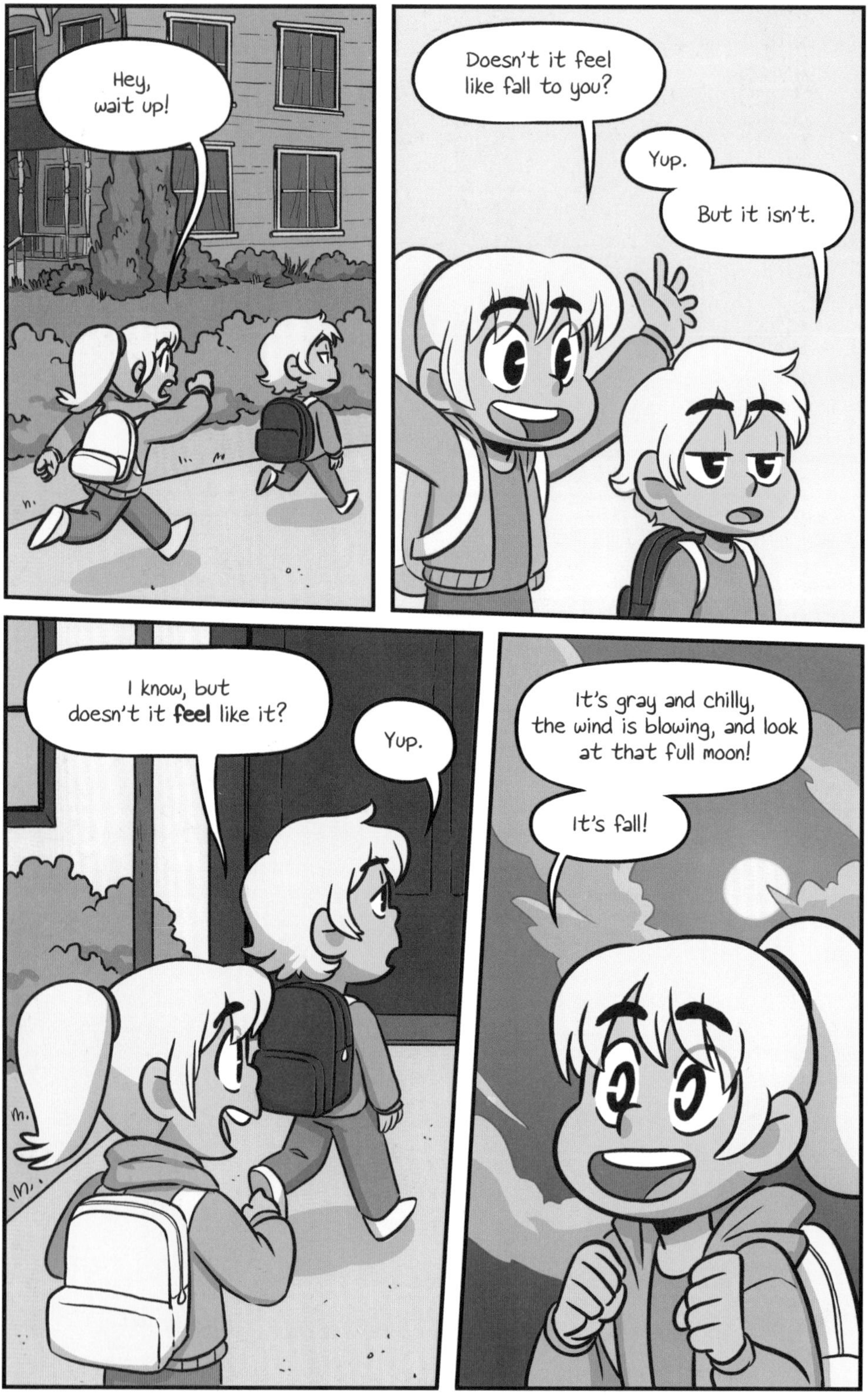
Hey,
wait up!
Doesn't it feel
like fall to you?
Yup.
But it isn't.
I know, but
doesn't it **feel** like it?
Yup.
It's gray and chilly,
the wind is blowing, and look
at that full moon!
It's fall!

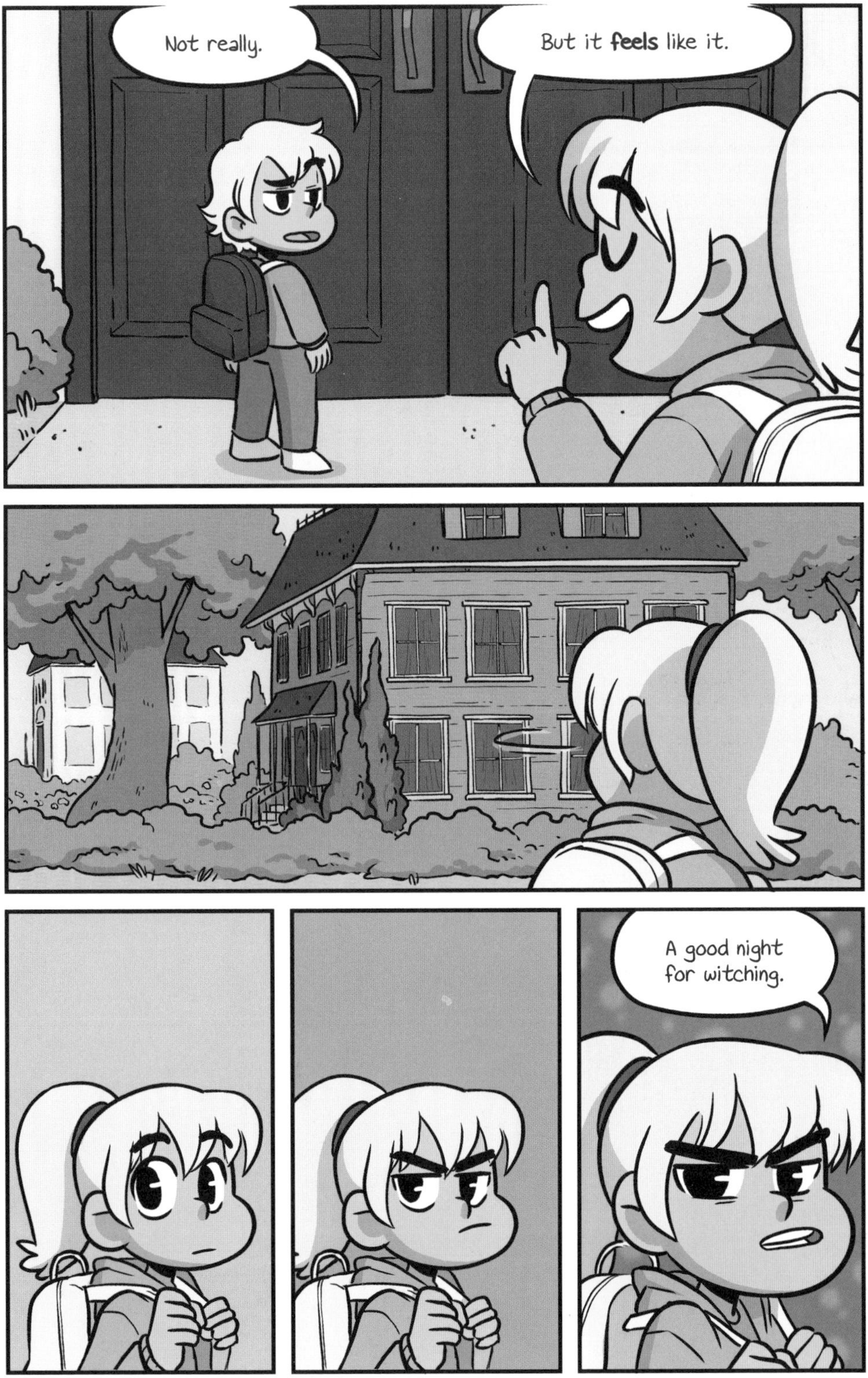
Not really.
But it **feels** like it.
A good night for witching.

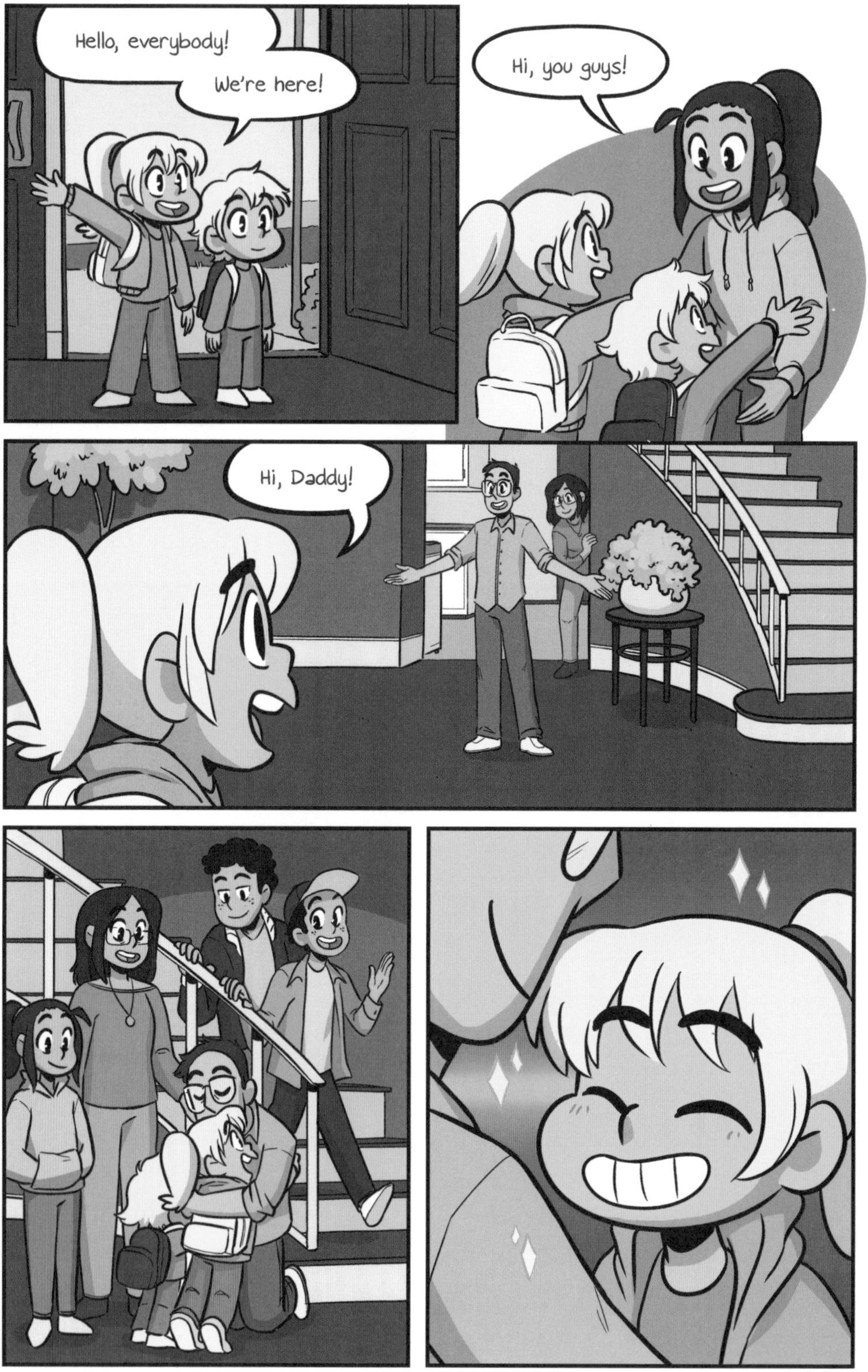
Hello, everybody!
We're here!
Hi, you guys!
Hi, Daddy!

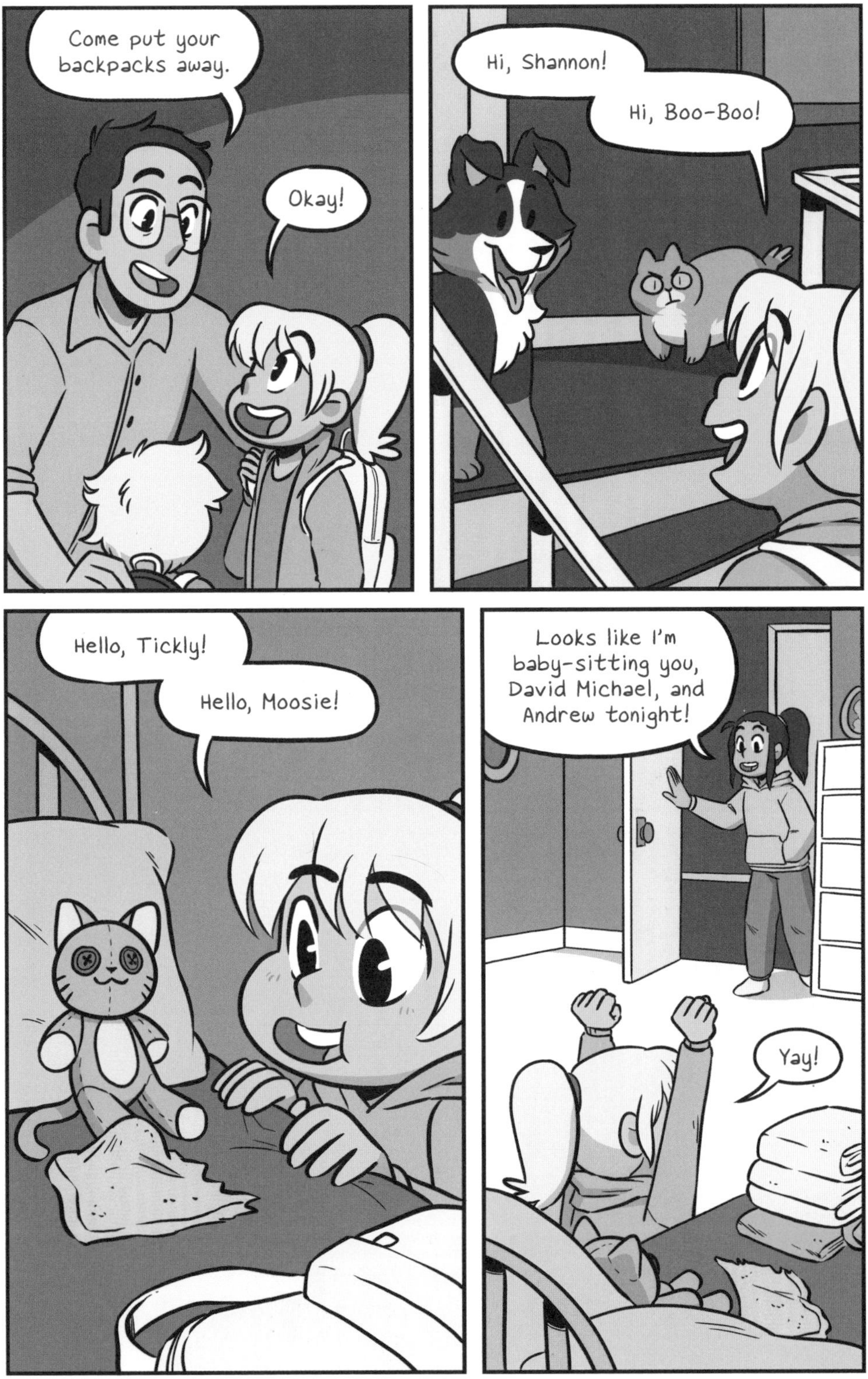
Come put your backpacks away.
Okay!
Hi, Shannon!
Hi, Boo-Boo!
Hello, Tickly!
Hello, Moosie!
Looks like I'm baby-sitting you, David Michael, and Andrew tonight!
Yay!

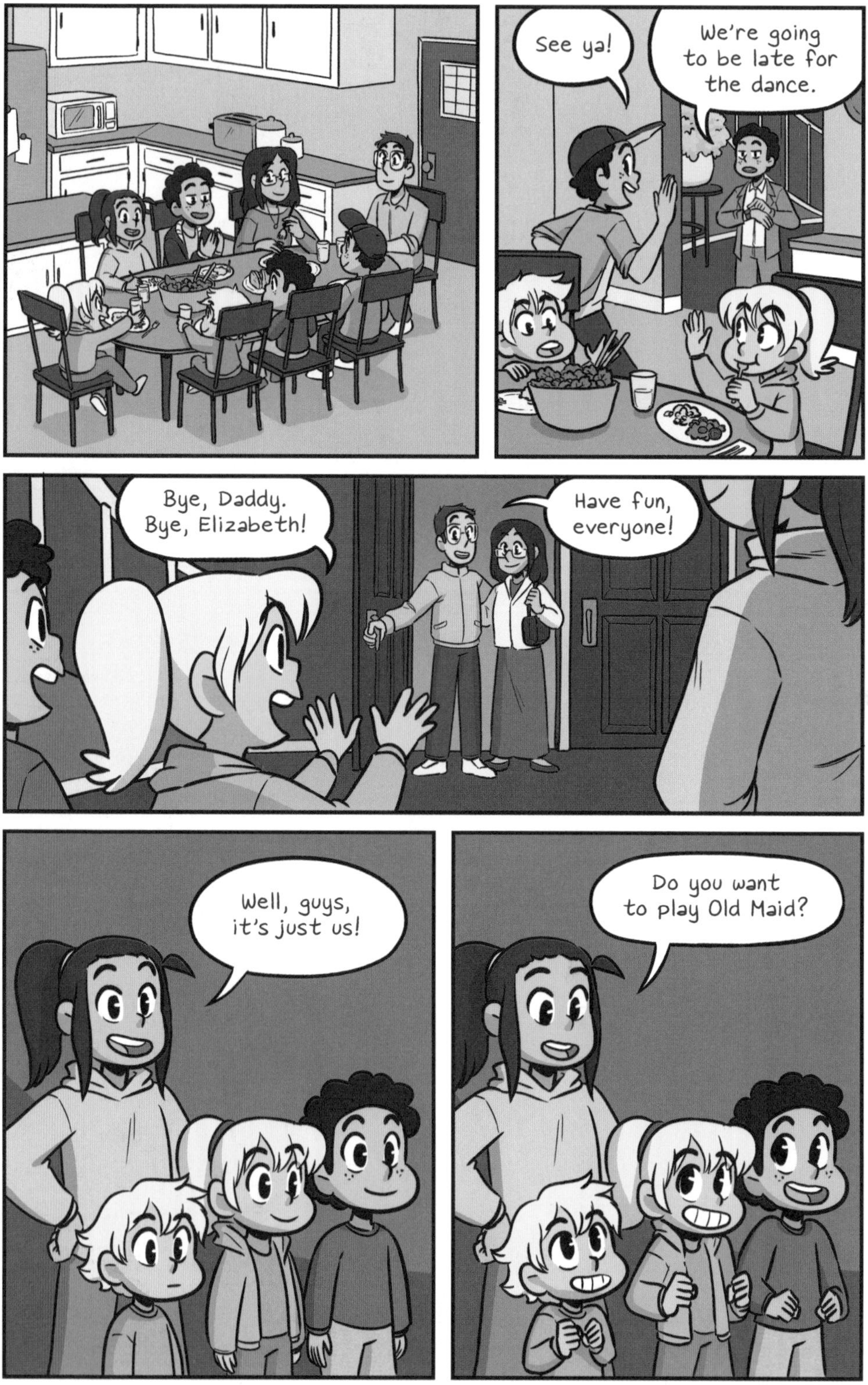
See ya!
We're going to be late for the dance.
Bye, Daddy. Bye, Elizabeth!
Have fun, everyone!
Well, guys, it's just us!
Do you want to play Old Maid?

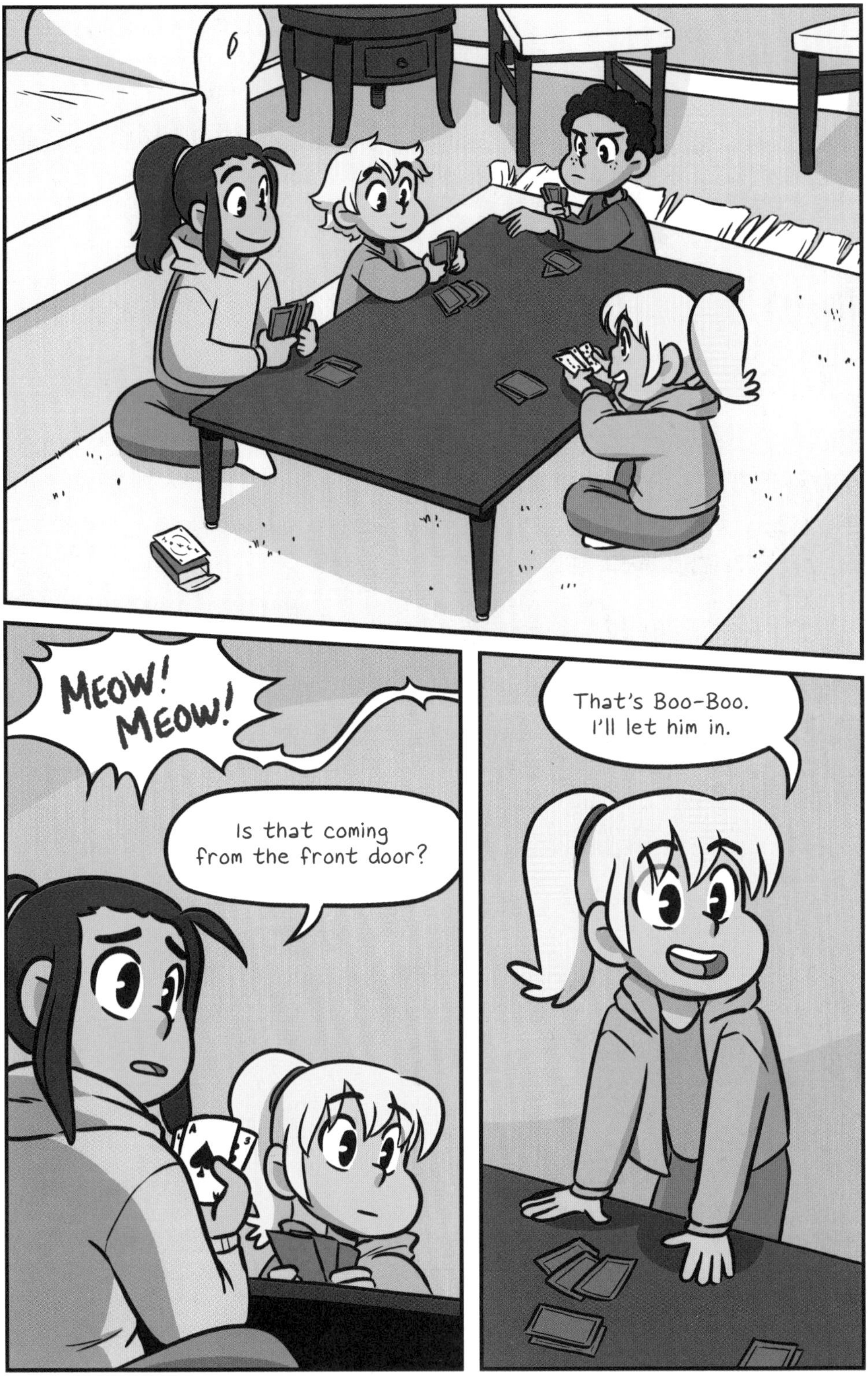
MEOW! MEOW!
Is that coming from the front door?
That's Boo-Boo. I'll let him in.

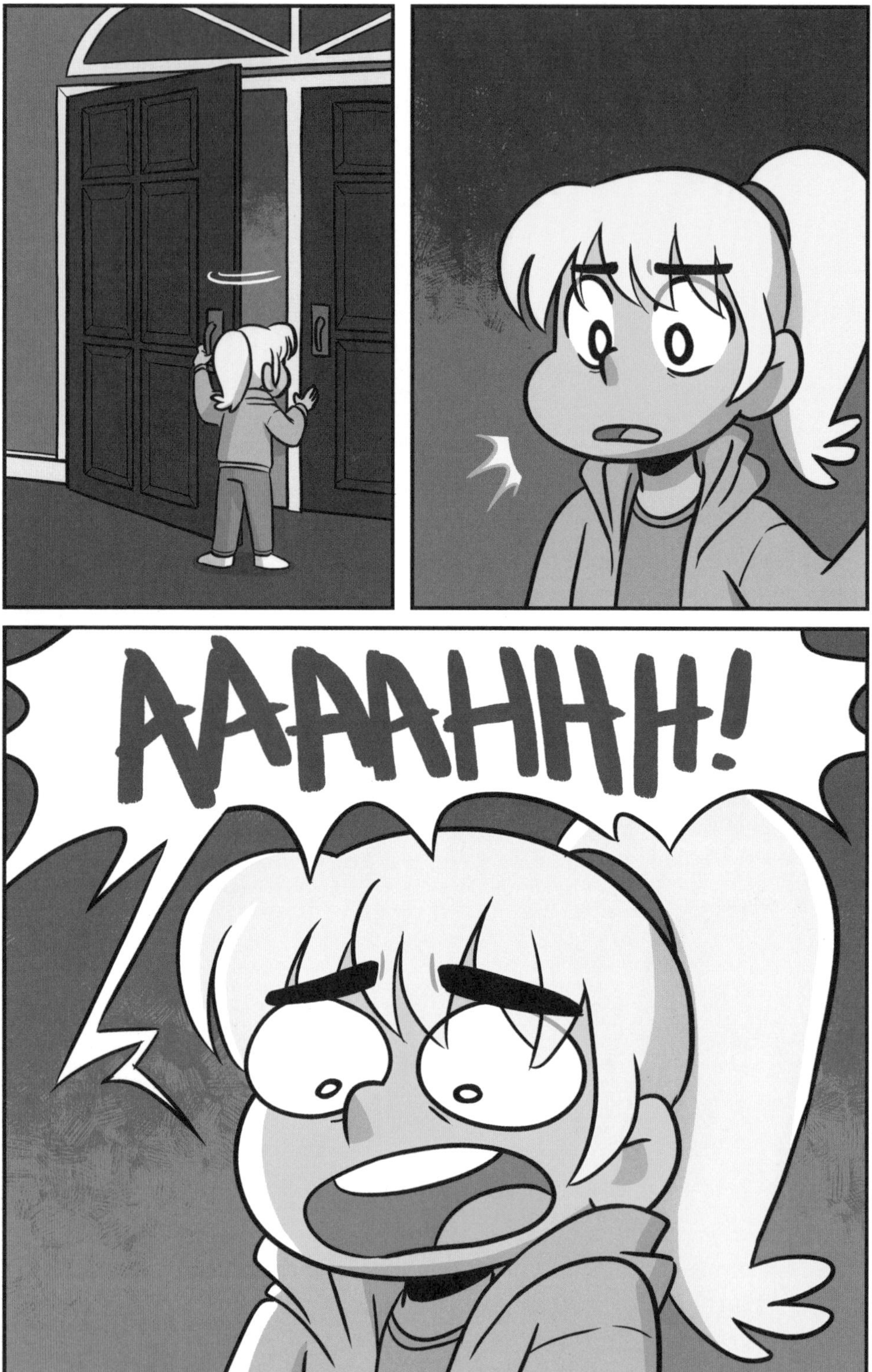
AAAAHHH!

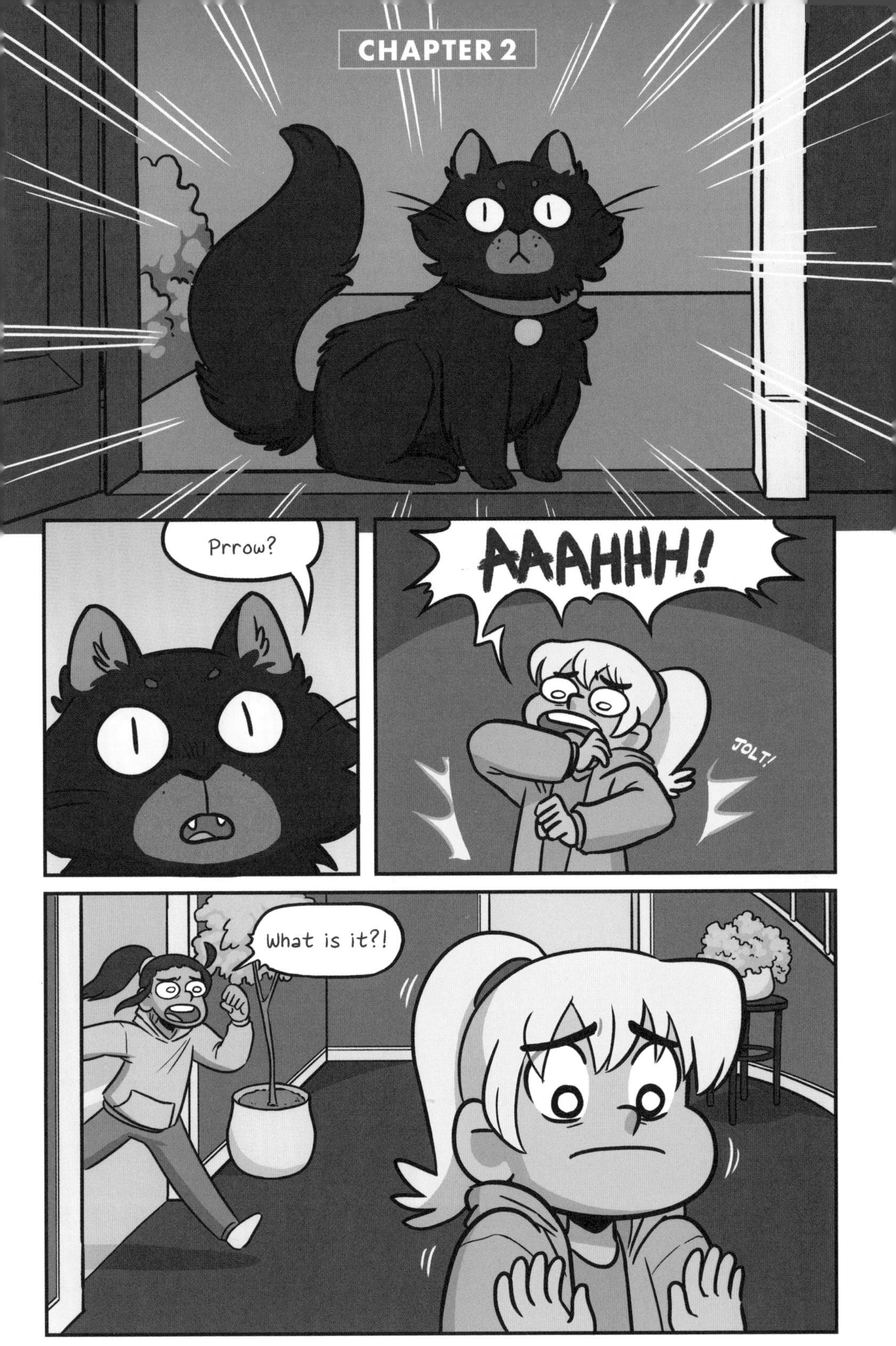
CHAPTER 2
Prrow?
AAAHHH!
JOLT!
What is it?!

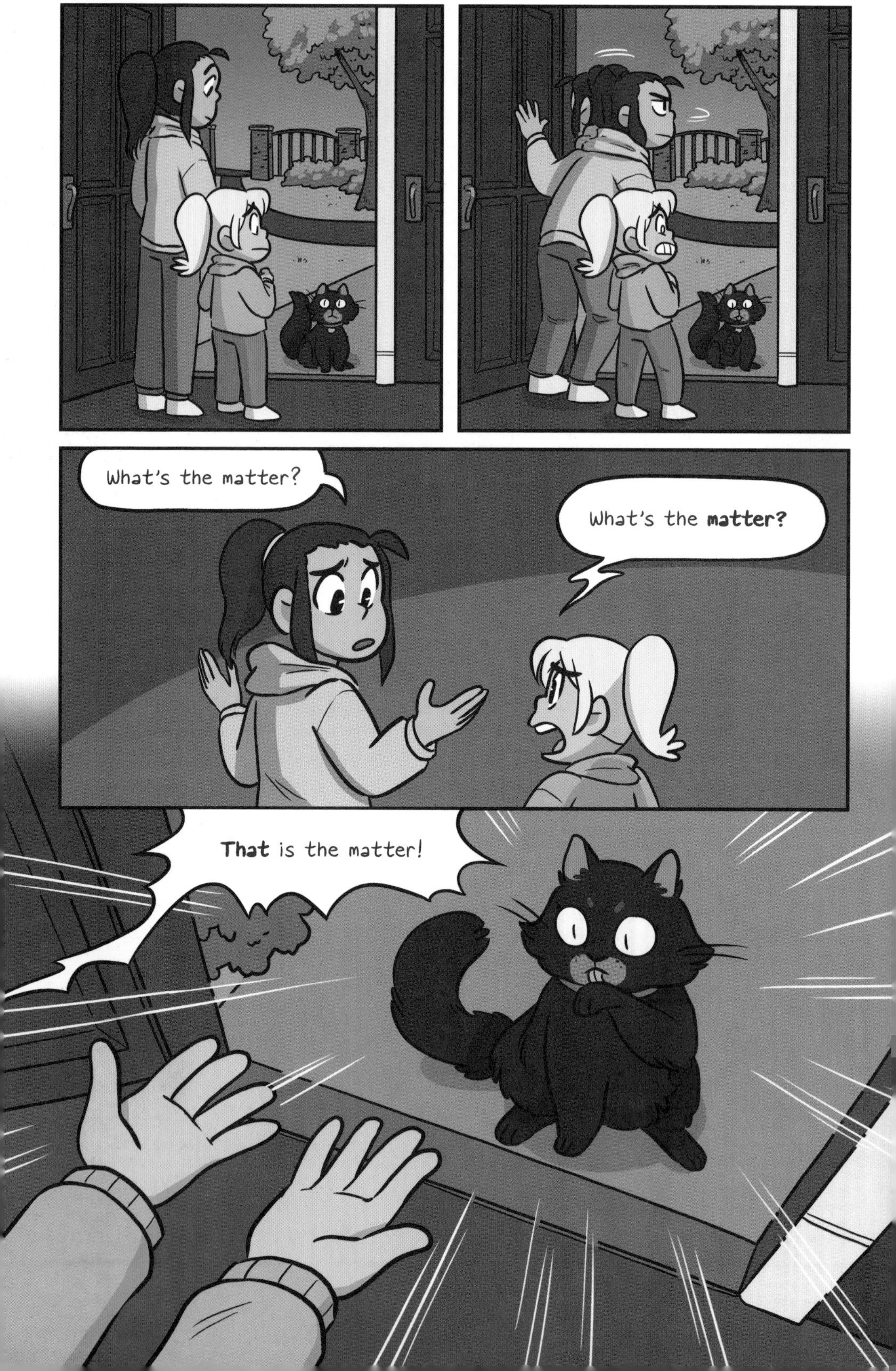
What's the matter?
What's the **matter?**
That is the matter!

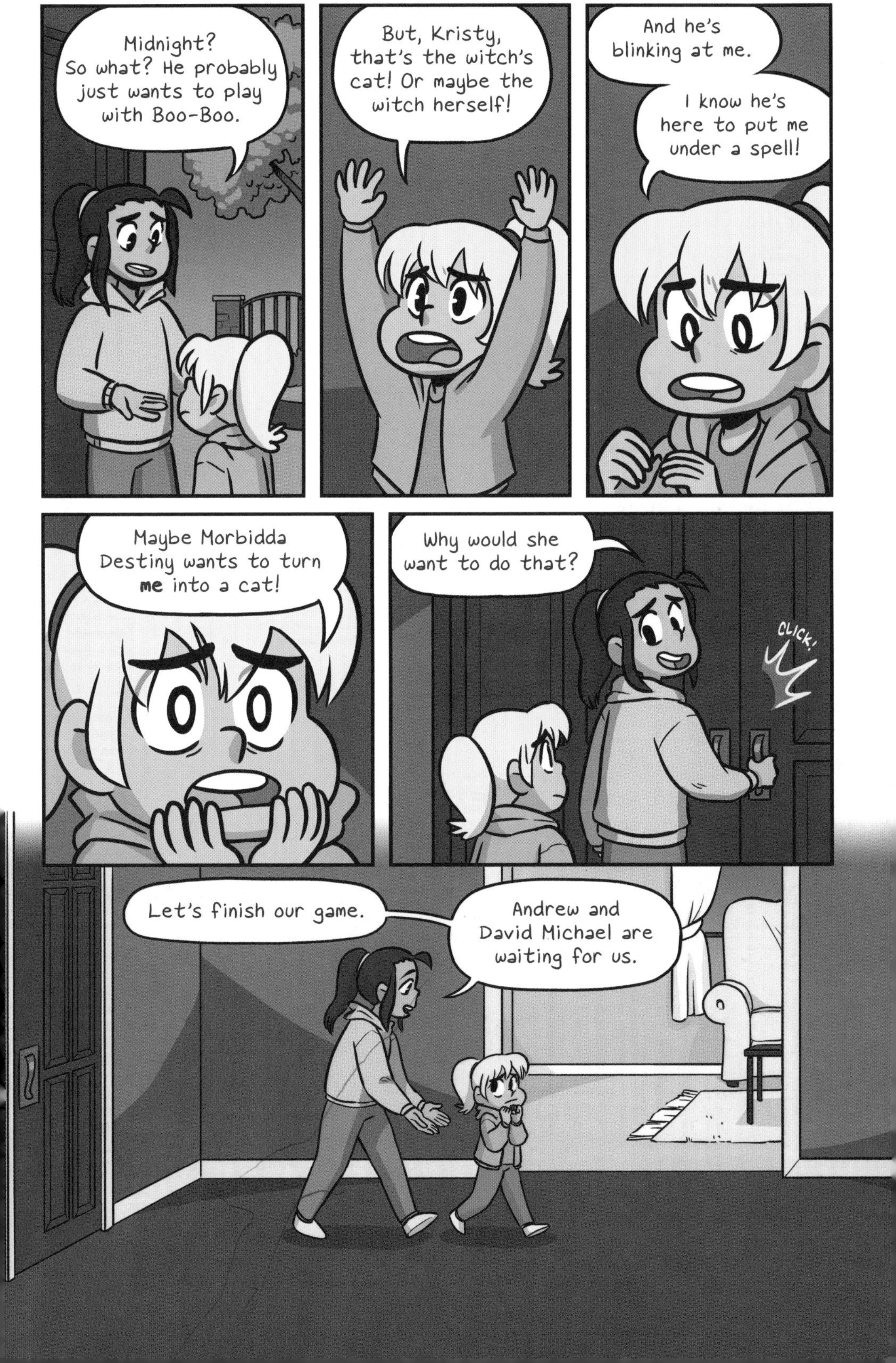
Midnight? So what? He probably just wants to play with Boo-Boo.
But, Kristy, that's the witch's cat! Or maybe the witch herself!
And he's blinking at me.
I know he's here to put me under a spell!
Maybe Morbidda Destiny wants to turn **me** into a cat!
Why would she want to do that?
CLICK!
Let's finish our game.
Andrew and David Michael are waiting for us.

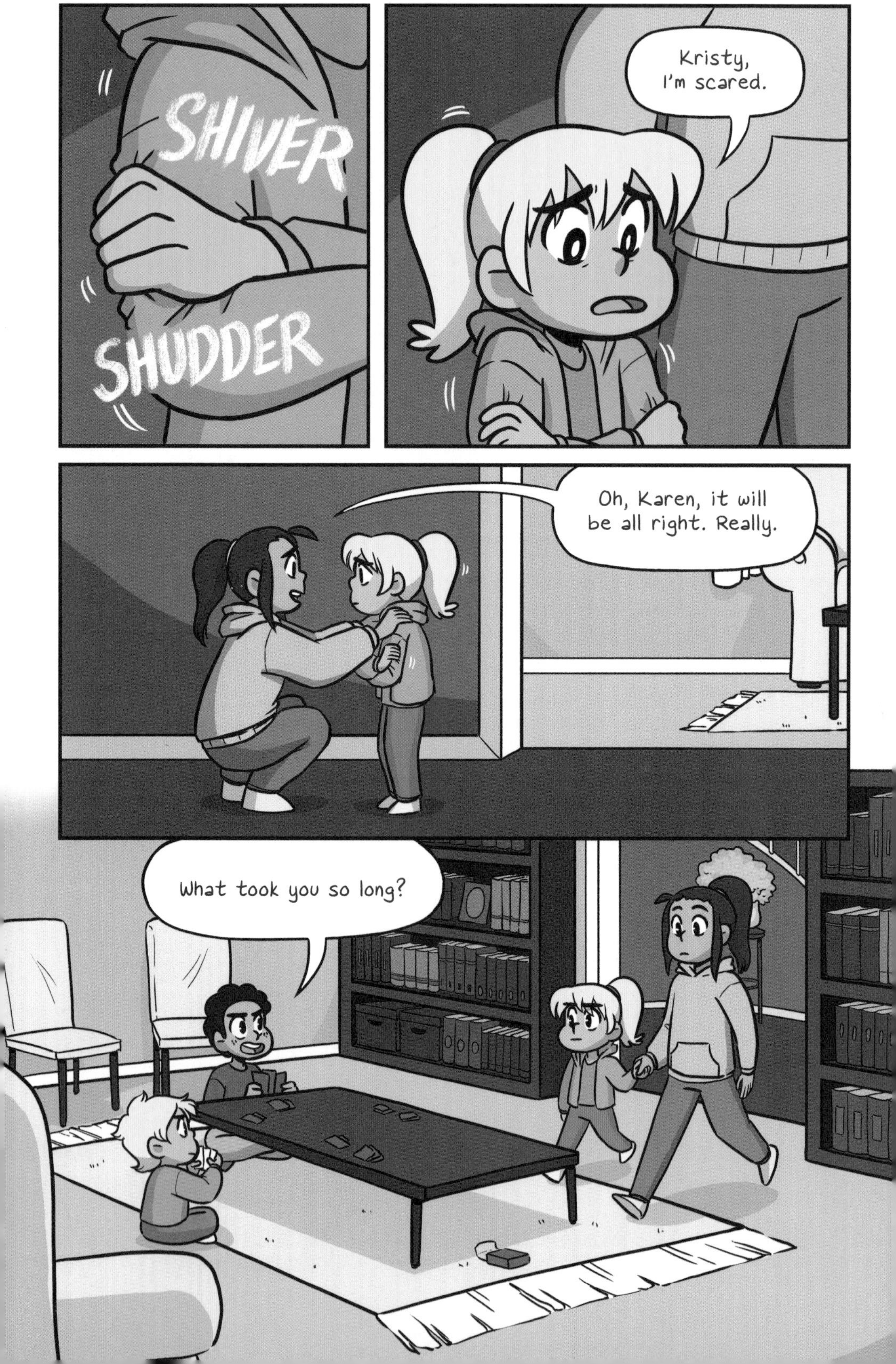
SHIVER
SHUDDER
Kristy, I'm scared.
Oh, Karen, it will be all right. Really.
What took you so long?

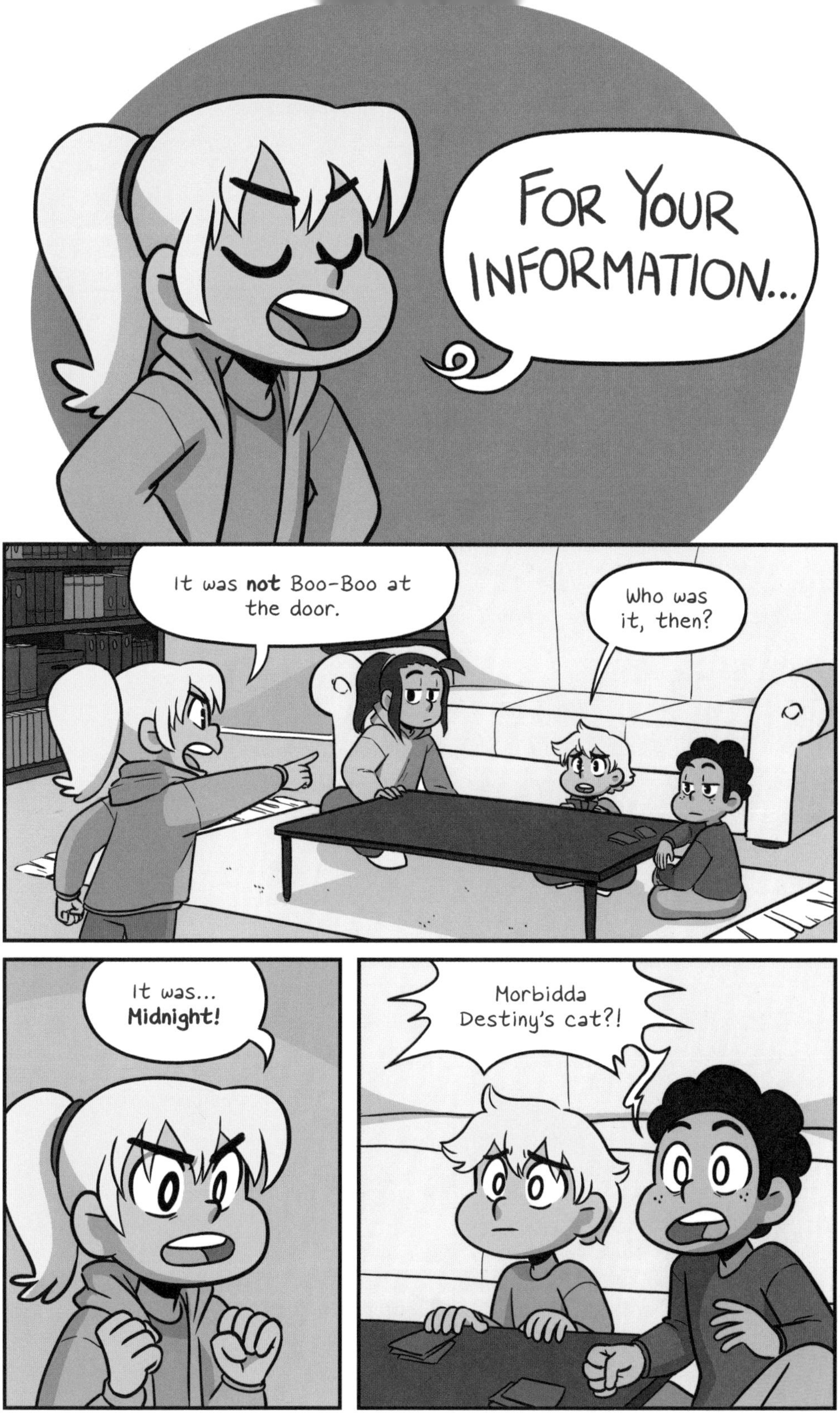
FOR YOUR INFORMATION...
It was **not** Boo-Boo at the door.
Who was it, then?
It was... **Midnight!**
Morbidda Destiny's cat?!

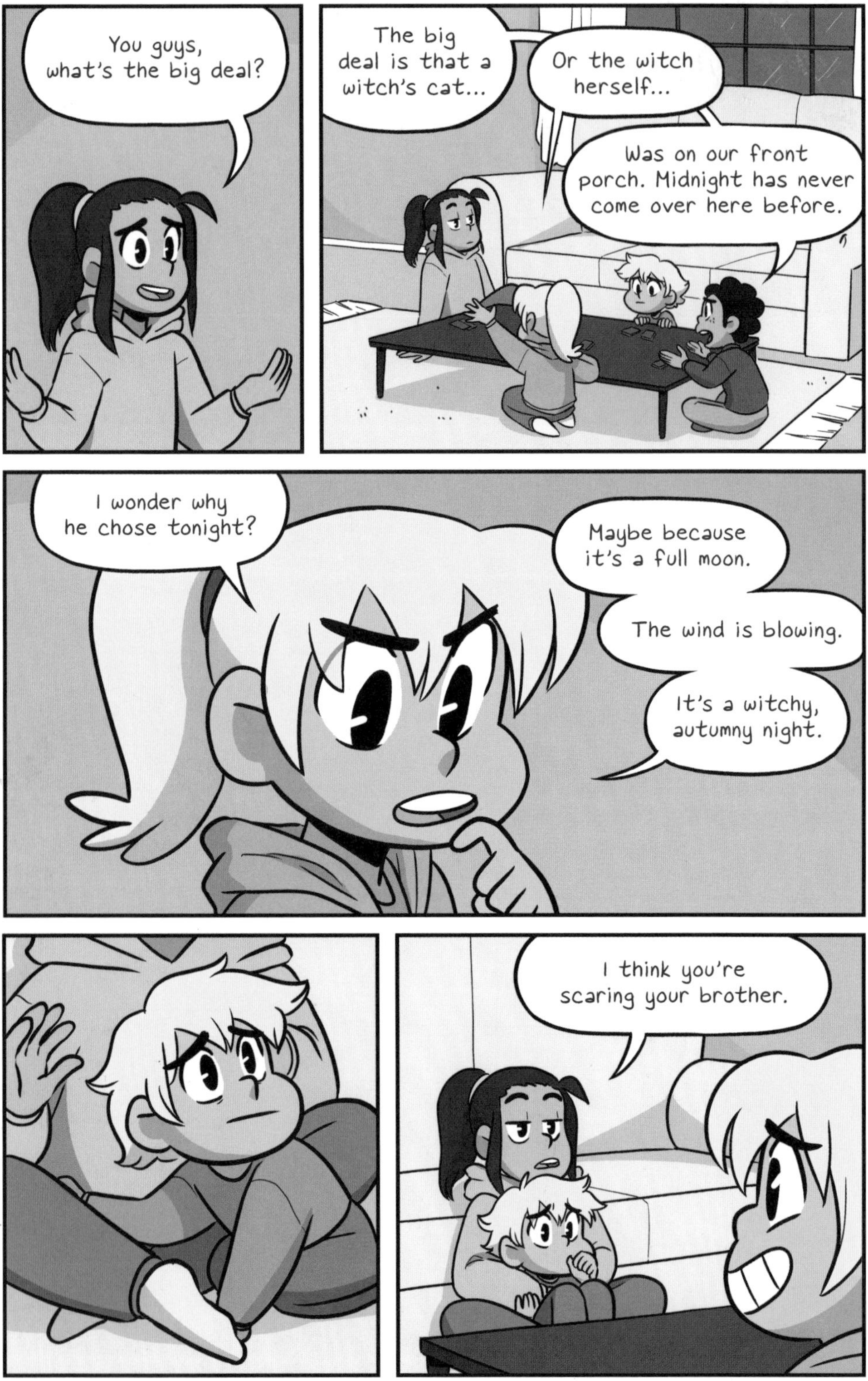
You guys, what's the big deal?
The big deal is that a witch's cat...
Or the witch herself...
Was on our front porch. Midnight has never come over here before.
I wonder why he chose tonight?
Maybe because it's a full moon.
The wind is blowing.
It's a witchy, autumny night.
I think you're scaring your brother.

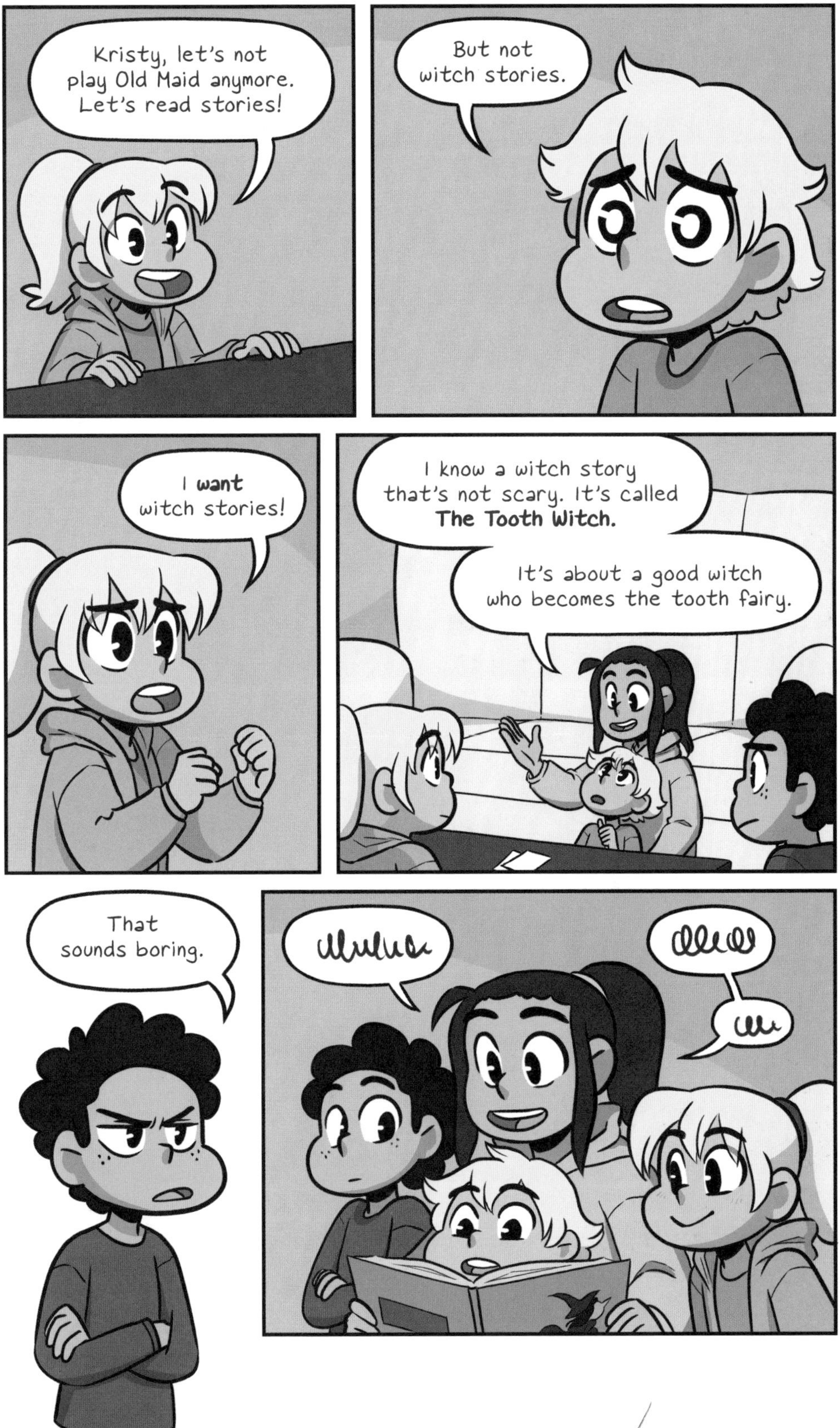
Kristy, let's not play Old Maid anymore. Let's read stories!
But not witch stories.
I **want** witch stories!
I know a witch story that's not scary. It's called **The Tooth Witch.**
It's about a good witch who becomes the tooth fairy.
That sounds boring.

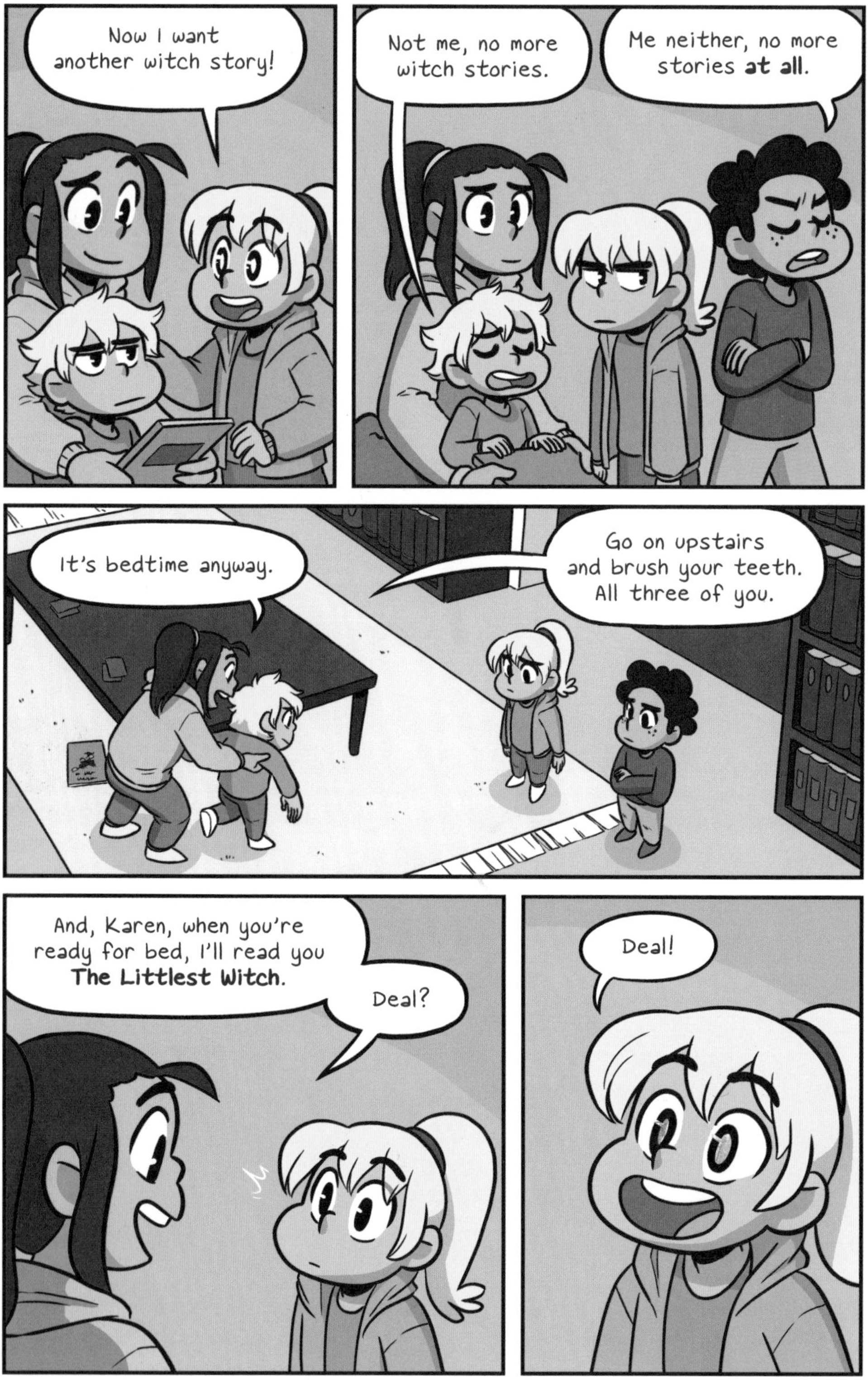

Now I want another witch story!
Not me, no more witch stories.
Me neither, no more stories **at all**.
It's bedtime anyway.
Go on upstairs and brush your teeth. All three of you.
And, Karen, when you're ready for bed, I'll read you **The Littlest Witch**.
Deal?
Deal!

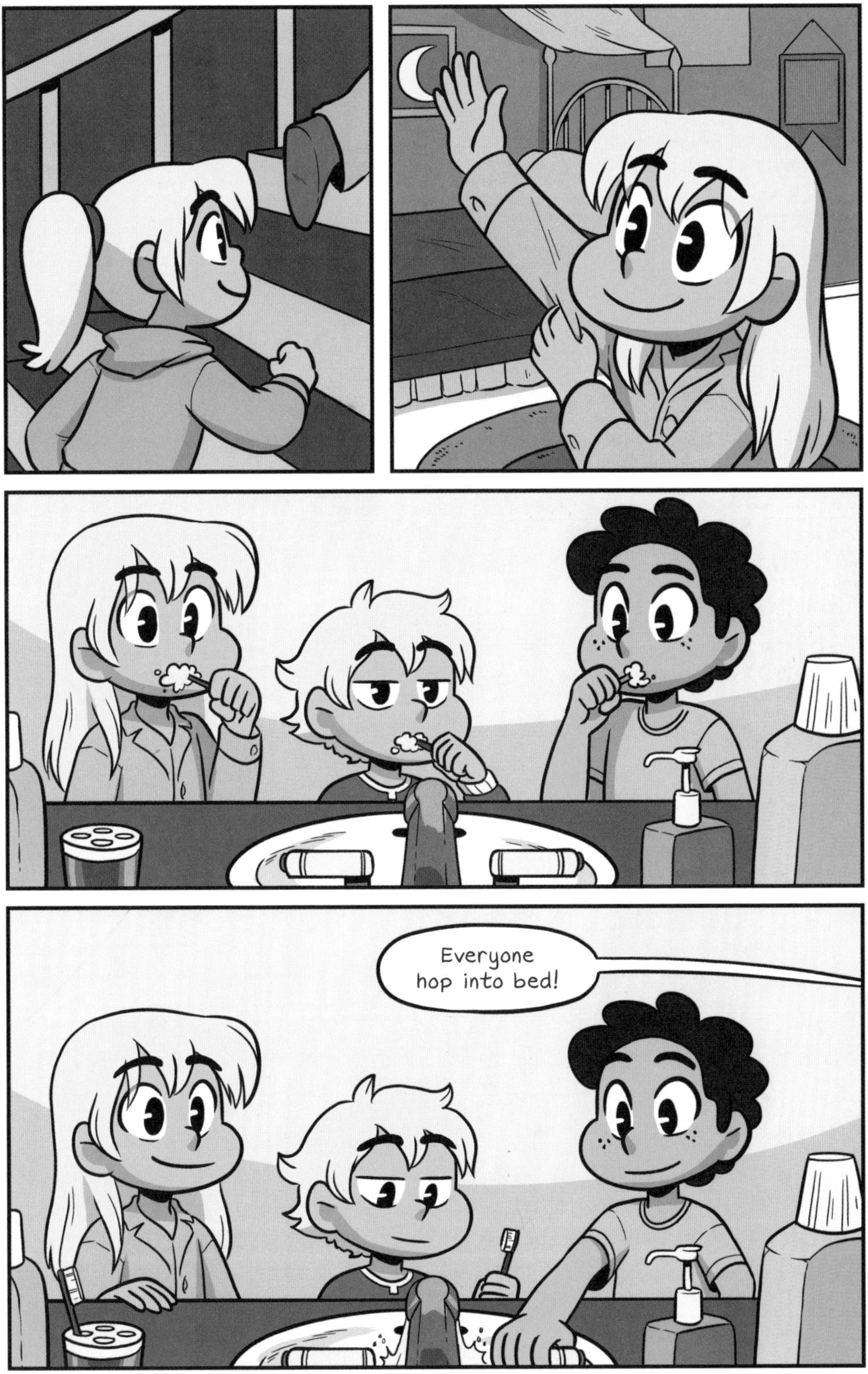
Everyone hop into bed!

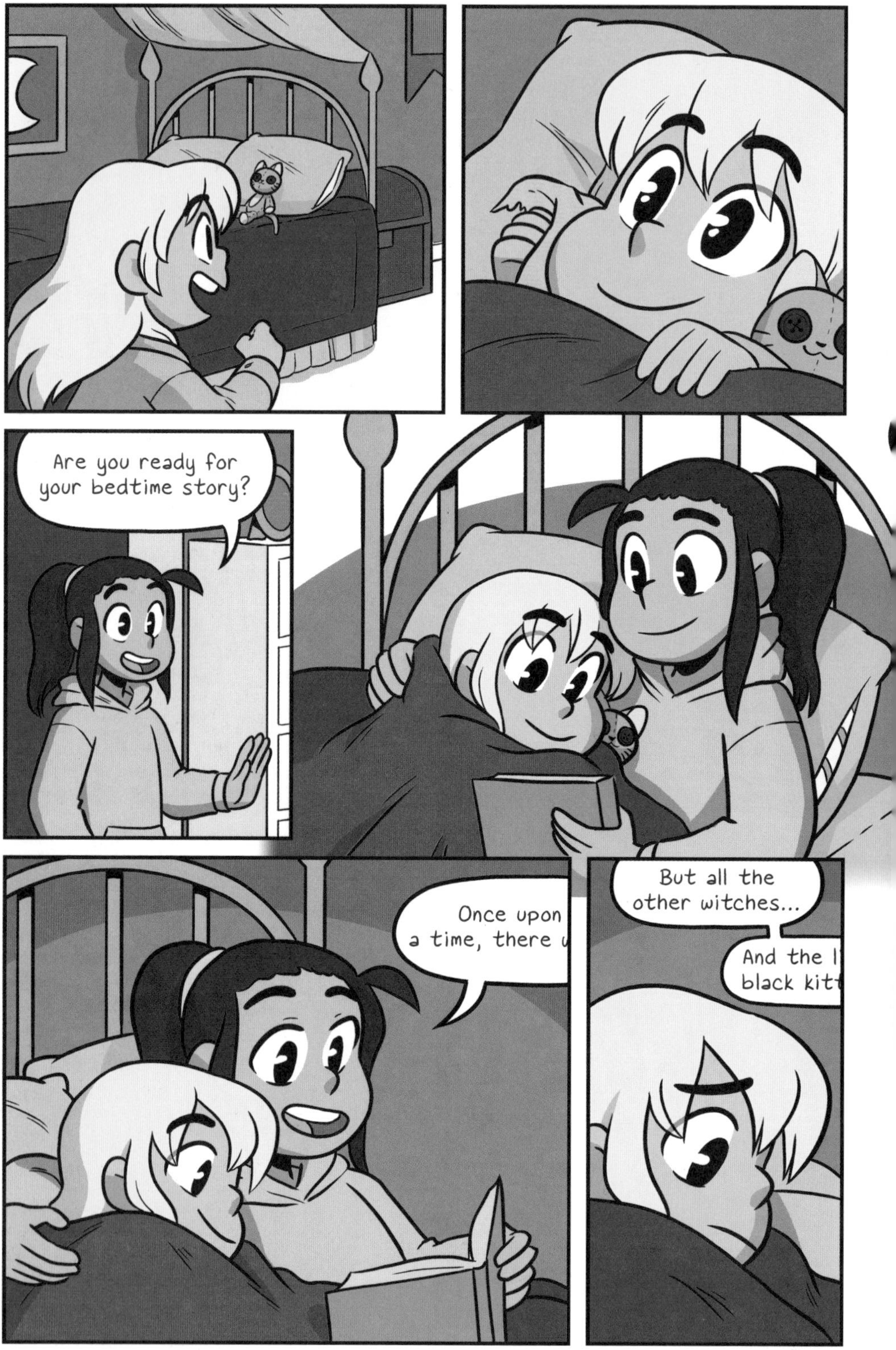
Are you ready for your bedtime story?
Once upon a time, there
But all the other witches...
And the l
black kit

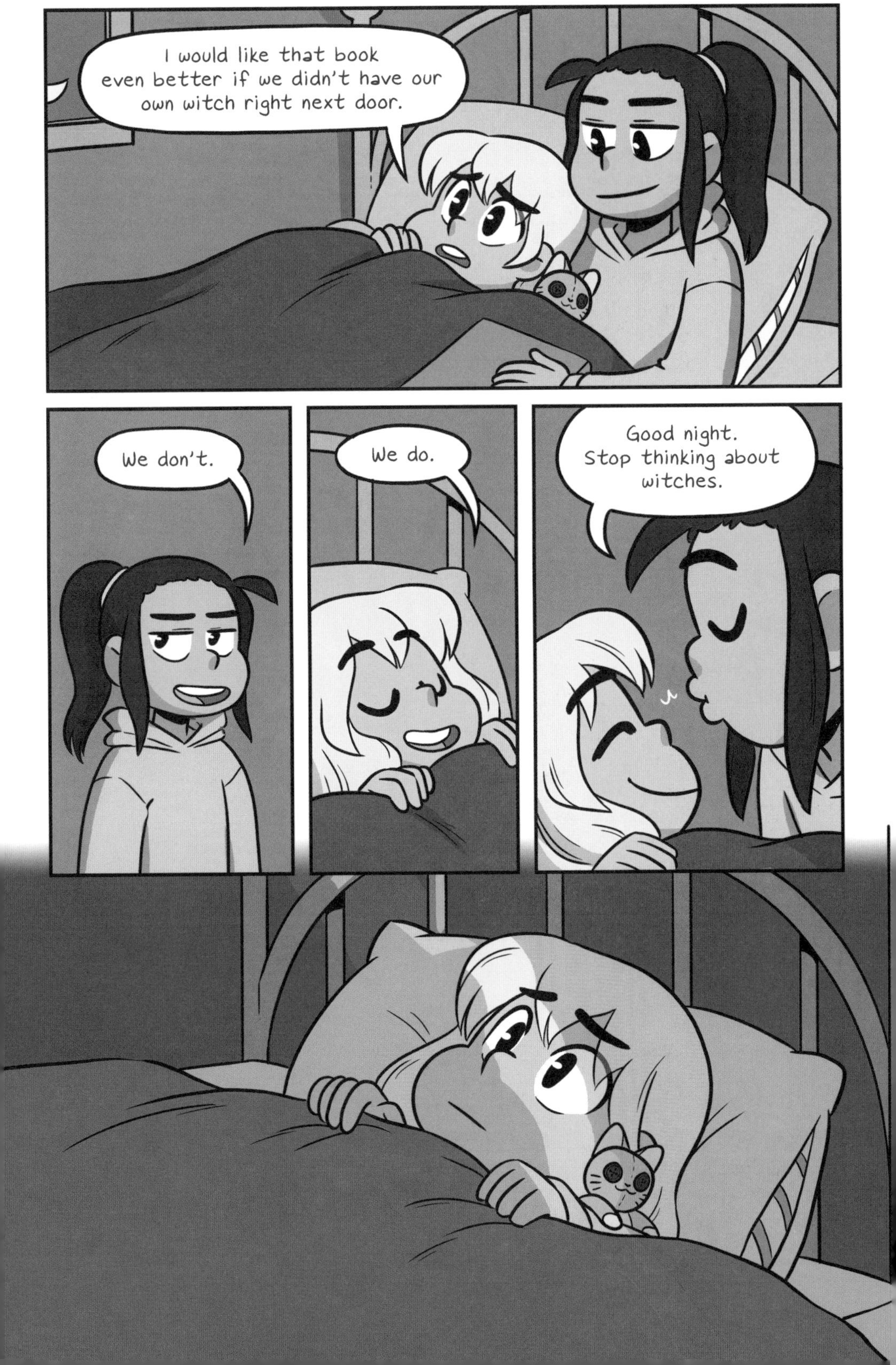
I would like that book even better if we didn't have our own witch right next door.
We don't.
We do.
Good night. Stop thinking about witches.

CHAPTER 3

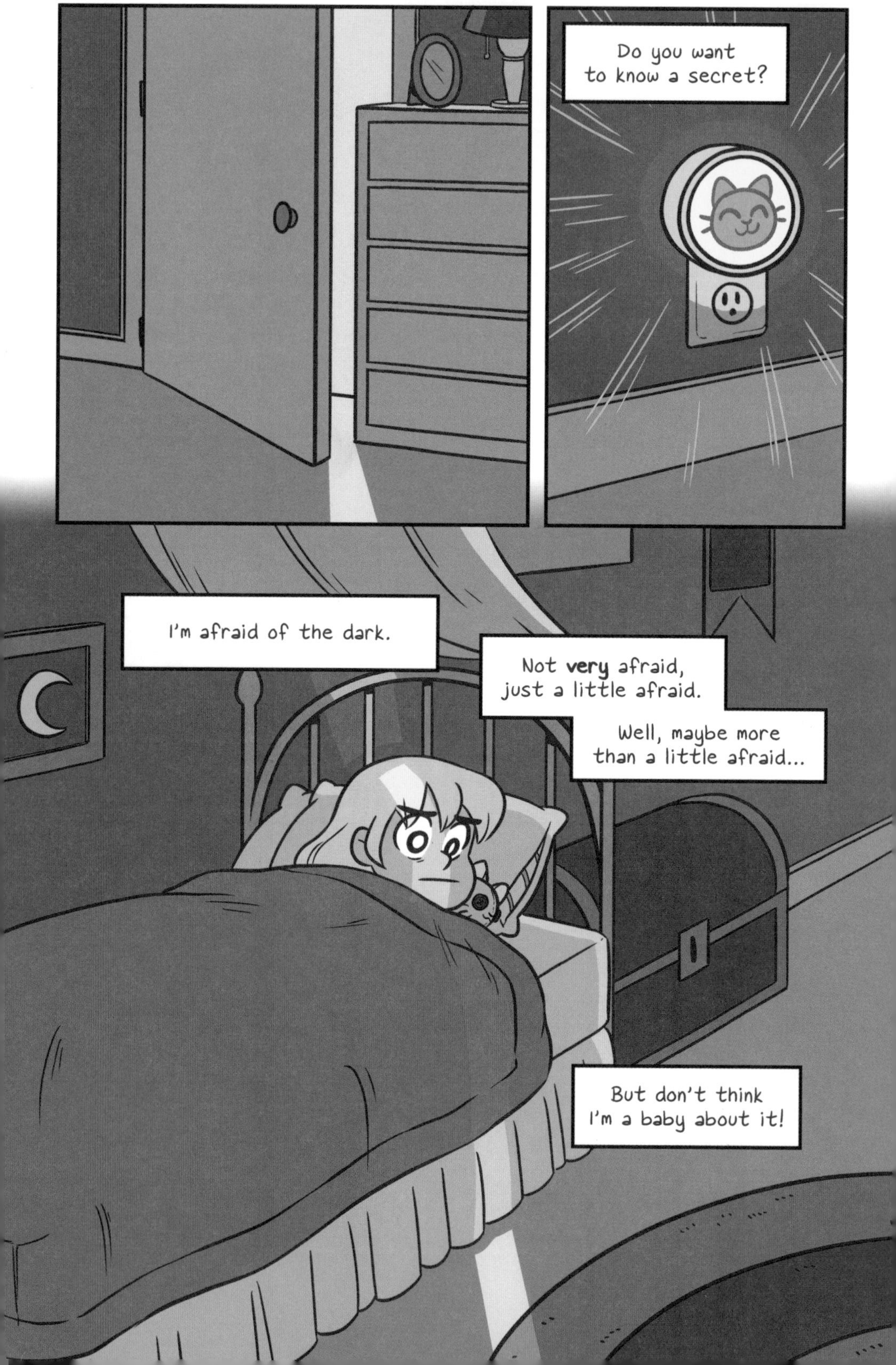
Do you want to know a secret?
I'm afraid of the dark.
Not **very** afraid, just a little afraid.
Well, maybe more than a little afraid...
But don't think I'm a baby about it!

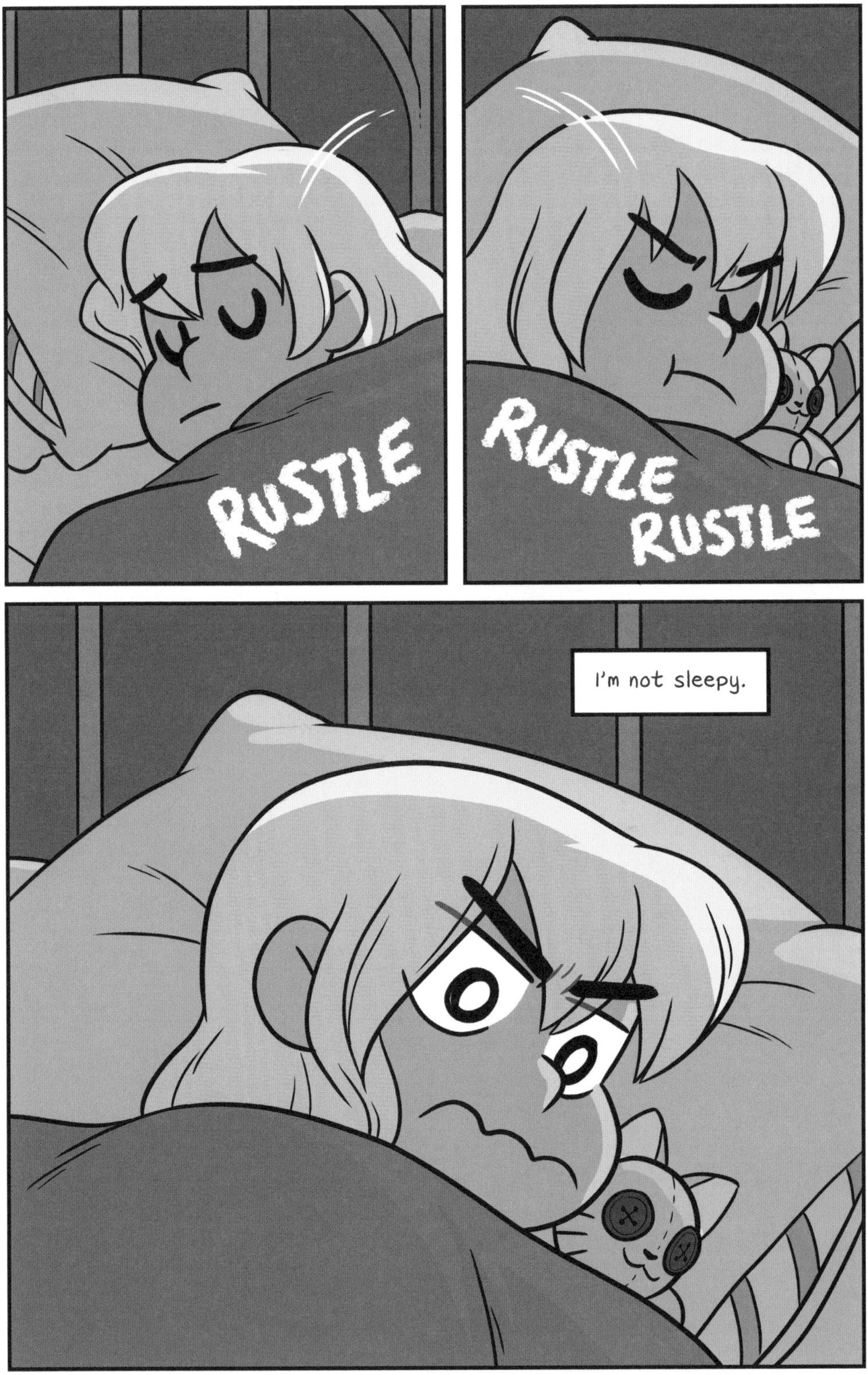
RUSTLE
RUSTLE
RUSTLE
I'm not sleepy.

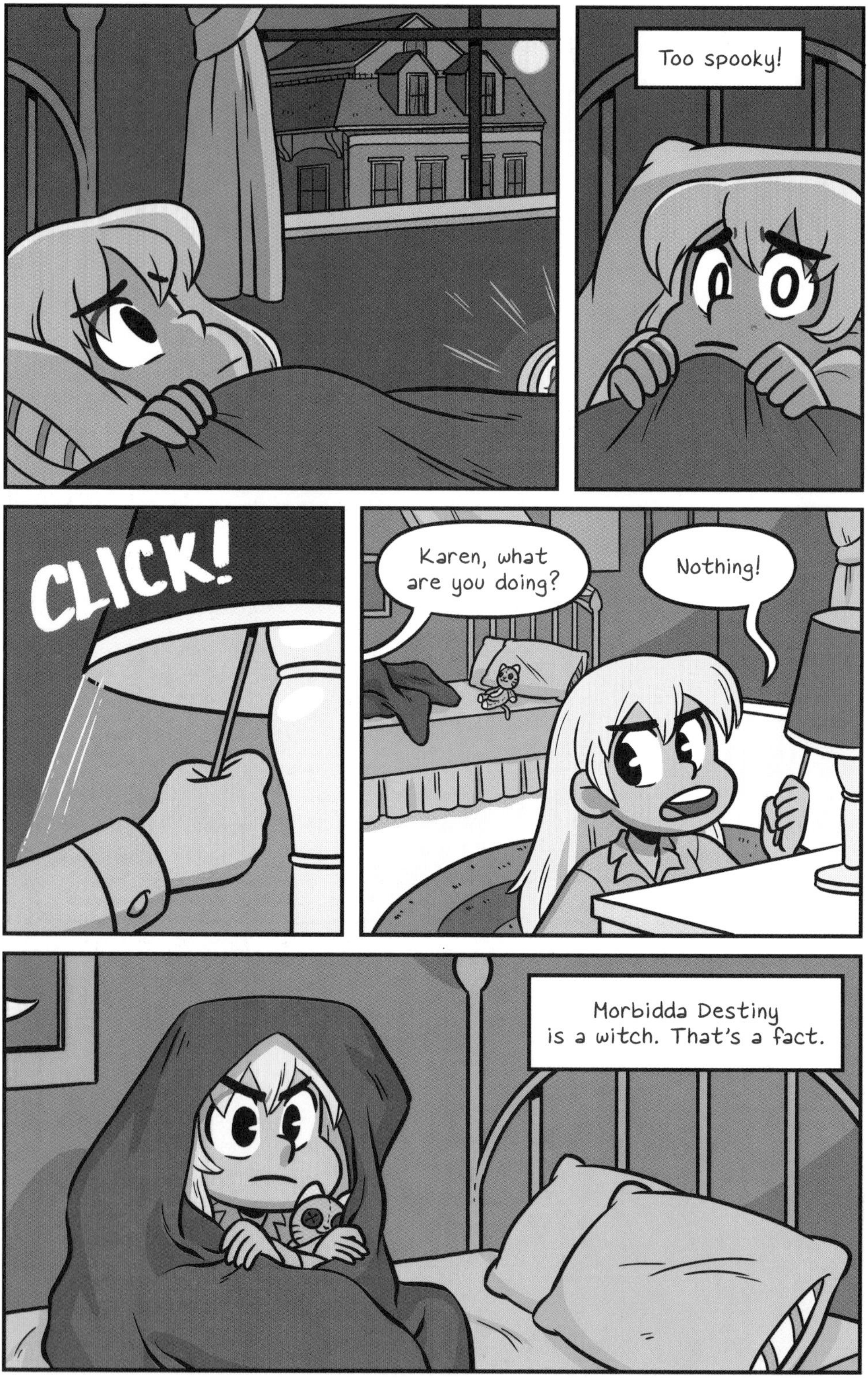
Too spooky!
CLICK!
Karen, what are you doing?
Nothing!
Morbidda Destiny is a witch. That's a fact.

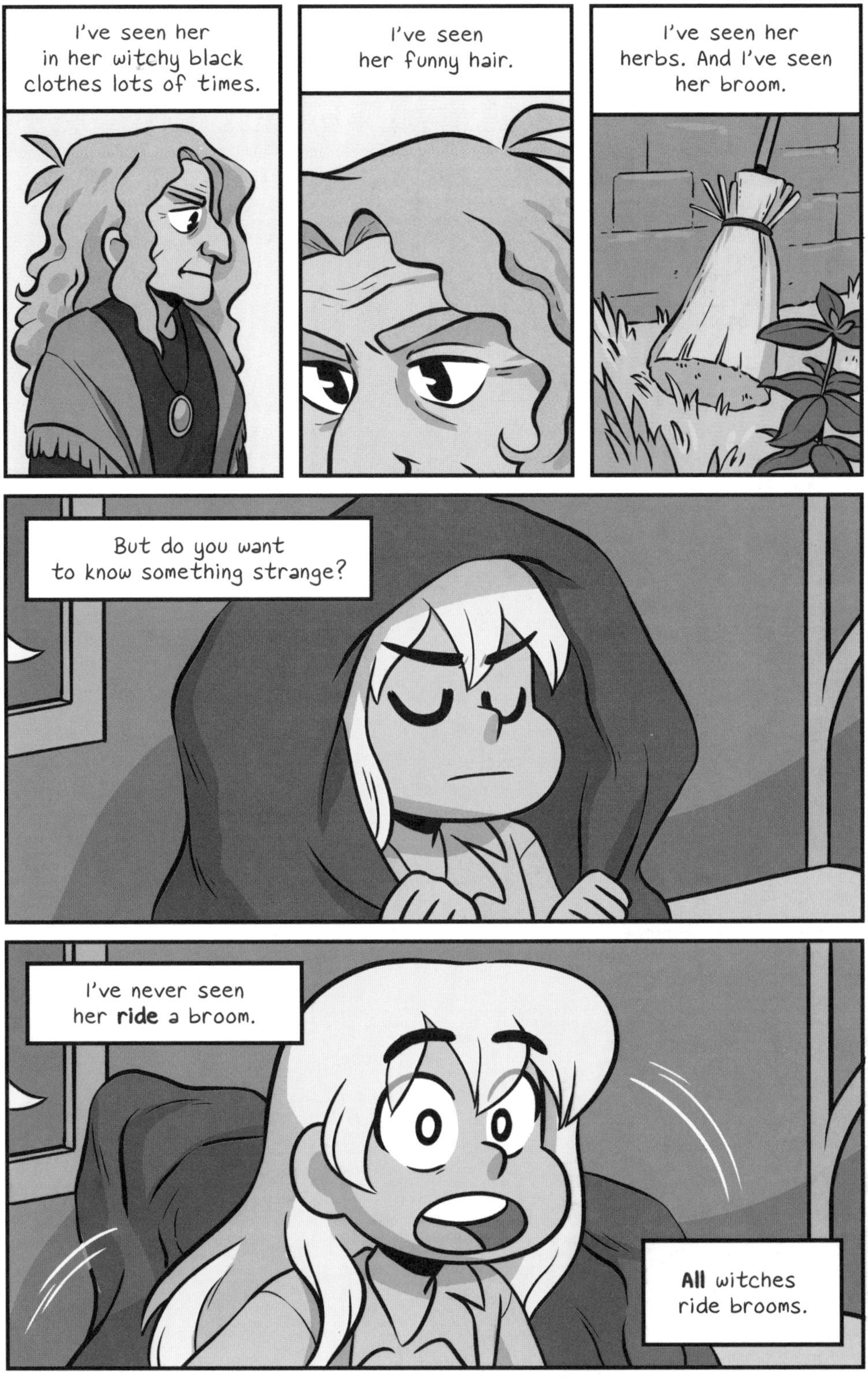
I've seen her in her witchy black clothes lots of times.
I've seen her funny hair.
I've seen her herbs. And I've seen her broom.
But do you want to know something strange?
I've never seen her **ride** a broom.
All witches ride brooms.

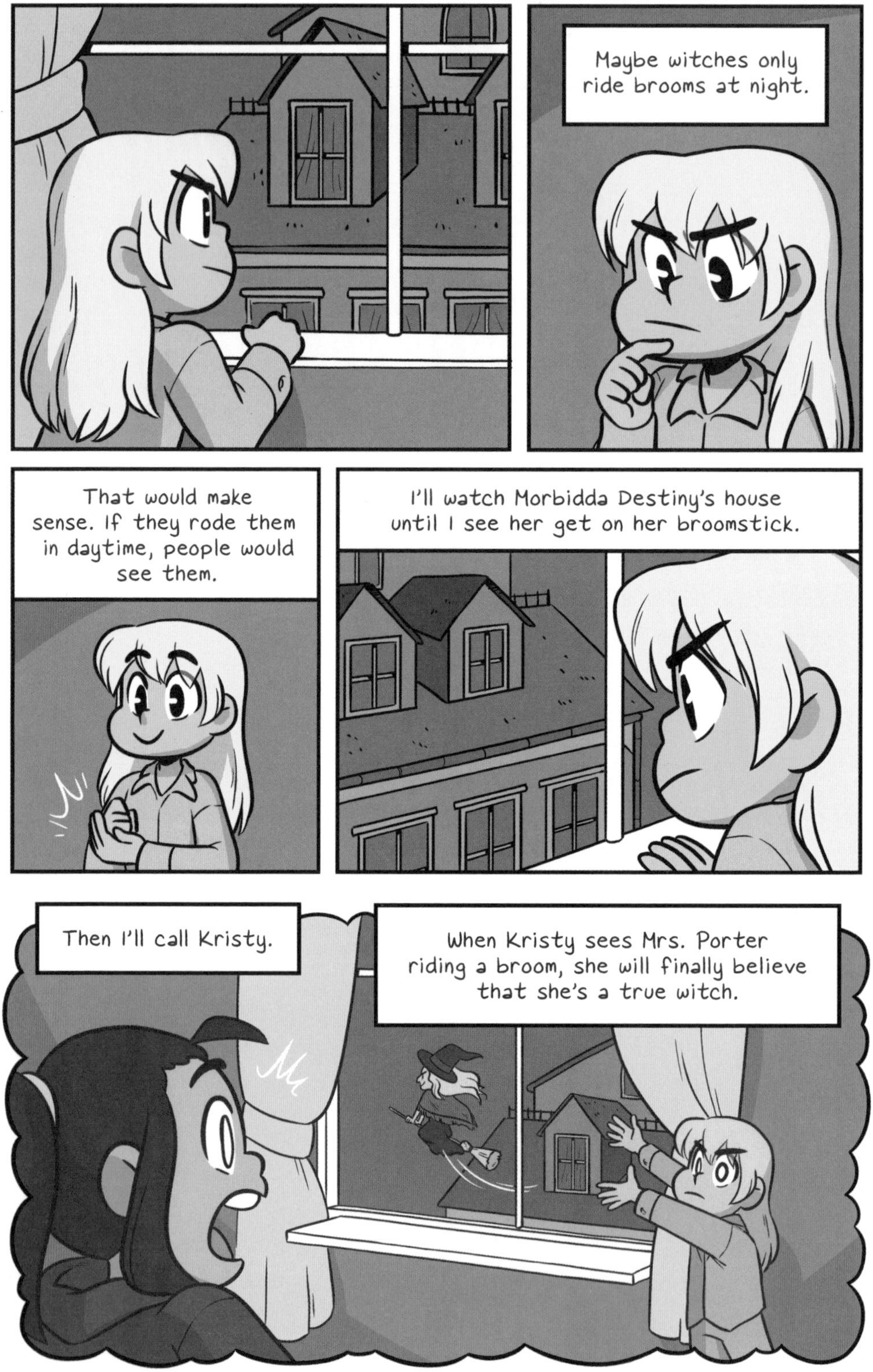
Maybe witches only ride brooms at night.
That would make sense. If they rode them in daytime, people would see them.
I'll watch Morbidda Destiny's house until I see her get on her broomstick.
Then I'll call Kristy.
When Kristy sees Mrs. Porter riding a broom, she will finally believe that she's a true witch.

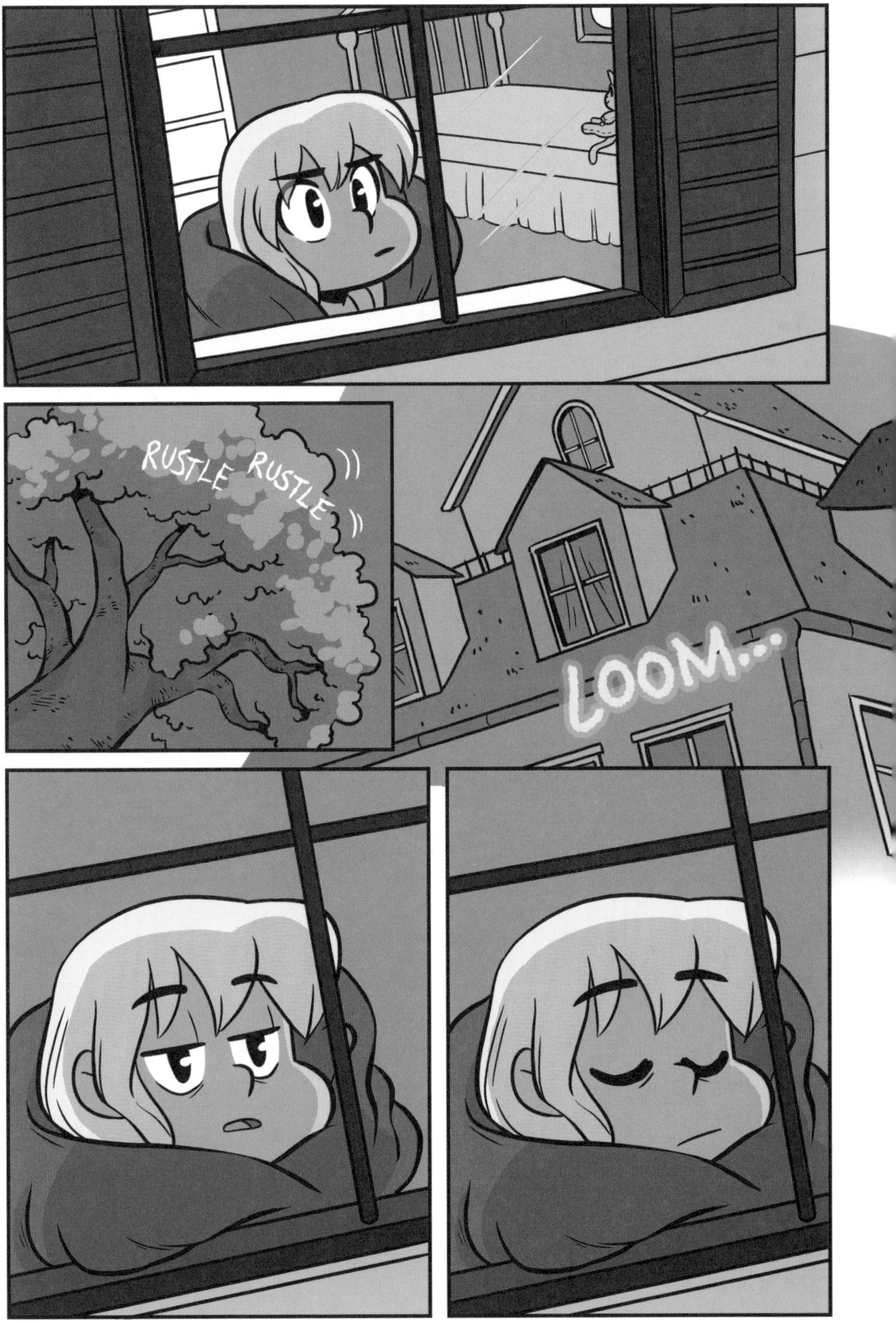
RUSTLE RUSTLE
LOOM...

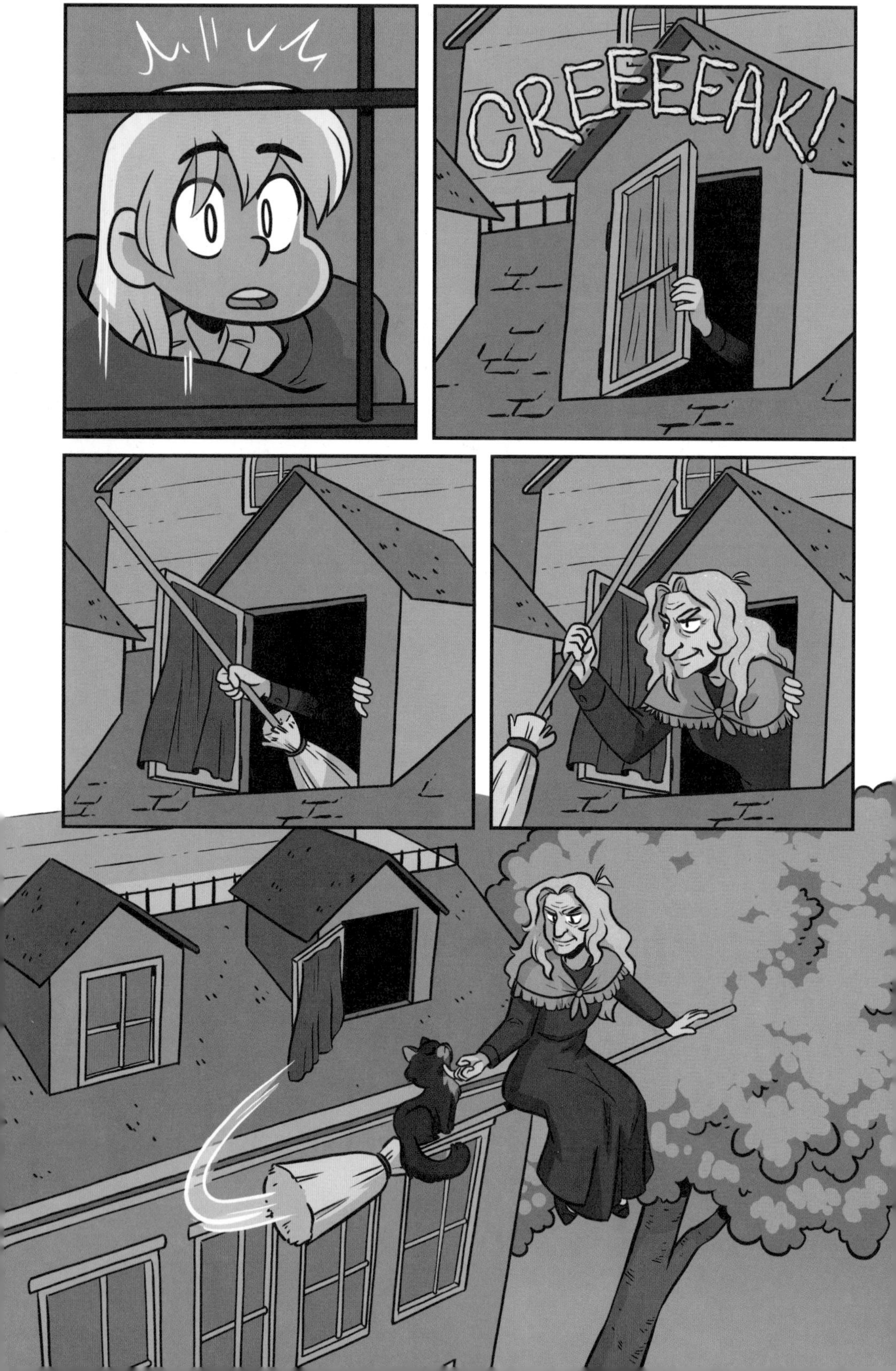
CREEEEAK!

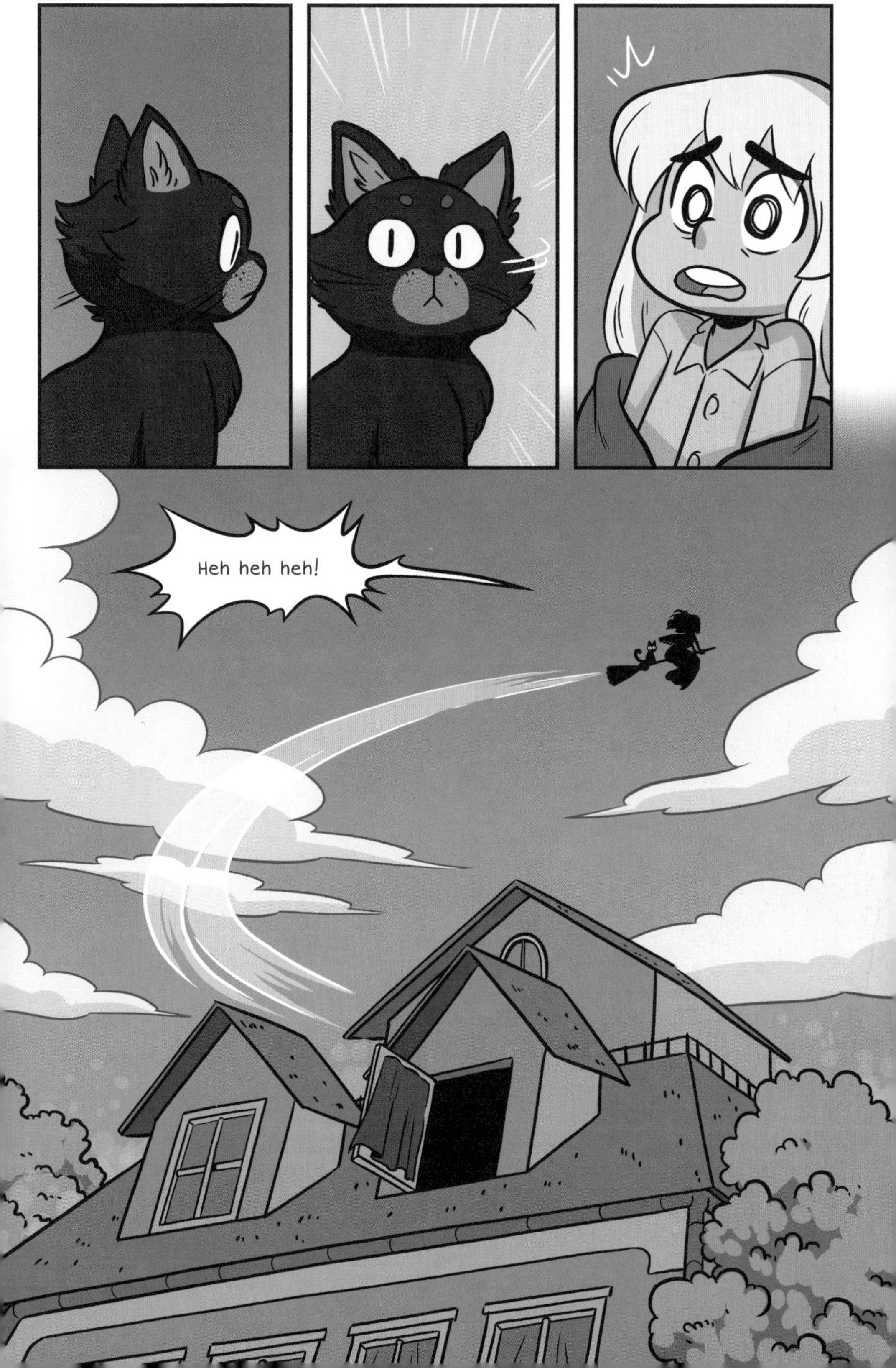
Heh heh heh!

AAAHHHHHH!

Karen, Karen! What's wrong?

Are you sick? Did you hurt yourself?

Turn off the light.

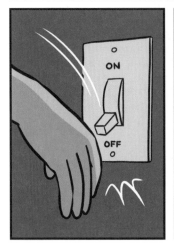

ON

OFF

Now come look out the window.

Hurry!

?

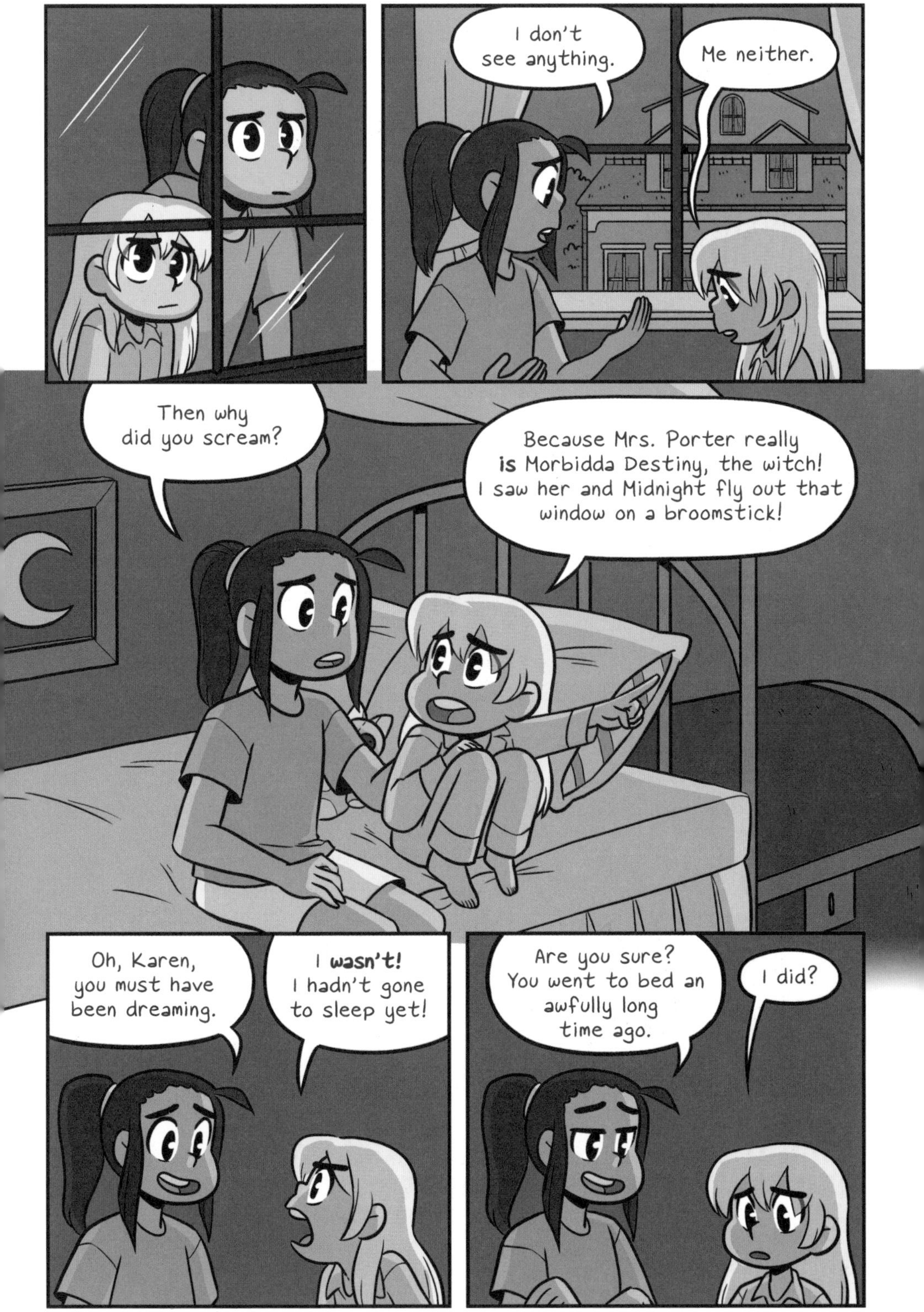

I don't see anything.
Me neither.
Then why did you scream?
Because Mrs. Porter really **is** Morbidda Destiny, the witch! I saw her and Midnight fly out that window on a broomstick!
Oh, Karen, you must have been dreaming.
I **wasn't!** I hadn't gone to sleep yet!
Are you sure? You went to bed an awfully long time ago.
I did?

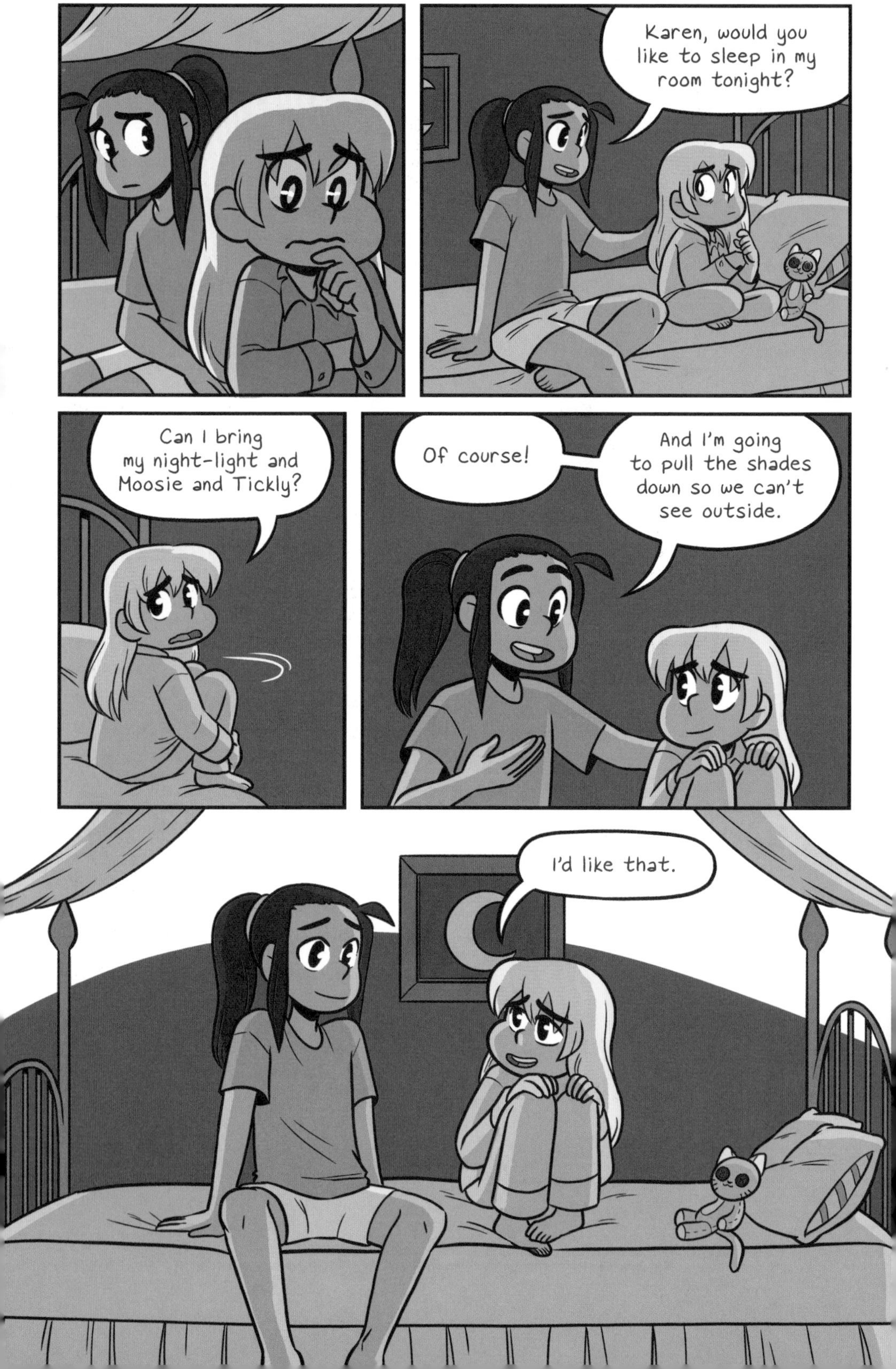
Karen, would you like to sleep in my room tonight?
Can I bring my night-light and Moosie and Tickly?
Of course!
And I'm going to pull the shades down so we can't see outside.
I'd like that.

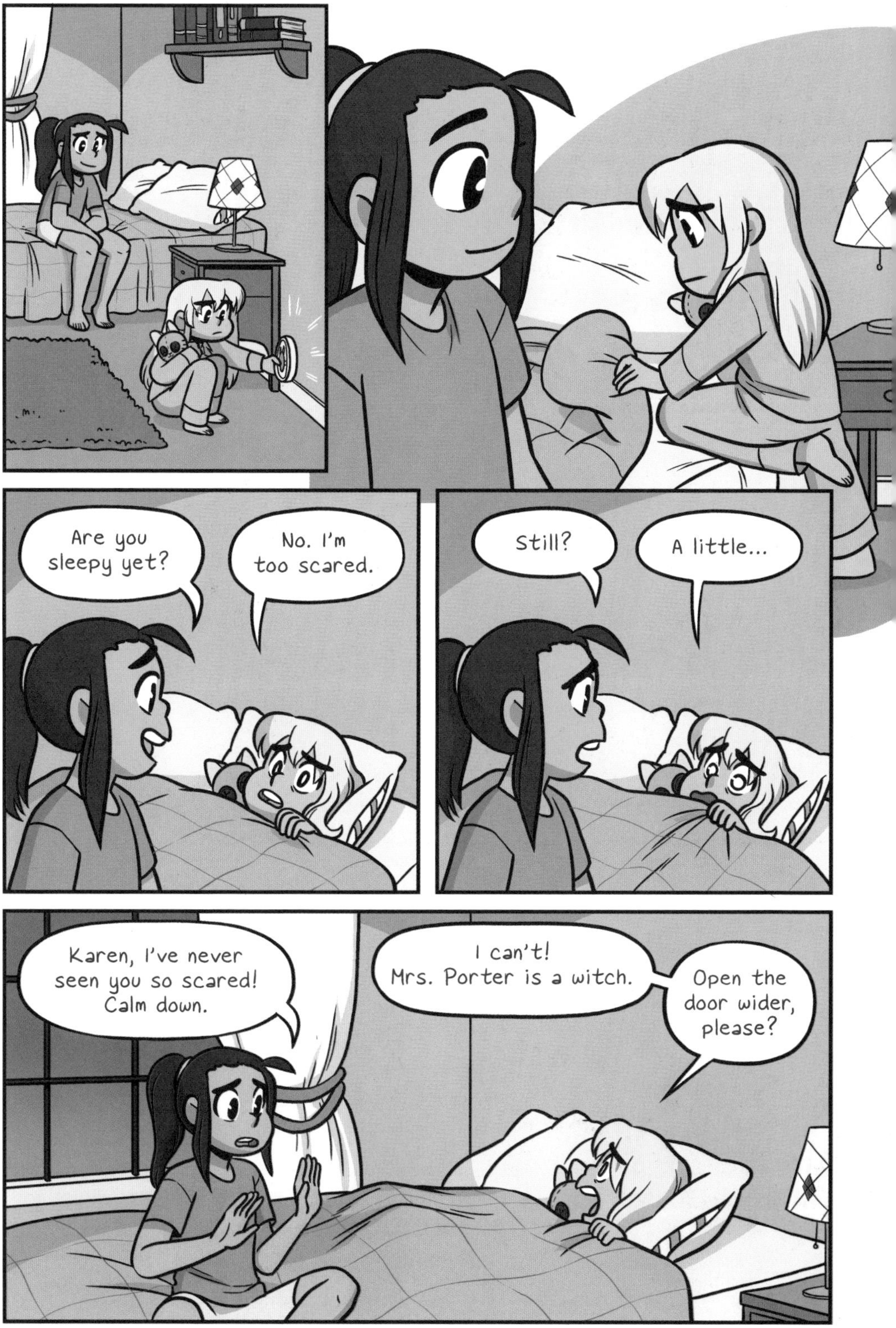

Are you sleepy yet?
No. I'm too scared.
Still?
A little...
Karen, I've never seen you so scared! Calm down.
I can't! Mrs. Porter is a witch.
Open the door wider, please?

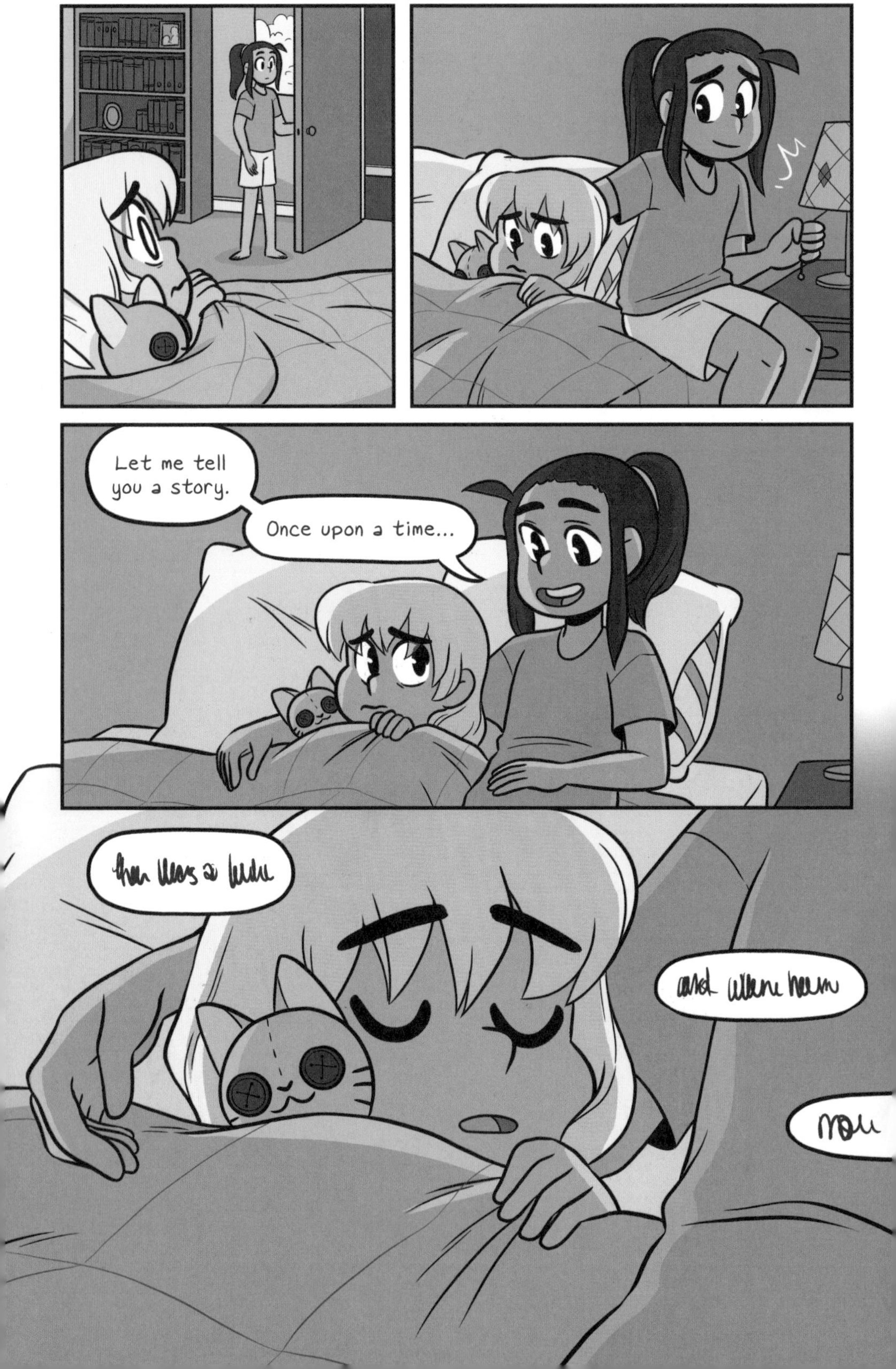

Let me tell you a story.
Once upon a time...

CHAPTER 4

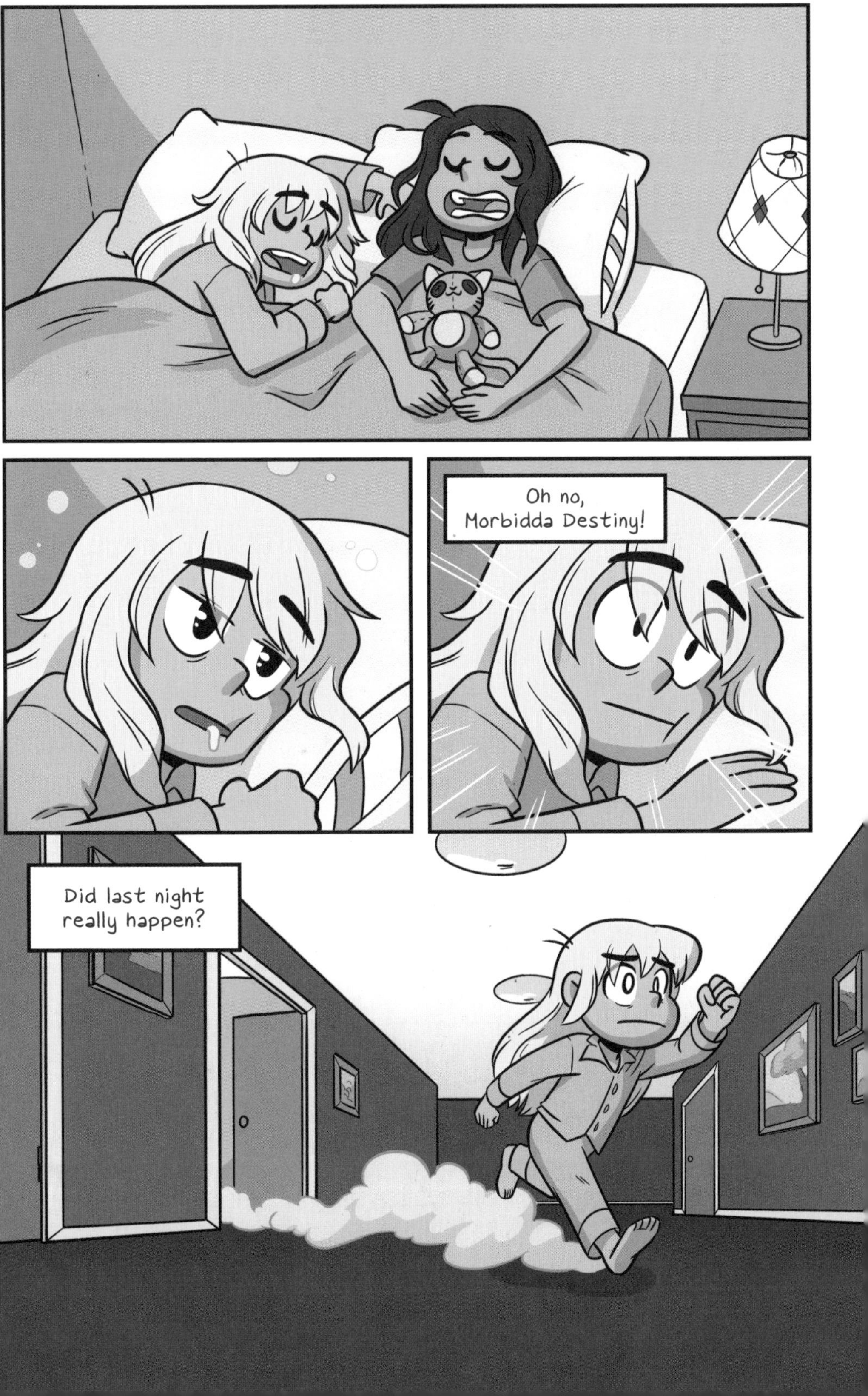
Oh no,
Morbidda Destiny!
Did last night
really happen?

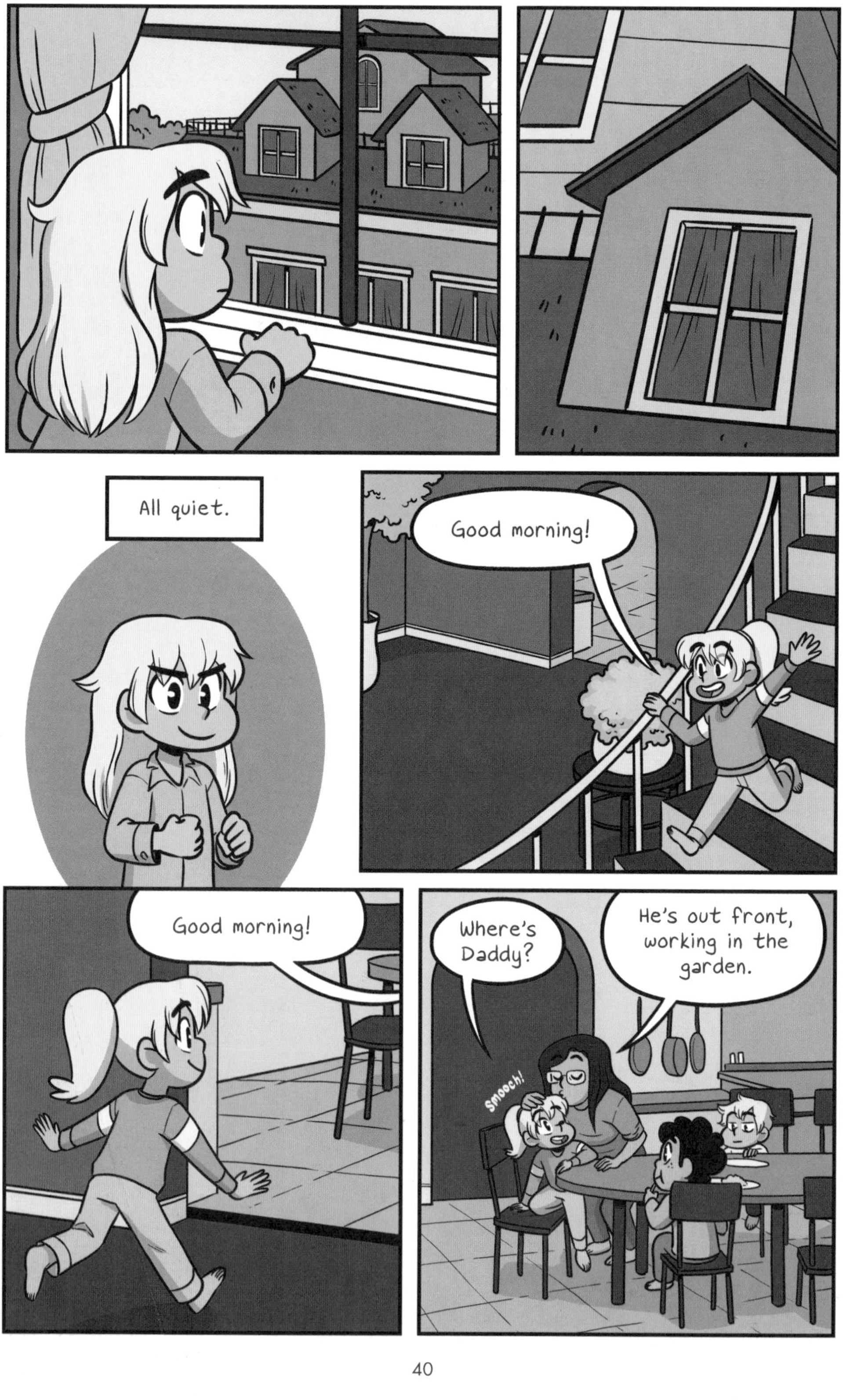
All quiet.
Good morning!
Good morning!
Where's Daddy?
Smooch!
He's out front, working in the garden.

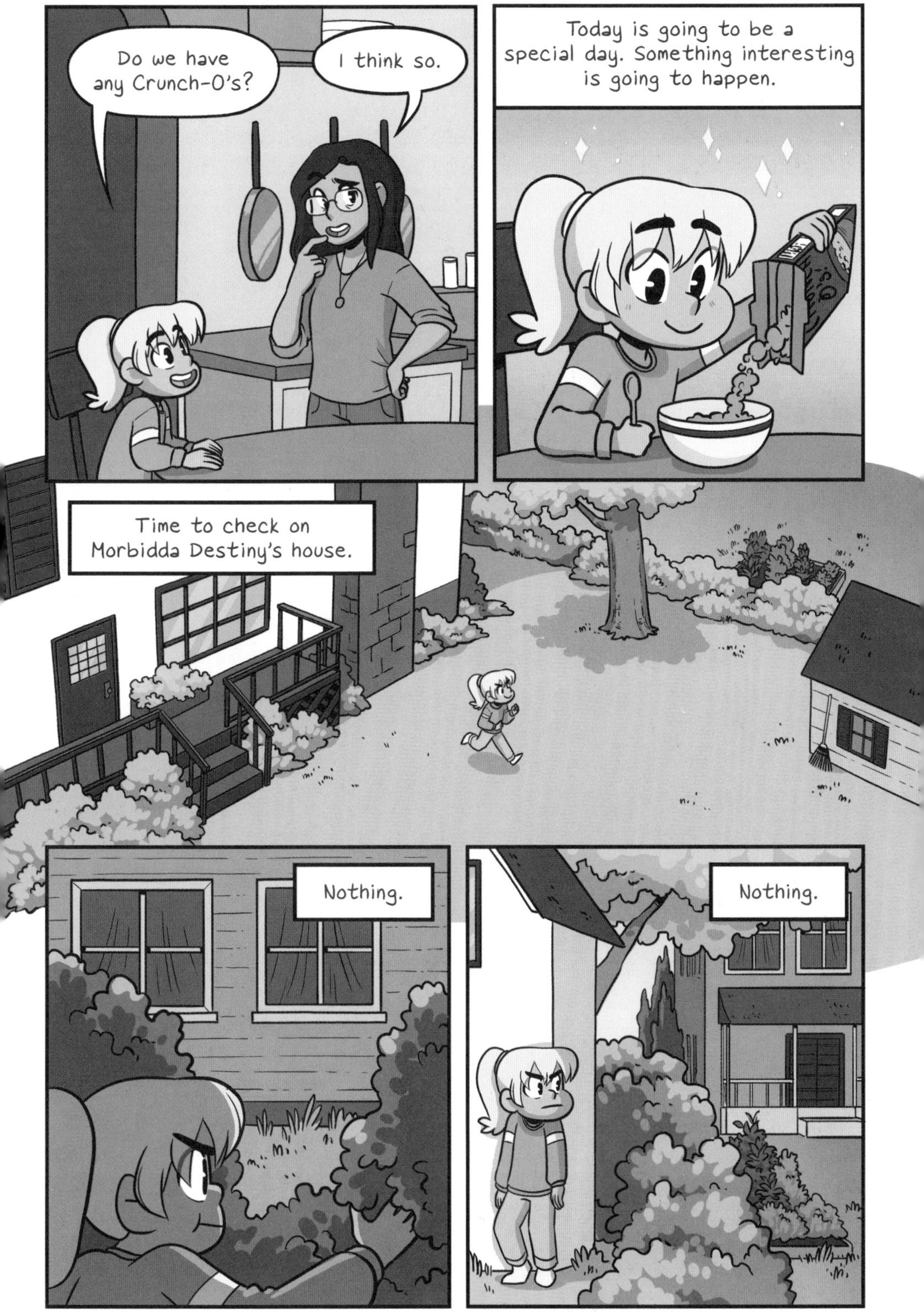
Do we have any Crunch-O's?
I think so.
Today is going to be a special day. Something interesting is going to happen.
Time to check on Morbidda Destiny's house.
Nothing.
Nothing.

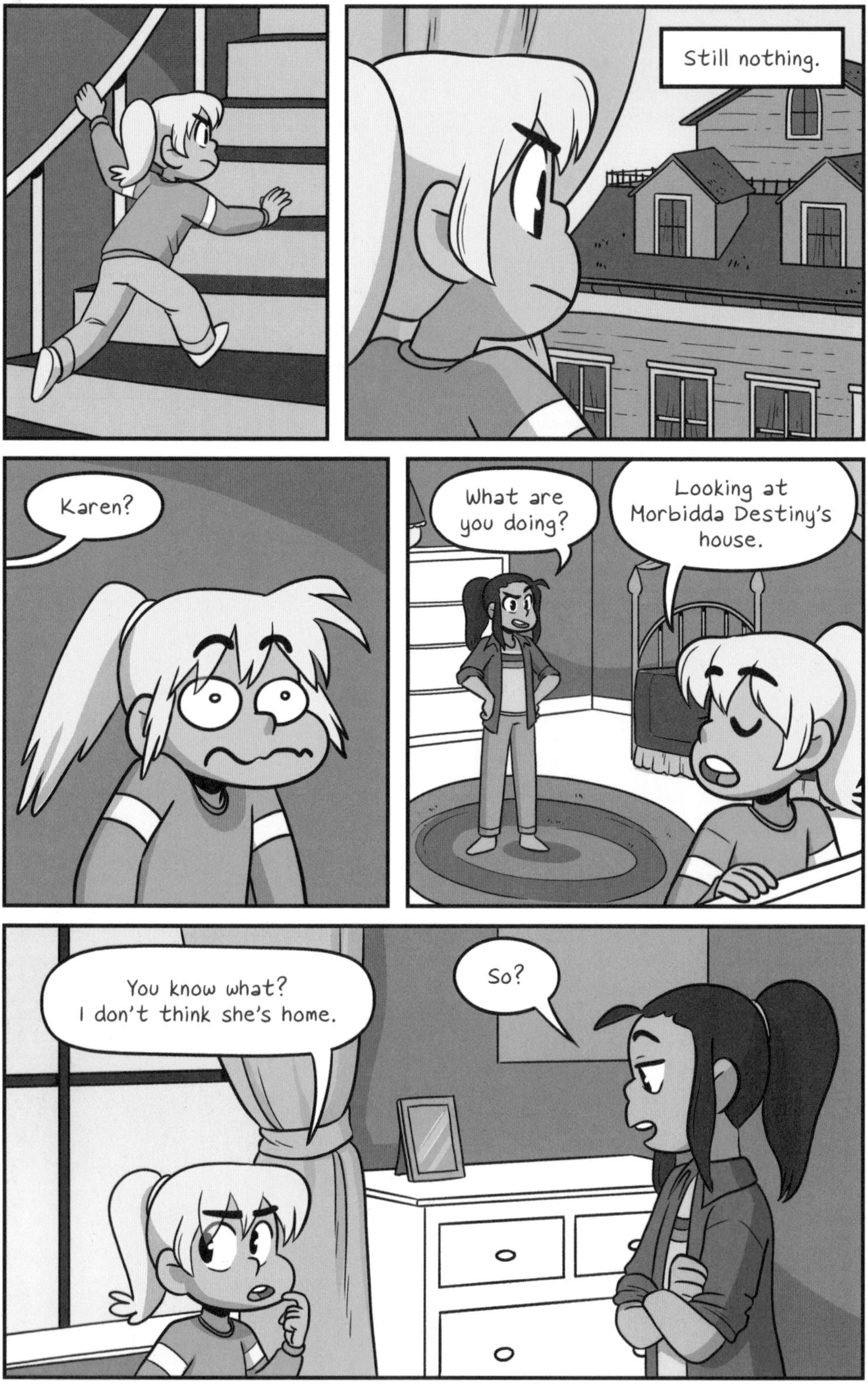

Still nothing.
Karen?
What are you doing?
Looking at Morbidda Destiny's house.
You know what? I don't think she's home.
So?

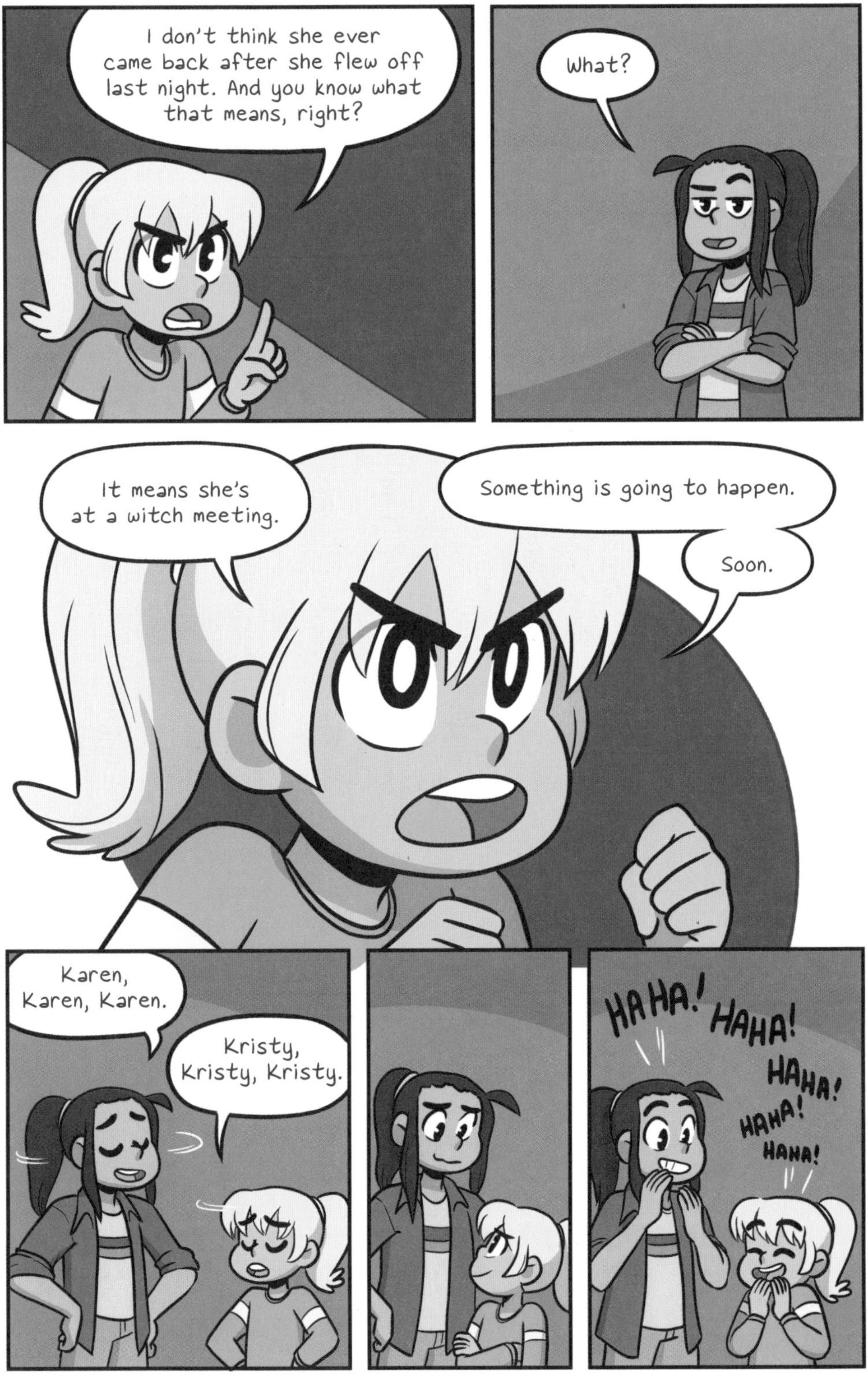
I don't think she ever came back after she flew off last night. And you know what that means, right?
What?
It means she's at a witch meeting.
Something is going to happen.
Soon.
Karen, Karen, Karen.
Kristy, Kristy, Kristy.
HAHA! HAHA!
HAHA!
HAHA!
HAHA!

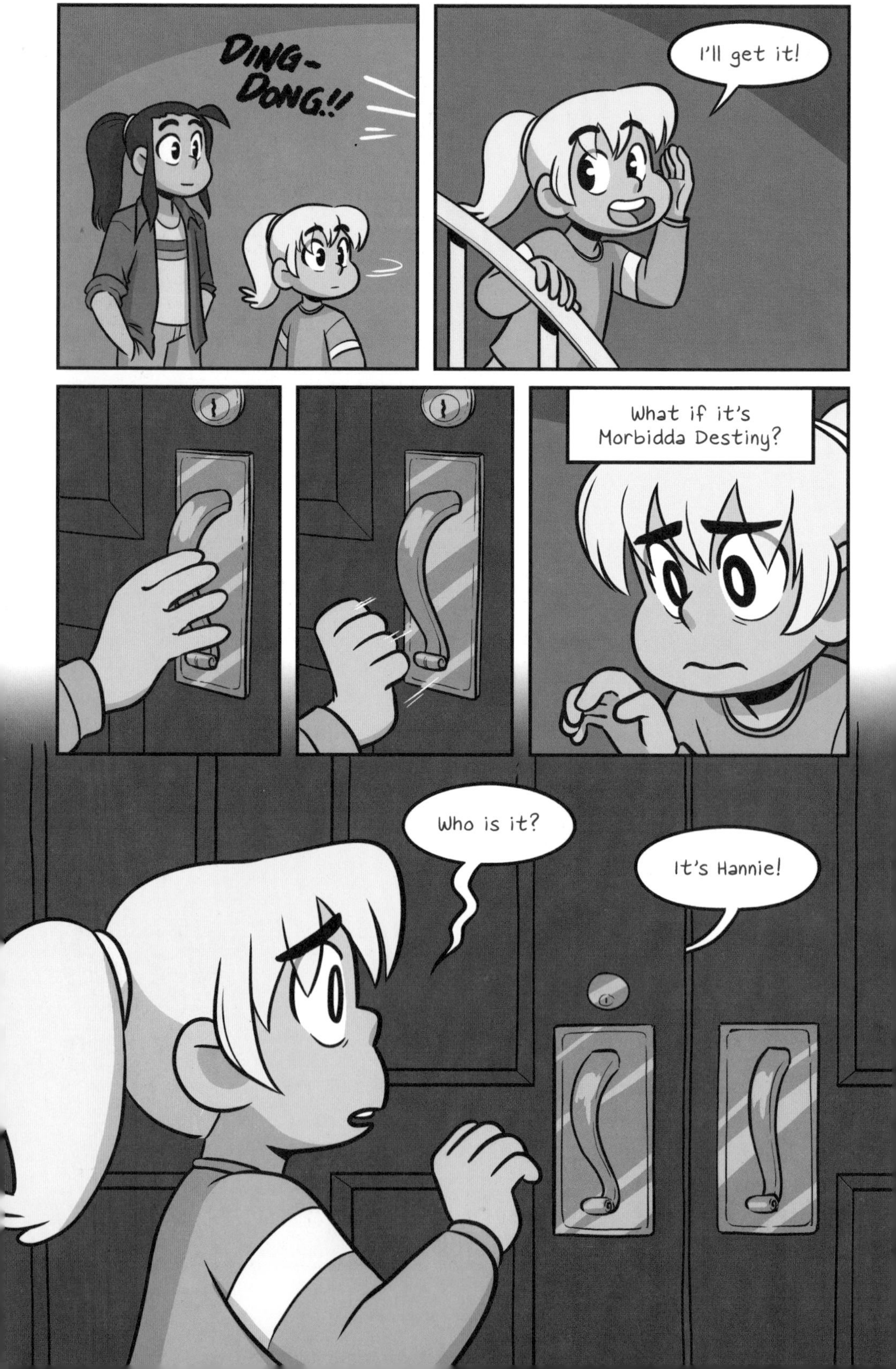
DING-DONG.!!
I'll get it!
What if it's Morbidda Destiny?
Who is it?
It's Hannie!

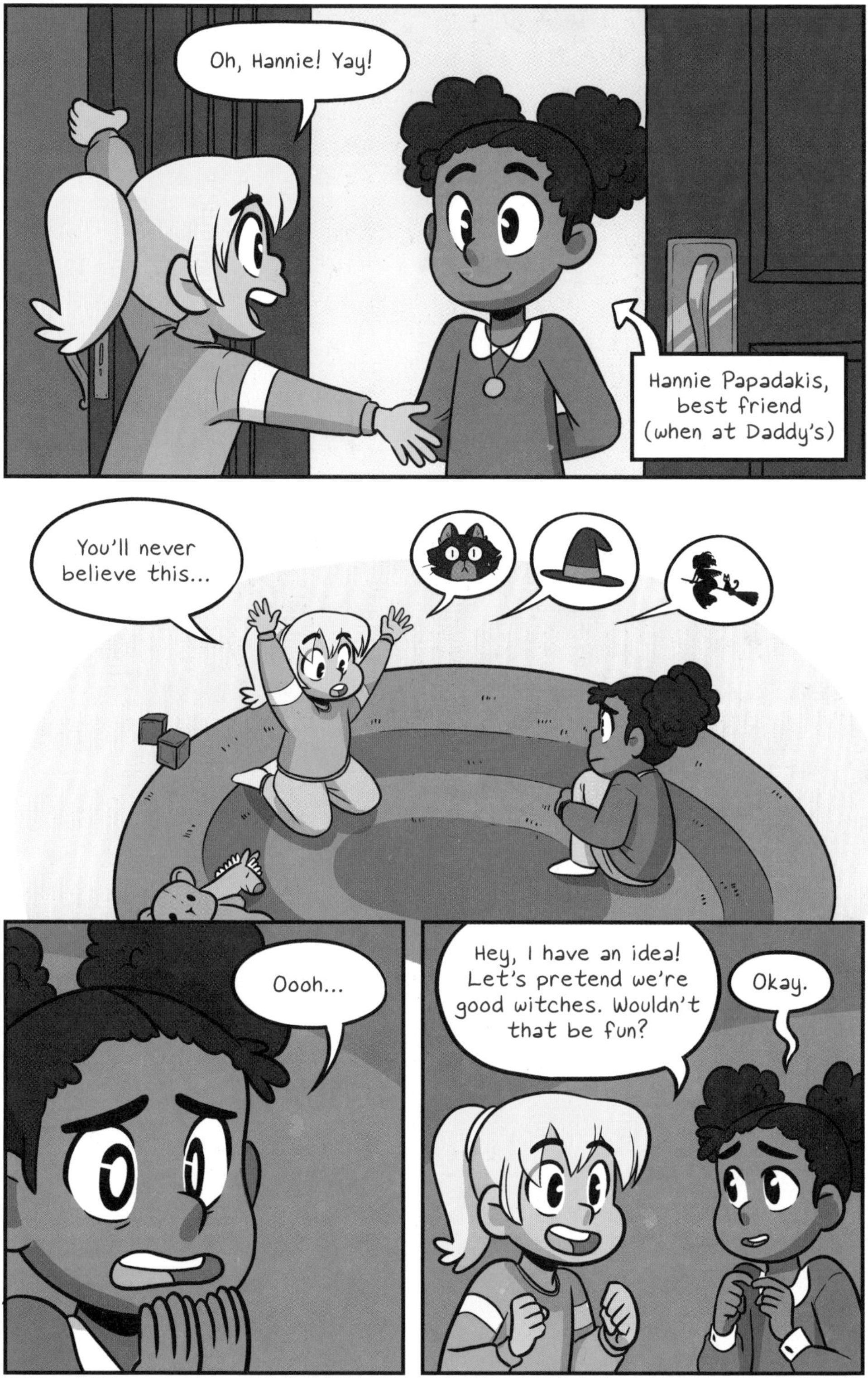
Oh, Hannie! Yay!
Hannie Papadakis, best friend (when at Daddy's)
You'll never believe this...
Oooh...
Hey, I have an idea! Let's pretend we're good witches. Wouldn't that be fun?
Okay.

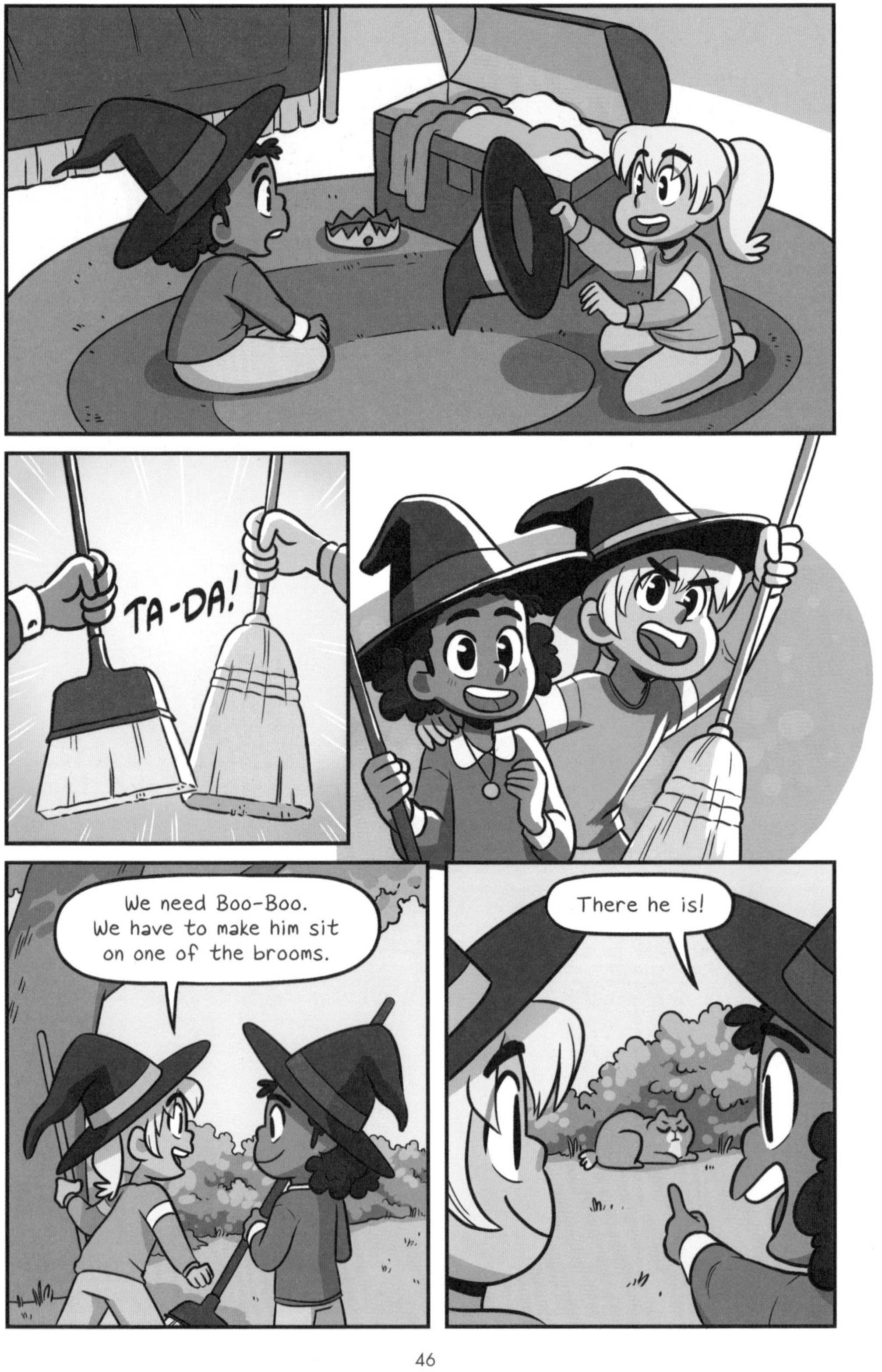
TA-DA!
We need Boo-Boo.
We have to make him sit
on one of the brooms.
There he is!

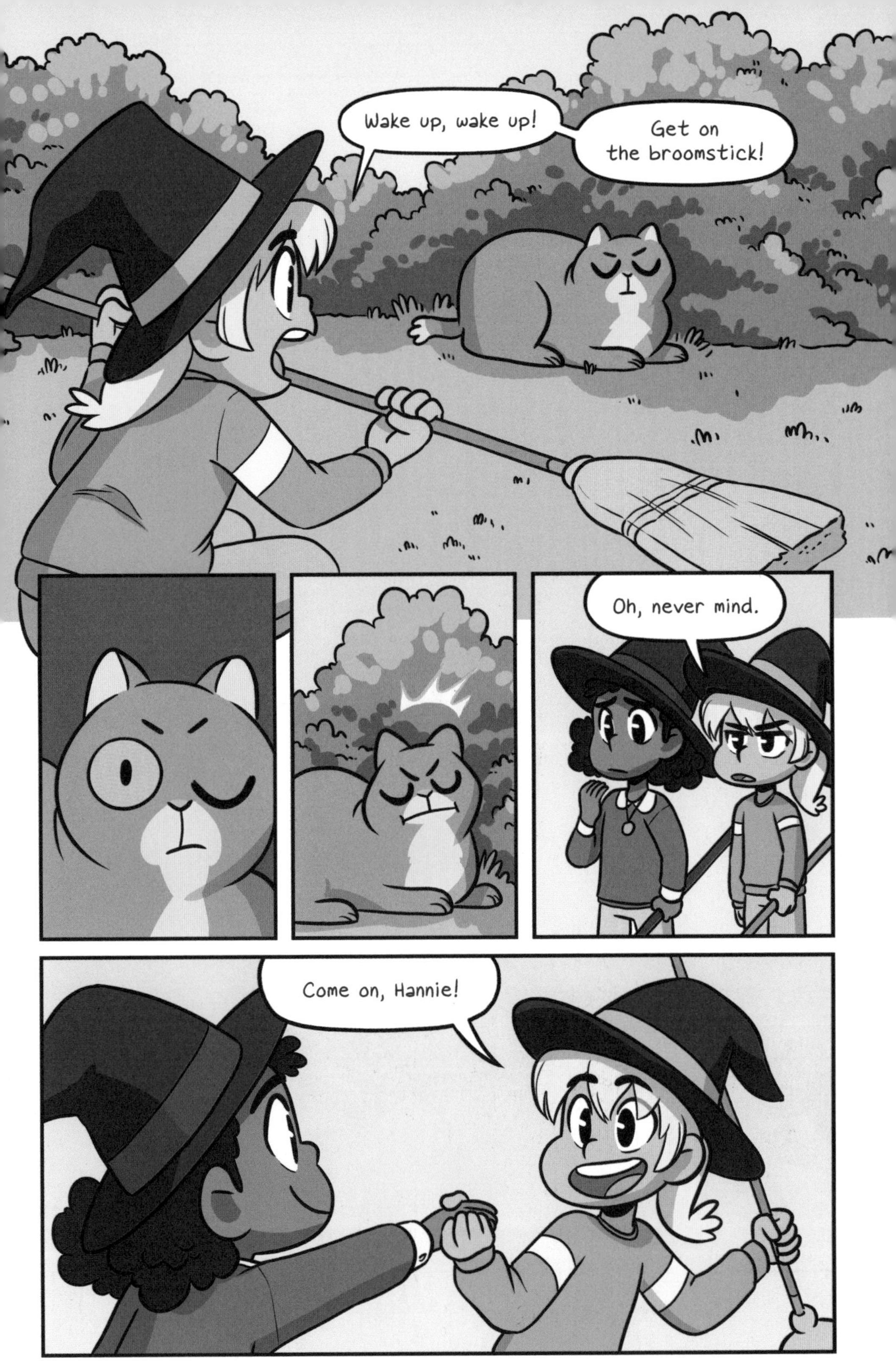
Wake up, wake up!
Get on the broomstick!
Oh, never mind.
Come on, Hannie!

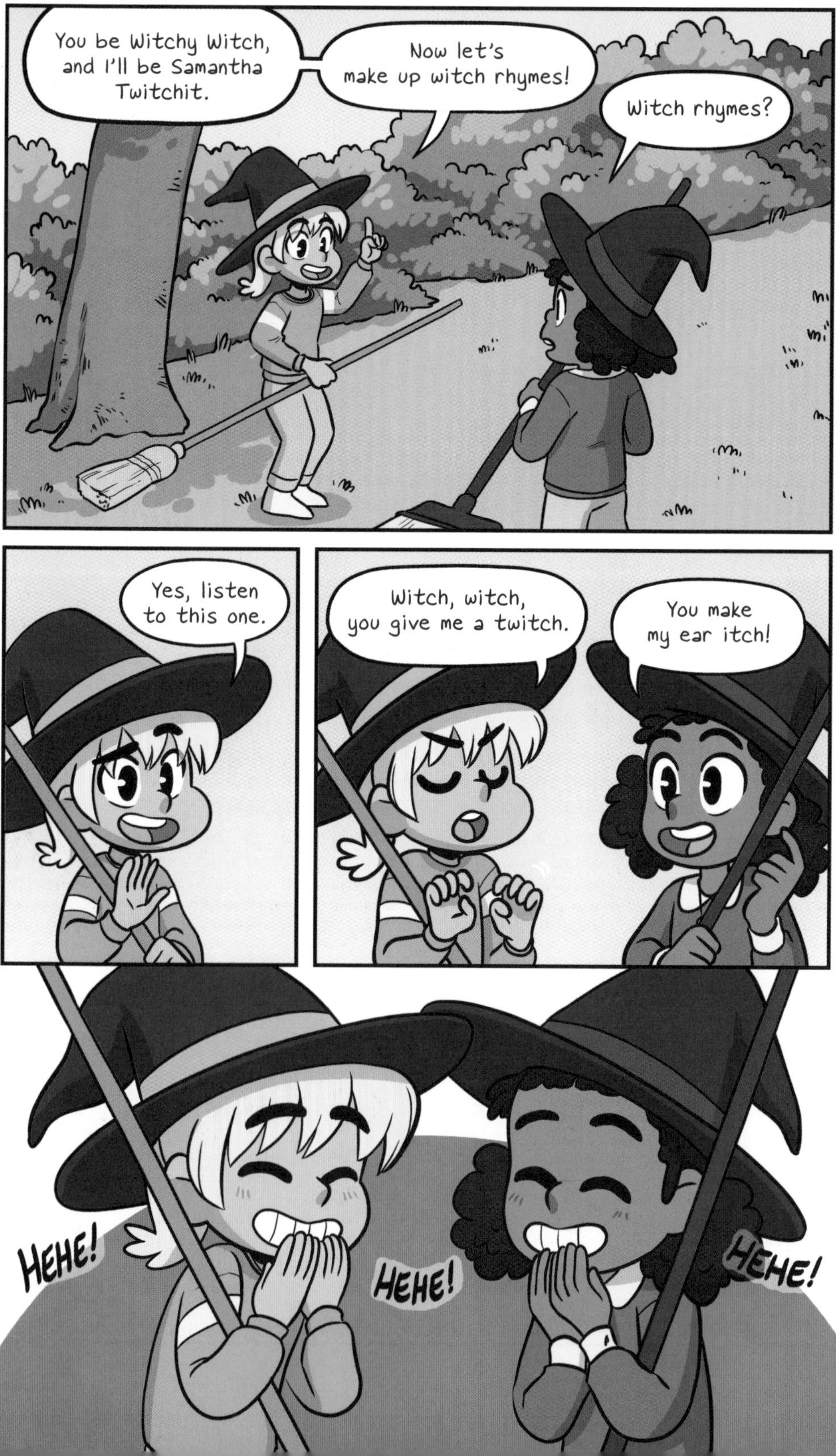
You be Witchy Witch, and I'll be Samantha Twitchit.
Now let's make up witch rhymes!
Witch rhymes?
Yes, listen to this one.
Witch, witch, you give me a twitch.
You make my ear itch!
HEHE!
HEHE!
HEHE!

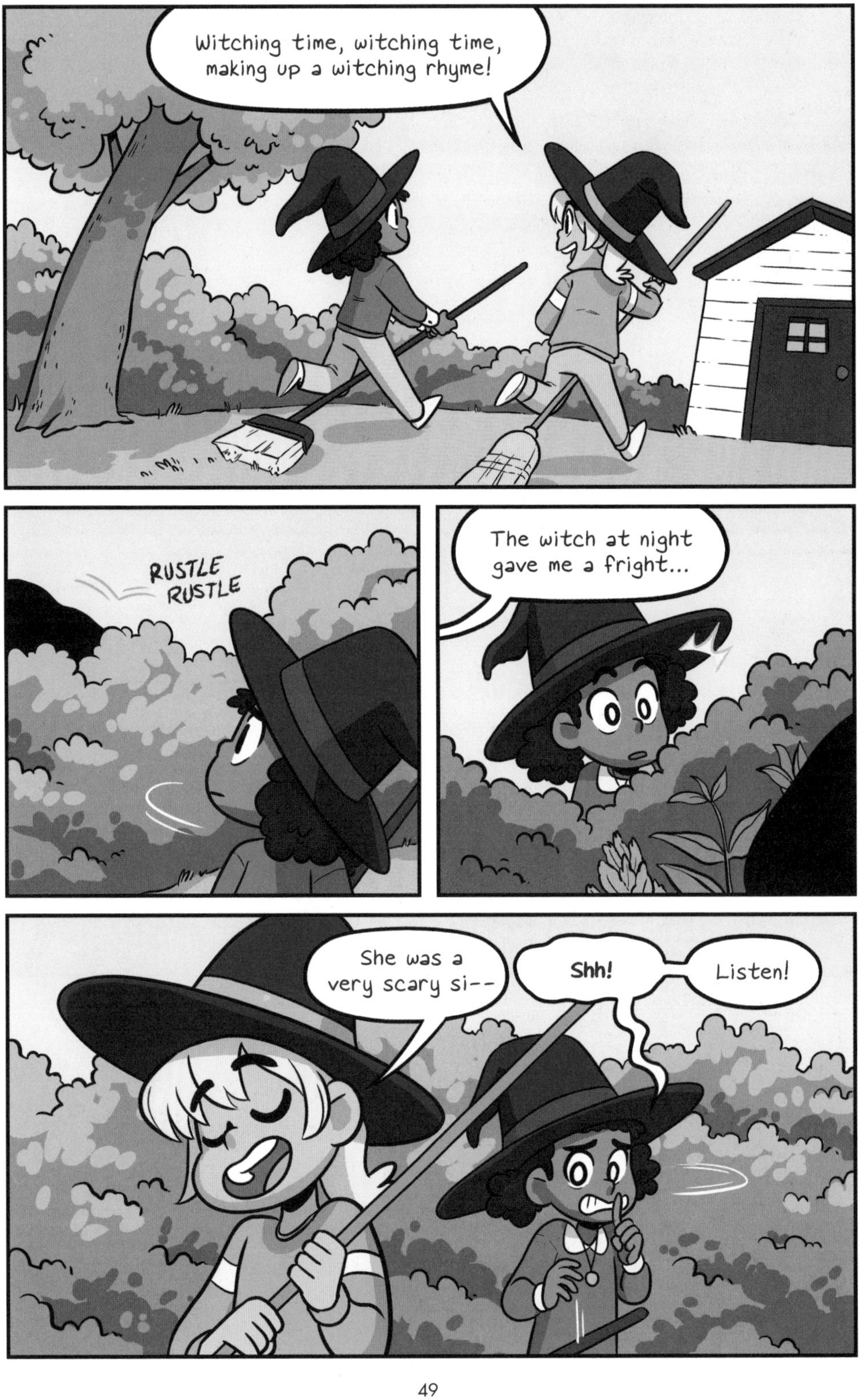
Witching time, witching time,
making up a witching rhyme!
RUSTLE
RUSTLE
The witch at night
gave me a fright...
She was a
very scary si--
Shh!
Listen!

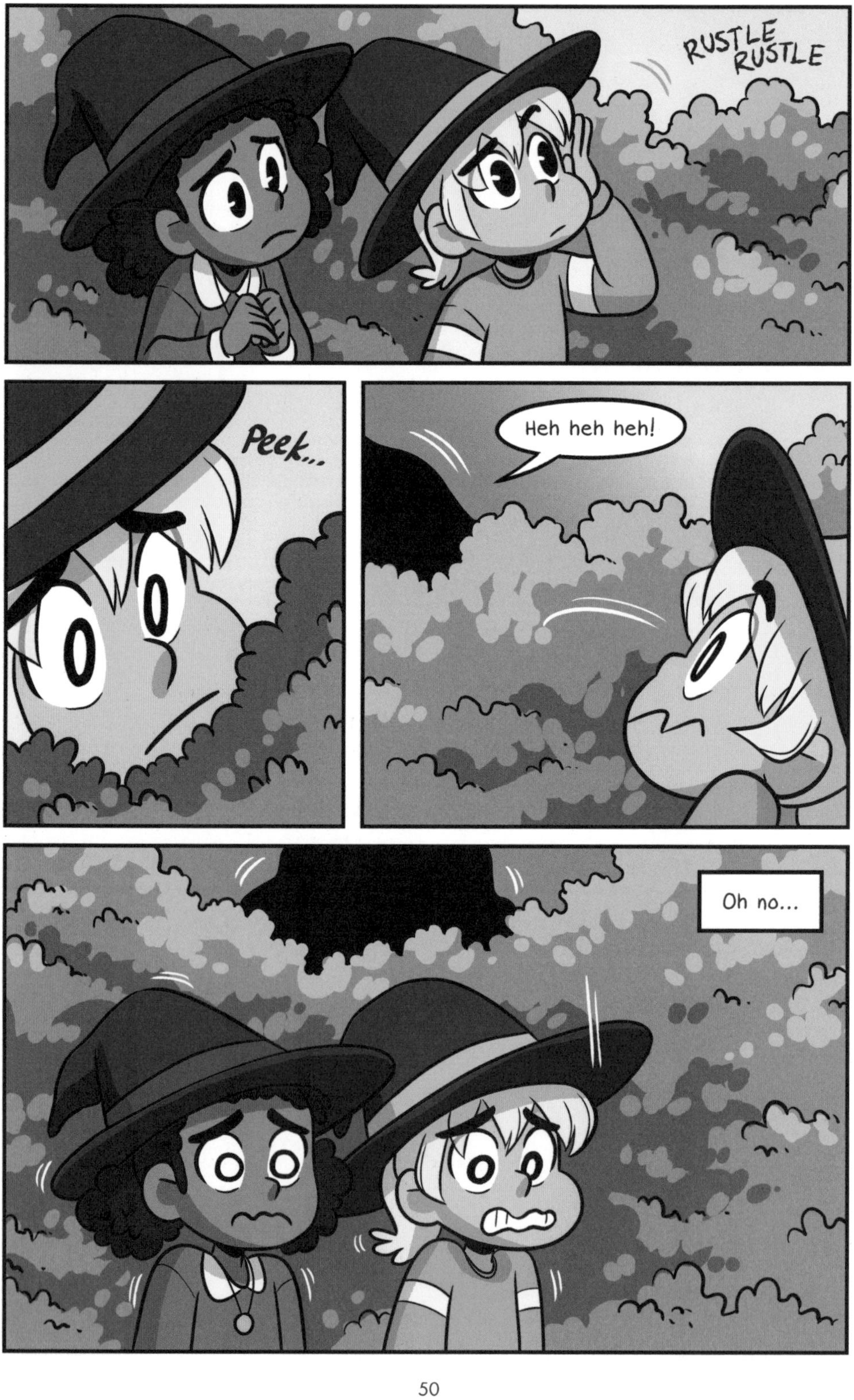
RUSTLE RUSTLE
Peek...
Heh heh heh!
Oh no...

CHAPTER 5

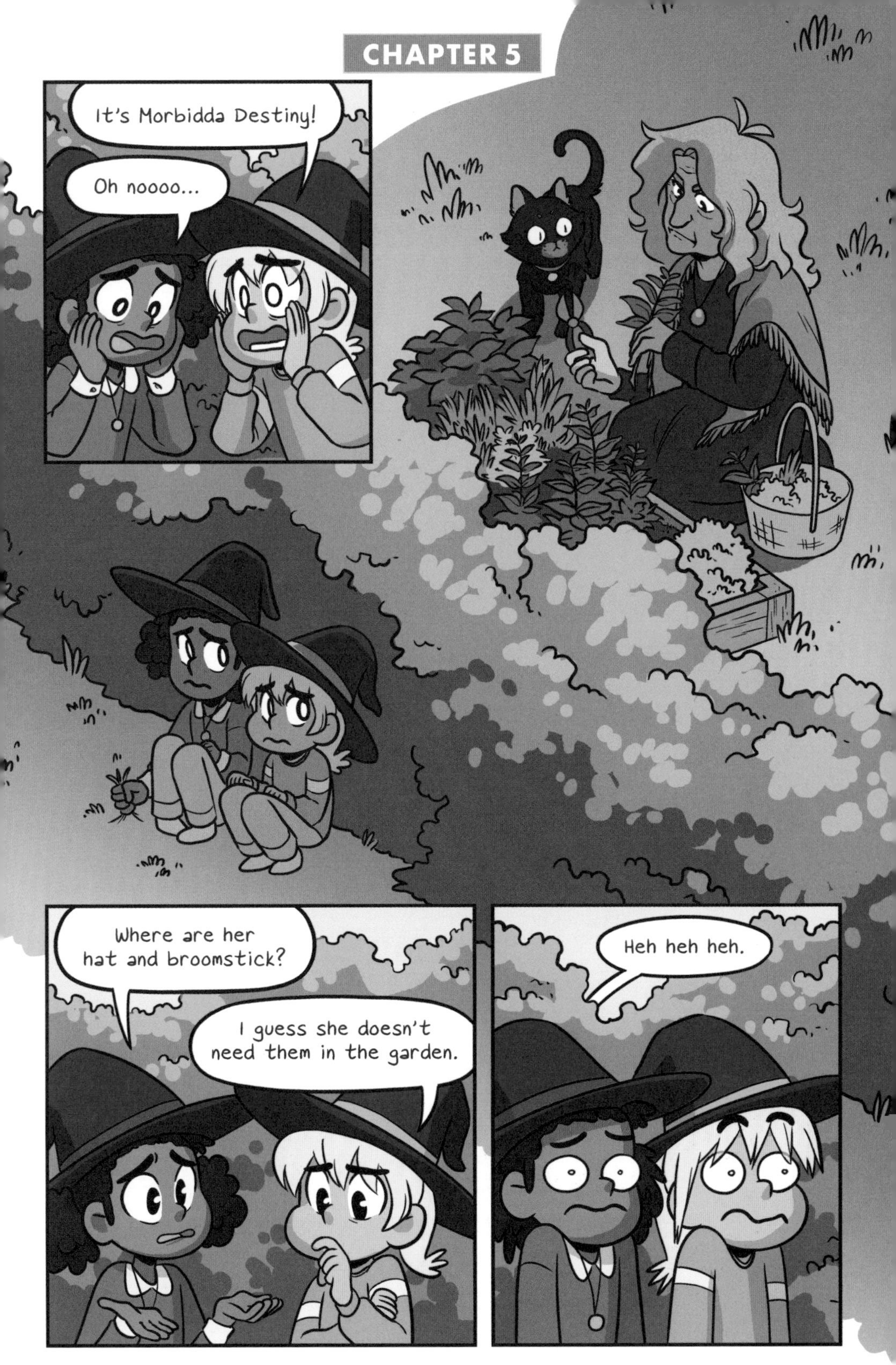

It's Morbidda Destiny!
Oh noooo...
Where are her hat and broomstick?
I guess she doesn't need them in the garden.
Heh heh heh.

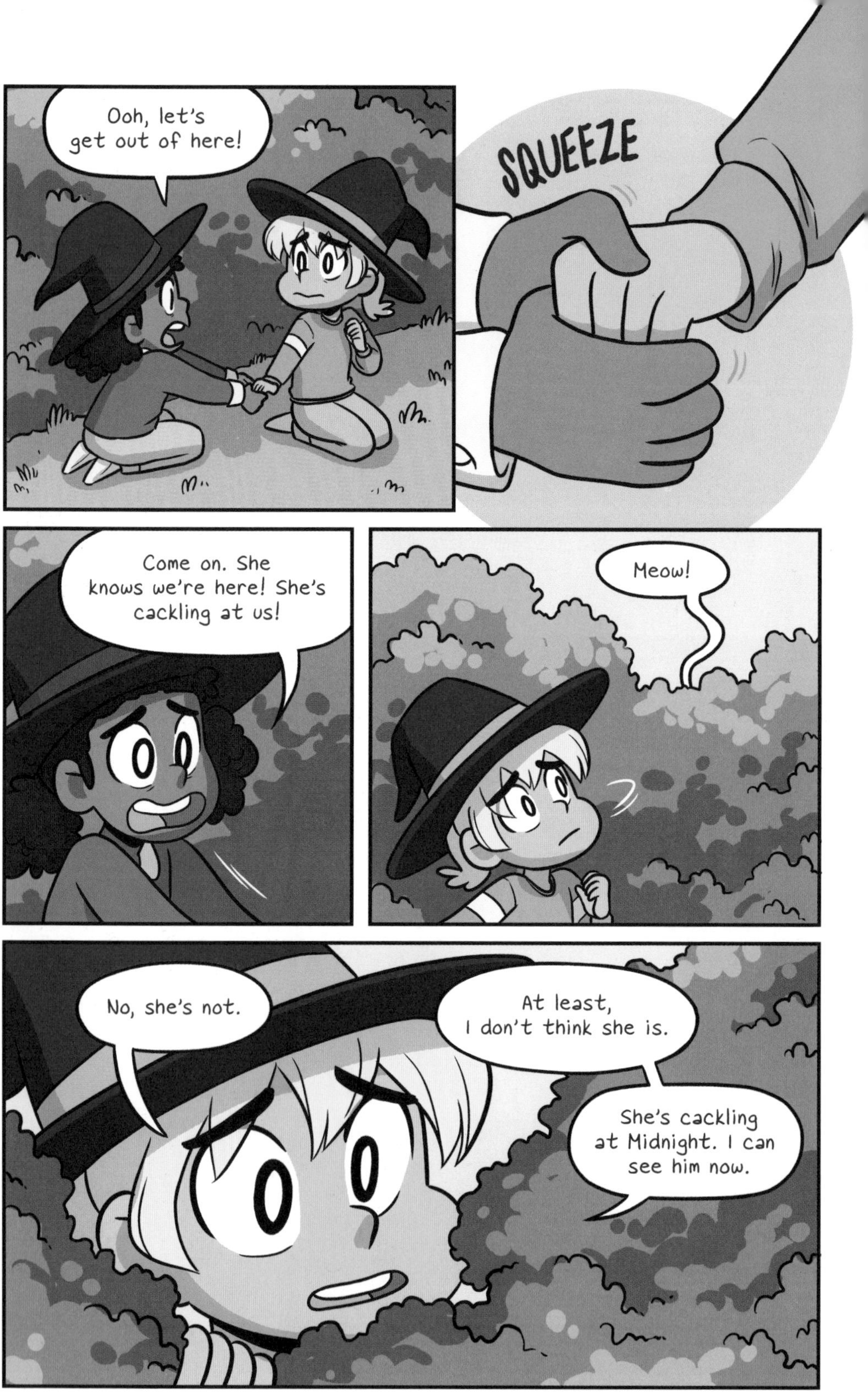
Ooh, let's get out of here!
SQUEEZE
Come on. She knows we're here! She's cackling at us!
Meow!
No, she's not.
At least, I don't think she is.
She's cackling at Midnight. I can see him now.

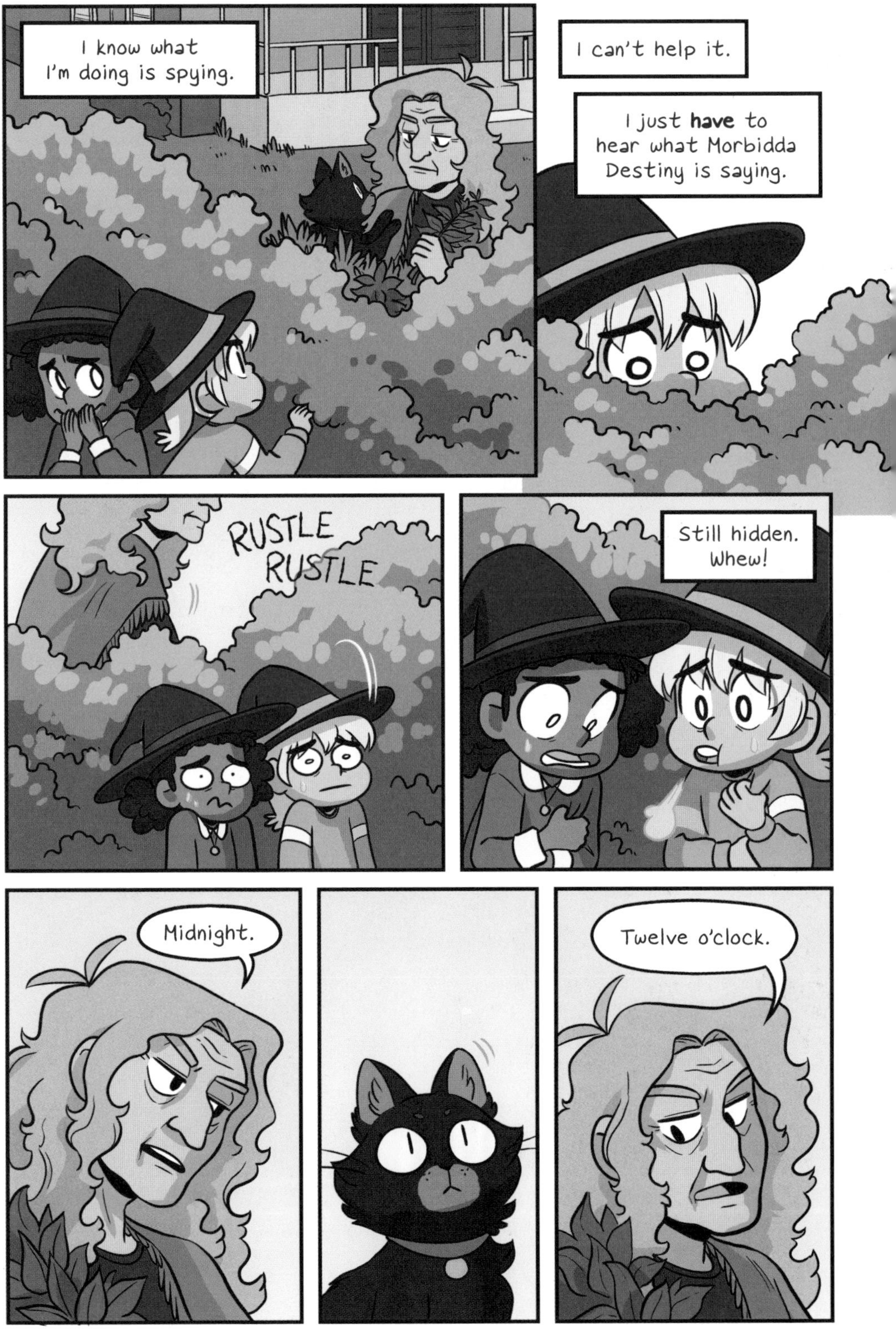

I know what I'm doing is spying.
I can't help it.
I just **have** to hear what Morbidda Destiny is saying.
RUSTLE RUSTLE
Still hidden. Whew!
Midnight.
Twelve o'clock.

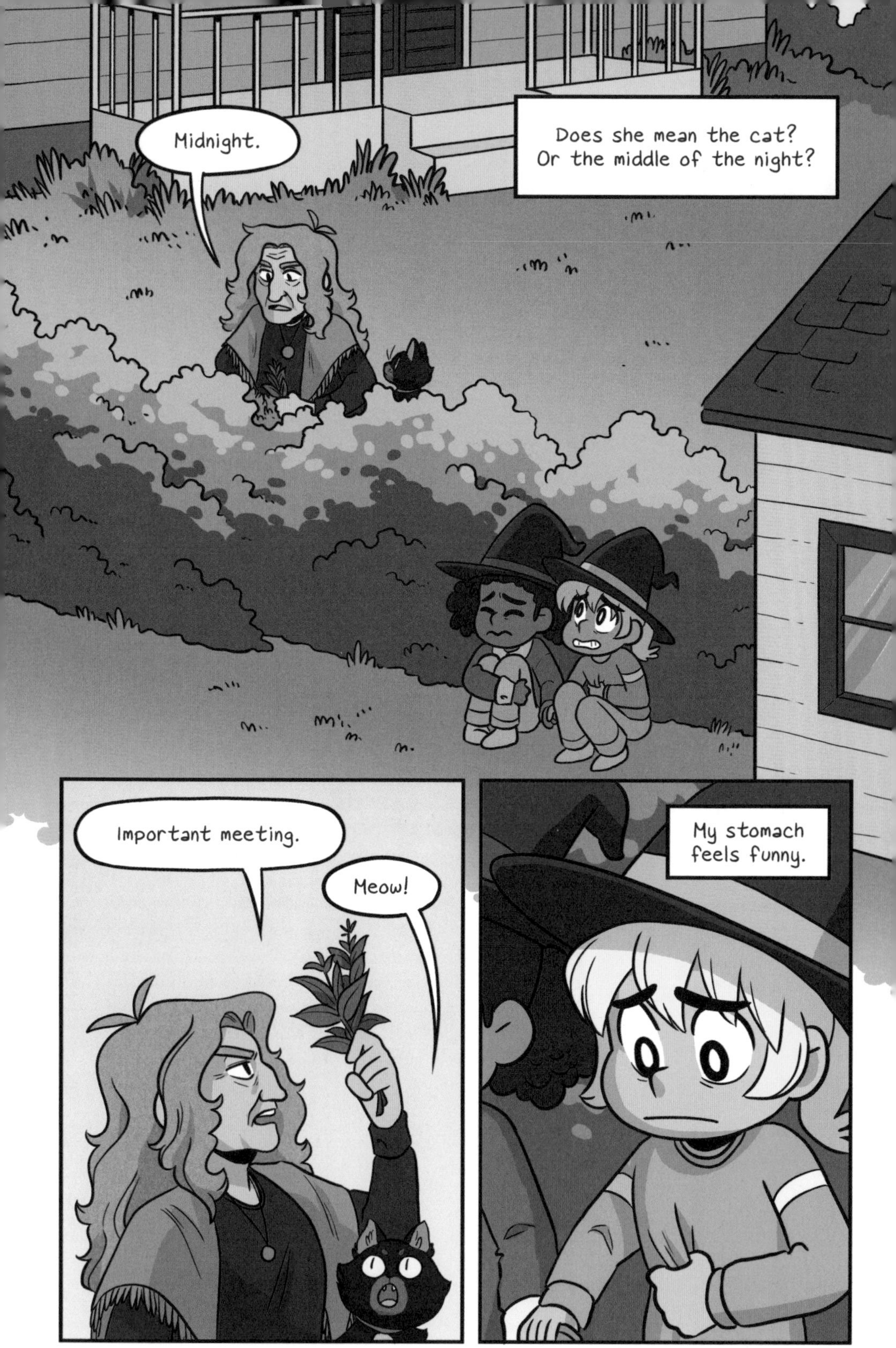
Midnight.
Does she mean the cat? Or the middle of the night?
Important meeting.
Meow!
My stomach feels funny.

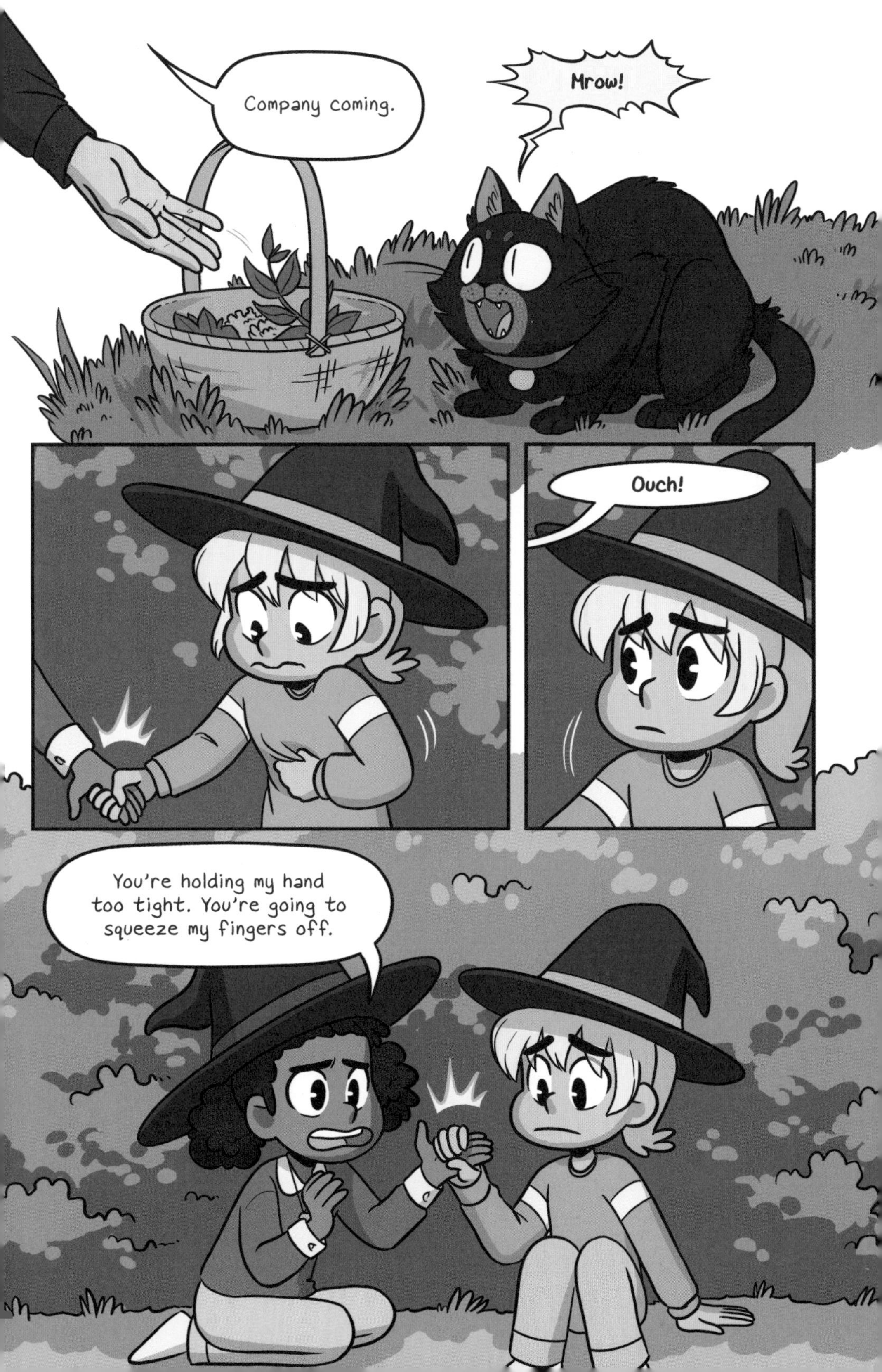
Company coming.
Mrow!
Ouch!
You're holding my hand too tight. You're going to squeeze my fingers off.

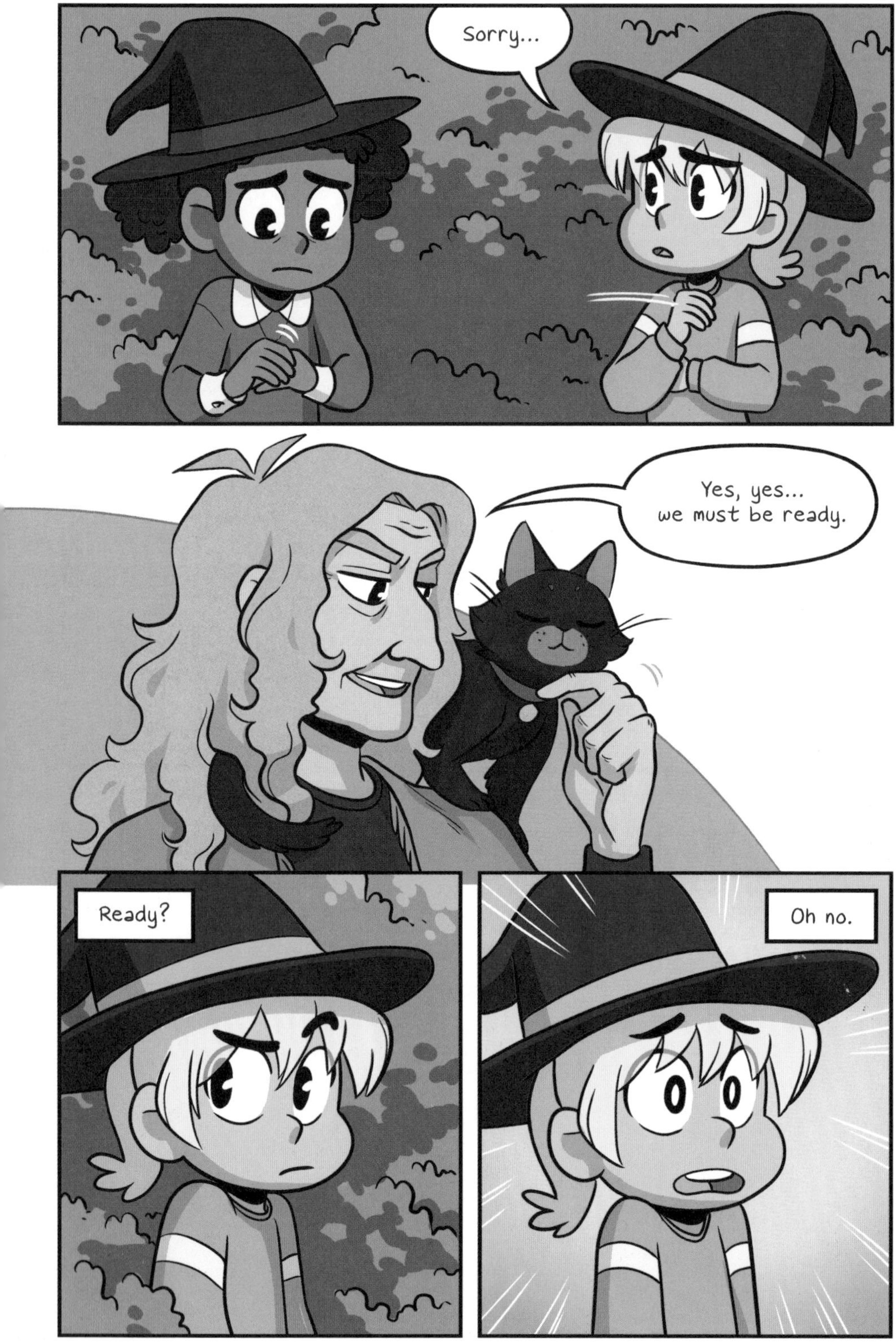
Sorry...
Yes, yes...
we must be ready.
Ready?
Oh no.

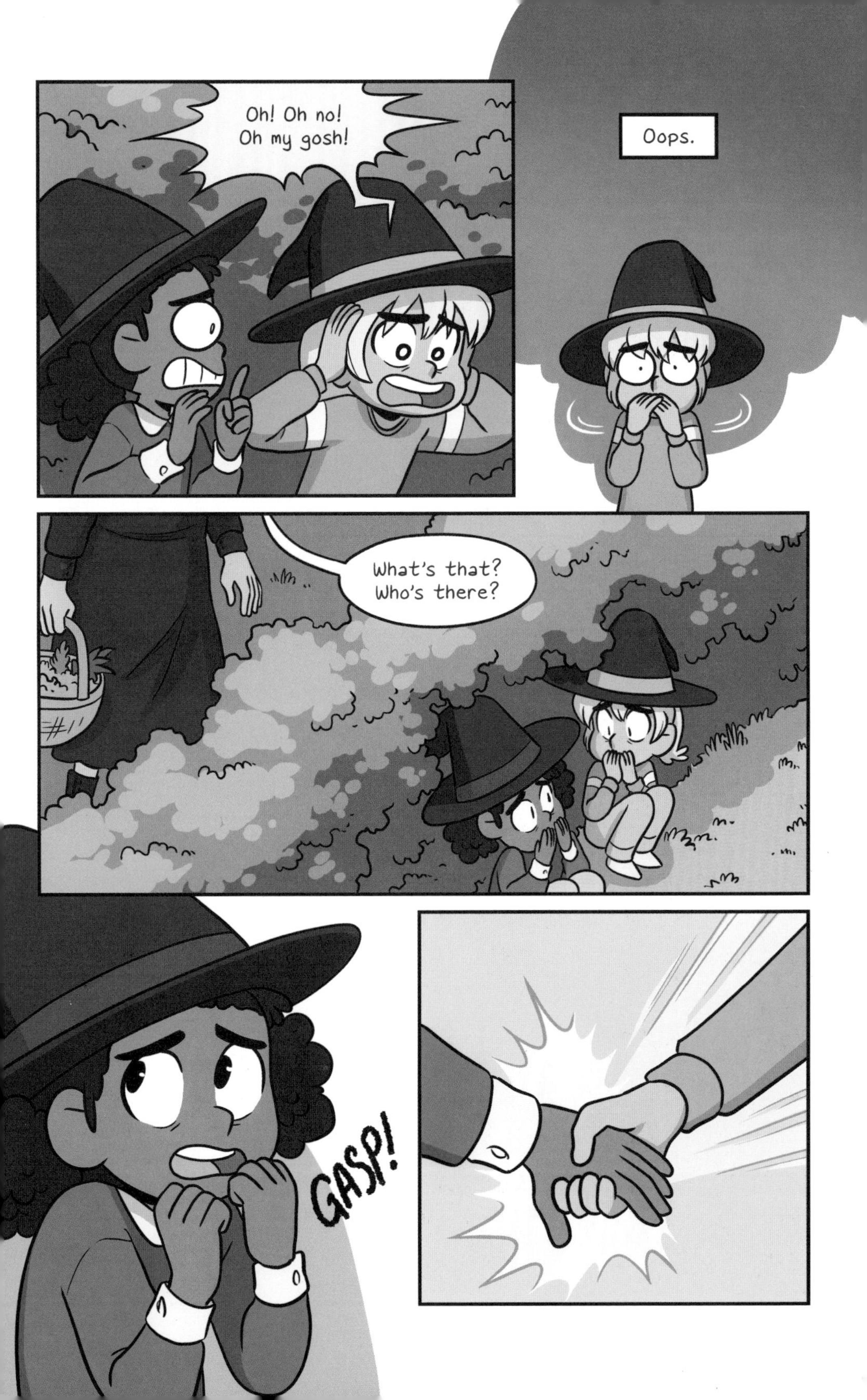
Oh! Oh no!
Oh my gosh!
Oops.
What's that?
Who's there?
GASP!

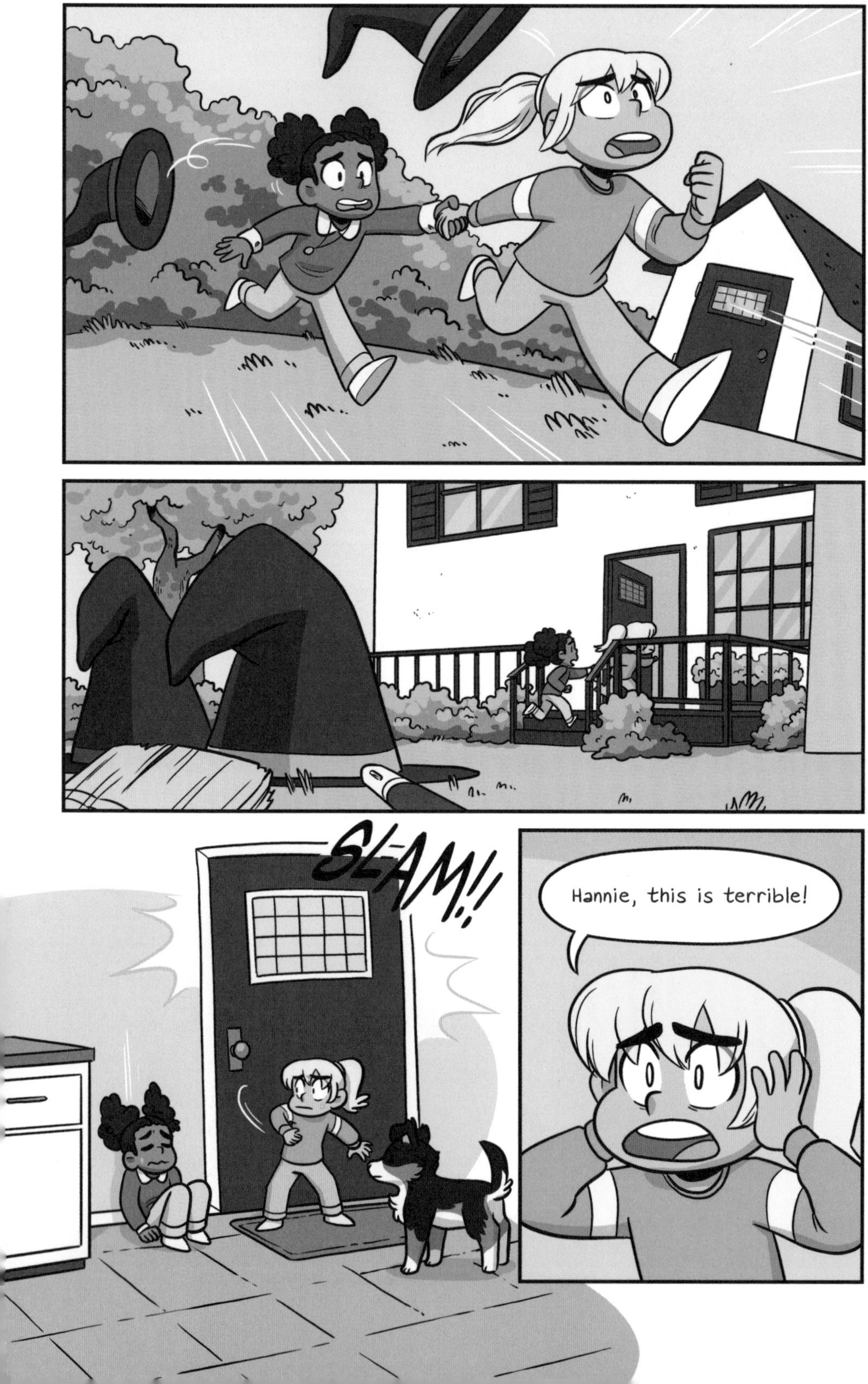
SLAM!!
Hannie, this is terrible!

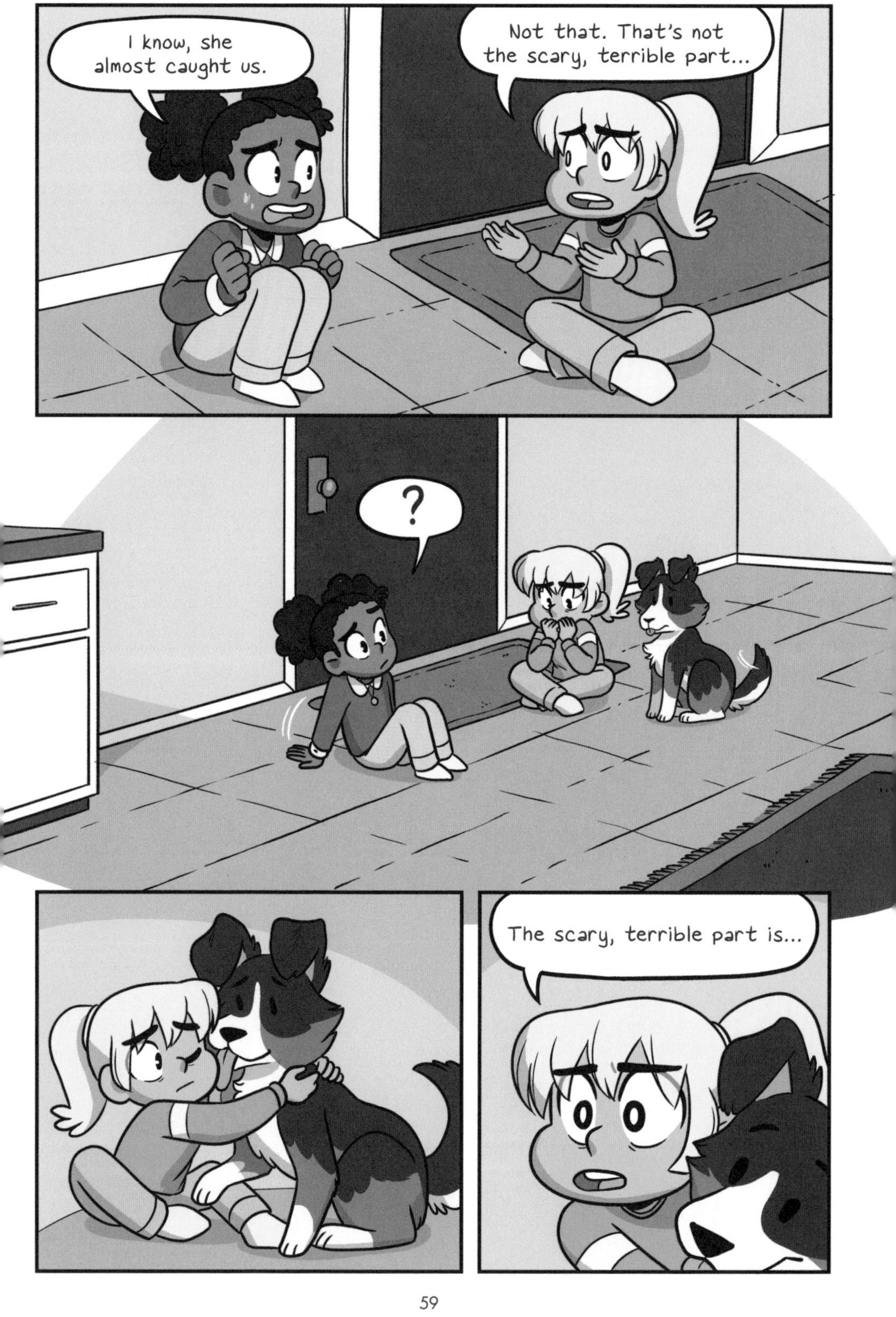
I know, she almost caught us.
Not that. That's not the scary, terrible part...
?
The scary, terrible part is...

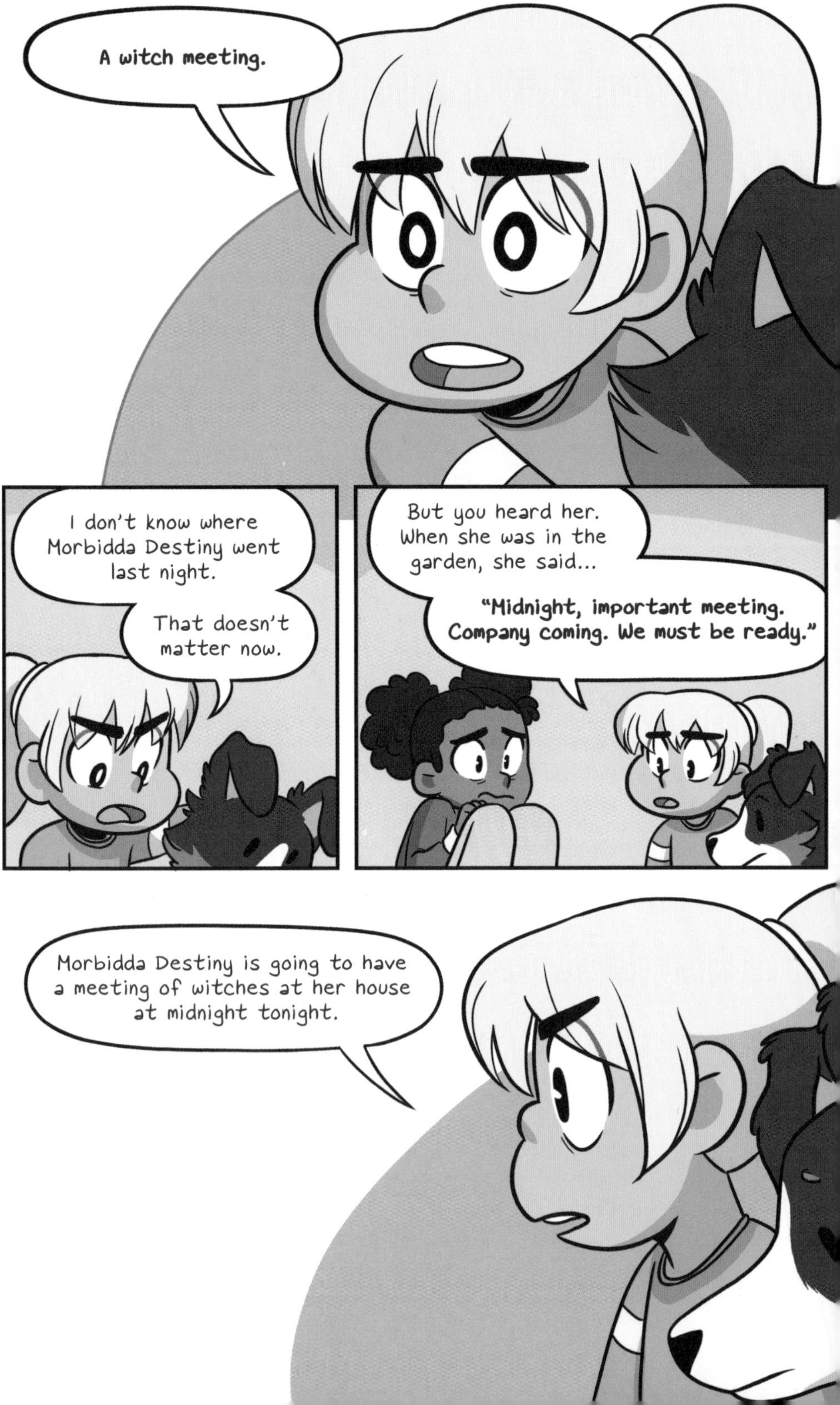
A witch meeting.
I don't know where Morbidda Destiny went last night.
That doesn't matter now.
But you heard her. When she was in the garden, she said...
"Midnight, important meeting. Company coming. We must be ready."
Morbidda Destiny is going to have a meeting of witches at her house at midnight tonight.

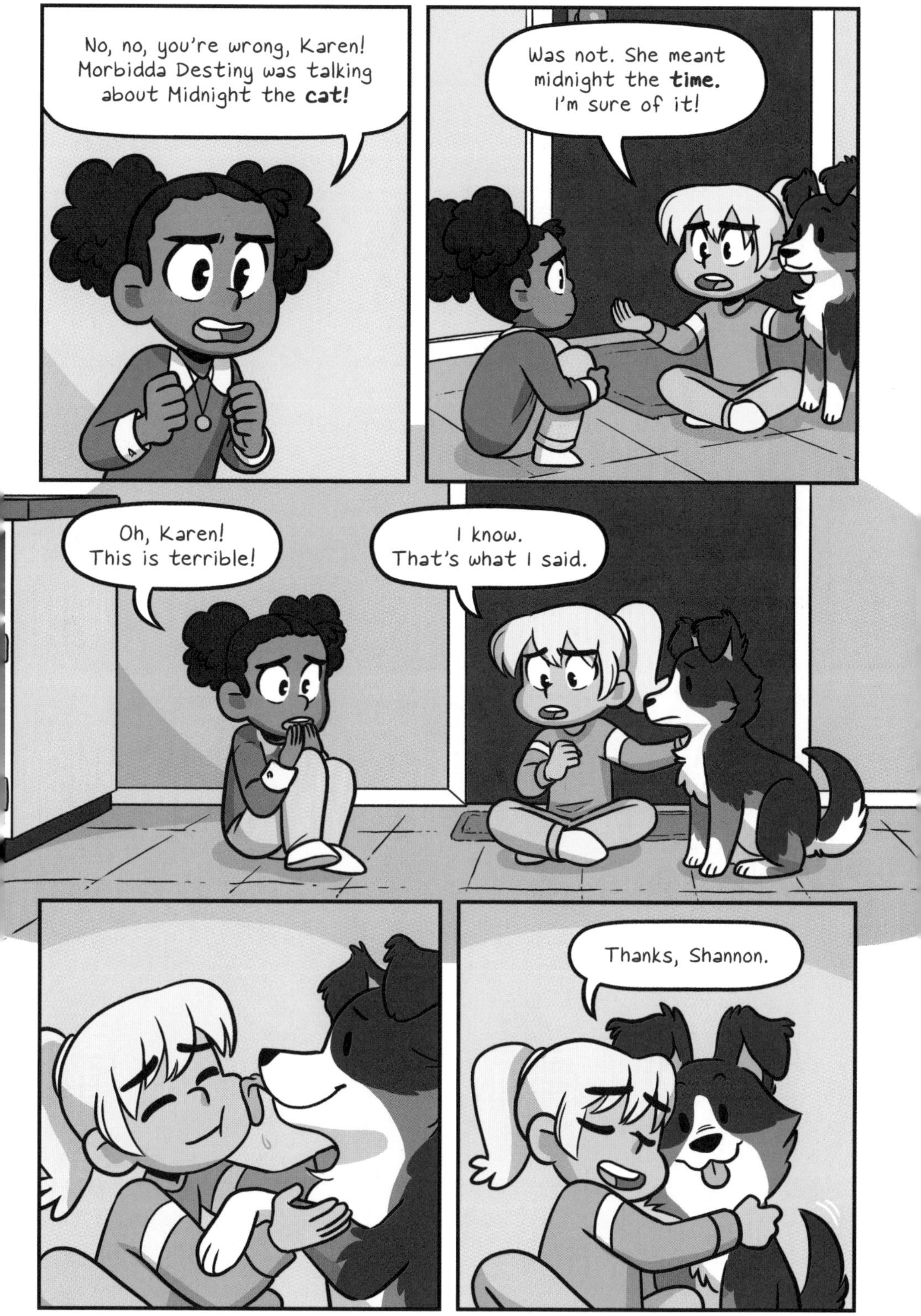
No, no, you're wrong, Karen! Morbidda Destiny was talking about Midnight the **cat!**
Was not. She meant midnight the **time.** I'm sure of it!
Oh, Karen! This is terrible!
I know. That's what I said.
Thanks, Shannon.

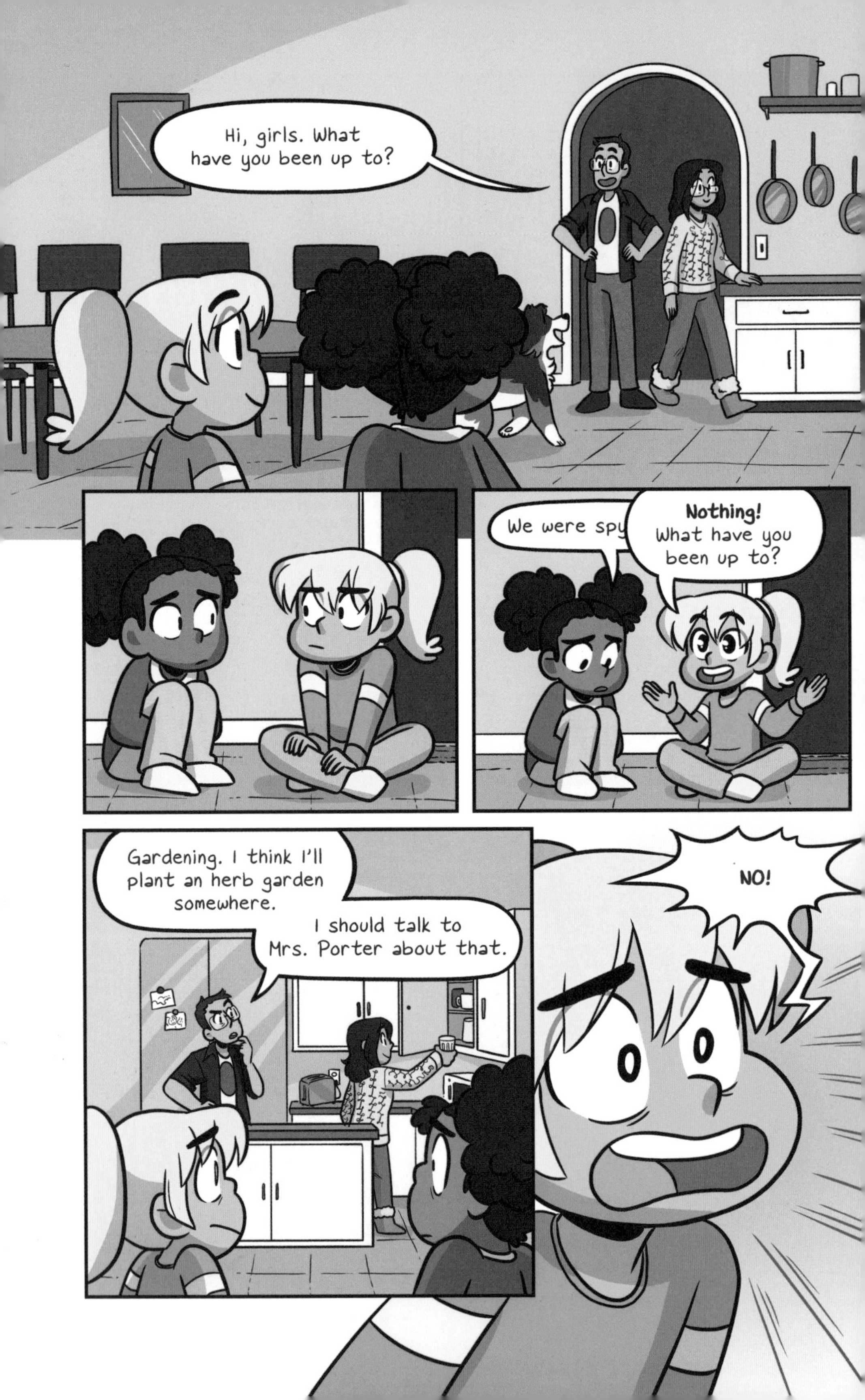
Hi, girls. What have you been up to?
We were spy
Nothing! What have you been up to?
Gardening. I think I'll plant an herb garden somewhere.
I should talk to Mrs. Porter about that.
NO!

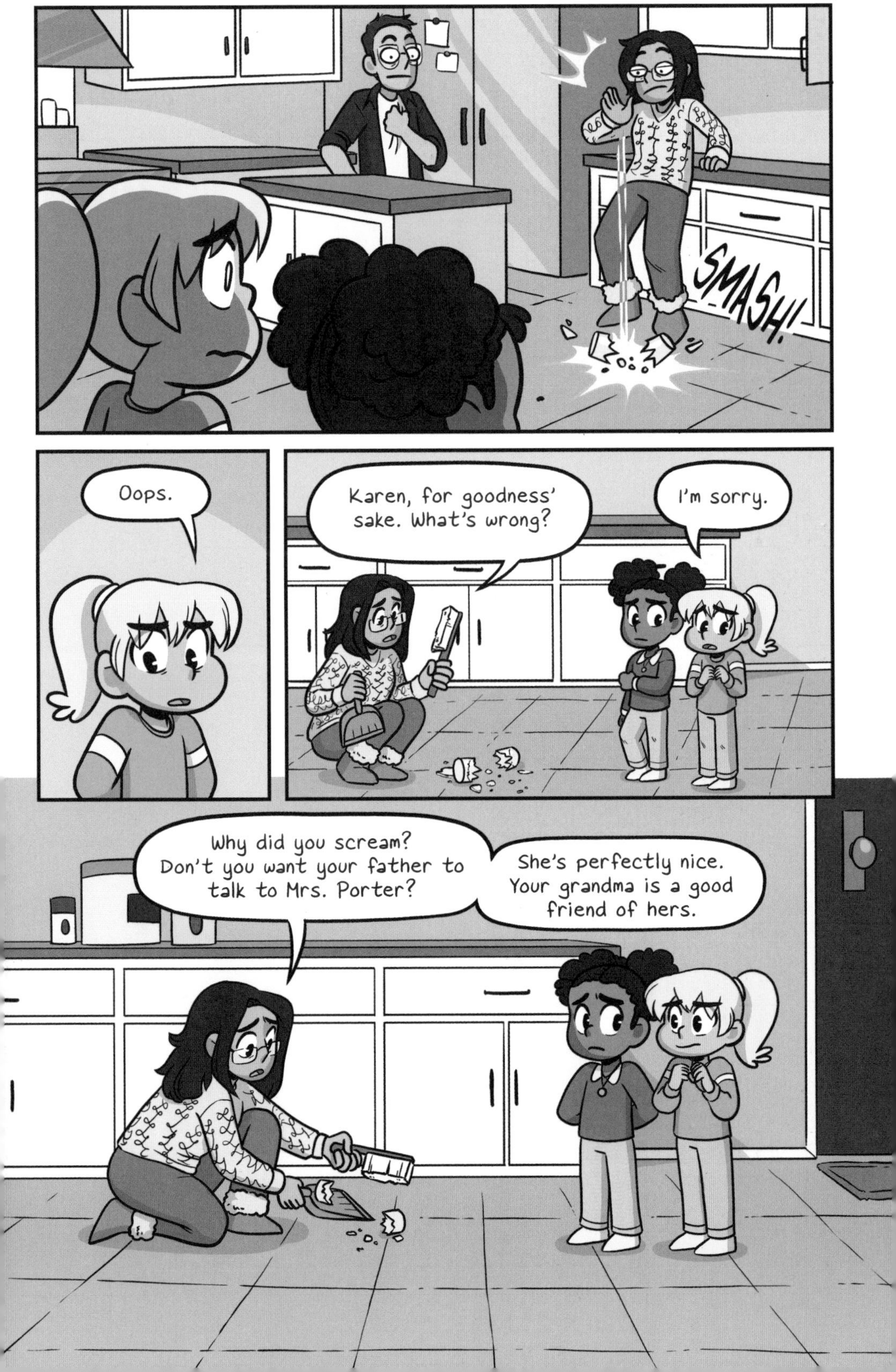
SMASH!
Oops.
Karen, for goodness' sake. What's wrong?
I'm sorry.
Why did you scream? Don't you want your father to talk to Mrs. Porter?
She's perfectly nice. Your grandma is a good friend of hers.

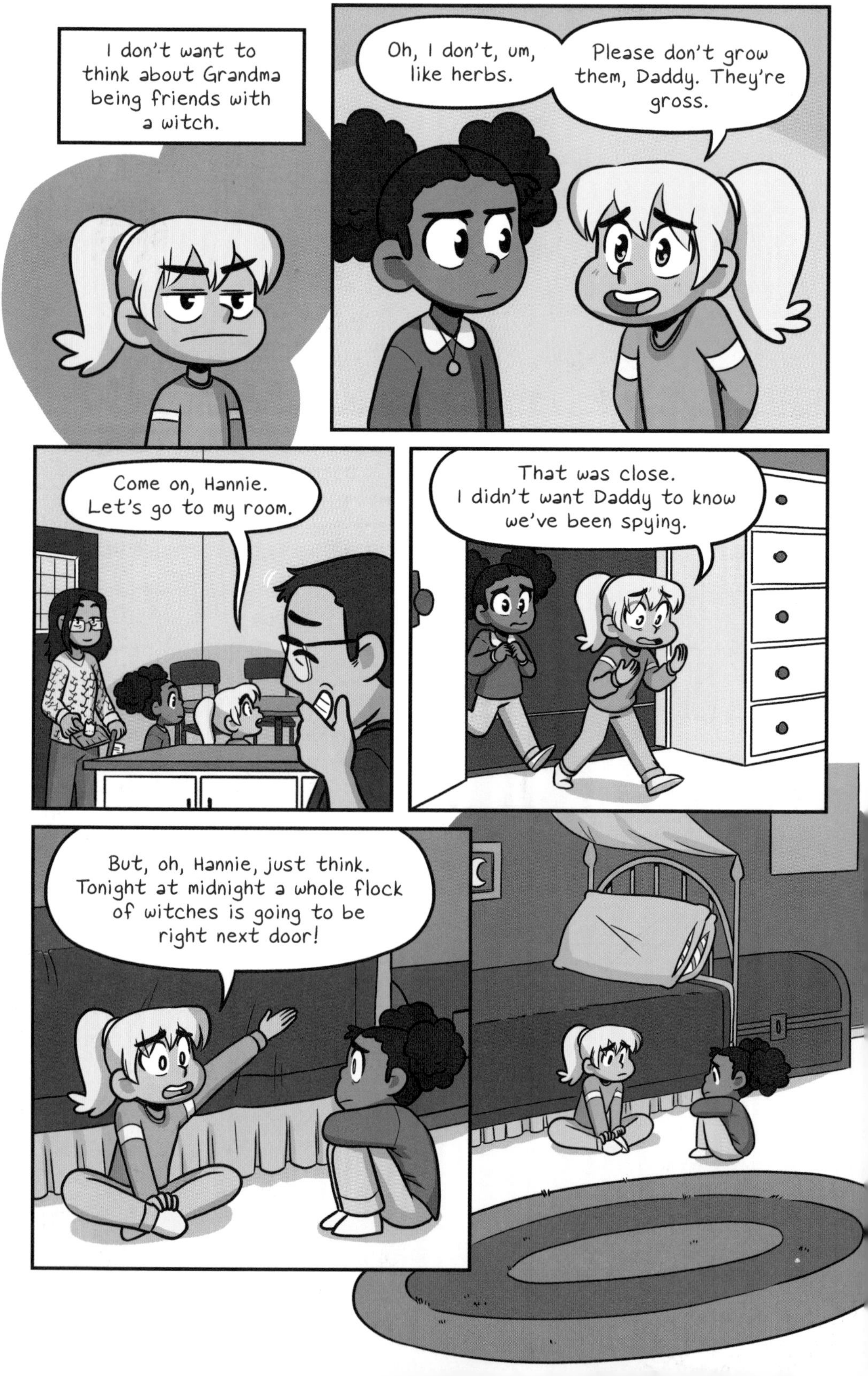
I don't want to think about Grandma being friends with a witch.
Oh, I don't, um, like herbs.
Please don't grow them, Daddy. They're gross.
Come on, Hannie. Let's go to my room.
That was close. I didn't want Daddy to know we've been spying.
But, oh, Hannie, just think. Tonight at midnight a whole flock of witches is going to be right next door!

CHAPTER 6

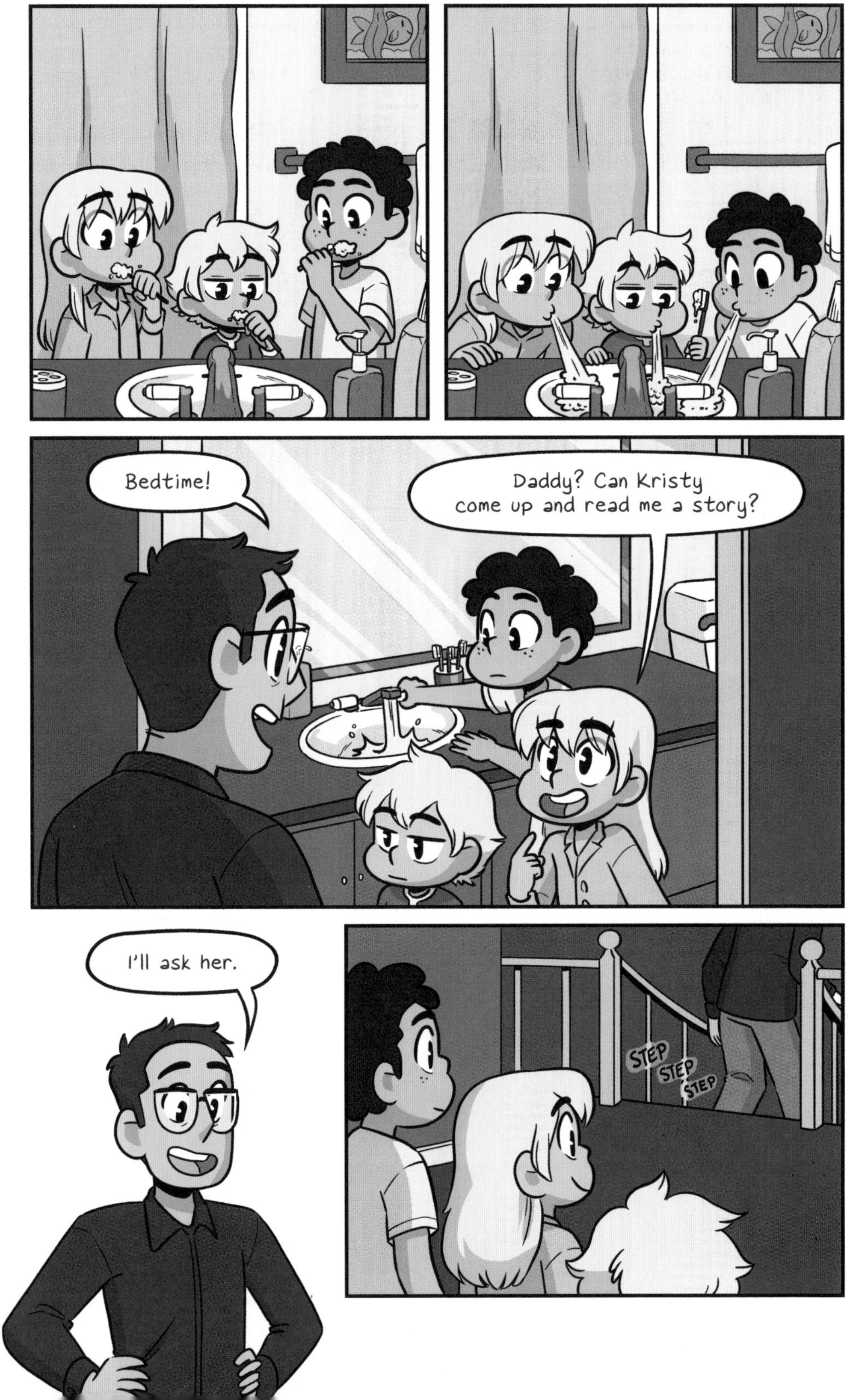

Bedtime!
Daddy? Can Kristy come up and read me a story?
I'll ask her.
STEP STEP STEP

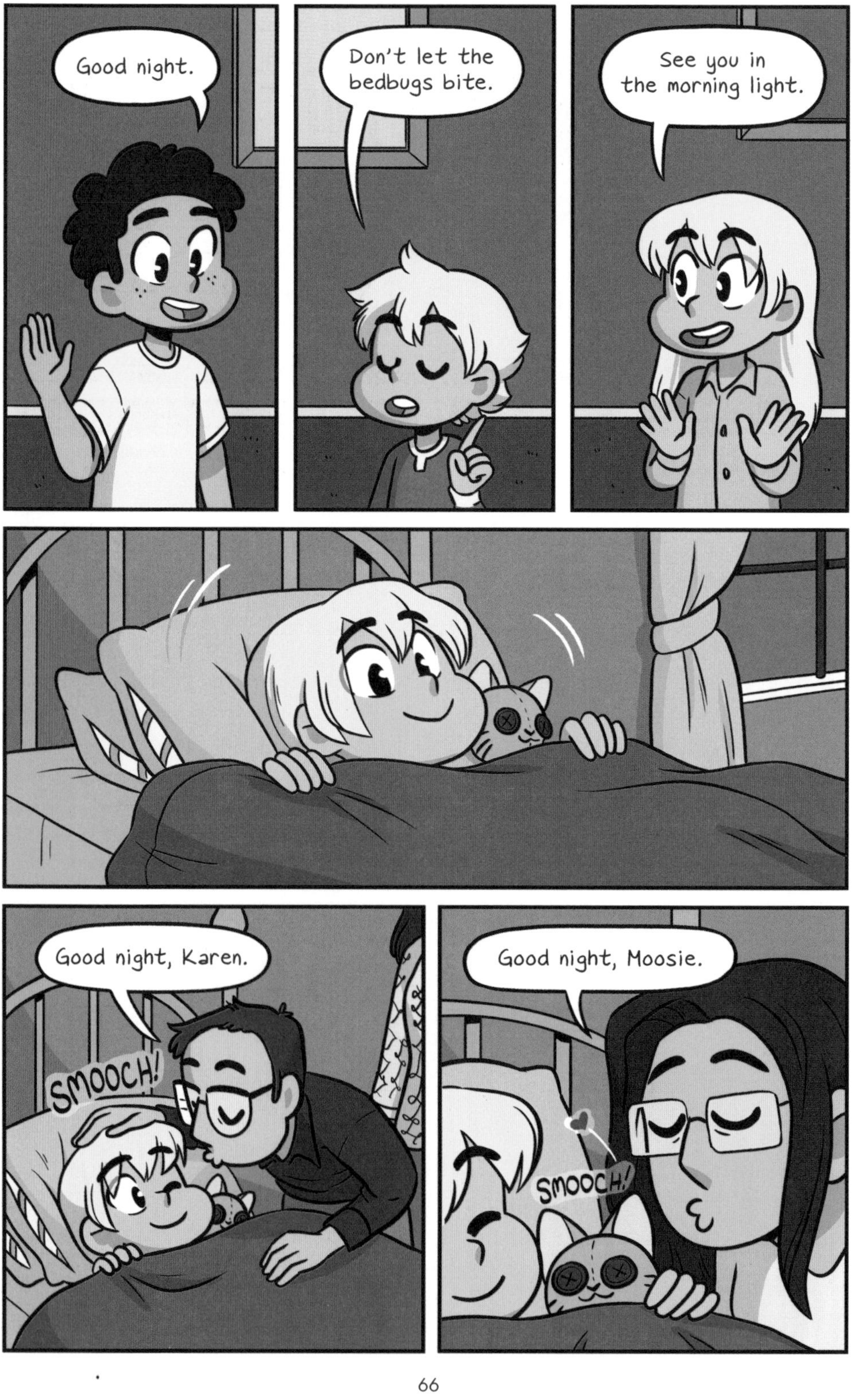
Good night.
Don't let the bedbugs bite.
See you in the morning light.
Good night, Karen.
SMOOCH!
Good night, Moosie.
SMOOCH!

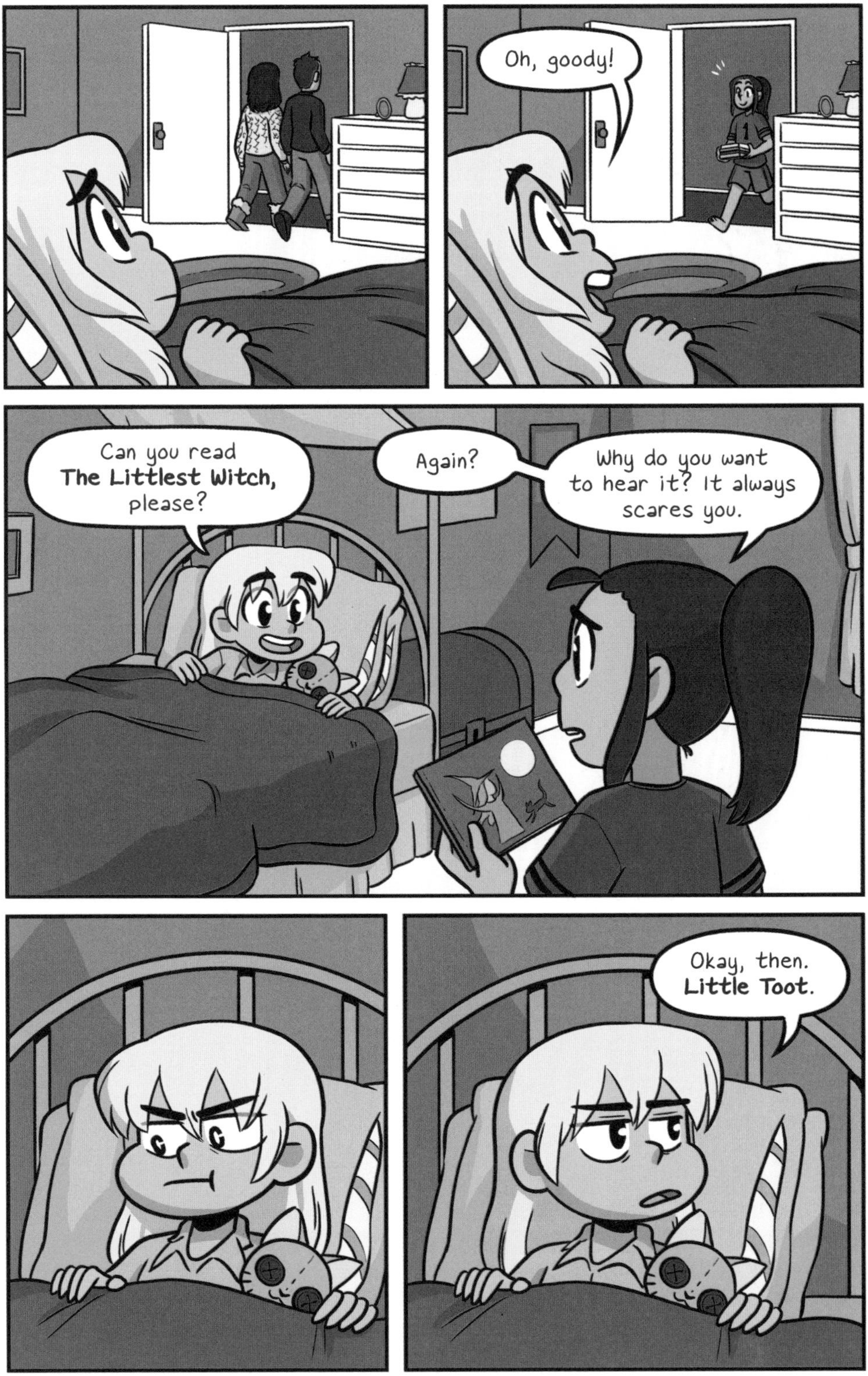
Oh, goody!
Can you read The Littlest Witch, please?
Again?
Why do you want to hear it? It always scares you.
Okay, then. Little Toot.

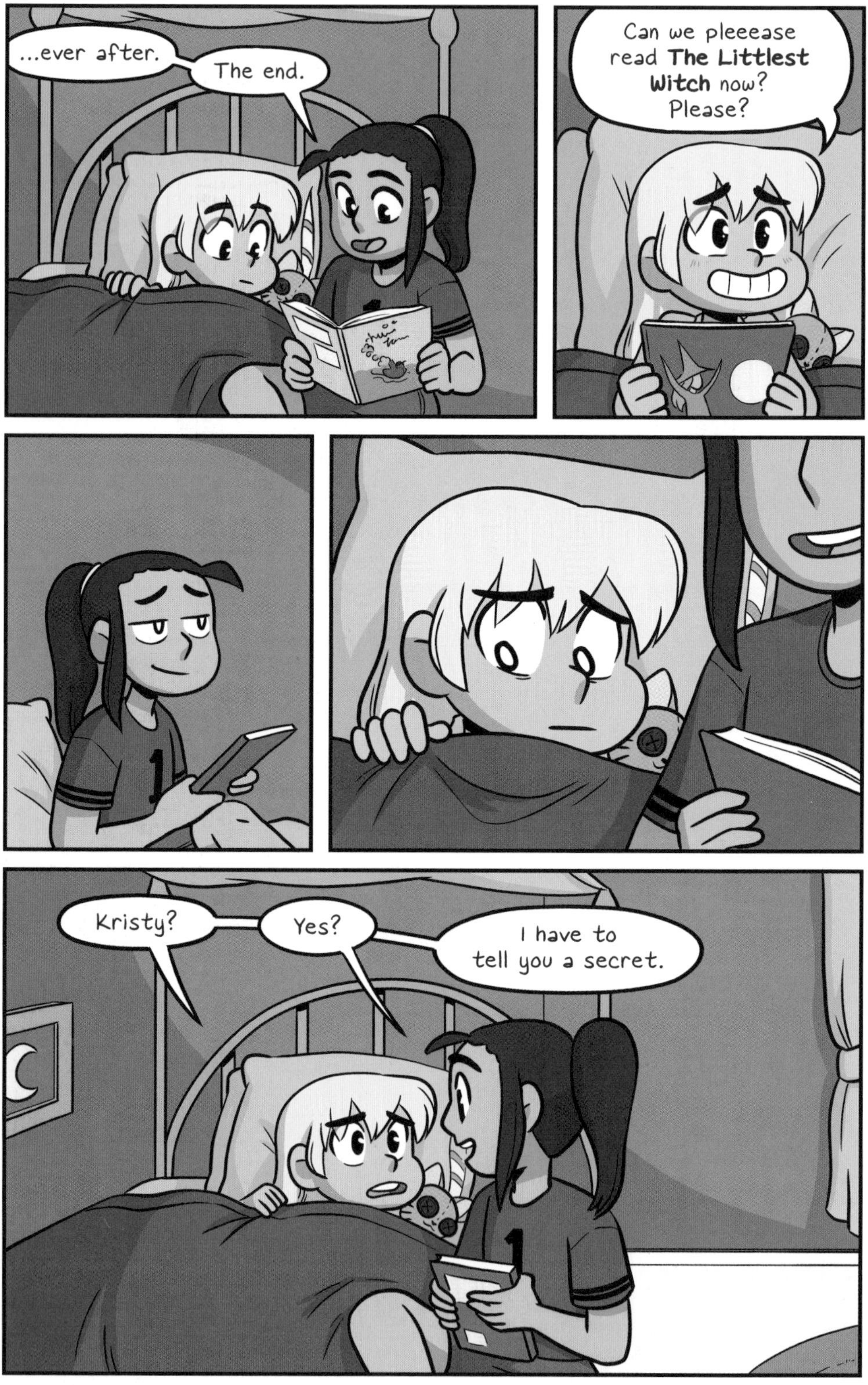
...ever after.
The end.
Can we pleeease read **The Littlest Witch** now? Please?
Kristy?
Yes?
I have to tell you a secret.

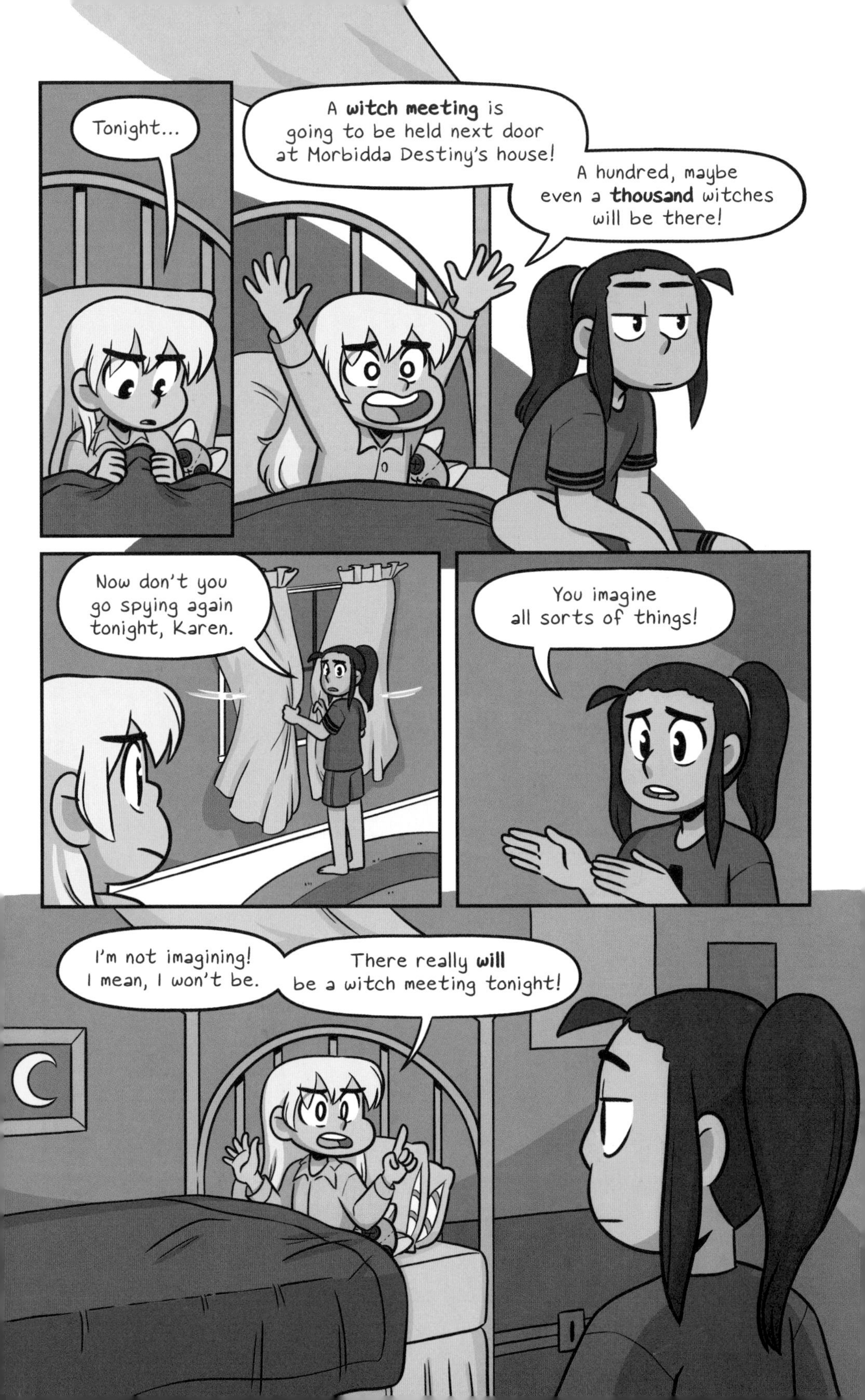
Tonight...
A **witch meeting** is going to be held next door at Morbidda Destiny's house!
A hundred, maybe even a **thousand** witches will be there!
Now don't you go spying again tonight, Karen.
You imagine all sorts of things!
I'm not imagining! I mean, I won't be.
There really **will** be a witch meeting tonight!

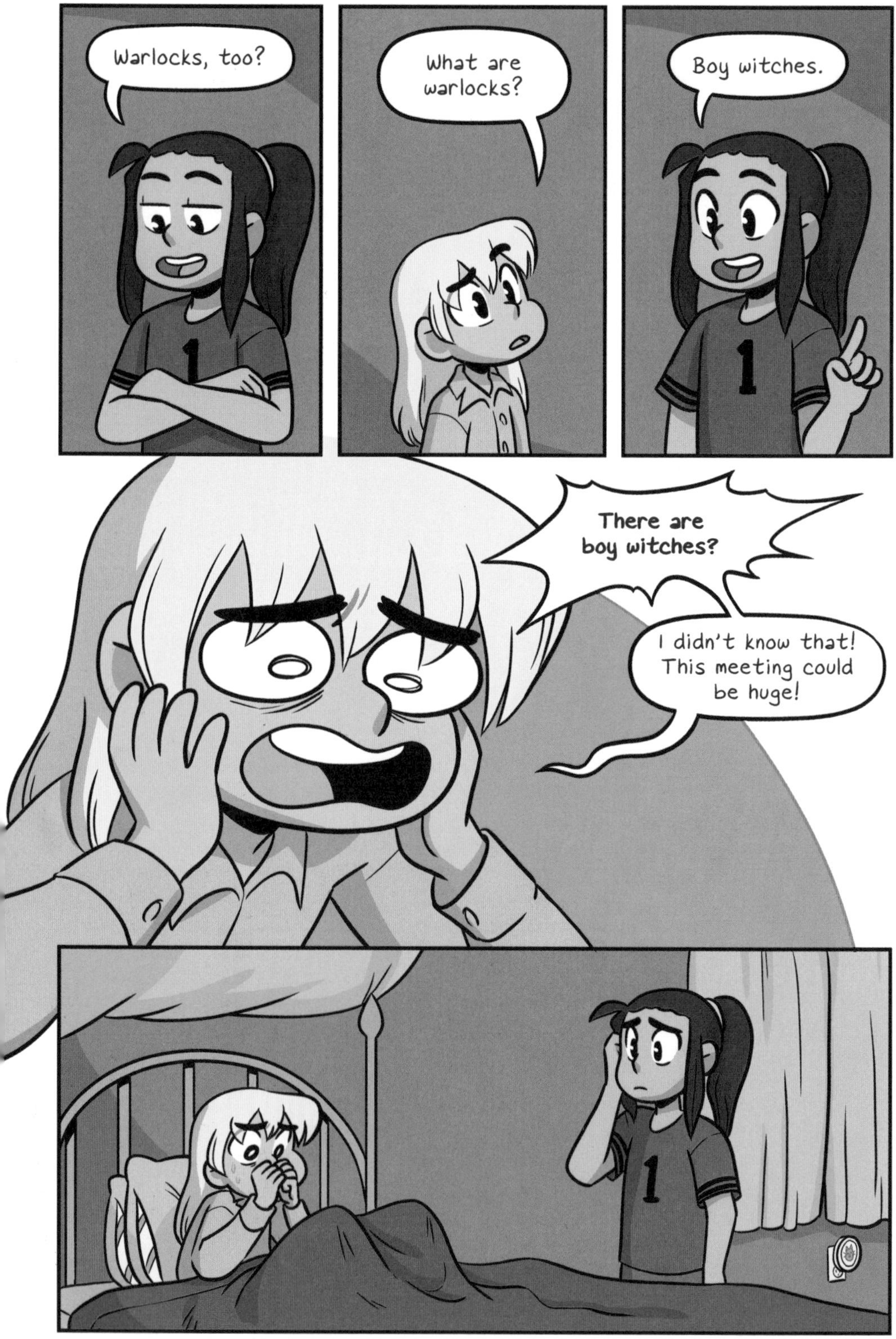
Warlocks, too?
What are warlocks?
Boy witches.
There are boy witches?
I didn't know that! This meeting could be huge!

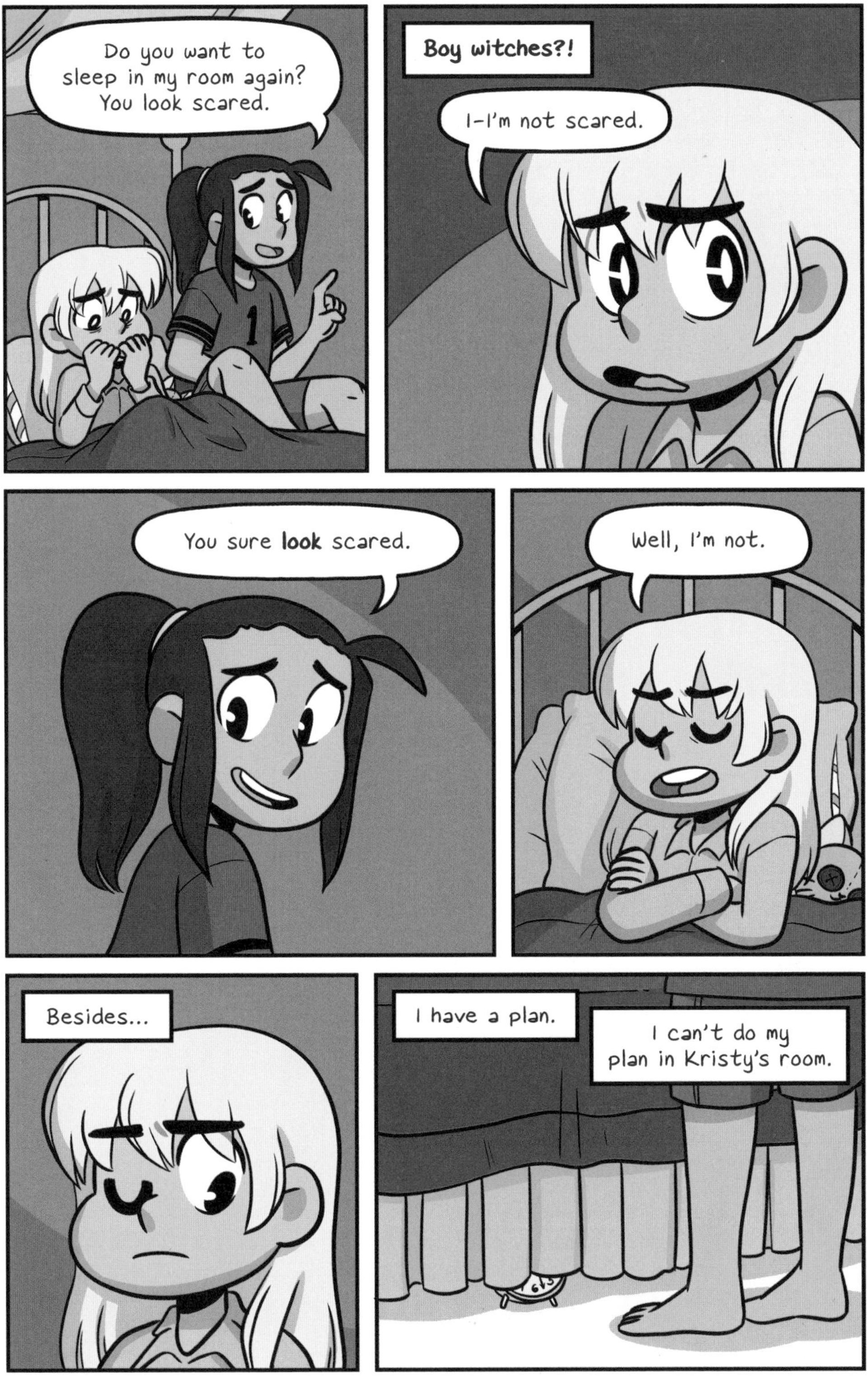
Do you want to sleep in my room again? You look scared.
Boy witches?!
I-I'm not scared.
You sure **look** scared.
Well, I'm not.
Besides...
I have a plan.
I can't do my plan in Kristy's room.

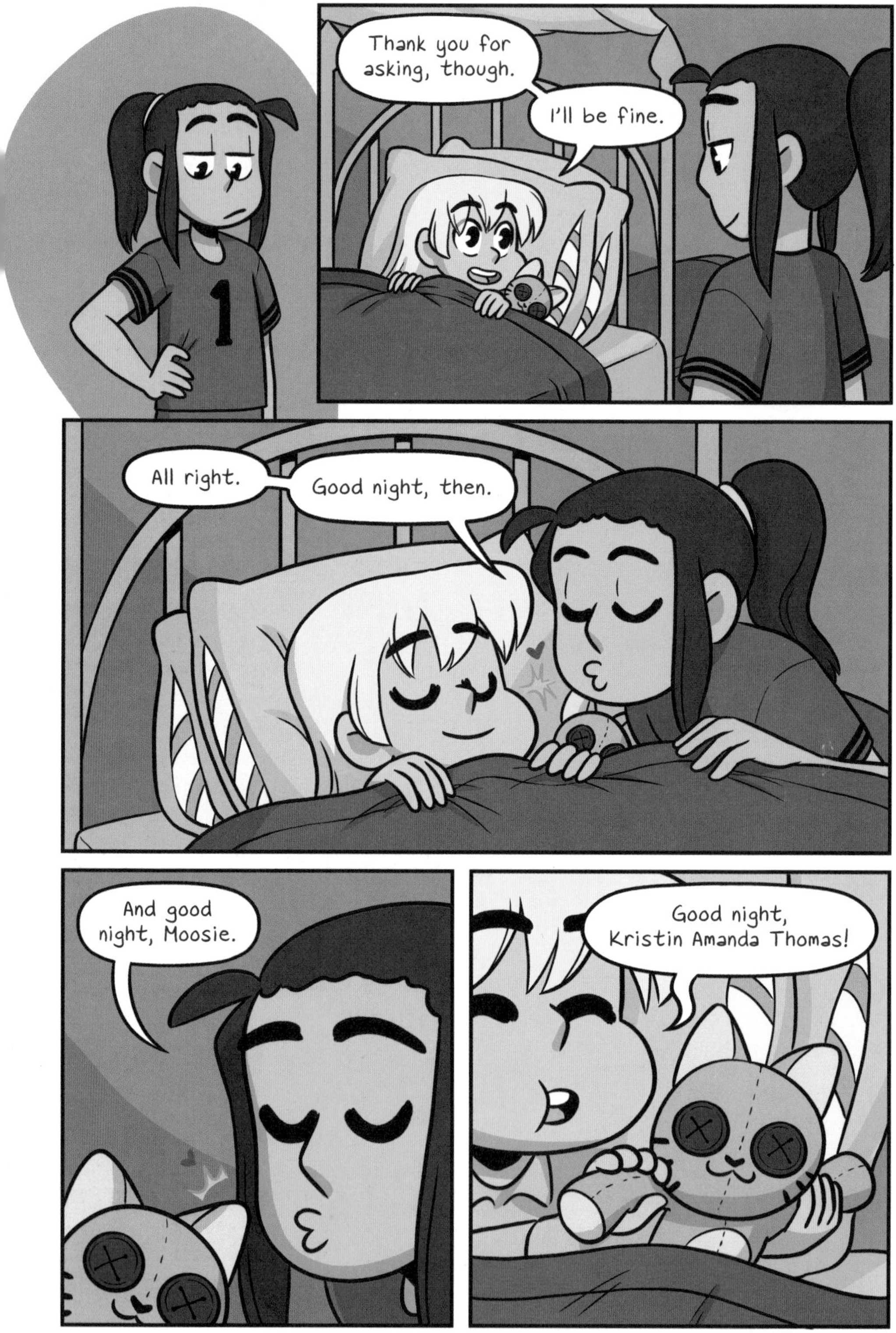
Thank you for asking, though.
I'll be fine.
All right.
Good night, then.
And good night, Moosie.
Good night, Kristin Amanda Thomas!

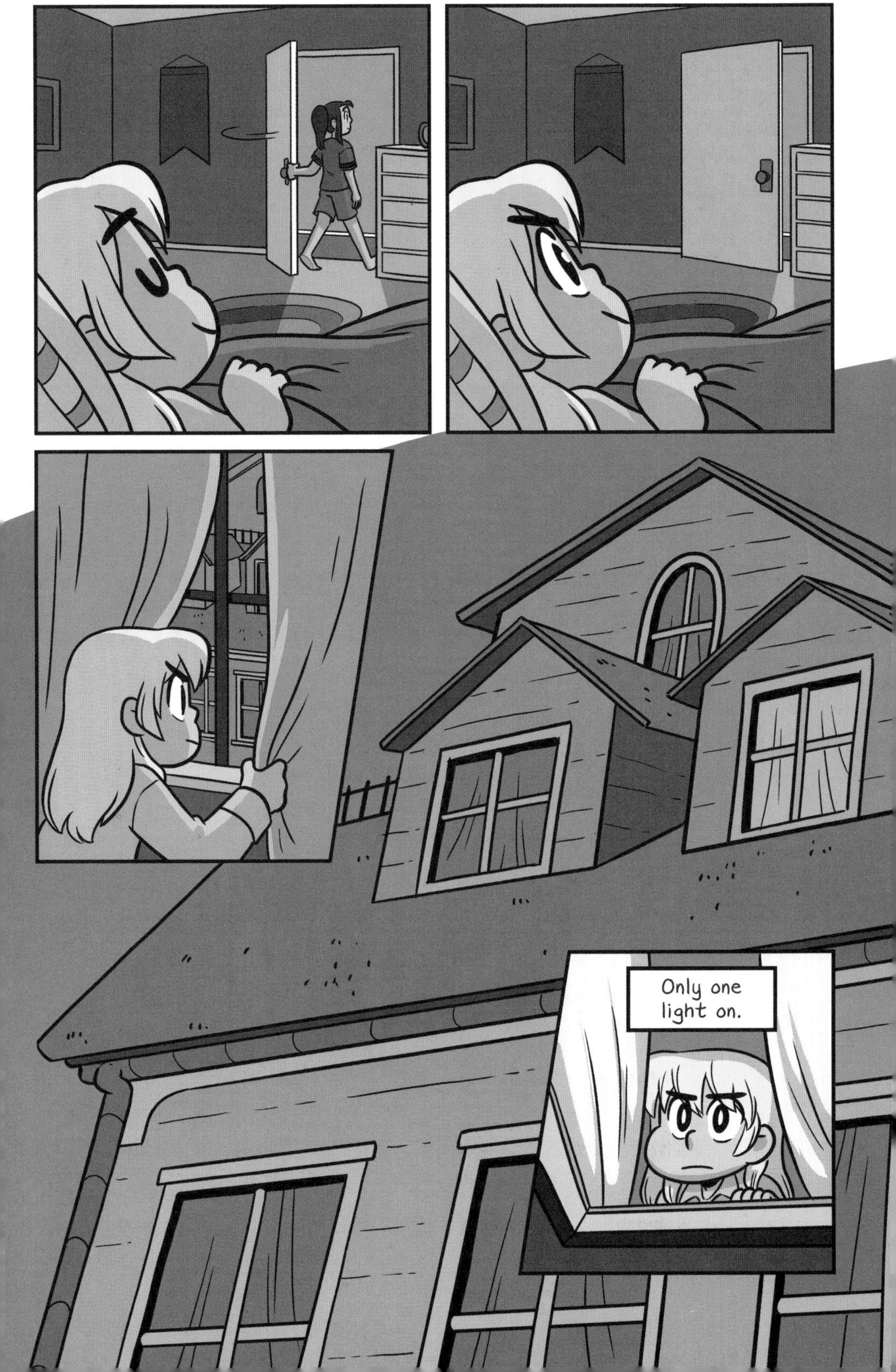
Only one
light on.

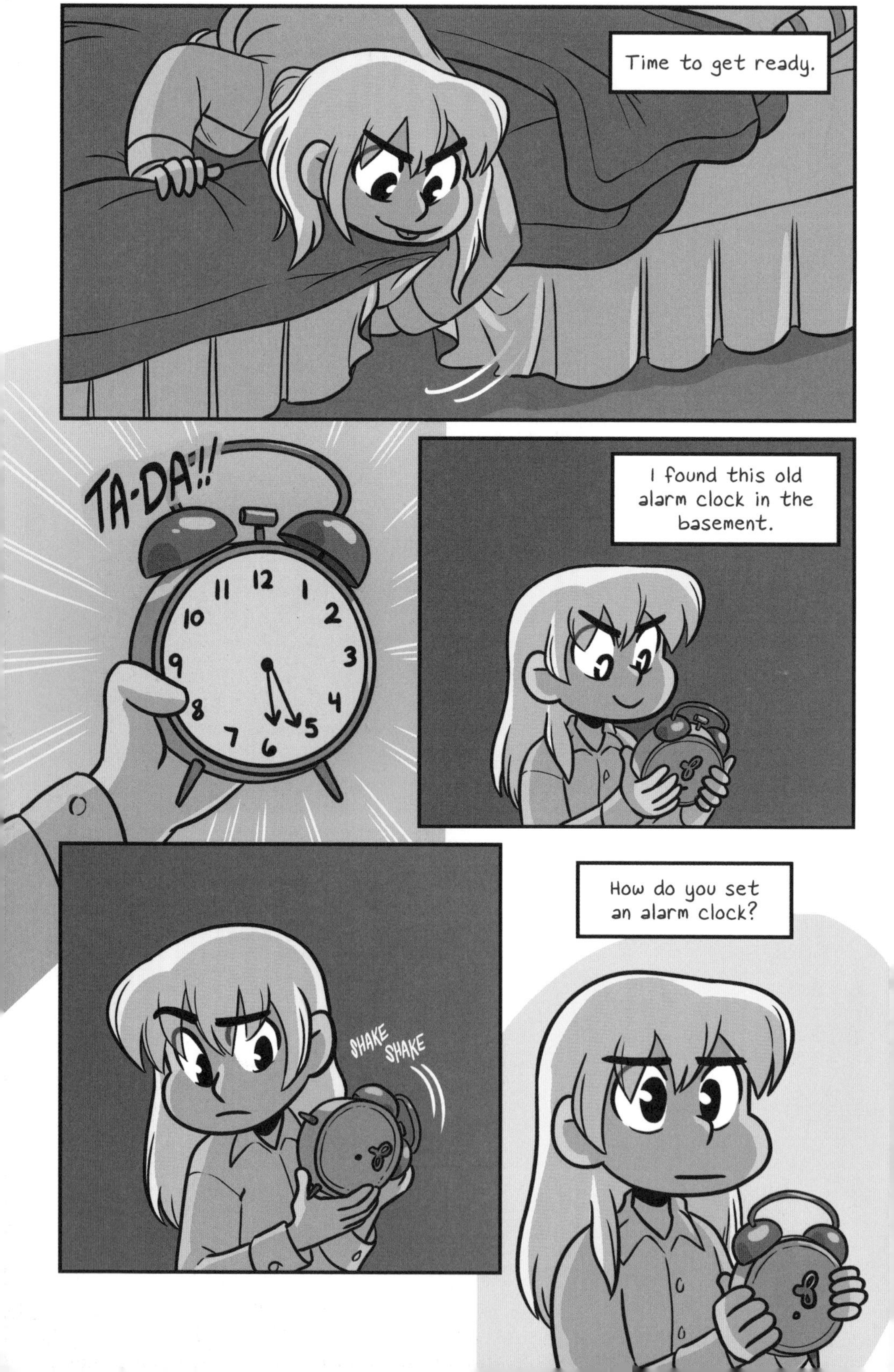
Time to get ready.
TA-DA!!
I found this old alarm clock in the basement.
SHAKE SHAKE
How do you set an alarm clock?

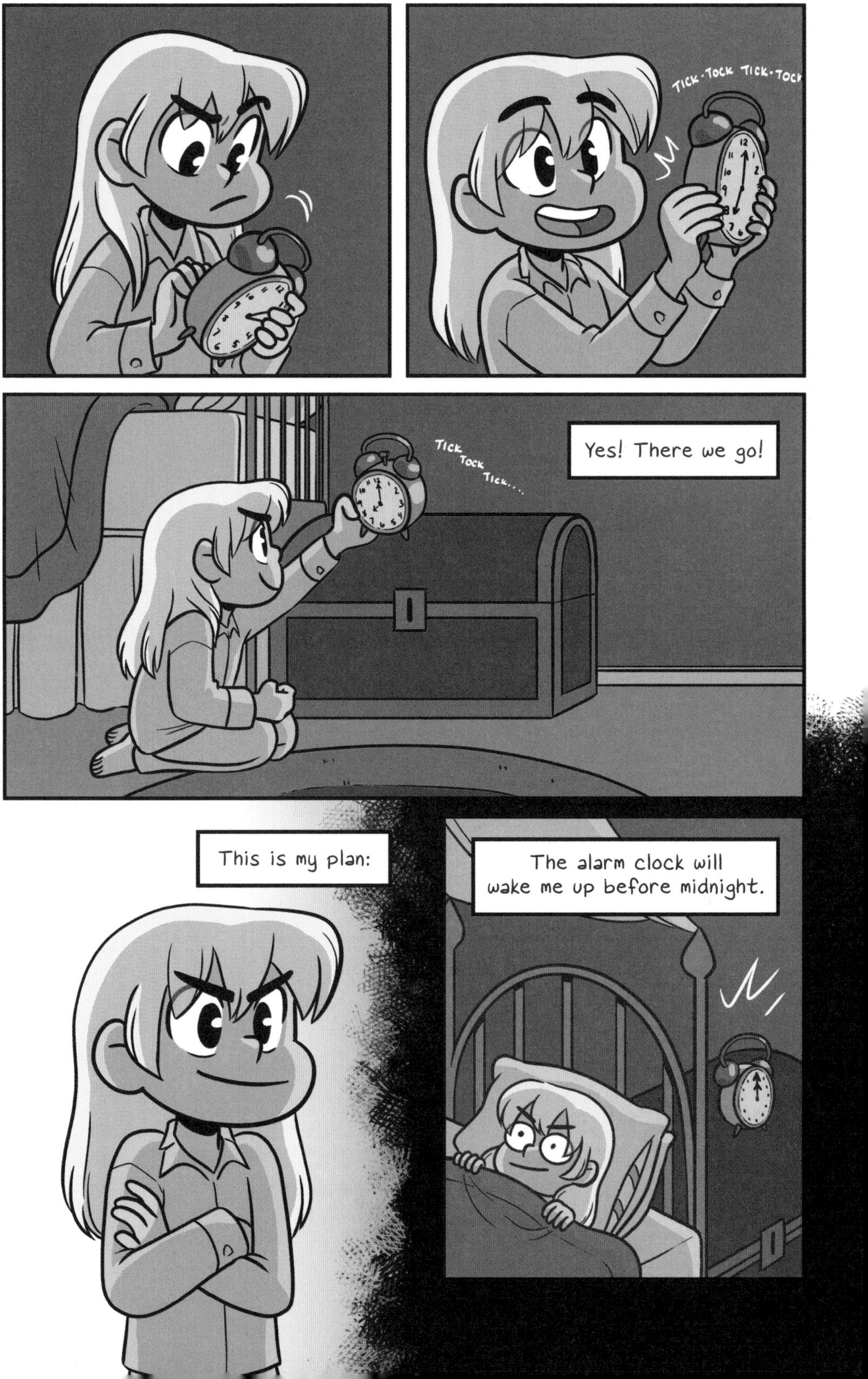
TICK-TOCK TICK-TOCK
Yes! There we go!
TICK TOCK TICK...
This is my plan:
The alarm clock will wake me up before midnight.

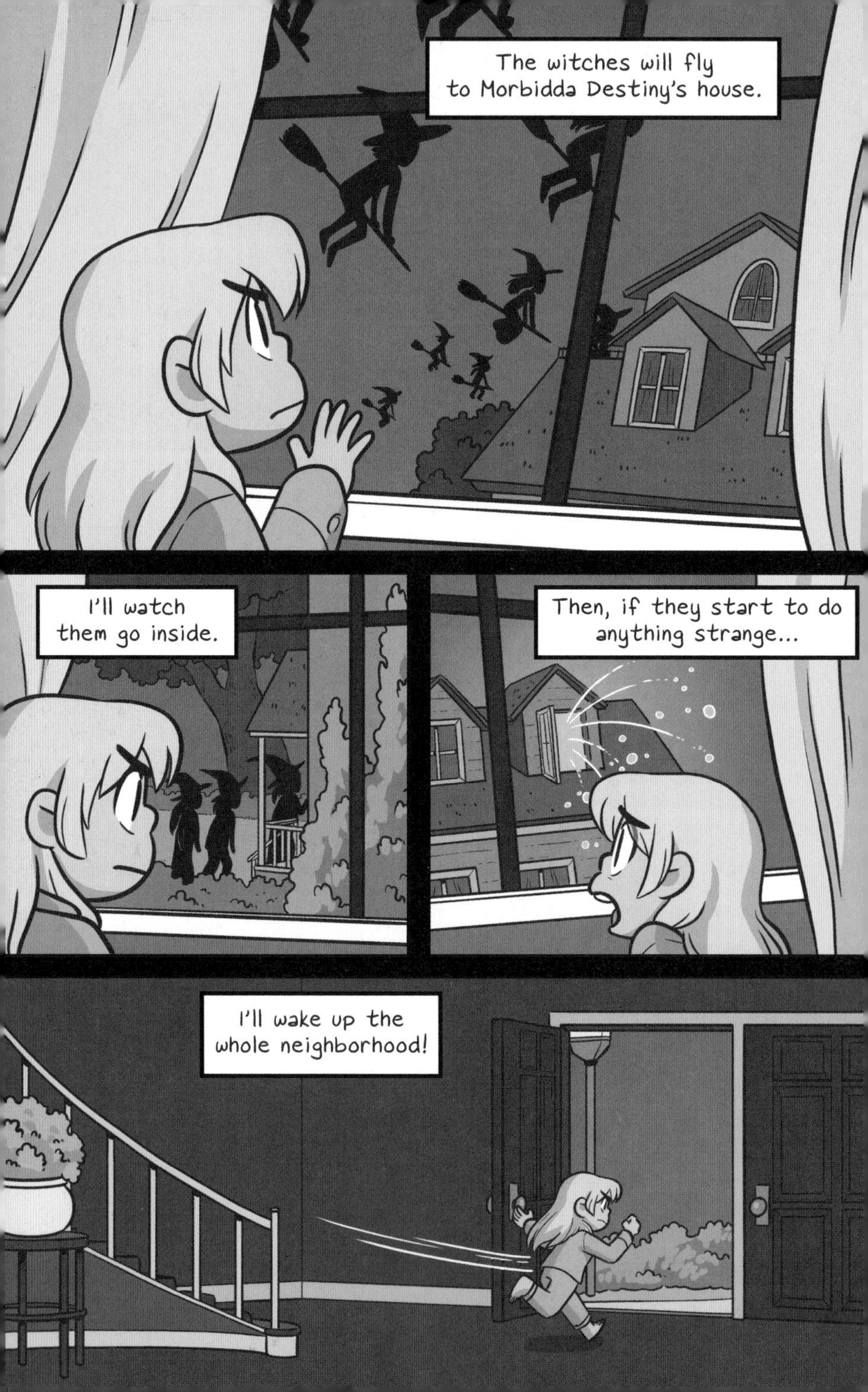
The witches will fly to Morbidda Destiny's house.
I'll watch them go inside.
Then, if they start to do anything strange...
I'll wake up the whole neighborhood!

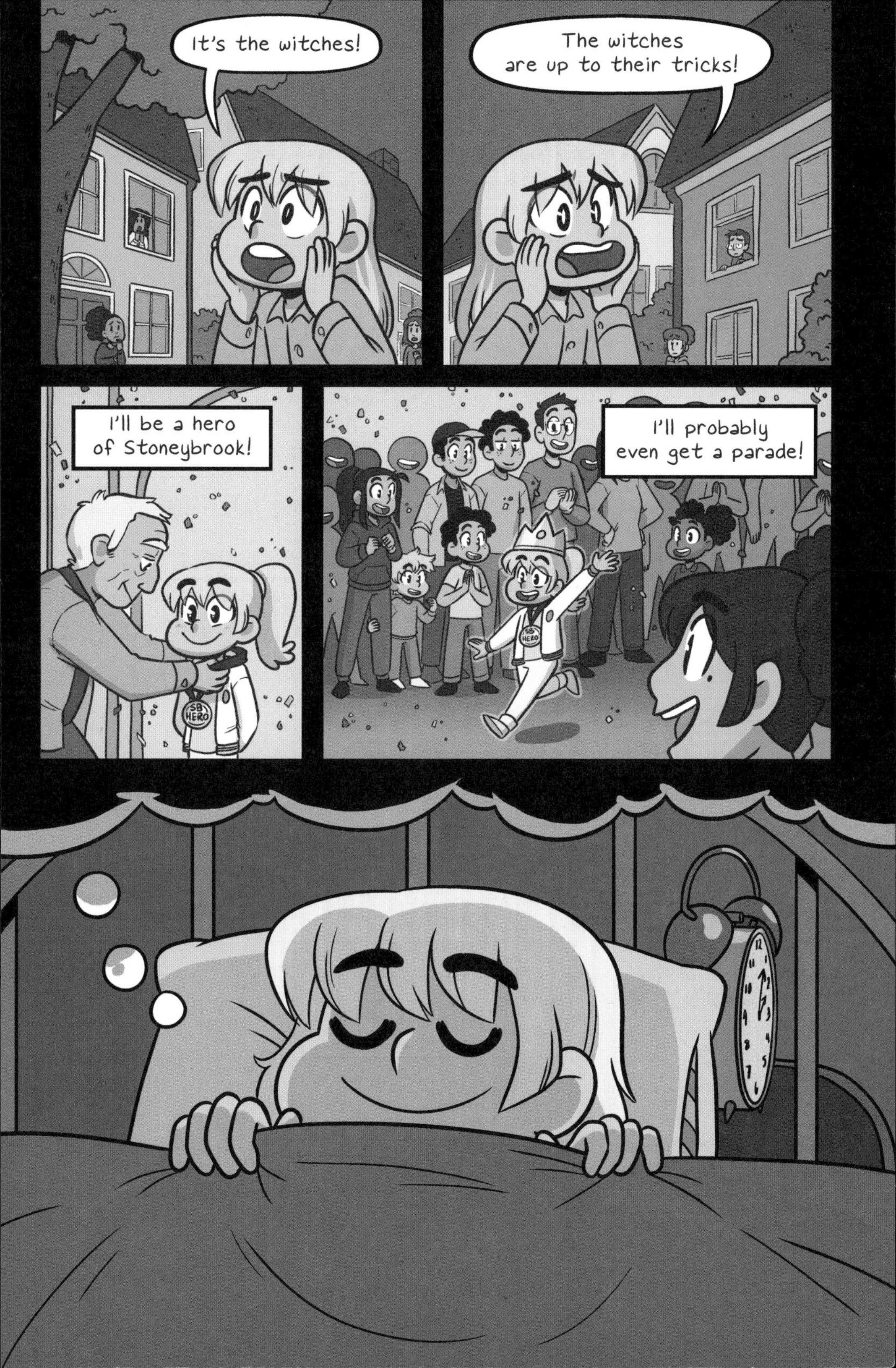
It's the witches!
The witches are up to their tricks!
I'll be a hero of Stoneybrook!
SB HERO
I'll probably even get a parade!
SB HERO

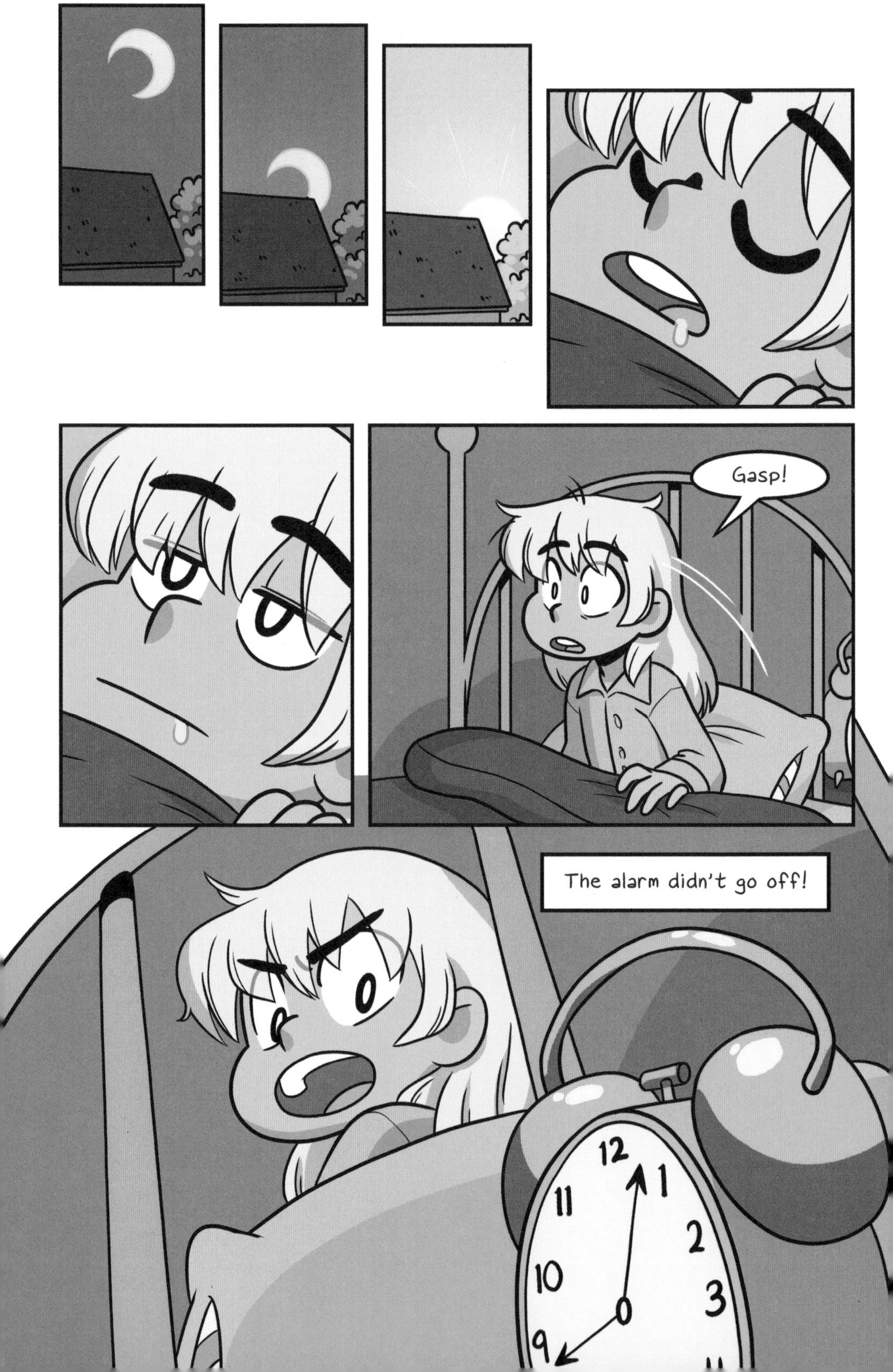
Gasp!
The alarm didn't go off!

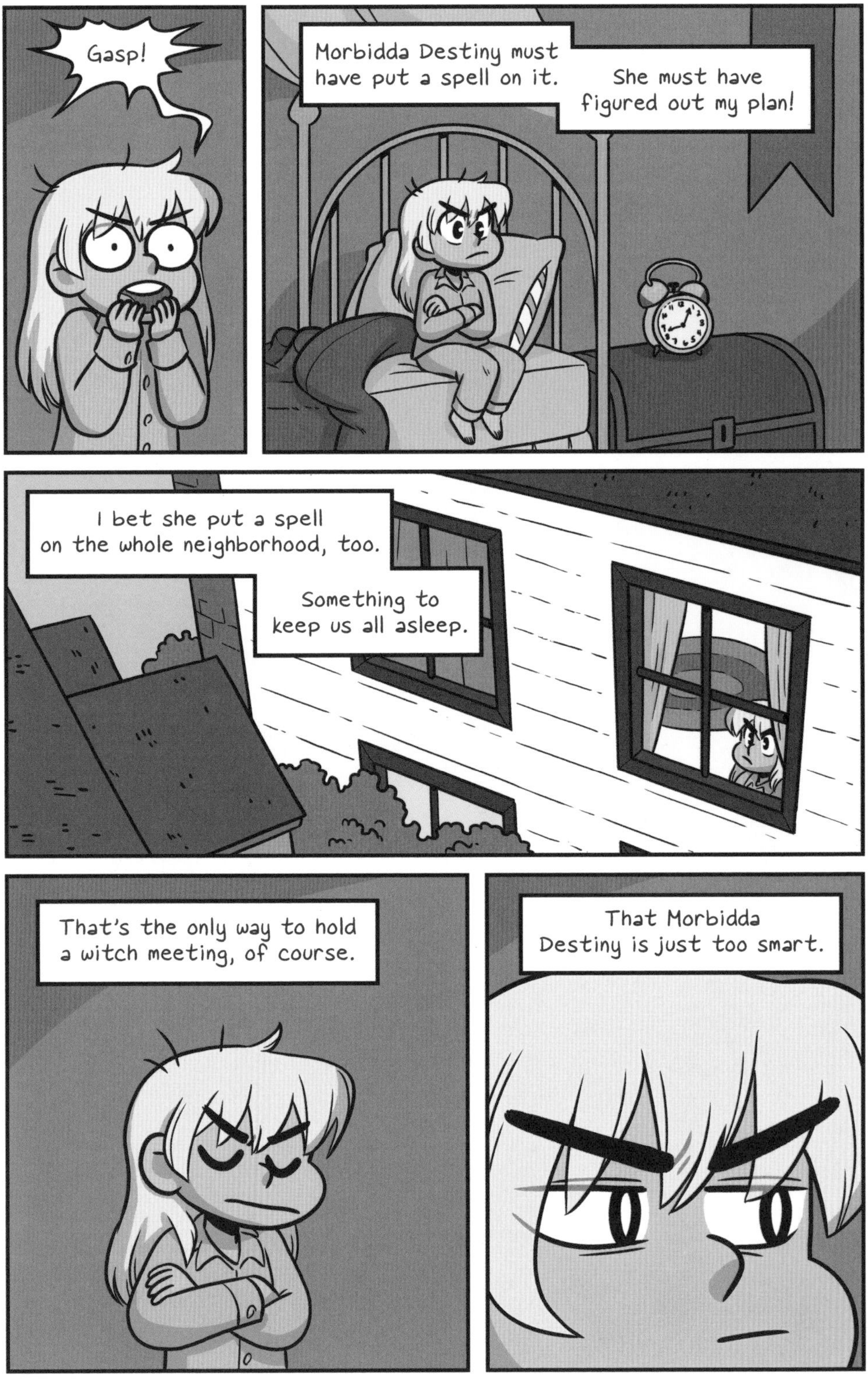
Gasp!
Morbidda Destiny must have put a spell on it.
She must have figured out my plan!
I bet she put a spell on the whole neighborhood, too.
Something to keep us all asleep.
That's the only way to hold a witch meeting, of course.
That Morbidda Destiny is just too smart.

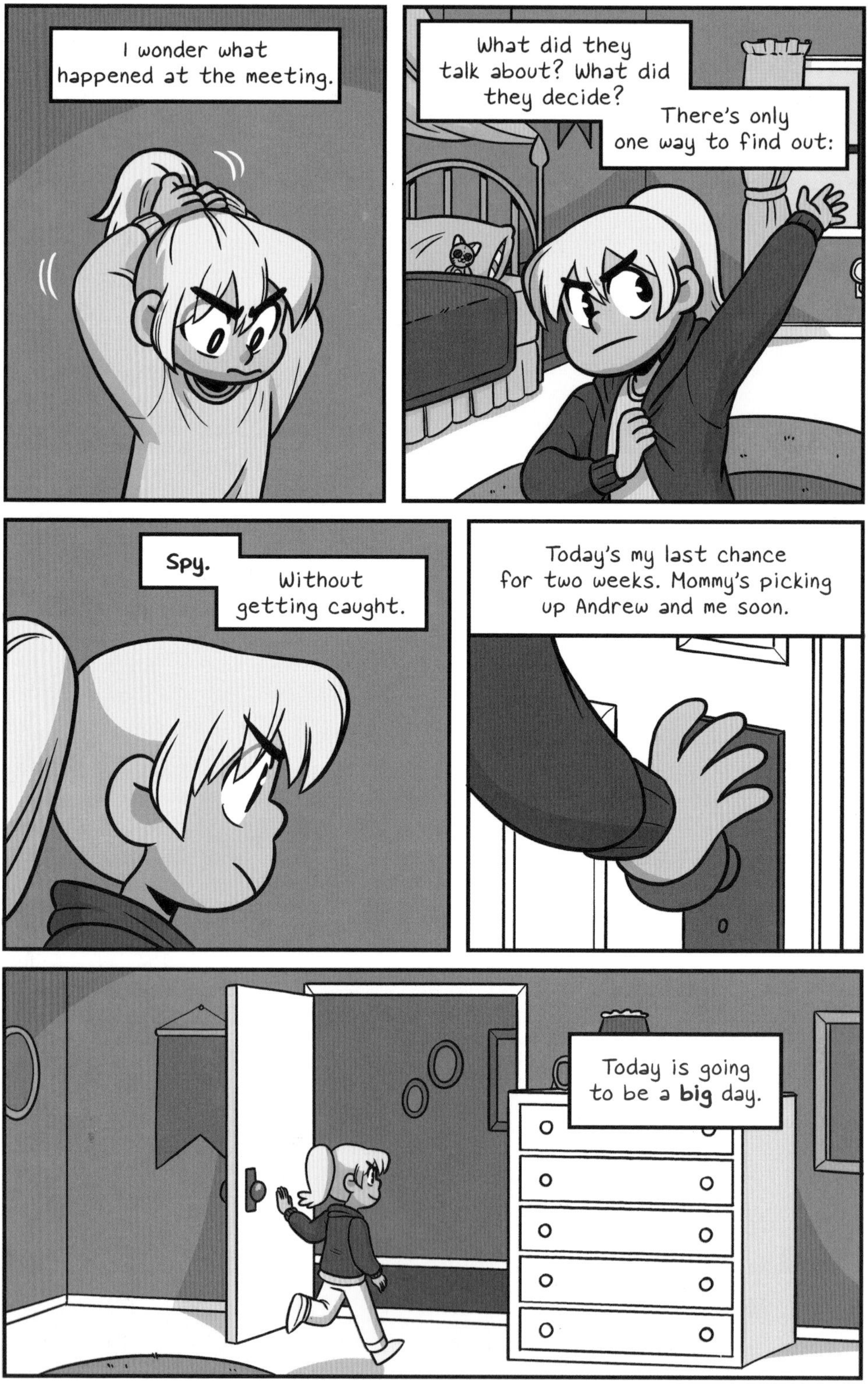
I wonder what happened at the meeting.
What did they talk about? What did they decide?
There's only one way to find out:
Spy.
Without getting caught.
Today's my last chance for two weeks. Mommy's picking up Andrew and me soon.
Today is going to be a **big** day.

CHAPTER 7

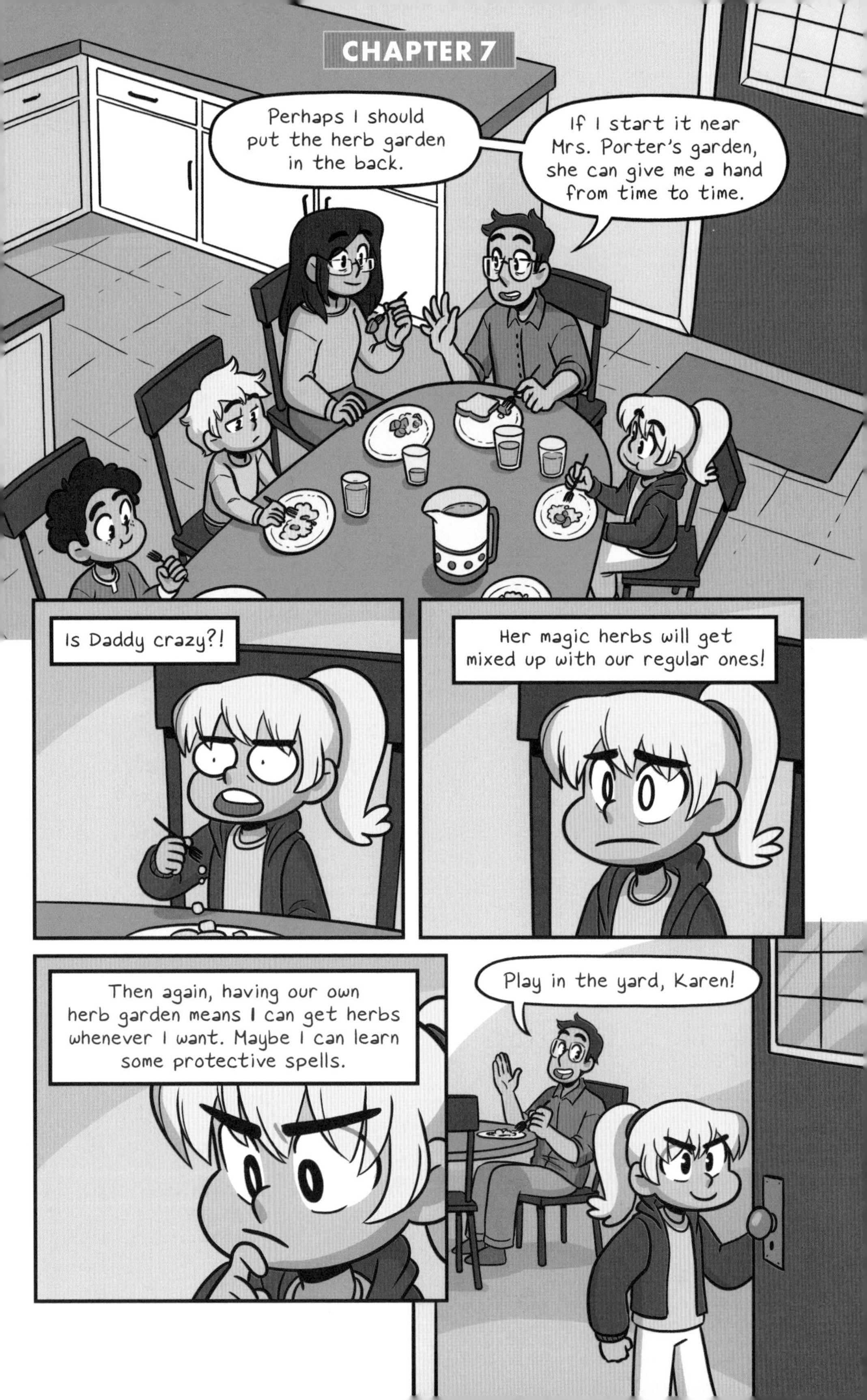
Perhaps I should put the herb garden in the back.
If I start it near Mrs. Porter's garden, she can give me a hand from time to time.
Is Daddy crazy?!
Her magic herbs will get mixed up with our regular ones!
Then again, having our own herb garden means I can get herbs whenever I want. Maybe I can learn some protective spells.
Play in the yard, Karen!

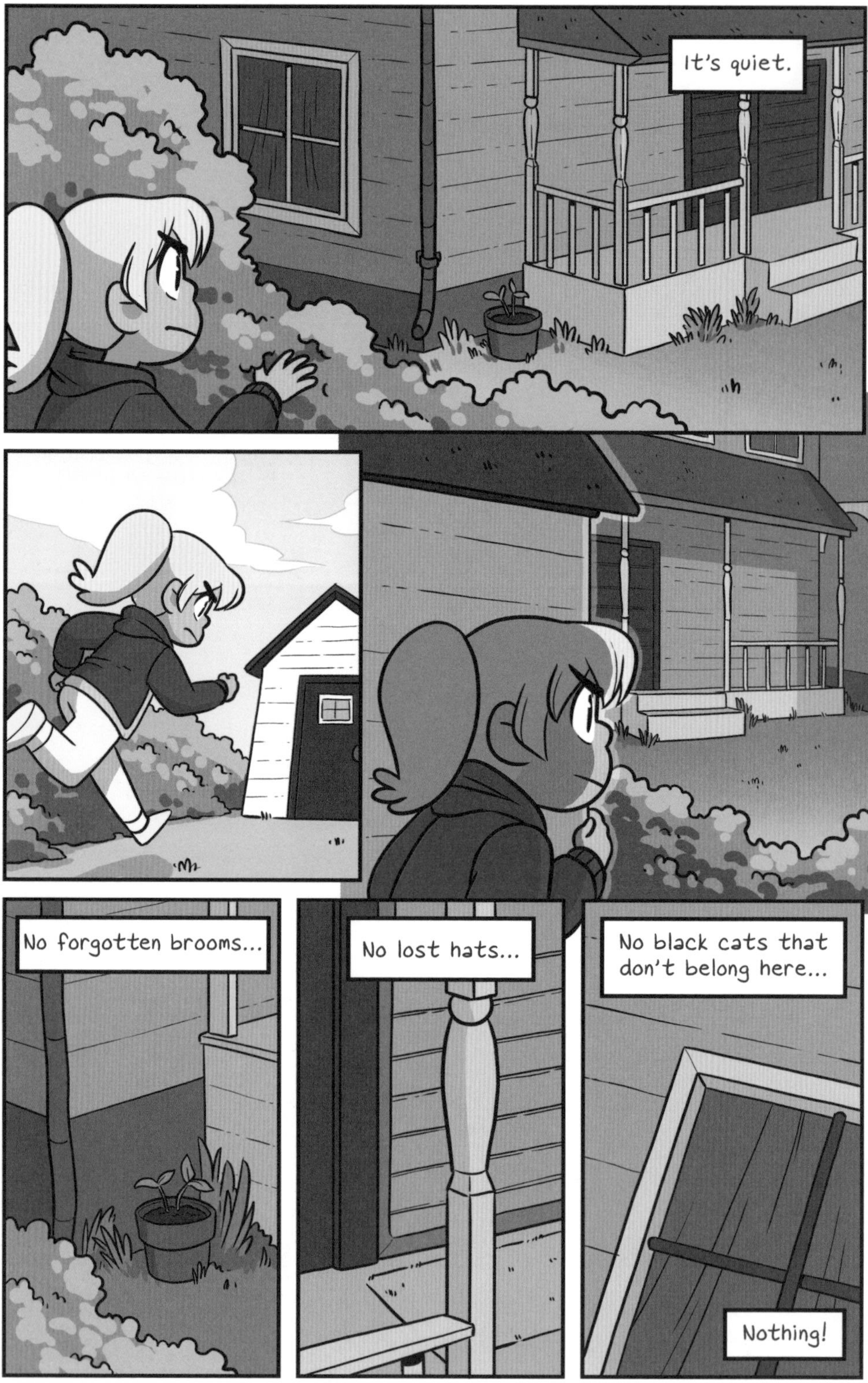
It's quiet.
No forgotten brooms...
No lost hats...
No black cats that don't belong here...
Nothing!

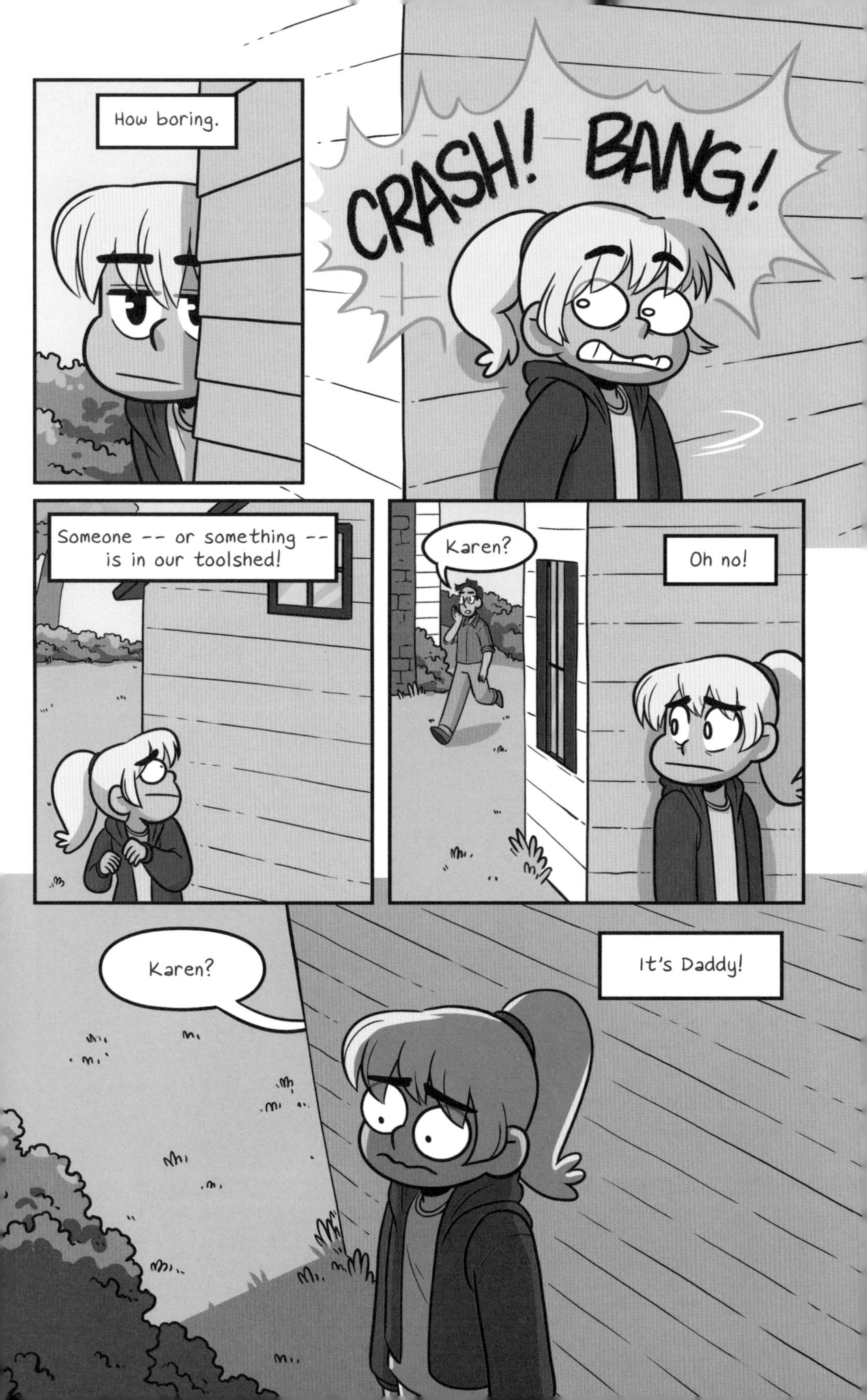
How boring.
CRASH! BANG!
Someone -- or something -- is in our toolshed!
Karen?
Oh no!
Karen?
It's Daddy!

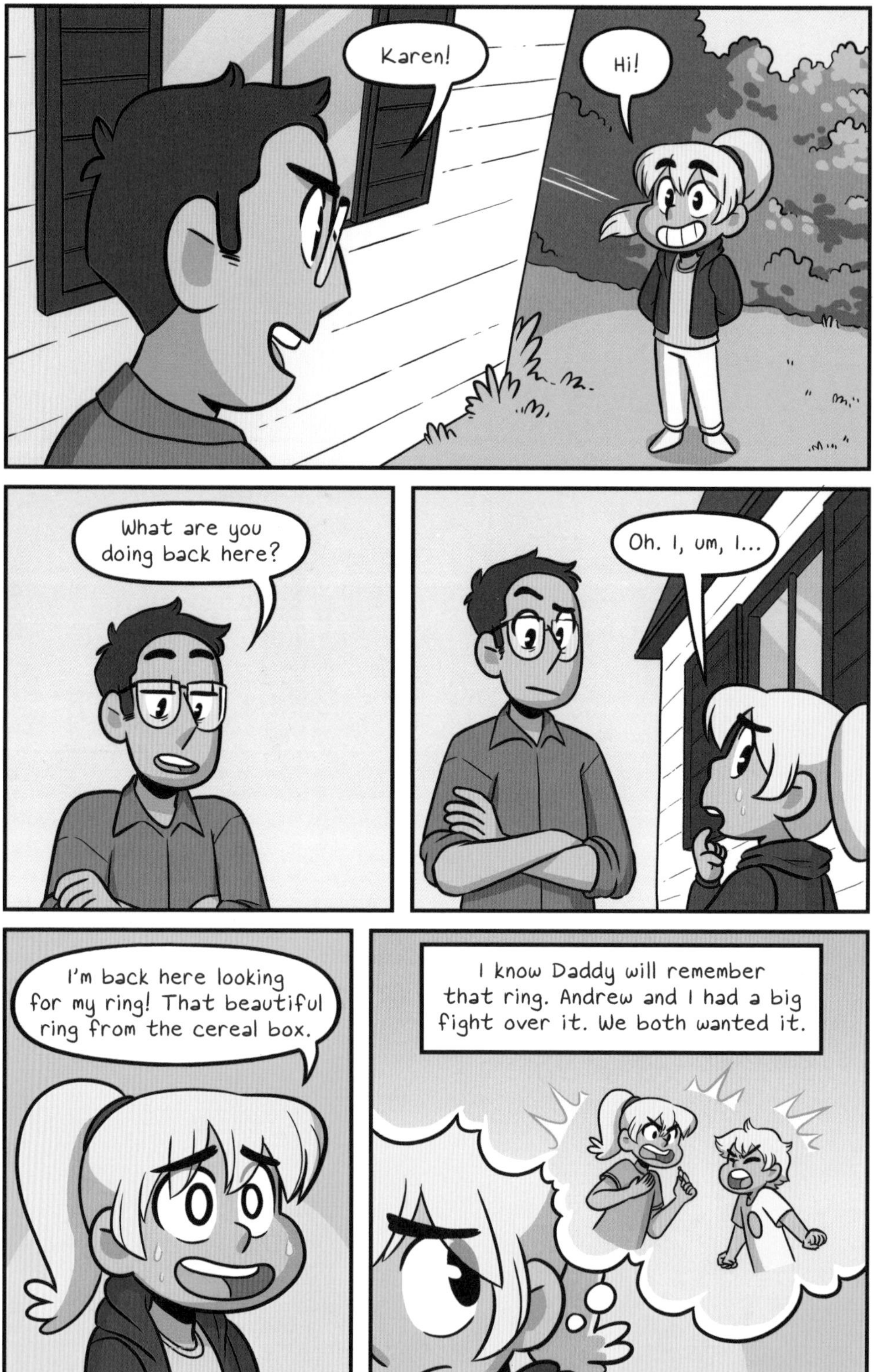
Karen!
Hi!
What are you doing back here?
Oh. I, um, I...
I'm back here looking for my ring! That beautiful ring from the cereal box.
I know Daddy will remember that ring. Andrew and I had a big fight over it. We both wanted it.

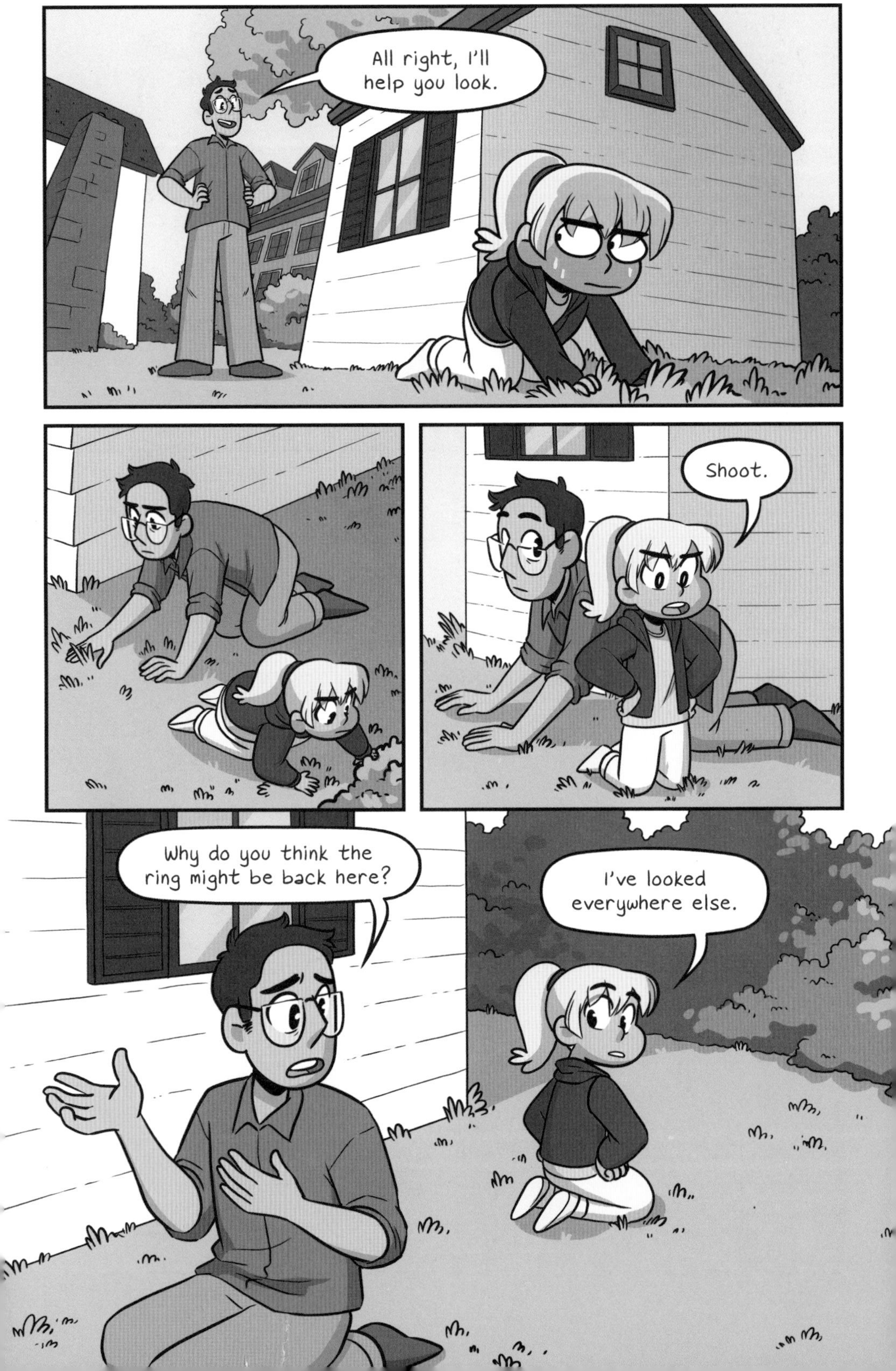
All right, I'll help you look.
Shoot.
Why do you think the ring might be back here?
I've looked everywhere else.

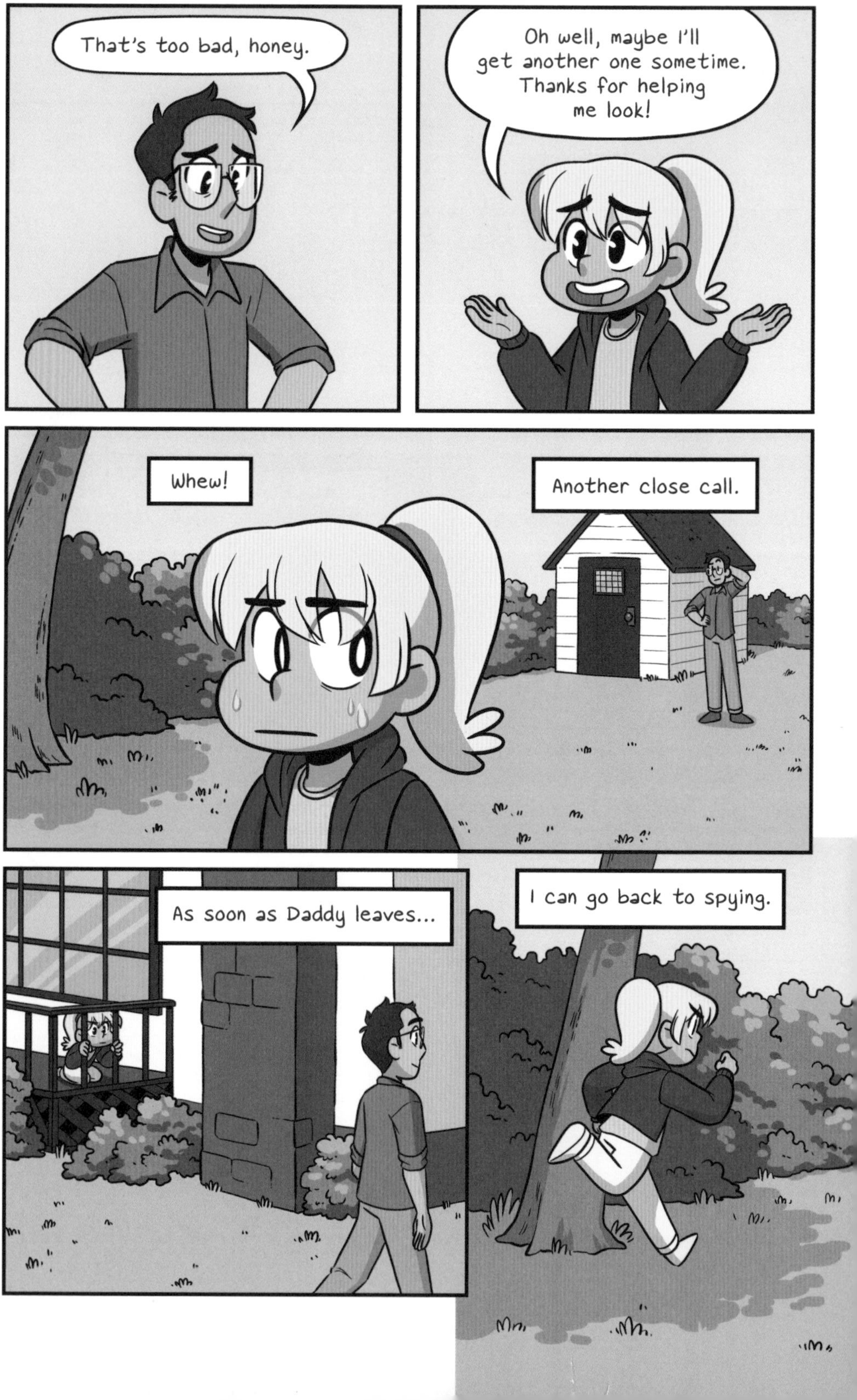
That's too bad, honey.
Oh well, maybe I'll get another one sometime. Thanks for helping me look!
Whew!
Another close call.
As soon as Daddy leaves...
I can go back to spying.

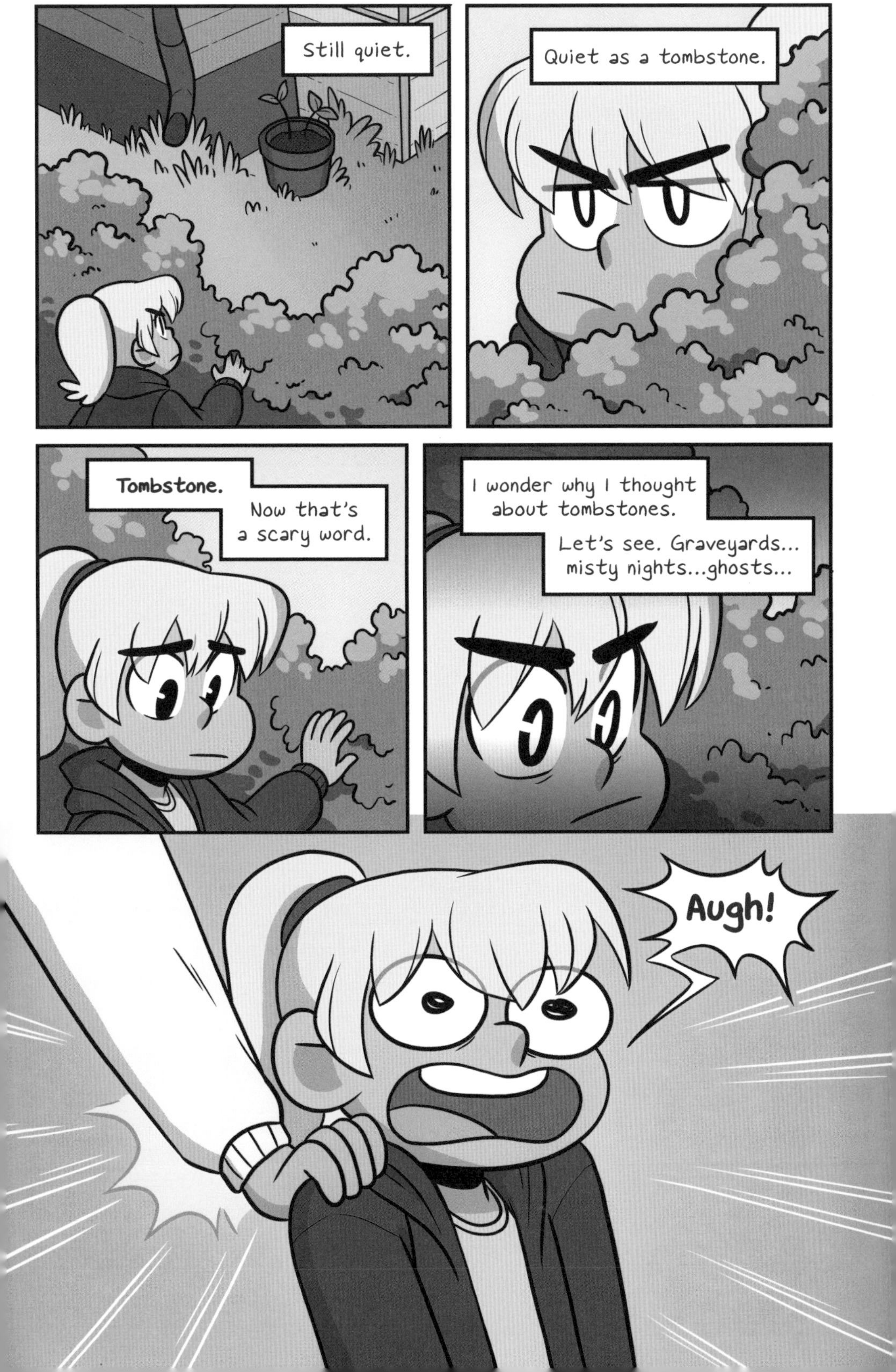
Still quiet.
Quiet as a tombstone.
Tombstone.
Now that's a scary word.
I wonder why I thought about tombstones.
Let's see. Graveyards... misty nights...ghosts...
Augh!

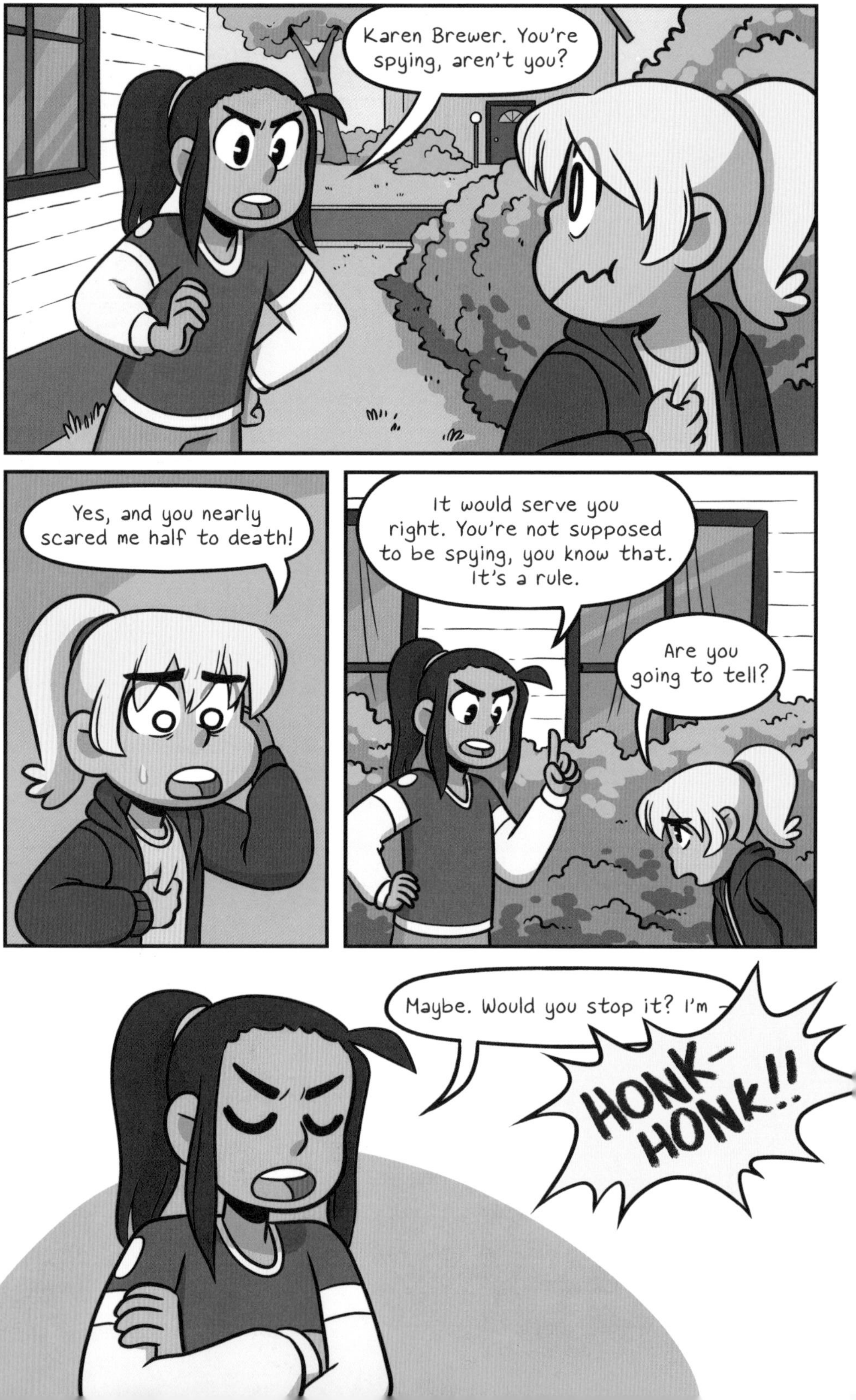
Karen Brewer. You're spying, aren't you?
Yes, and you nearly scared me half to death!
It would serve you right. You're not supposed to be spying, you know that. It's a rule.
Are you going to tell?
Maybe. Would you stop it? I'm —
HONK-HONK!!

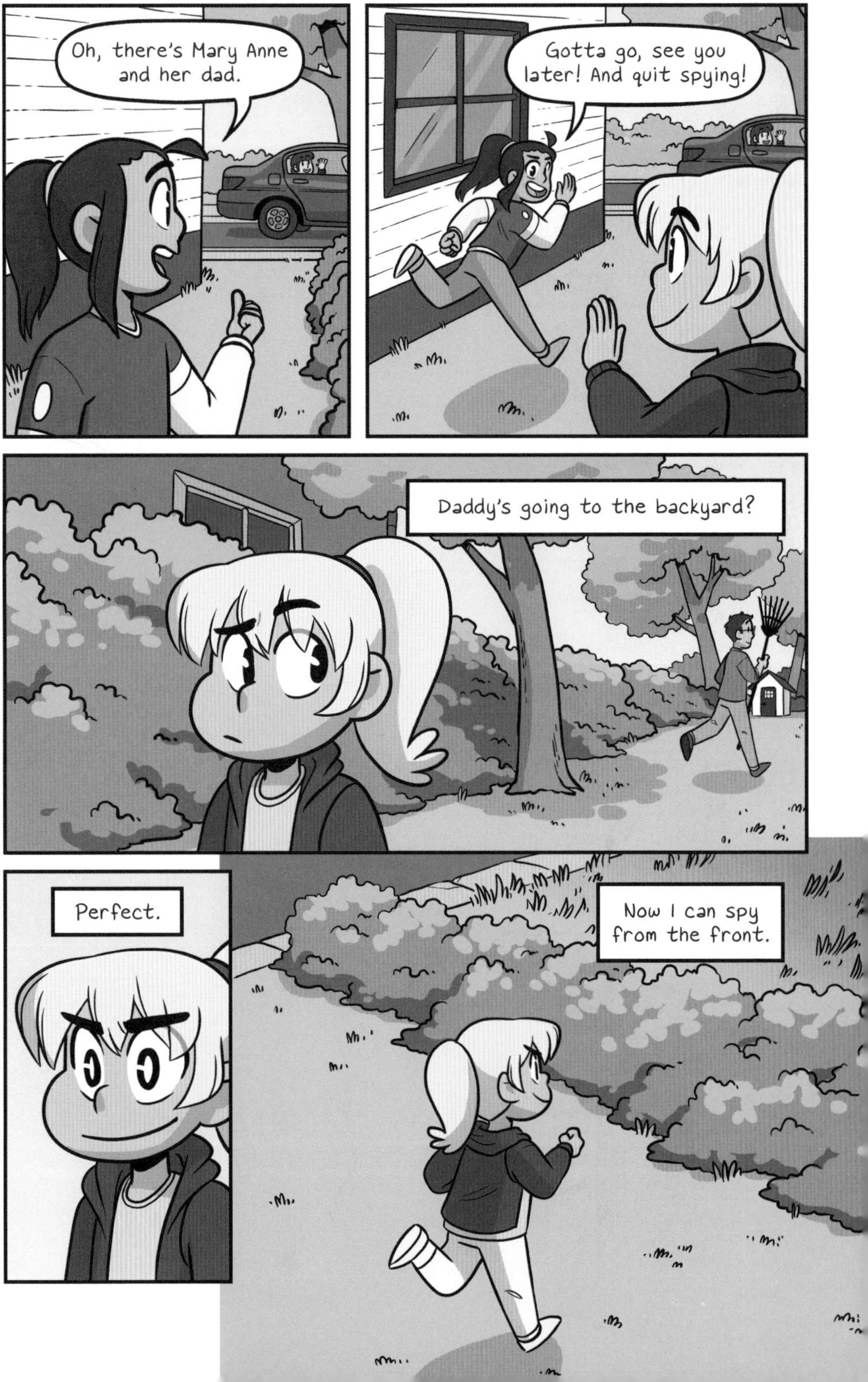
Oh, there's Mary Anne and her dad.
Gotta go, see you later! And quit spying!
Daddy's going to the backyard?
Perfect.
Now I can spy from the front.

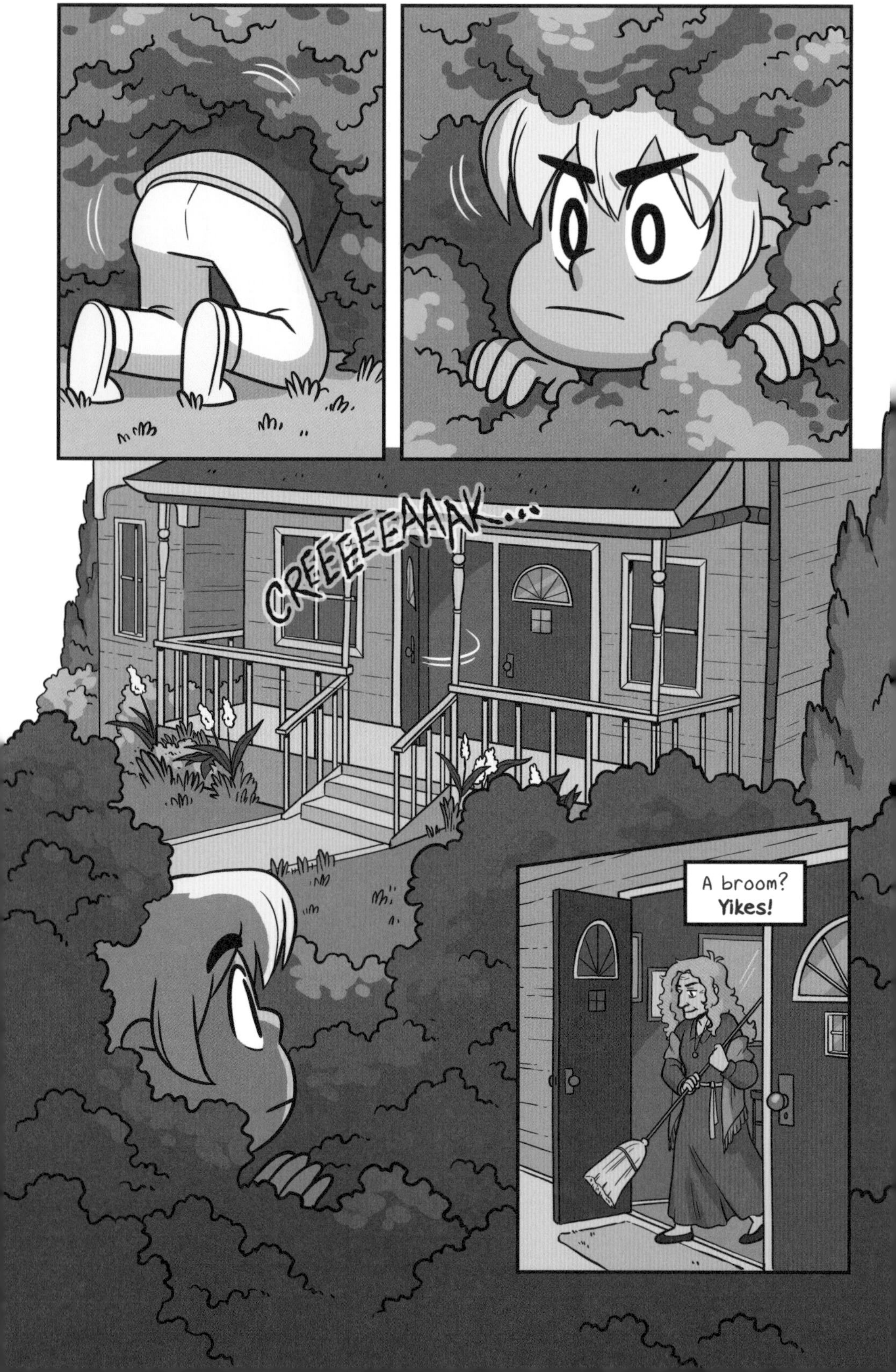
CREEEEEAAAK...
A broom?
Yikes!

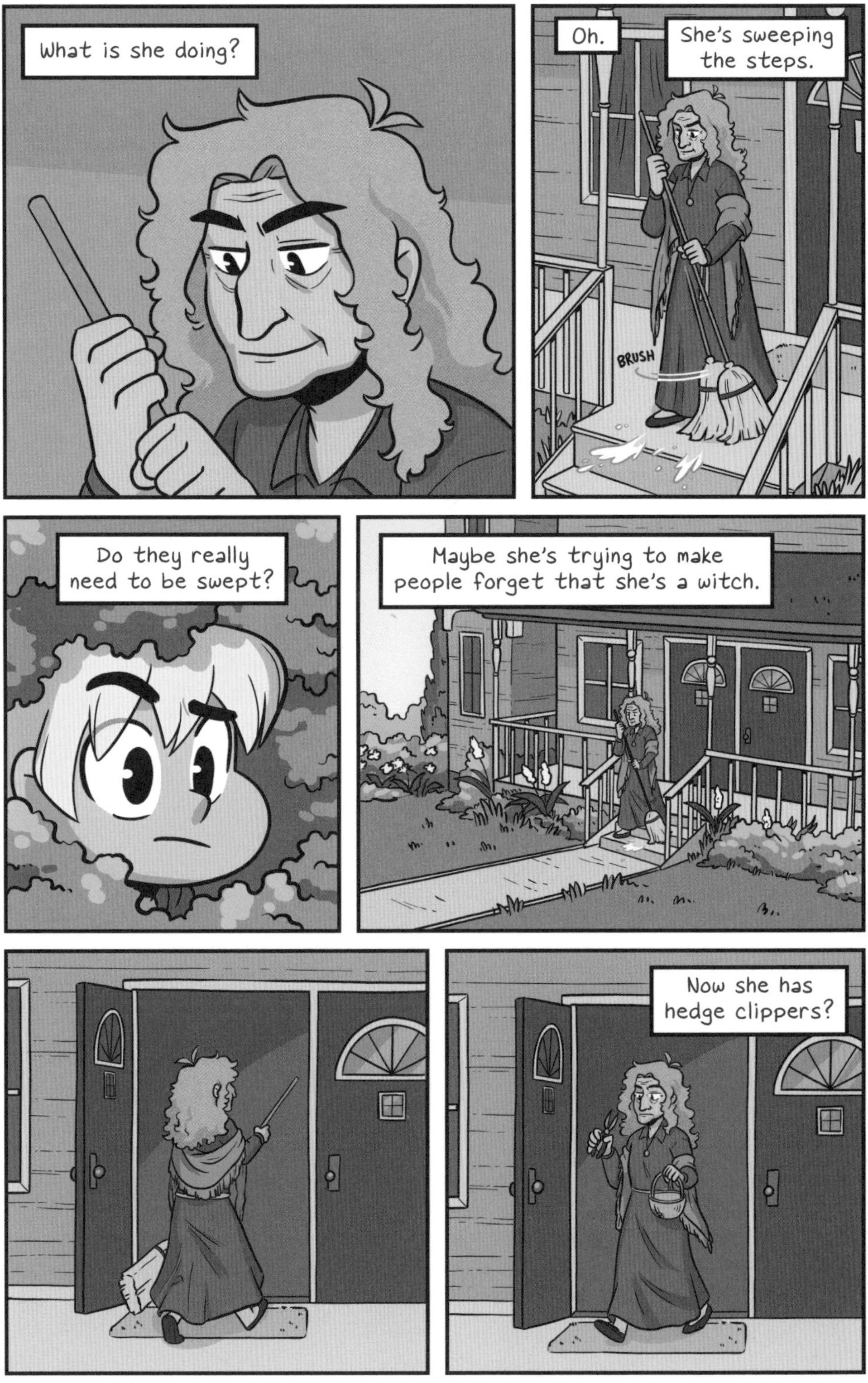
What is she doing?
Oh.
She's sweeping the steps.
BRUSH
Do they really need to be swept?
Maybe she's trying to make people forget that she's a witch.
Now she has hedge clippers?

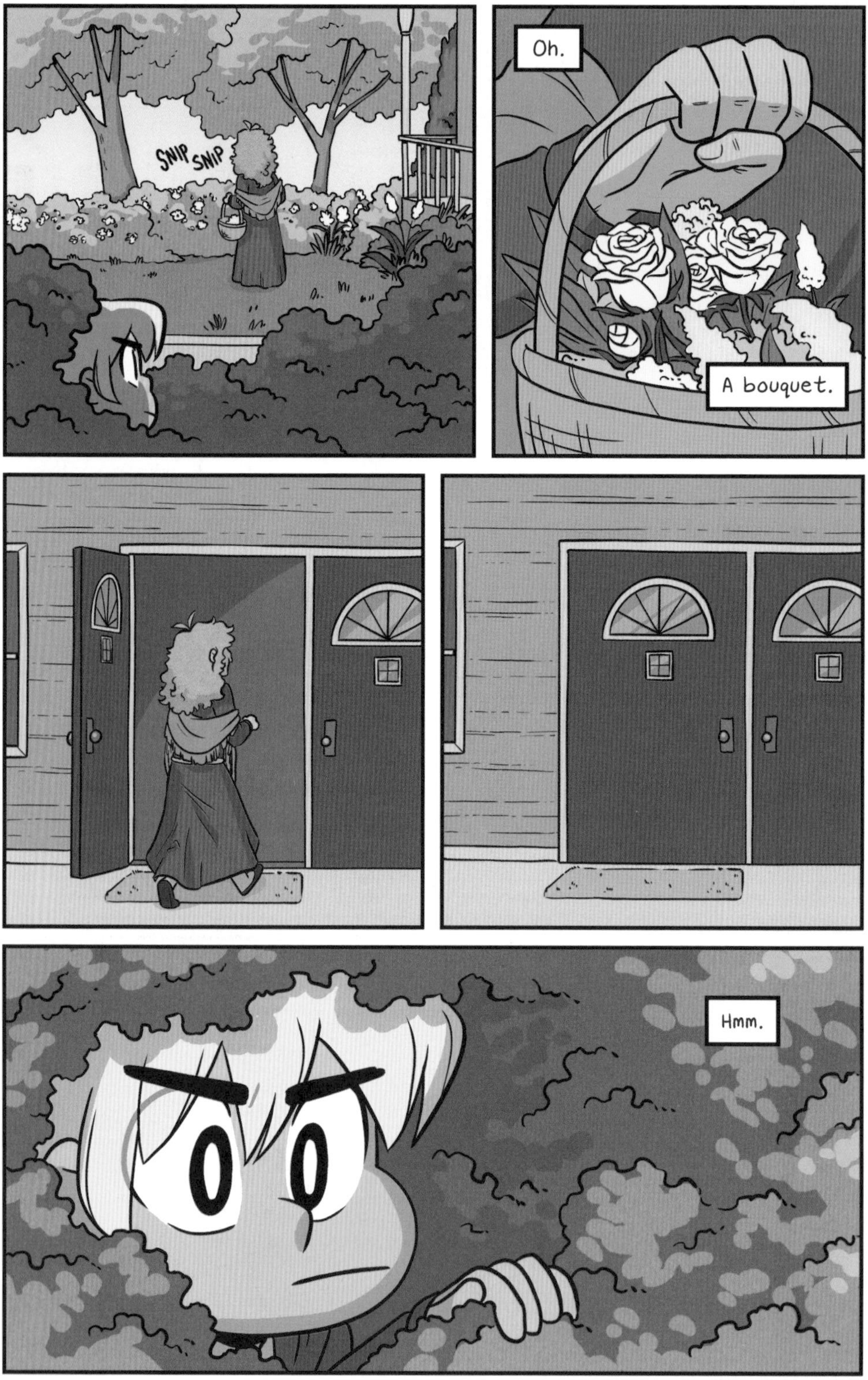
SNIP SNIP
Oh.
A bouquet.
Hmm.

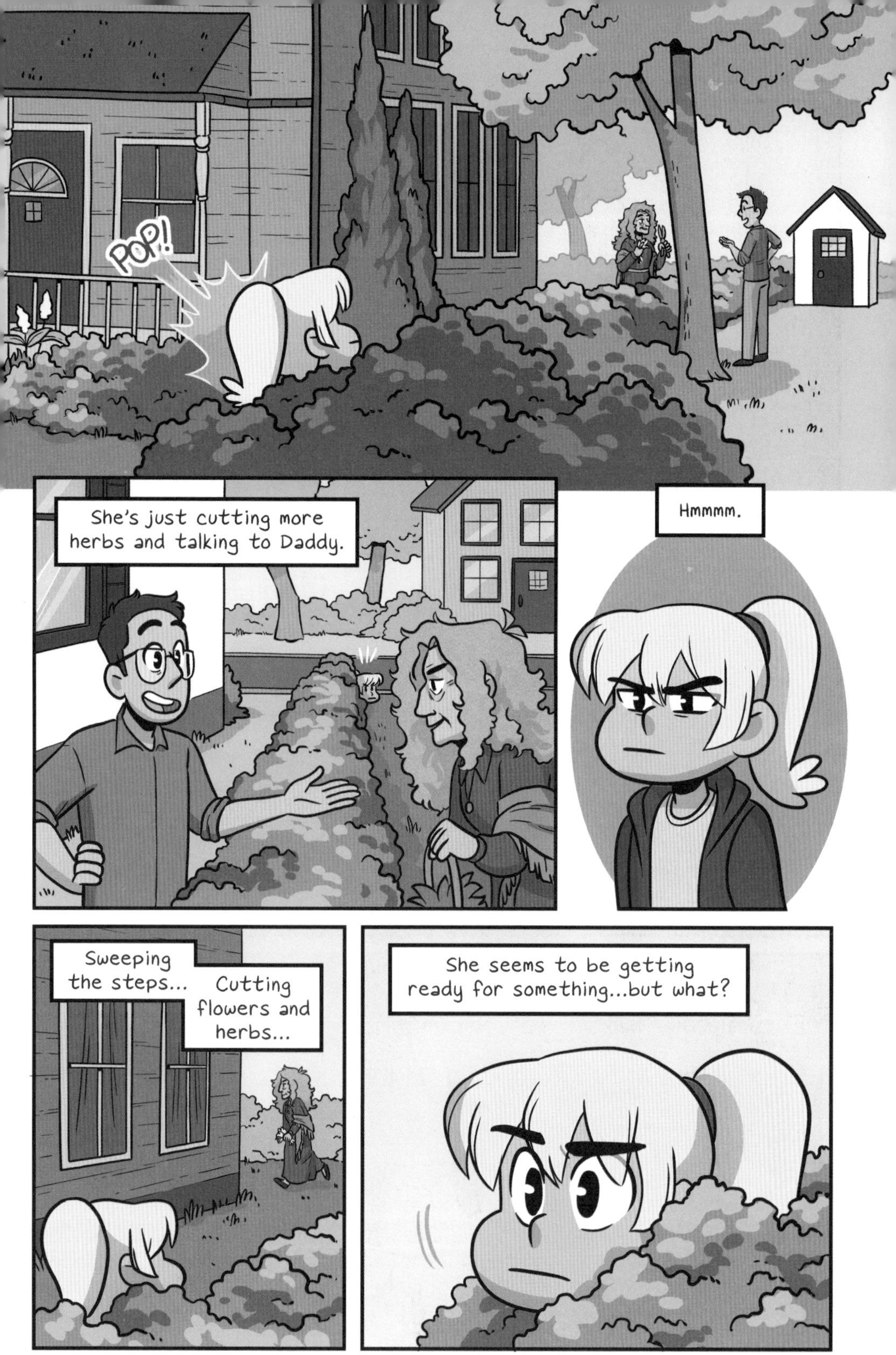

POP!
She's just cutting more herbs and talking to Daddy.
Hmmmm.
Sweeping the steps...
Cutting flowers and herbs...
She seems to be getting ready for something...but what?

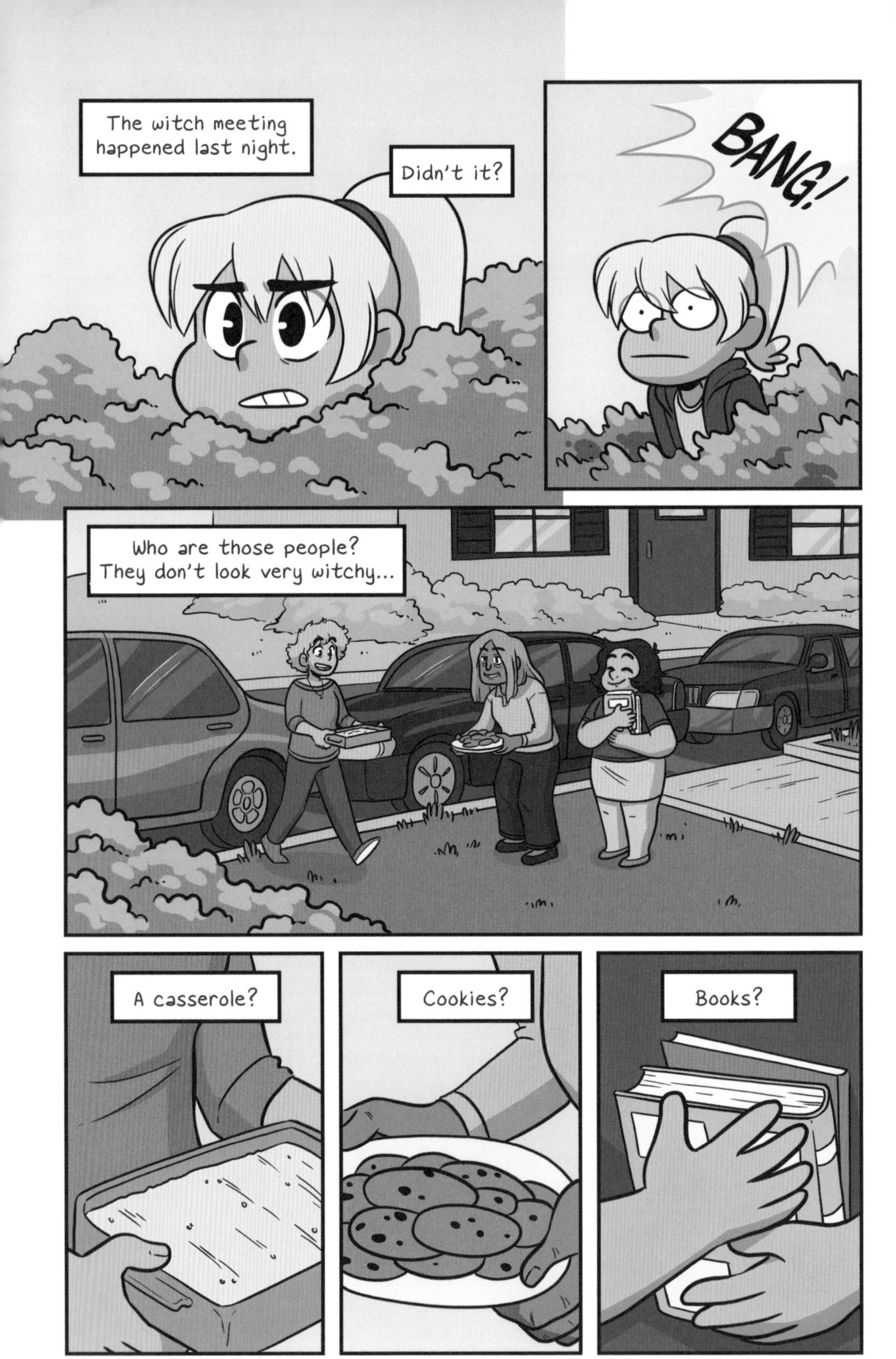

The witch meeting happened last night.
Didn't it?
BANG!
Who are those people? They don't look very witchy...
A casserole?
Cookies?
Books?

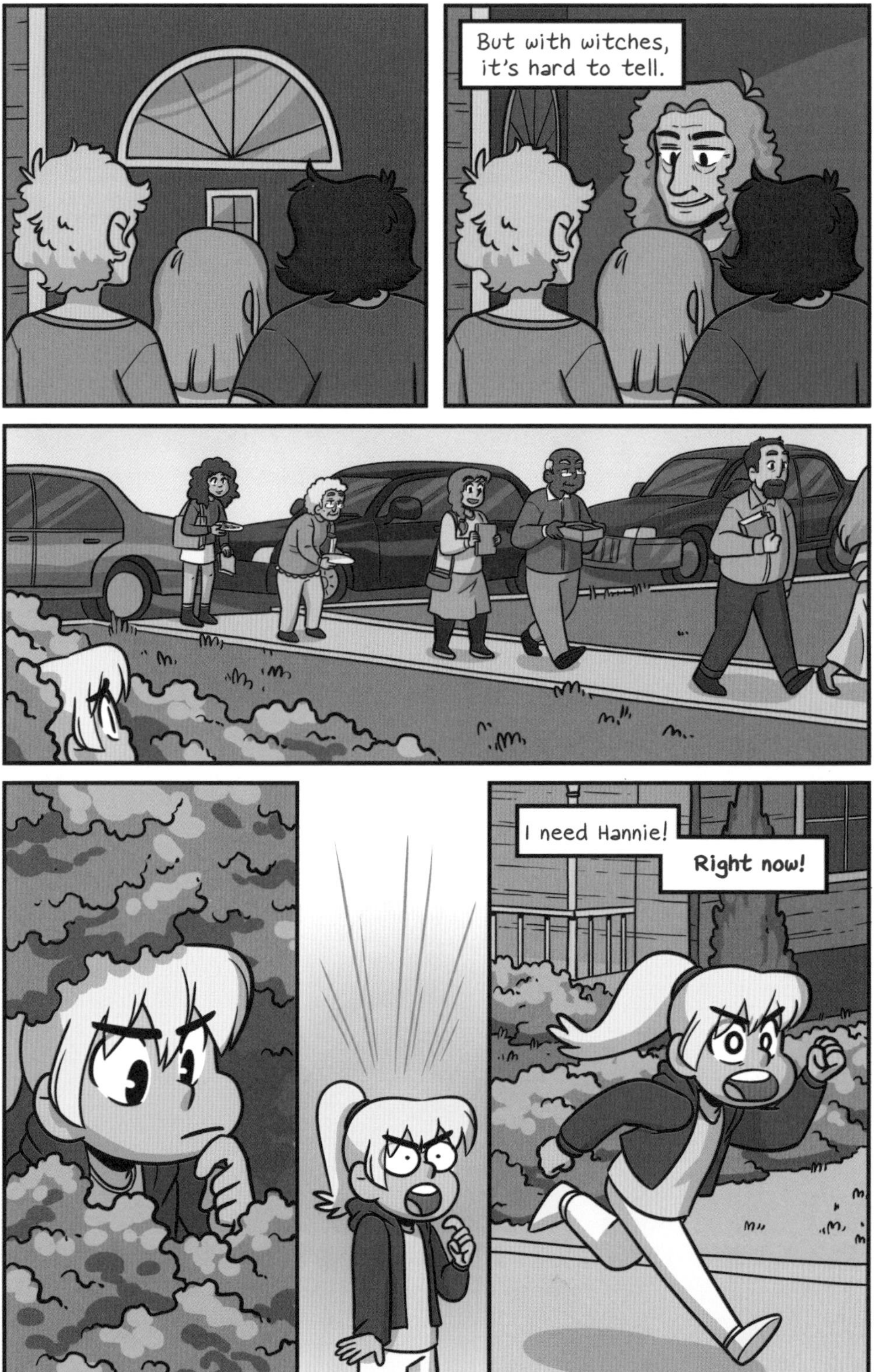
But with witches, it's hard to tell.
I need Hannie!
Right now!

CHAPTER 8

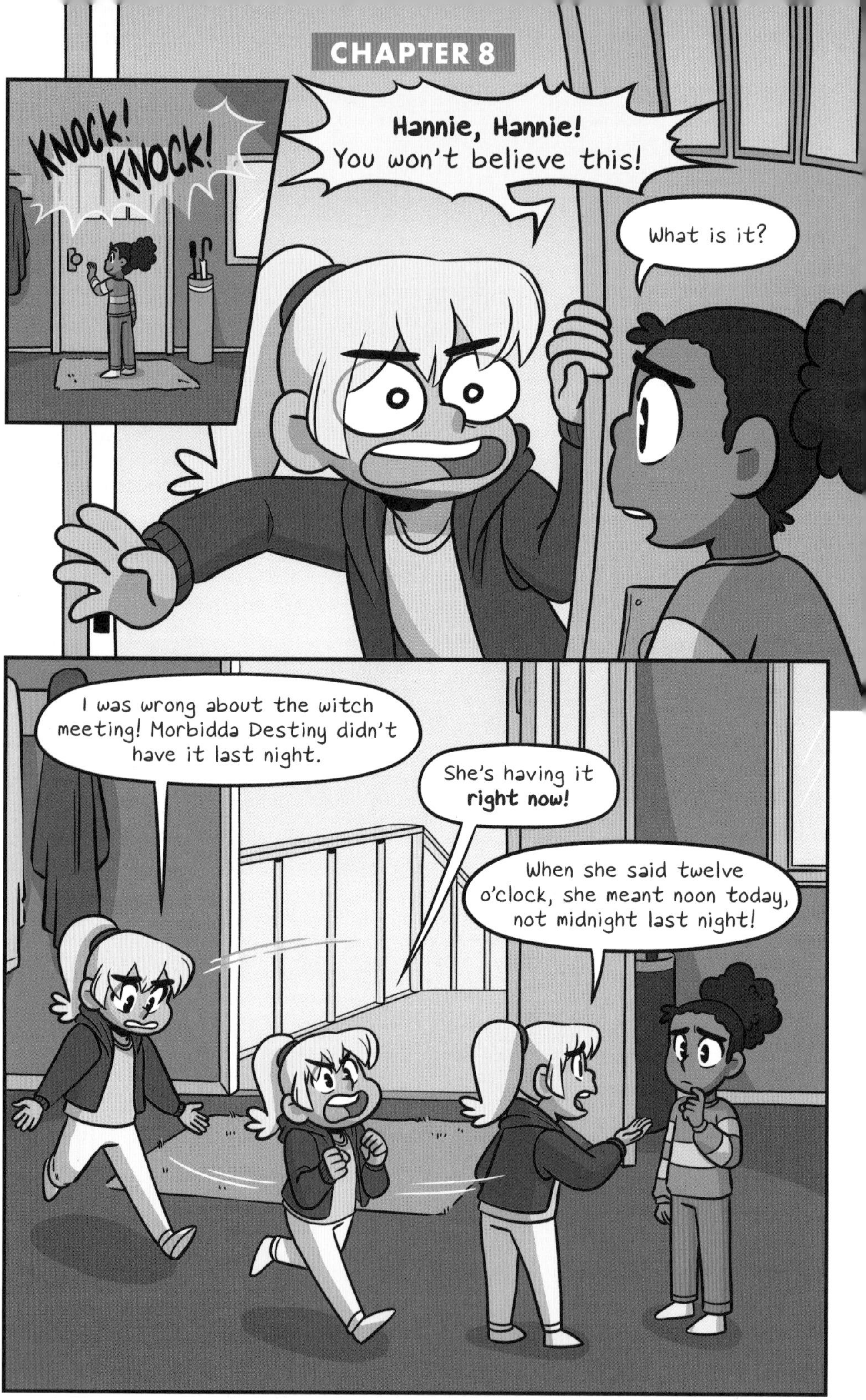

KNOCK! KNOCK!
Hannie, Hannie! You won't believe this!
What is it?
I was wrong about the witch meeting! Morbidda Destiny didn't have it last night.
She's having it **right now!**
When she said twelve o'clock, she meant noon today, not midnight last night!

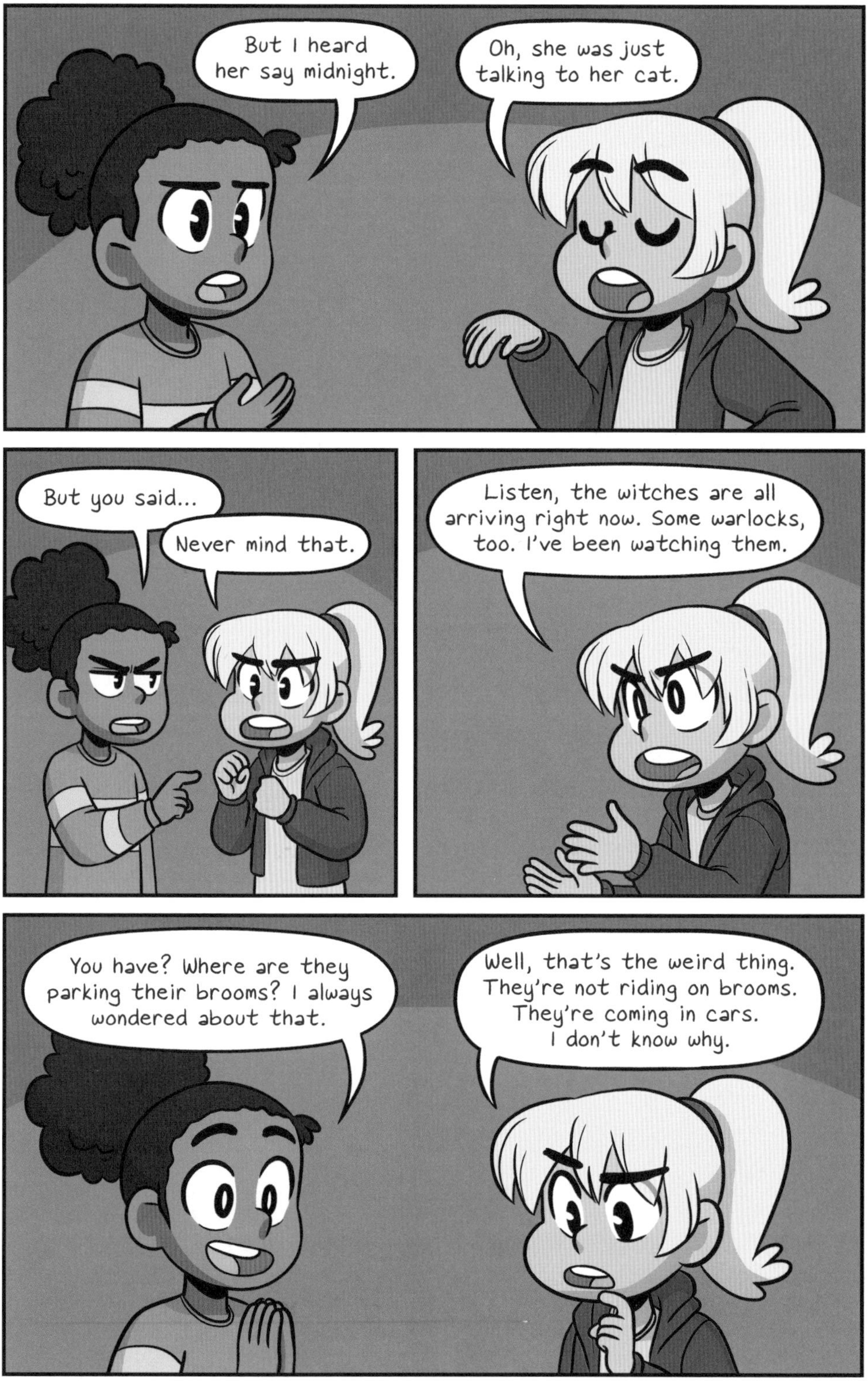
But I heard her say midnight.
Oh, she was just talking to her cat.
But you said...
Never mind that.
Listen, the witches are all arriving right now. Some warlocks, too. I've been watching them.
You have? Where are they parking their brooms? I always wondered about that.
Well, that's the weird thing. They're not riding on brooms. They're coming in cars. I don't know why.

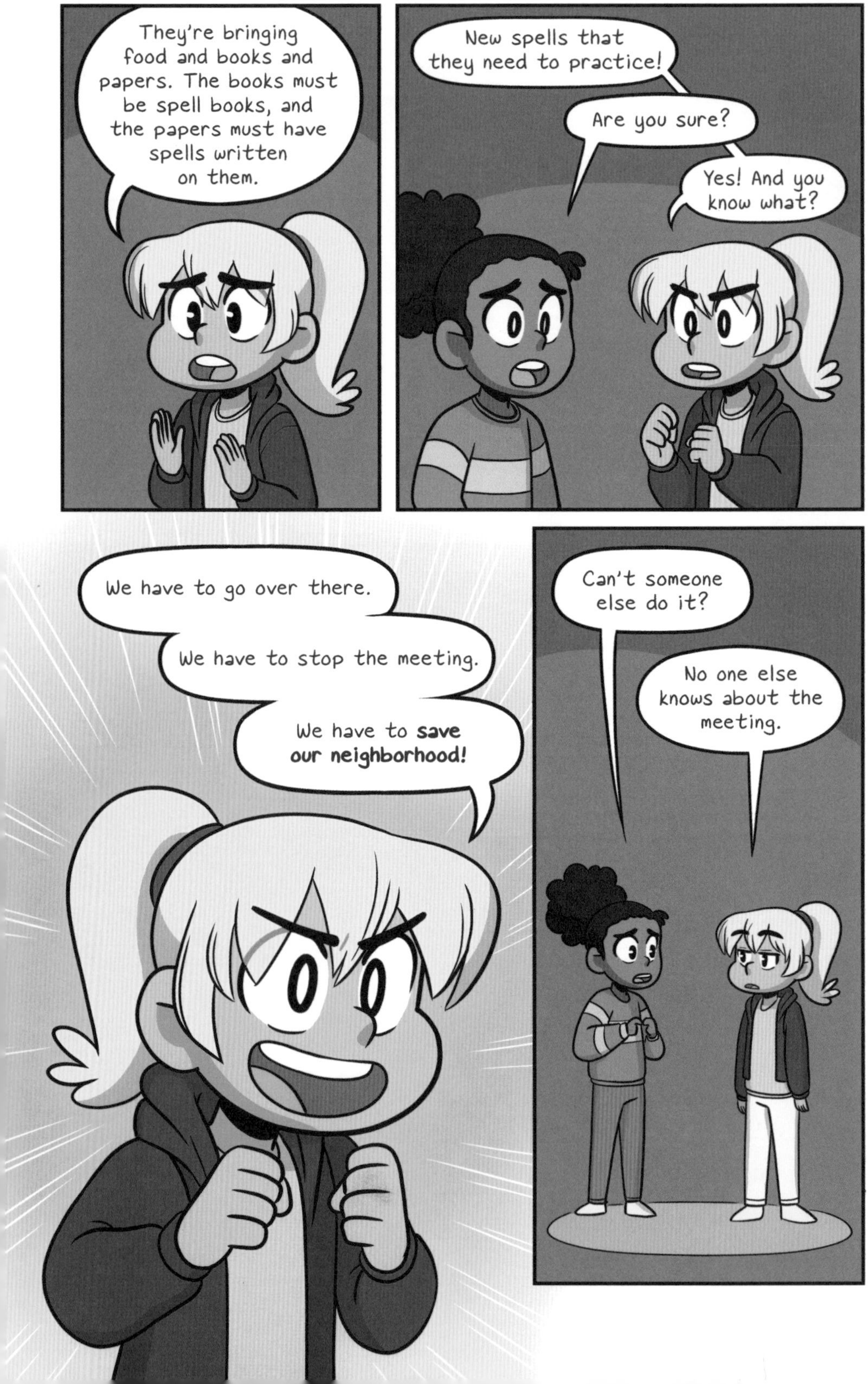
They're bringing food and books and papers. The books must be spell books, and the papers must have spells written on them.
New spells that they need to practice!
Are you sure?
Yes! And you know what?
We have to go over there.
We have to stop the meeting.
We have to **save our neighborhood!**
Can't someone else do it?
No one else knows about the meeting.

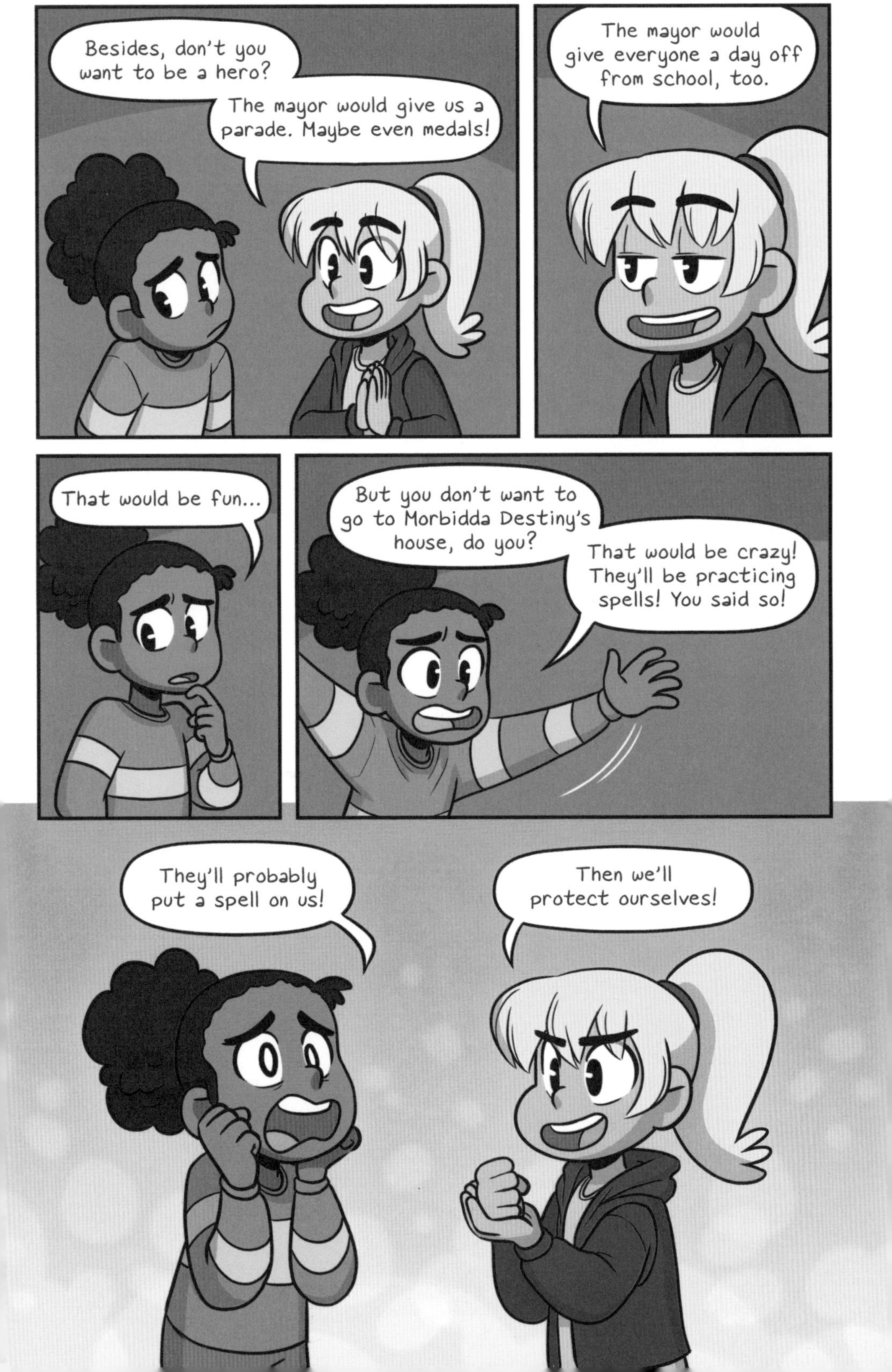
Besides, don't you want to be a hero?
The mayor would give us a parade. Maybe even medals!
The mayor would give everyone a day off from school, too.
That would be fun...
But you don't want to go to Morbidda Destiny's house, do you?
That would be crazy! They'll be practicing spells! You said so!
They'll probably put a spell on us!
Then we'll protect ourselves!

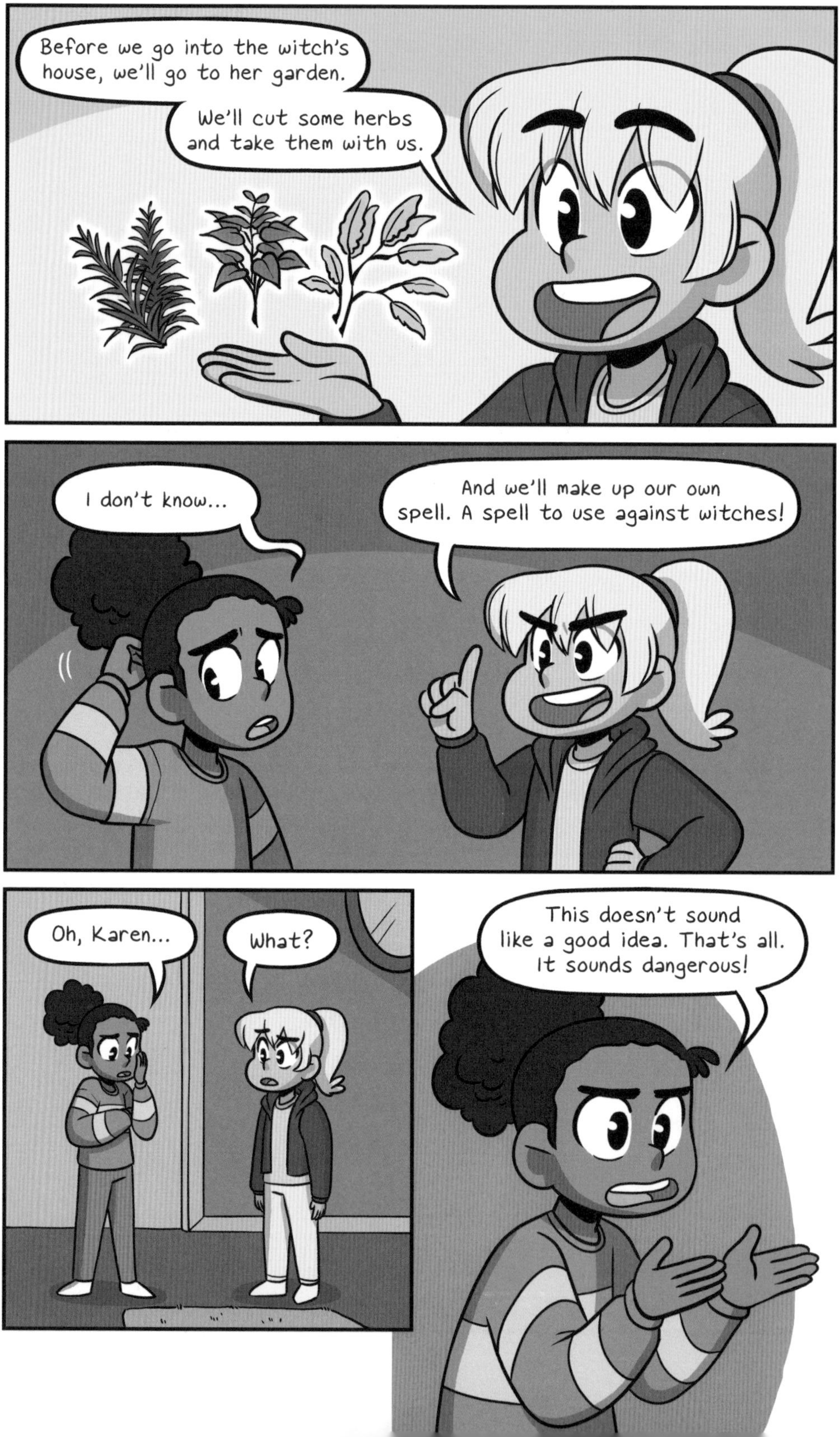

Before we go into the witch's house, we'll go to her garden.
We'll cut some herbs and take them with us.
I don't know...
And we'll make up our own spell. A spell to use against witches!
Oh, Karen...
What?
This doesn't sound like a good idea. That's all. It sounds dangerous!

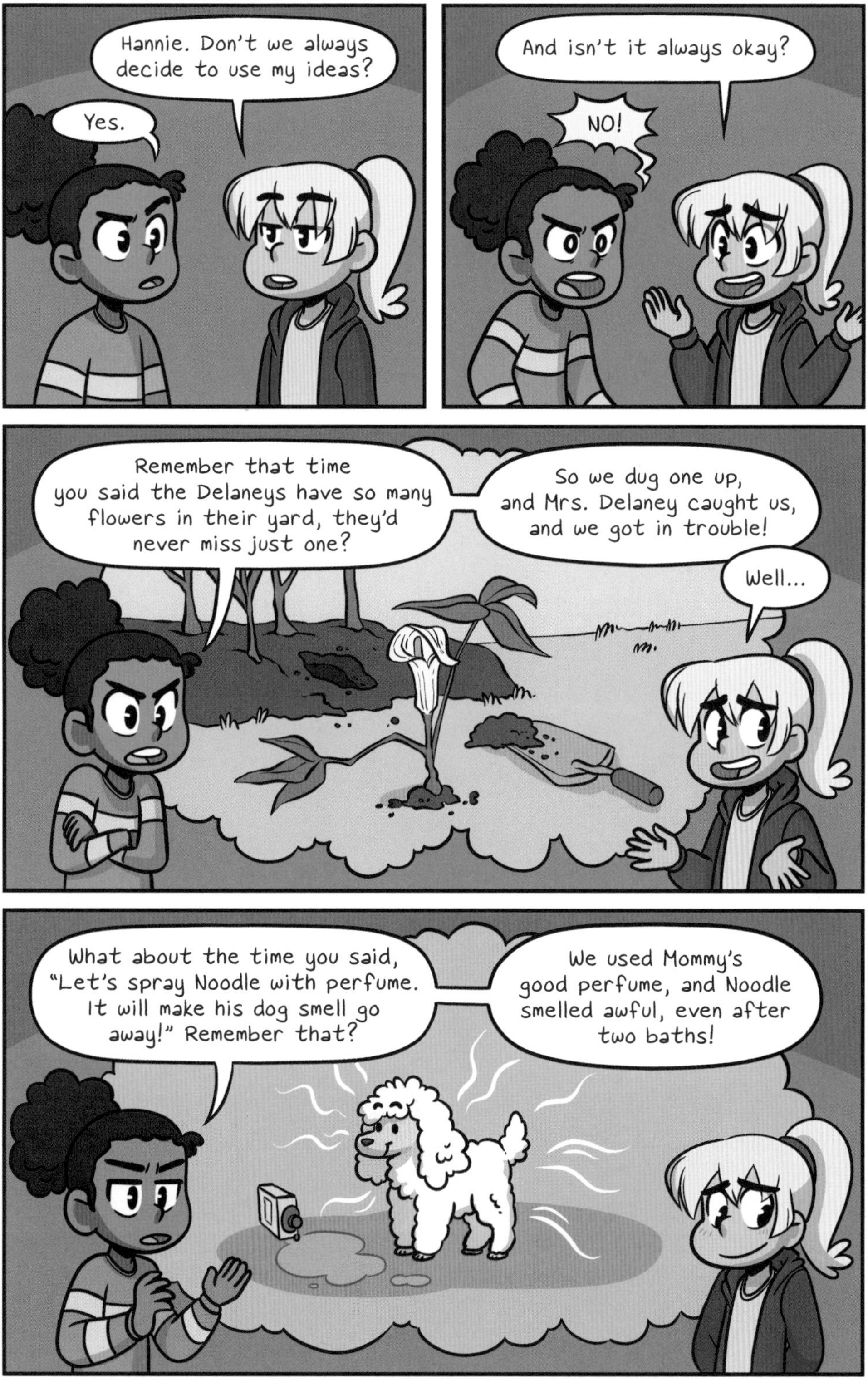

Hannie. Don't we always decide to use my ideas?
Yes.
And isn't it always okay?
NO!
Remember that time you said the Delaneys have so many flowers in their yard, they'd never miss just one?
So we dug one up, and Mrs. Delaney caught us, and we got in trouble!
Well...
What about the time you said, "Let's spray Noodle with perfume. It will make his dog smell go away!" Remember that?
We used Mommy's good perfume, and Noodle smelled awful, even after two baths!

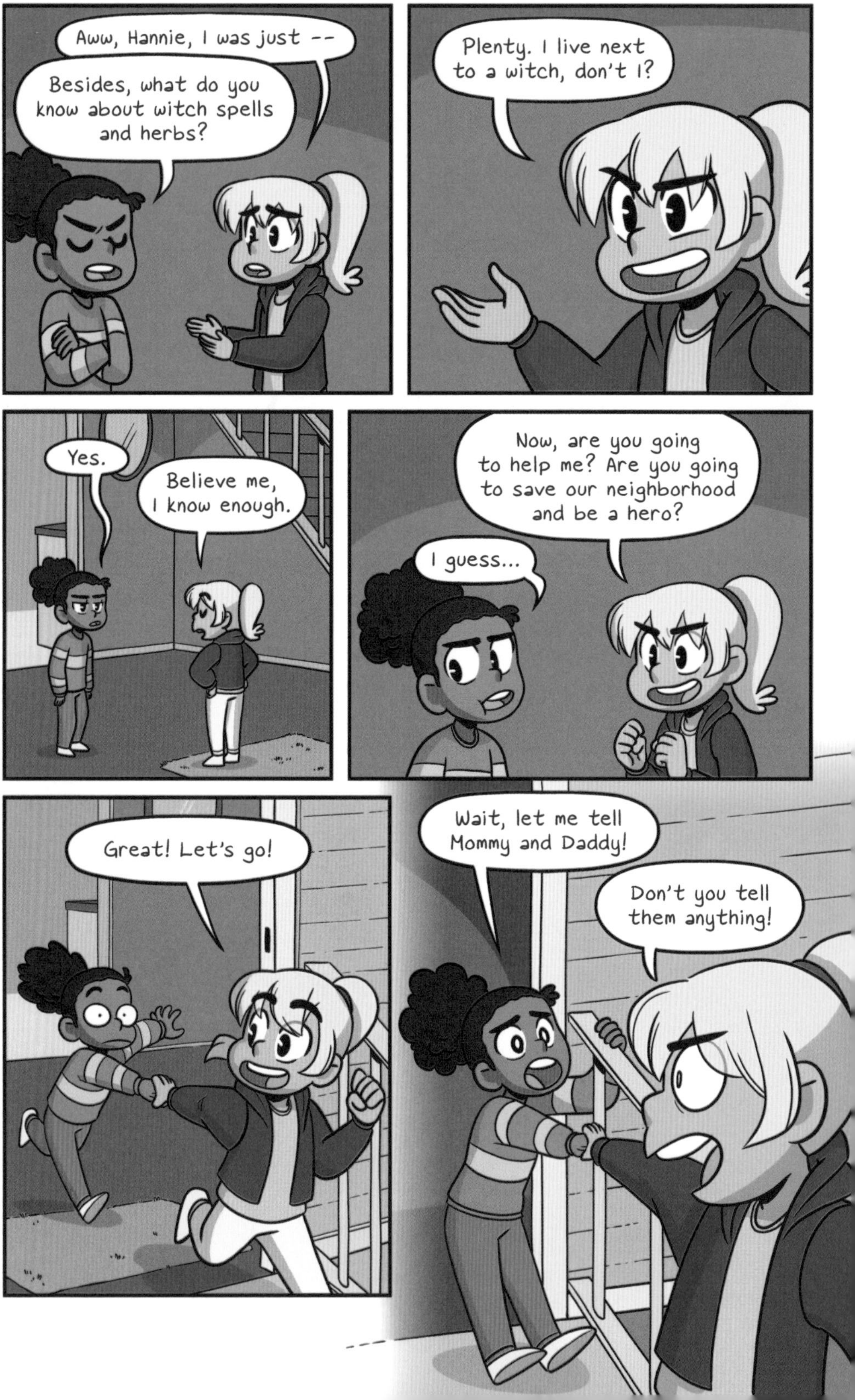
Aww, Hannie, I was just --
Besides, what do you know about witch spells and herbs?
Plenty. I live next to a witch, don't I?
Yes.
Believe me, I know enough.
Now, are you going to help me? Are you going to save our neighborhood and be a hero?
I guess...
Great! Let's go!
Wait, let me tell Mommy and Daddy!
Don't you tell them anything!

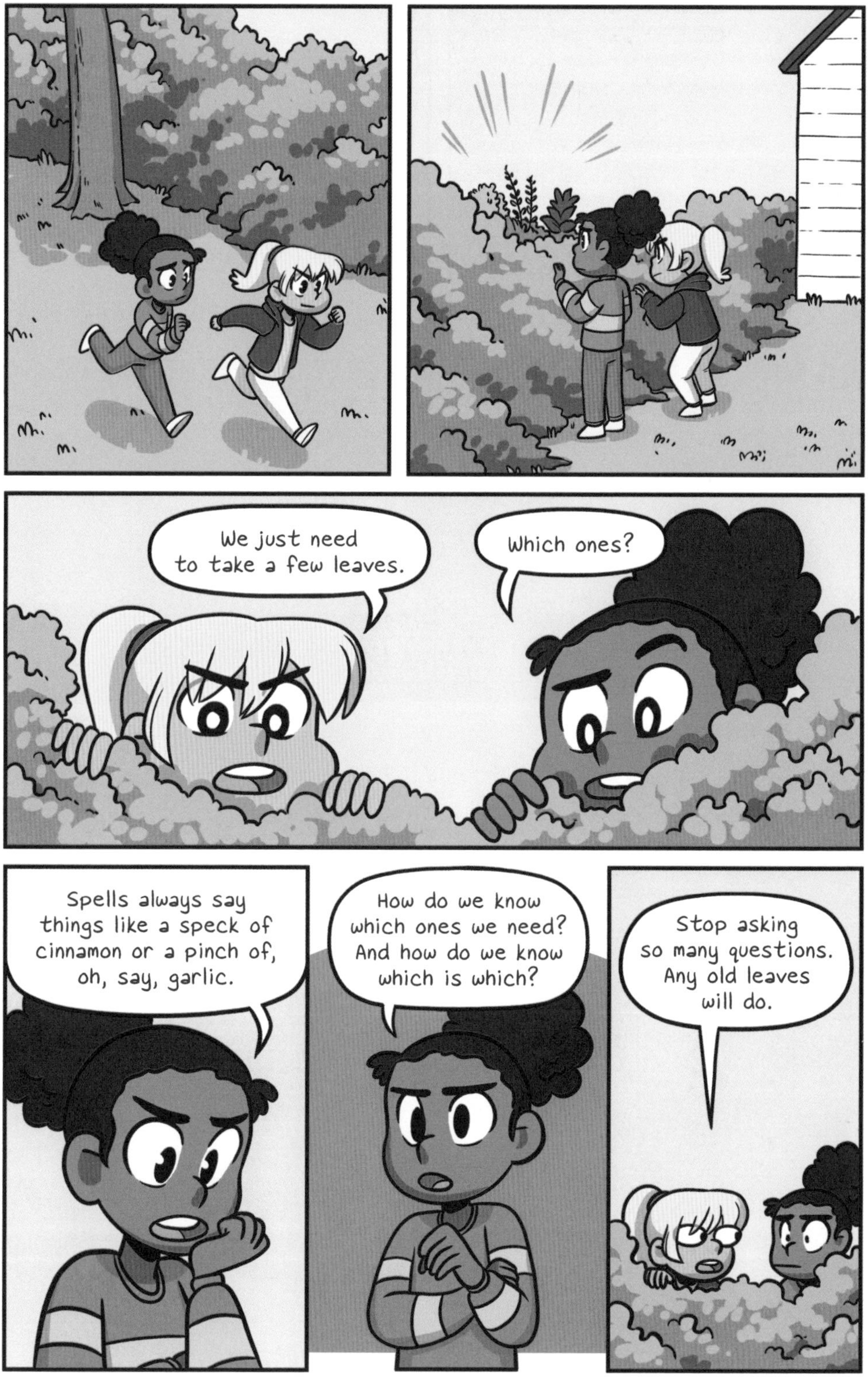

We just need to take a few leaves.
Which ones?
Spells always say things like a speck of cinnamon or a pinch of, oh, say, garlic.
How do we know which ones we need? And how do we know which is which?
Stop asking so many questions. Any old leaves will do.

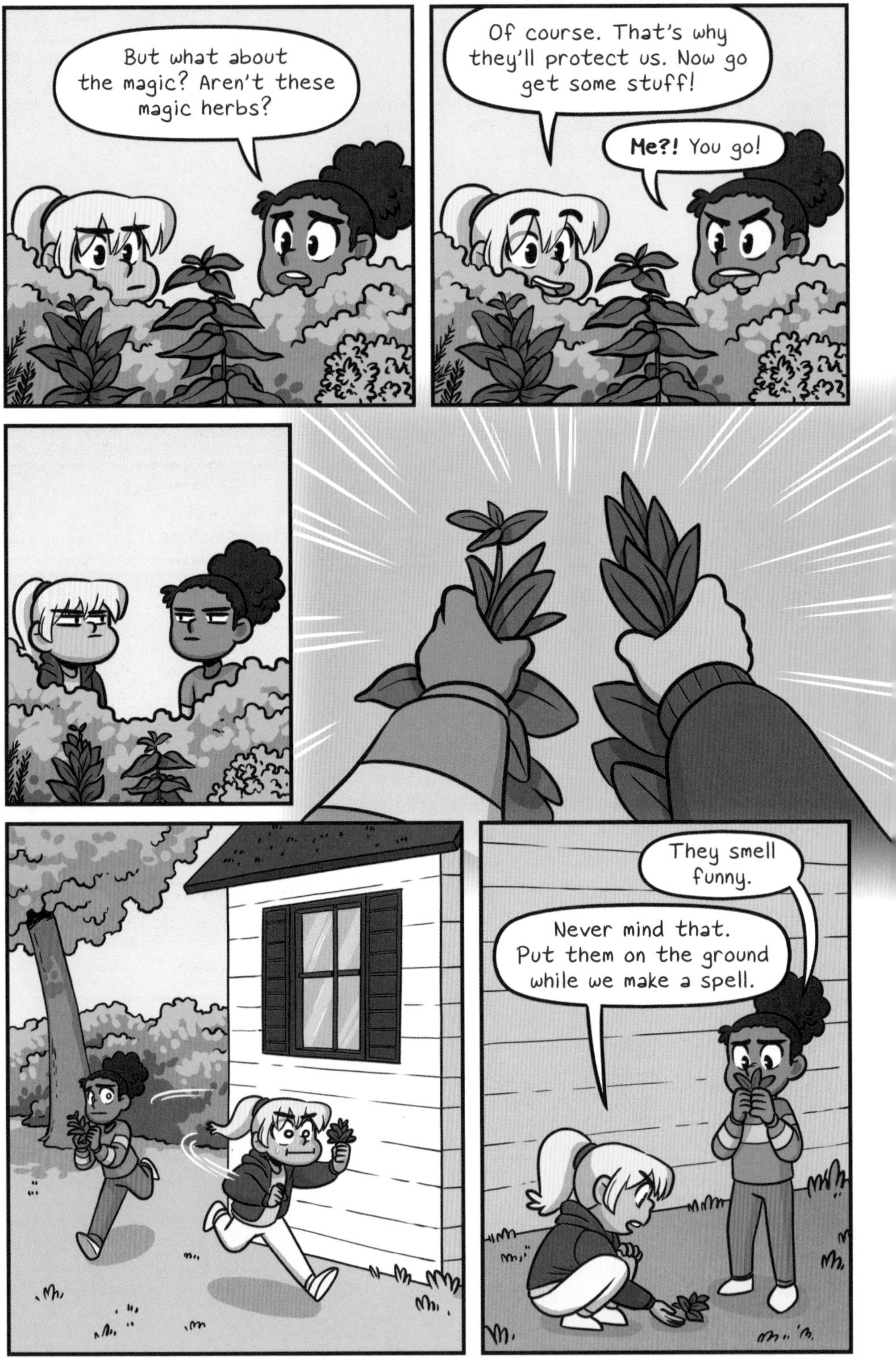
But what about the magic? Aren't these magic herbs?
Of course. That's why they'll protect us. Now go get some stuff!
Me?! You go!
They smell funny.
Never mind that. Put them on the ground while we make a spell.

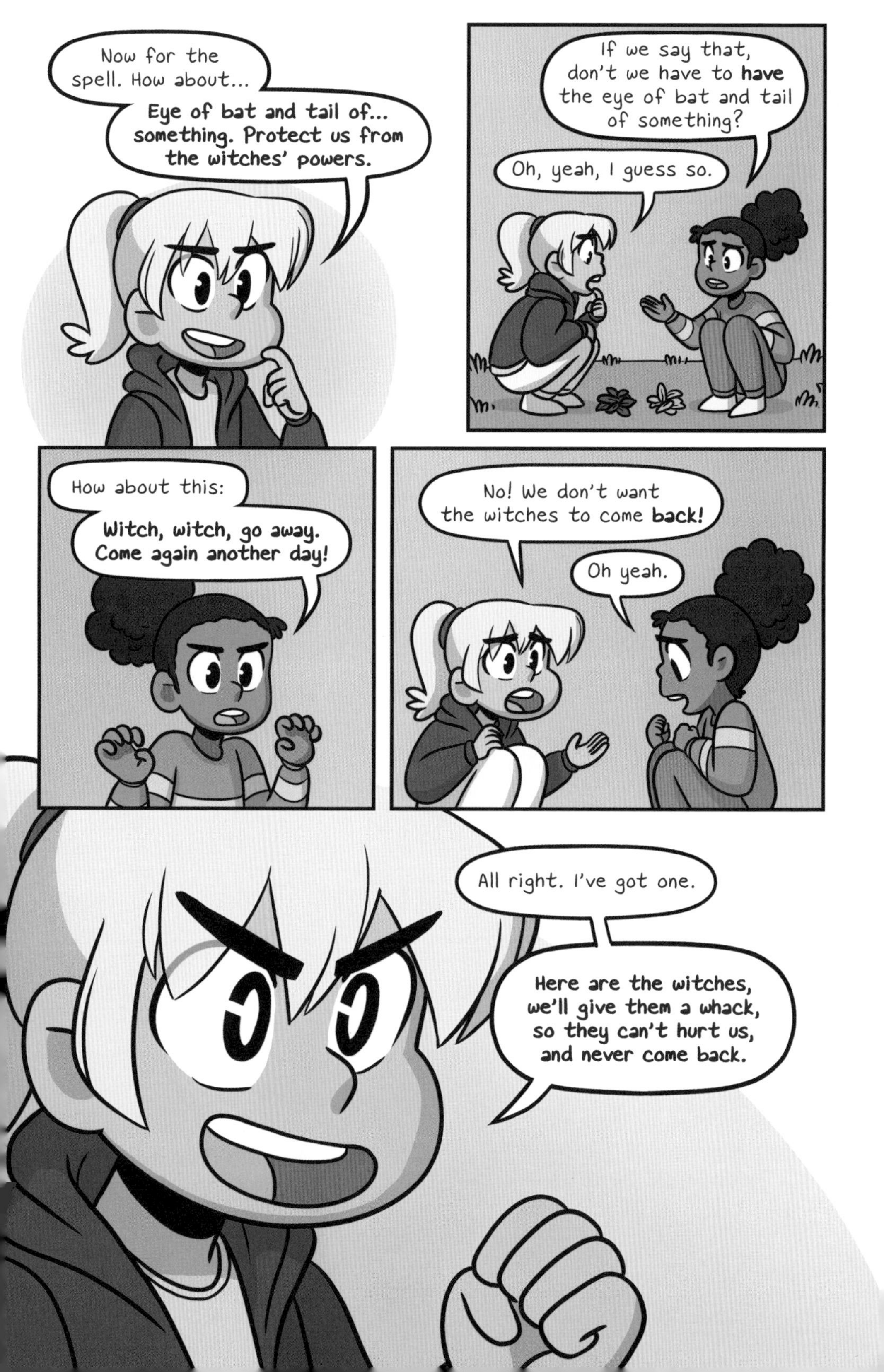
Now for the spell. How about...
Eye of bat and tail of... something. Protect us from the witches' powers.
If we say that, don't we have to **have** the eye of bat and tail of something?
Oh, yeah, I guess so.
How about this:
Witch, witch, go away. Come again another day!
No! We don't want the witches to come **back!**
Oh yeah.
All right. I've got one.
Here are the witches, we'll give them a whack, so they can't hurt us, and never come back.

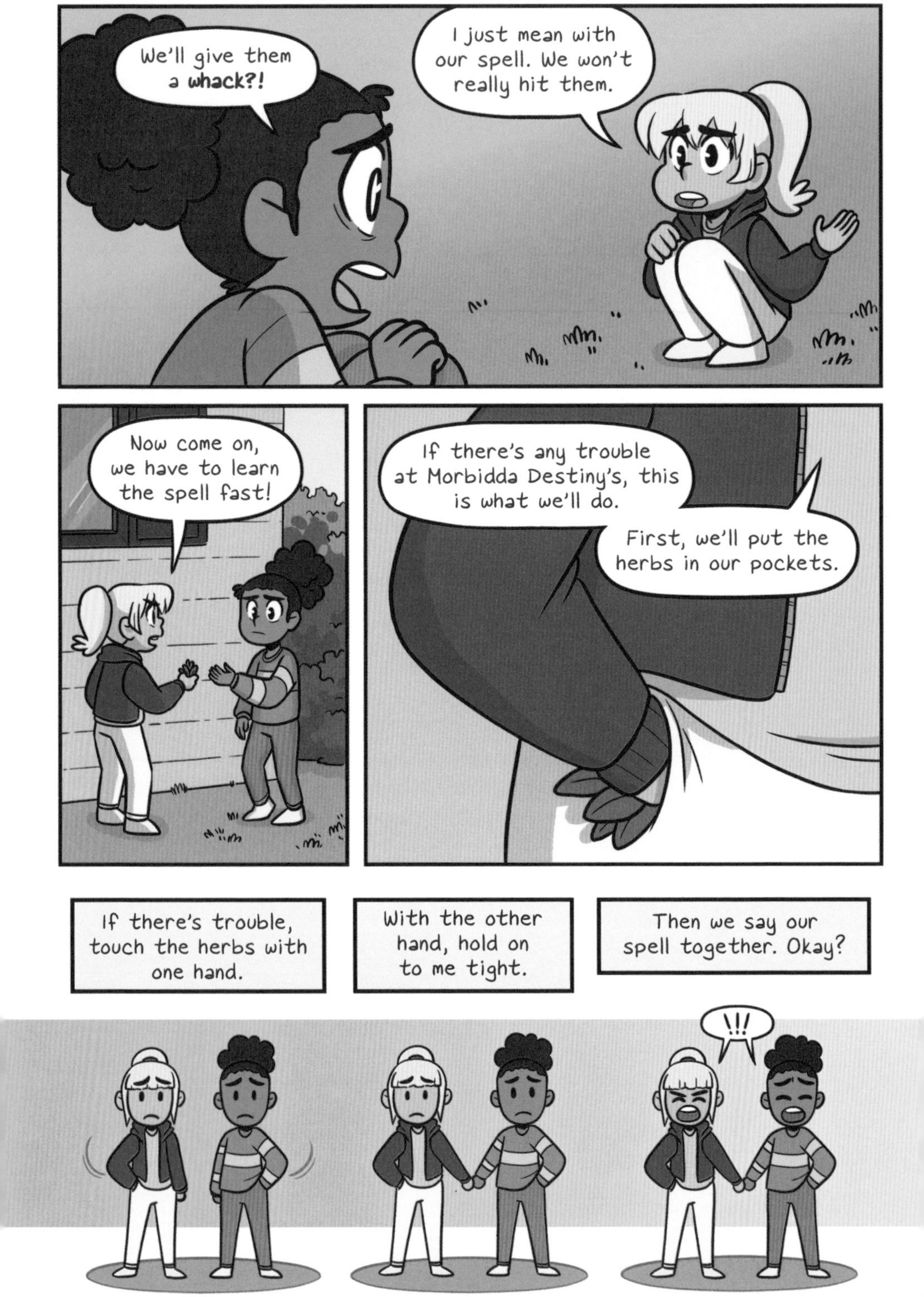
We'll give them a **whack?!**
I just mean with our spell. We won't really hit them.
Now come on, we have to learn the spell fast!
If there's any trouble at Morbidda Destiny's, this is what we'll do.
First, we'll put the herbs in our pockets.
If there's trouble, touch the herbs with one hand.
With the other hand, hold on to me tight.
Then we say our spell together. Okay?
!!!

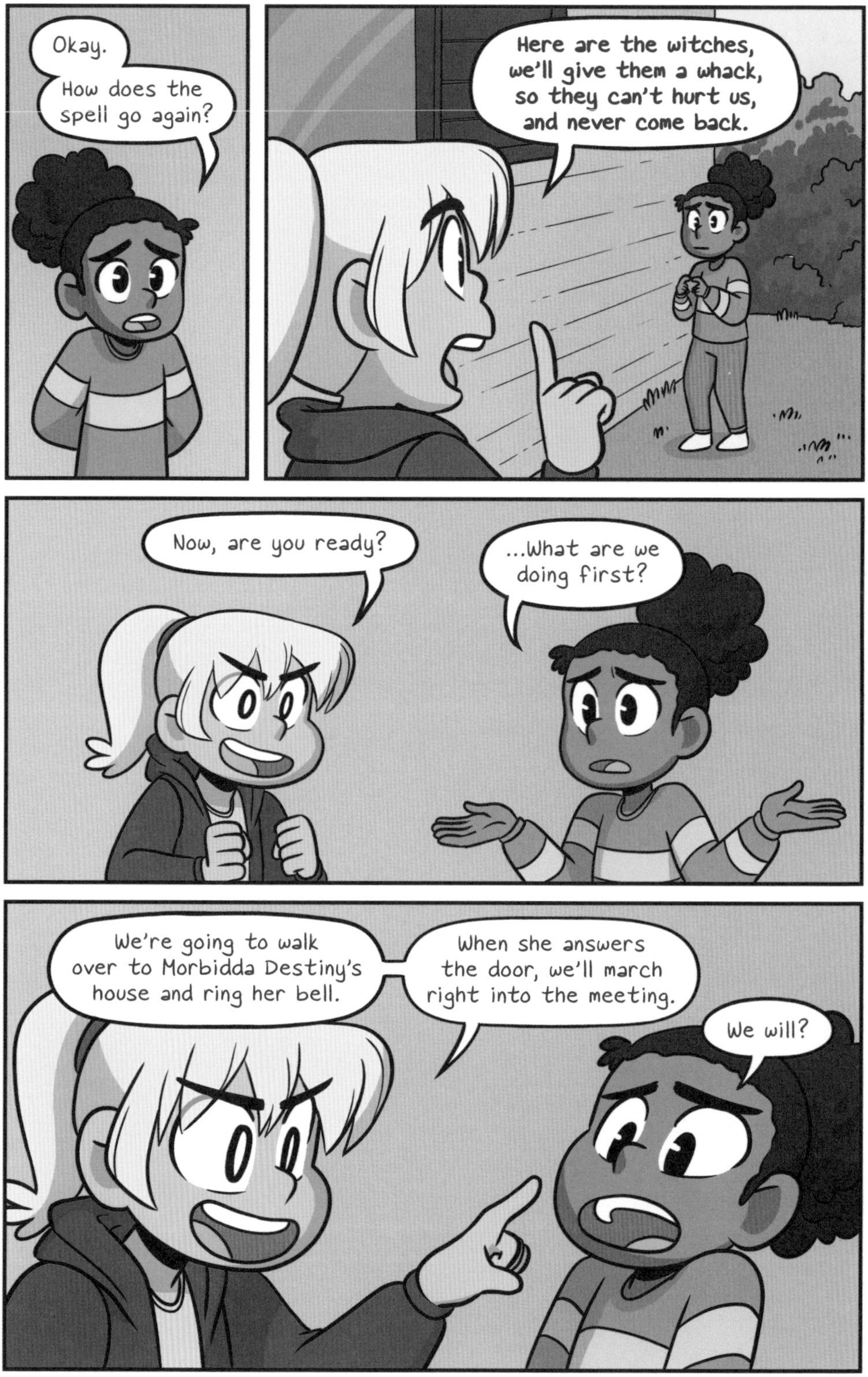
Okay.
How does the spell go again?
Here are the witches, we'll give them a whack, so they can't hurt us, and never come back.
Now, are you ready?
...What are we doing first?
We're going to walk over to Morbidda Destiny's house and ring her bell.
When she answers the door, we'll march right into the meeting.
We will?

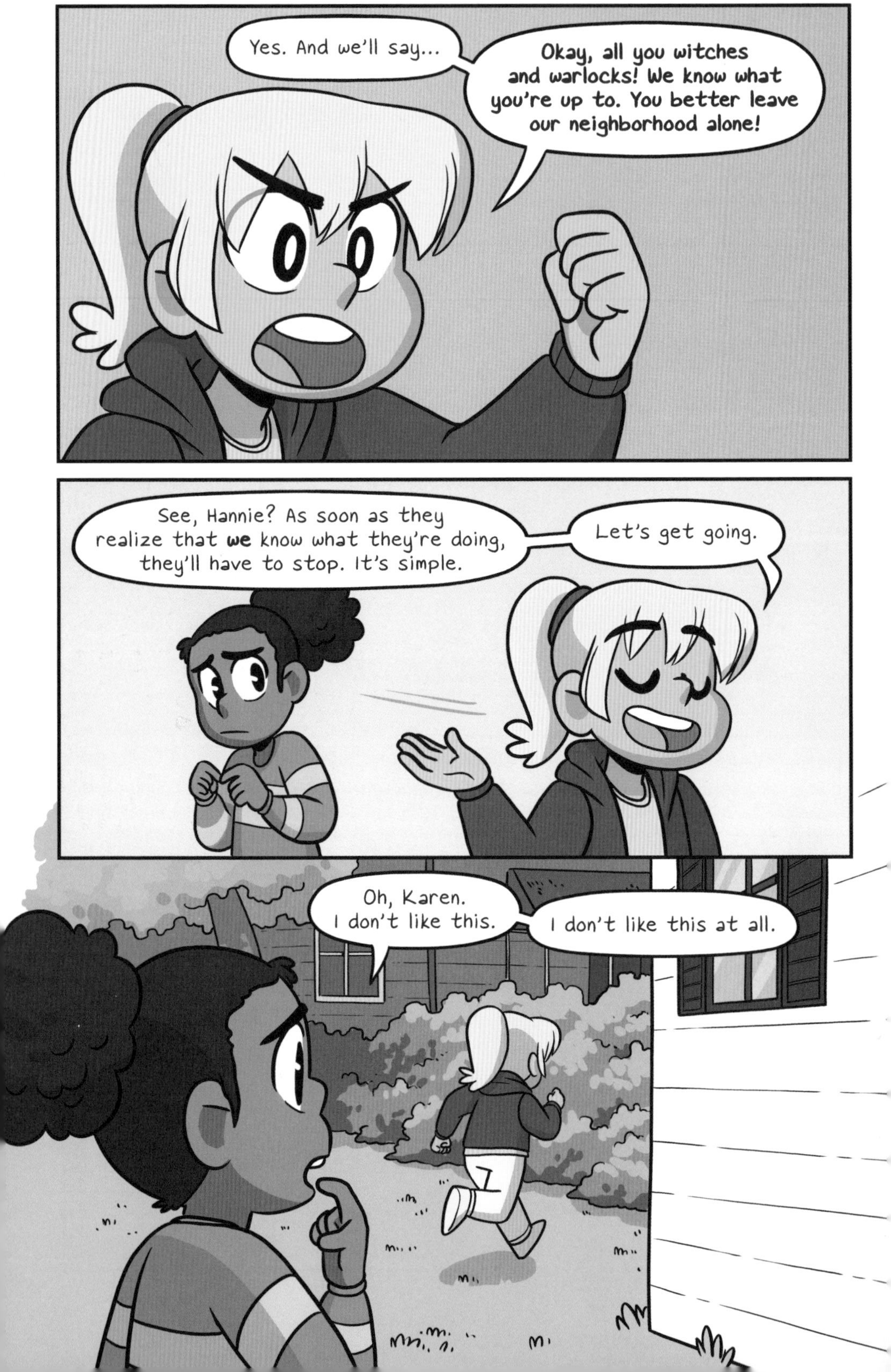
Yes. And we'll say...
Okay, all you witches and warlocks! We know what you're up to. You better leave our neighborhood alone!
See, Hannie? As soon as they realize that **we** know what they're doing, they'll have to stop. It's simple.
Let's get going.
Oh, Karen. I don't like this.
I don't like this at all.

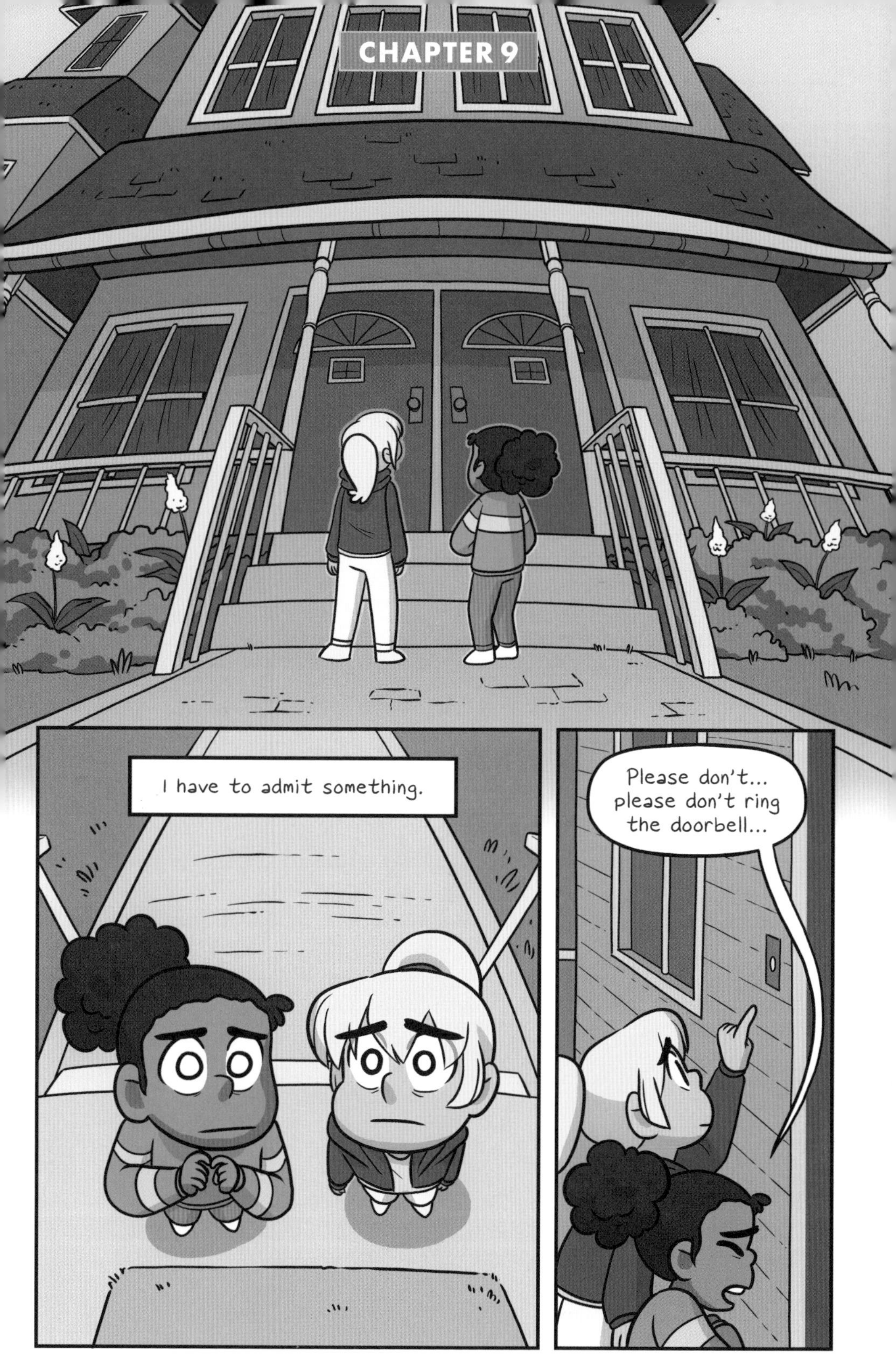
CHAPTER 9
I have to admit something.
Please don't... please don't ring the doorbell...

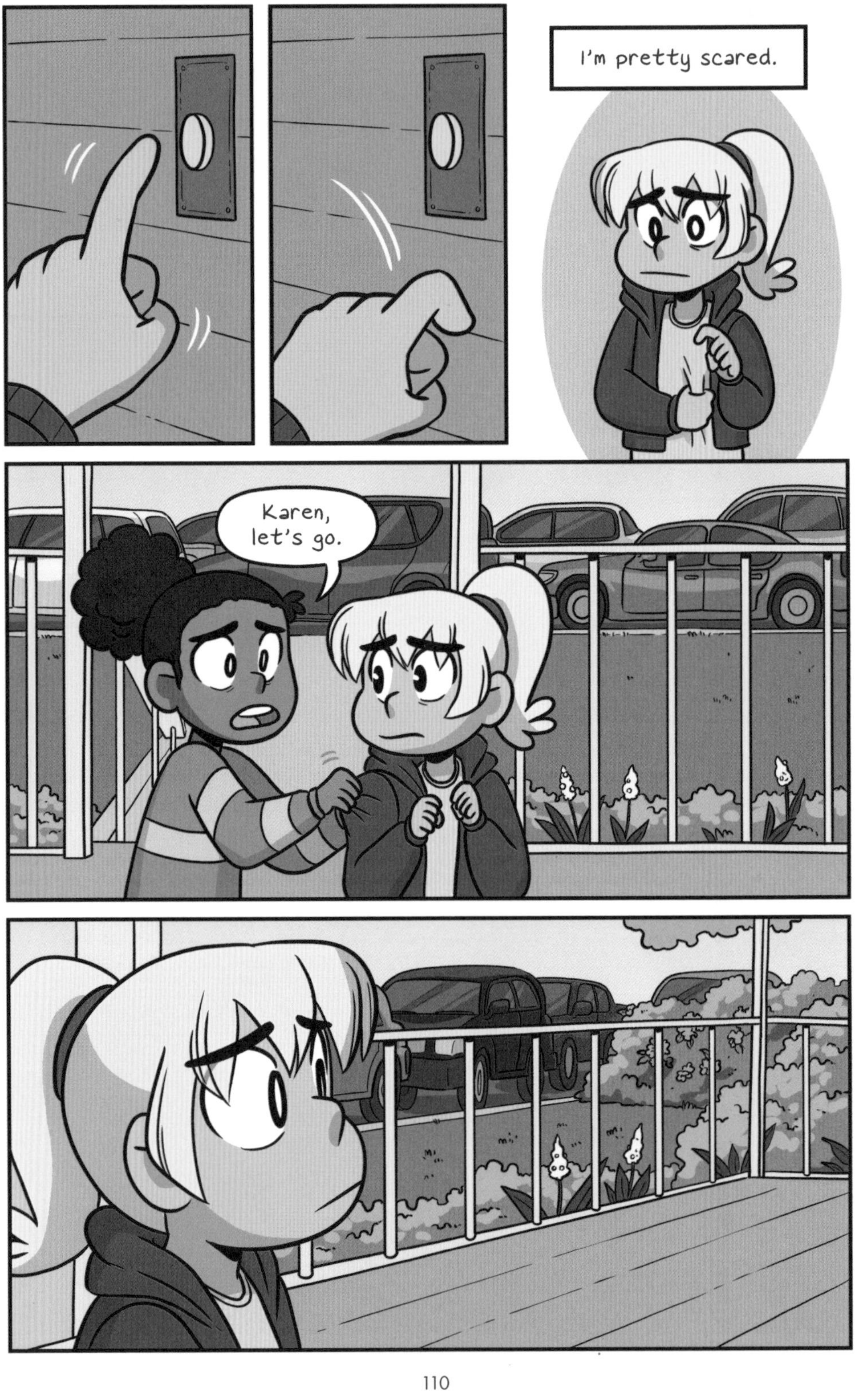
I'm pretty scared.
Karen, let's go.

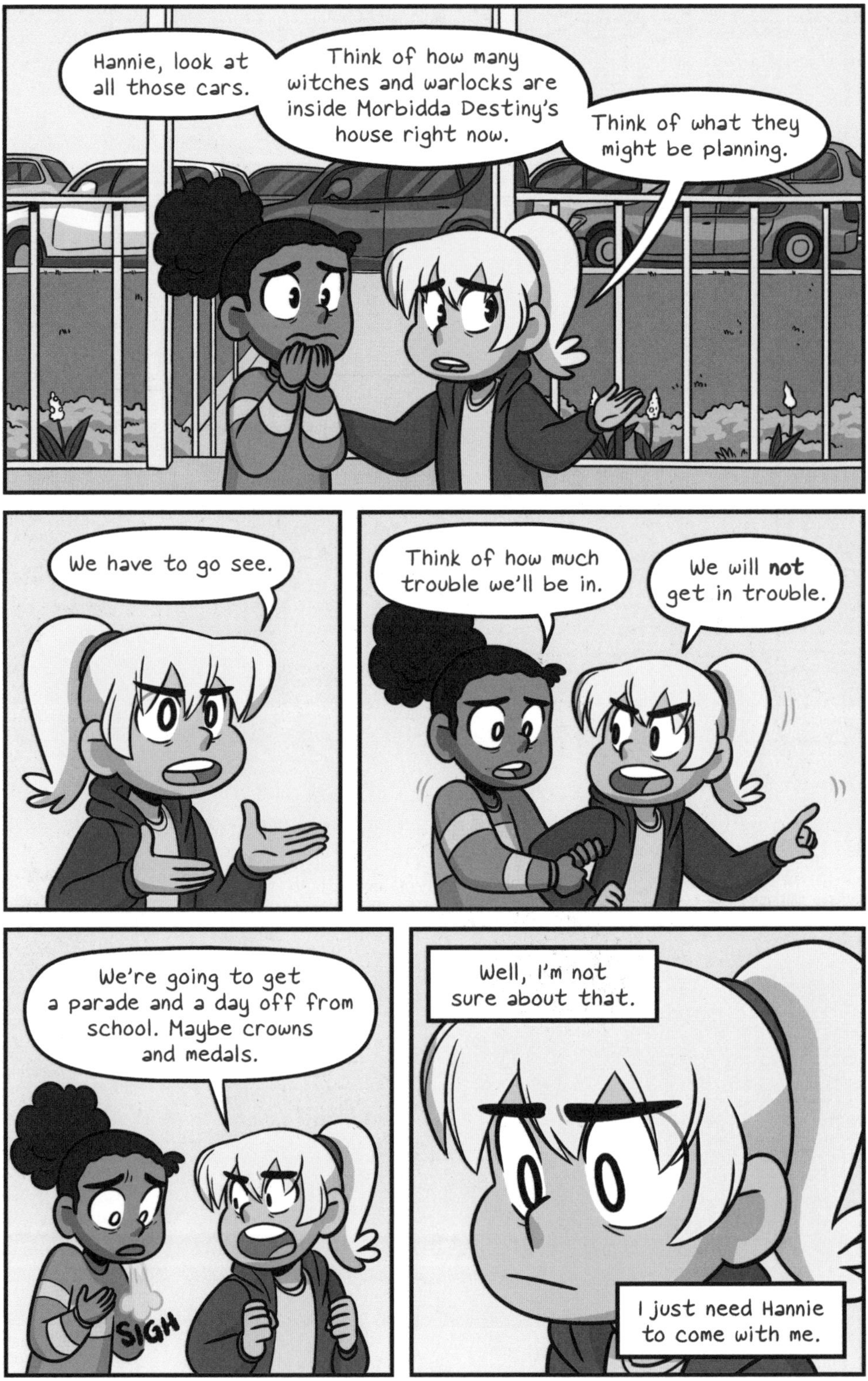
Hannie, look at all those cars.
Think of how many witches and warlocks are inside Morbidda Destiny's house right now.
Think of what they might be planning.
We have to go see.
Think of how much trouble we'll be in.
We will **not** get in trouble.
We're going to get a parade and a day off from school. Maybe crowns and medals.
SIGH
Well, I'm not sure about that.
I just need Hannie to come with me.

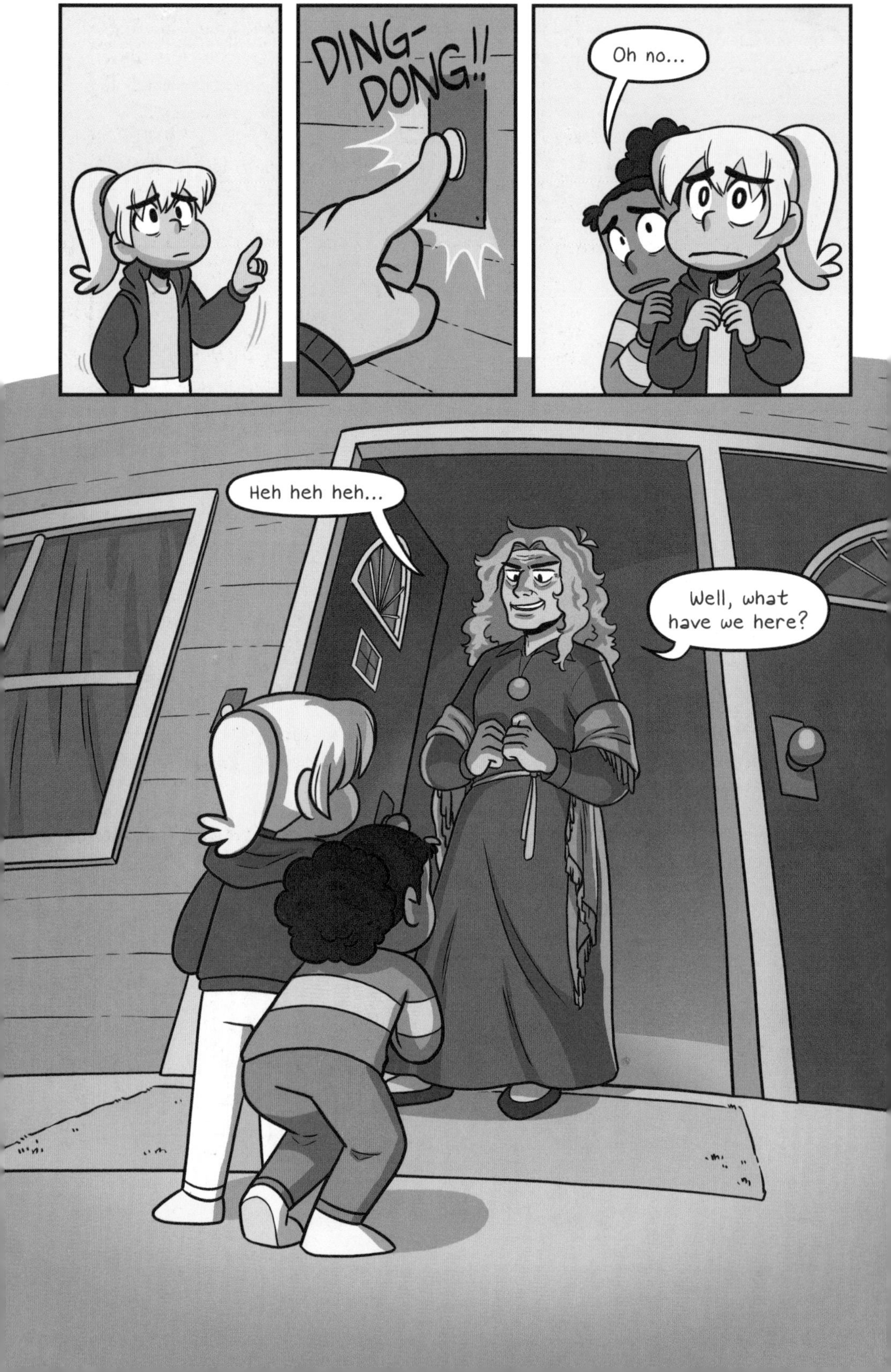
DING-DONG!!
Oh no...
Heh heh heh...
Well, what have we here?

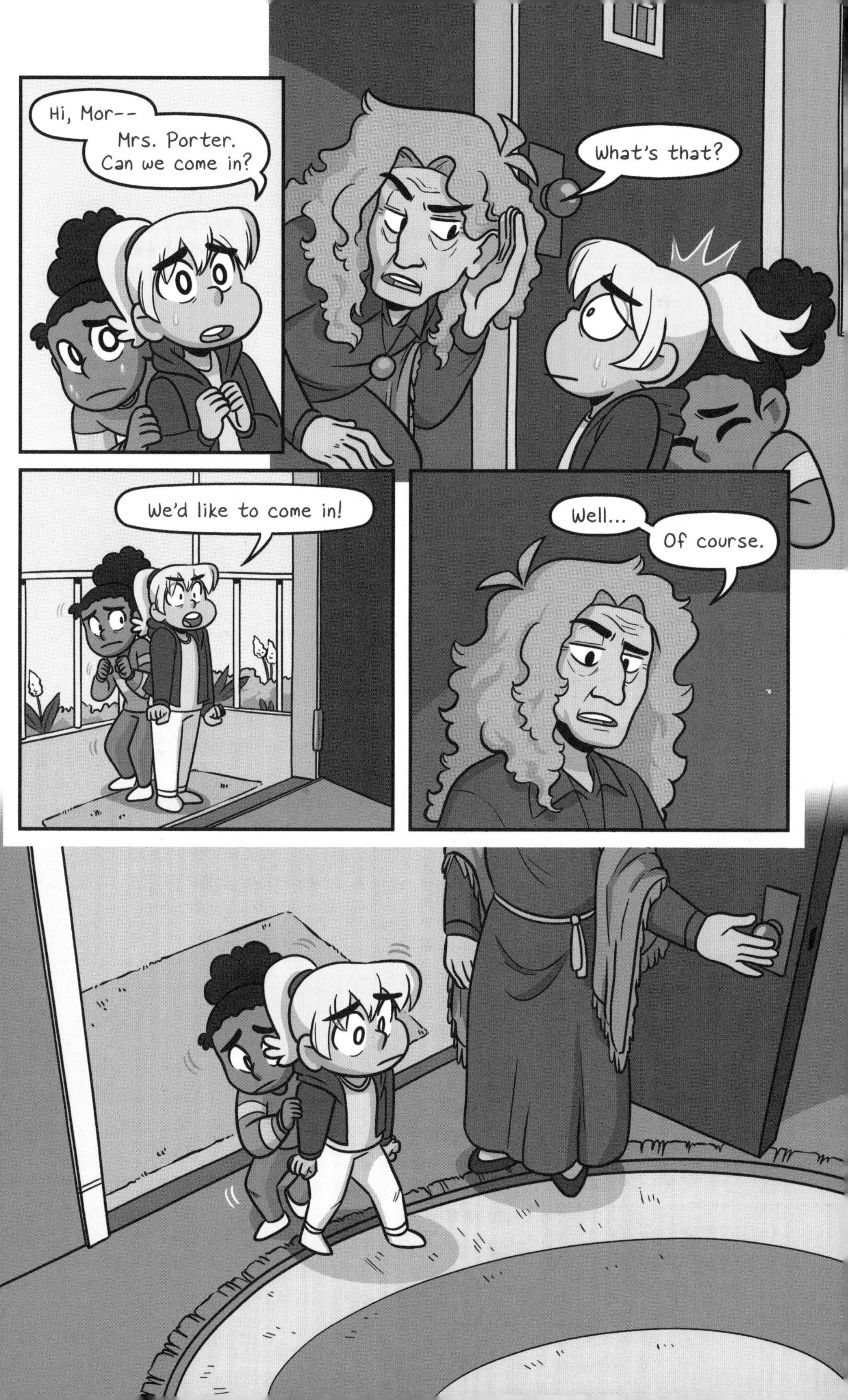
Hi, Mor--
Mrs. Porter. Can we come in?
What's that?
We'd like to come in!
Well...
Of course.

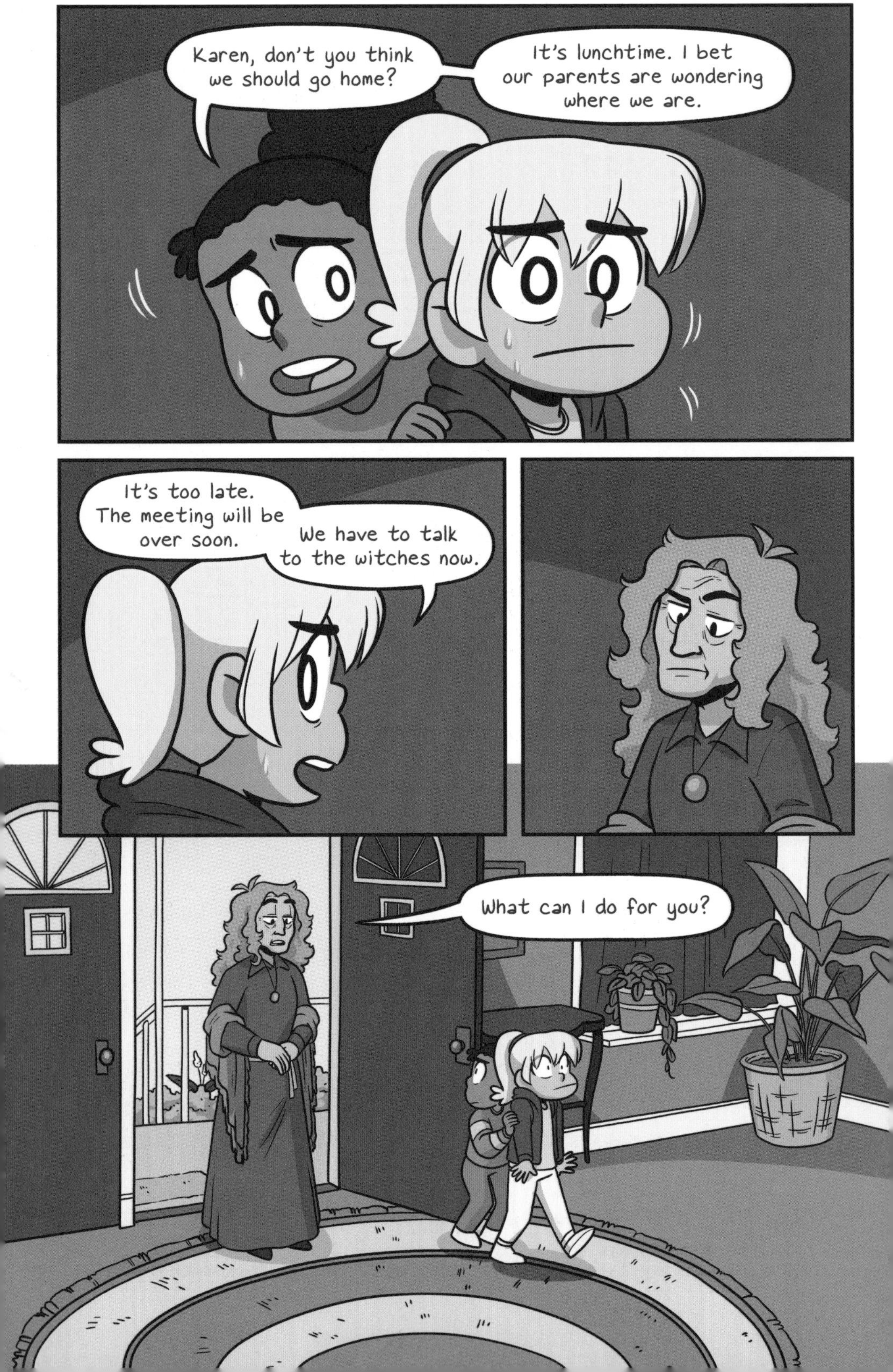
Karen, don't you think we should go home?
It's lunchtime. I bet our parents are wondering where we are.
It's too late. The meeting will be over soon.
We have to talk to the witches now.
What can I do for you?

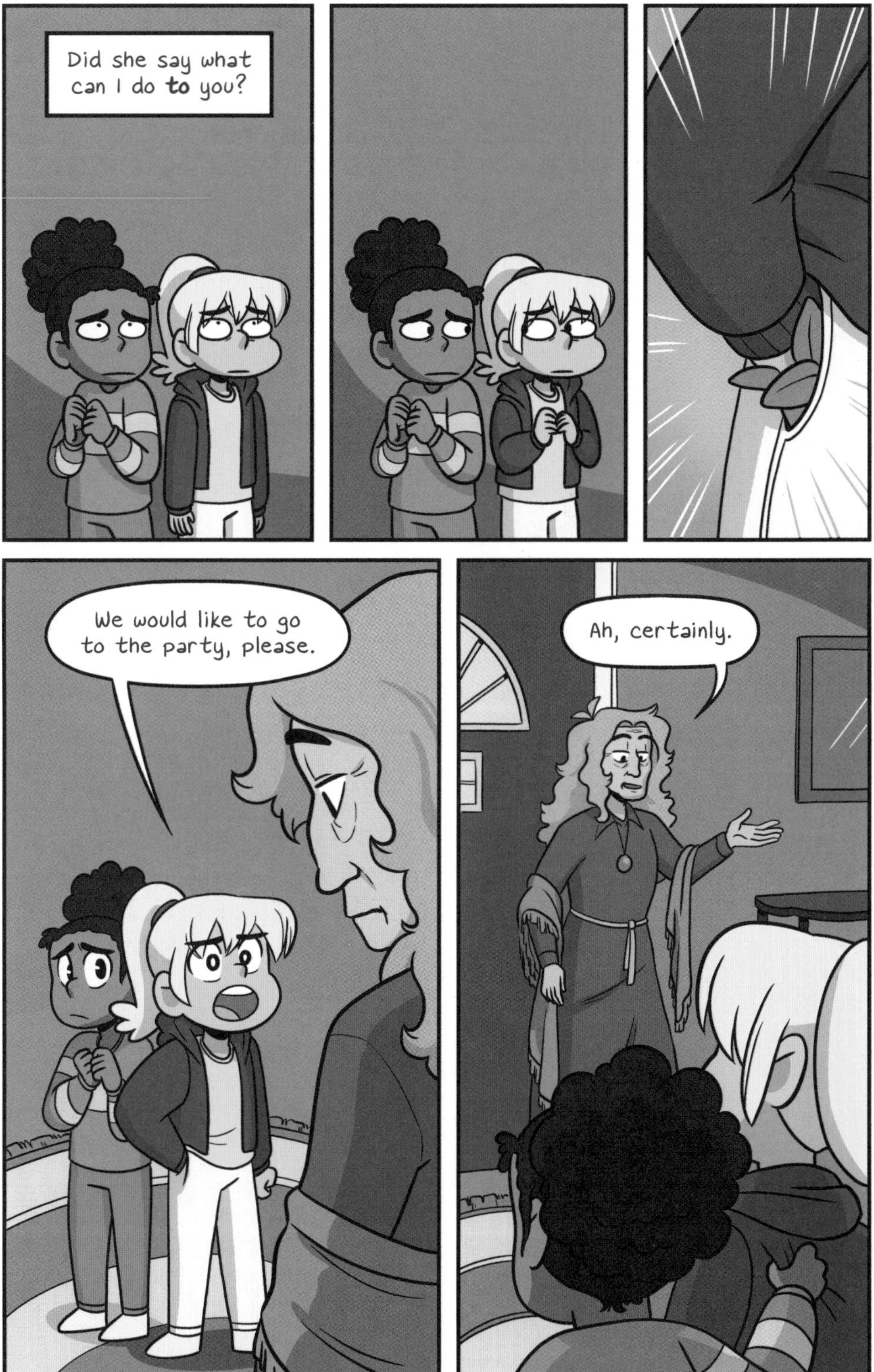
Did she say what can I do **to** you?
We would like to go to the party, please.
Ah, certainly.

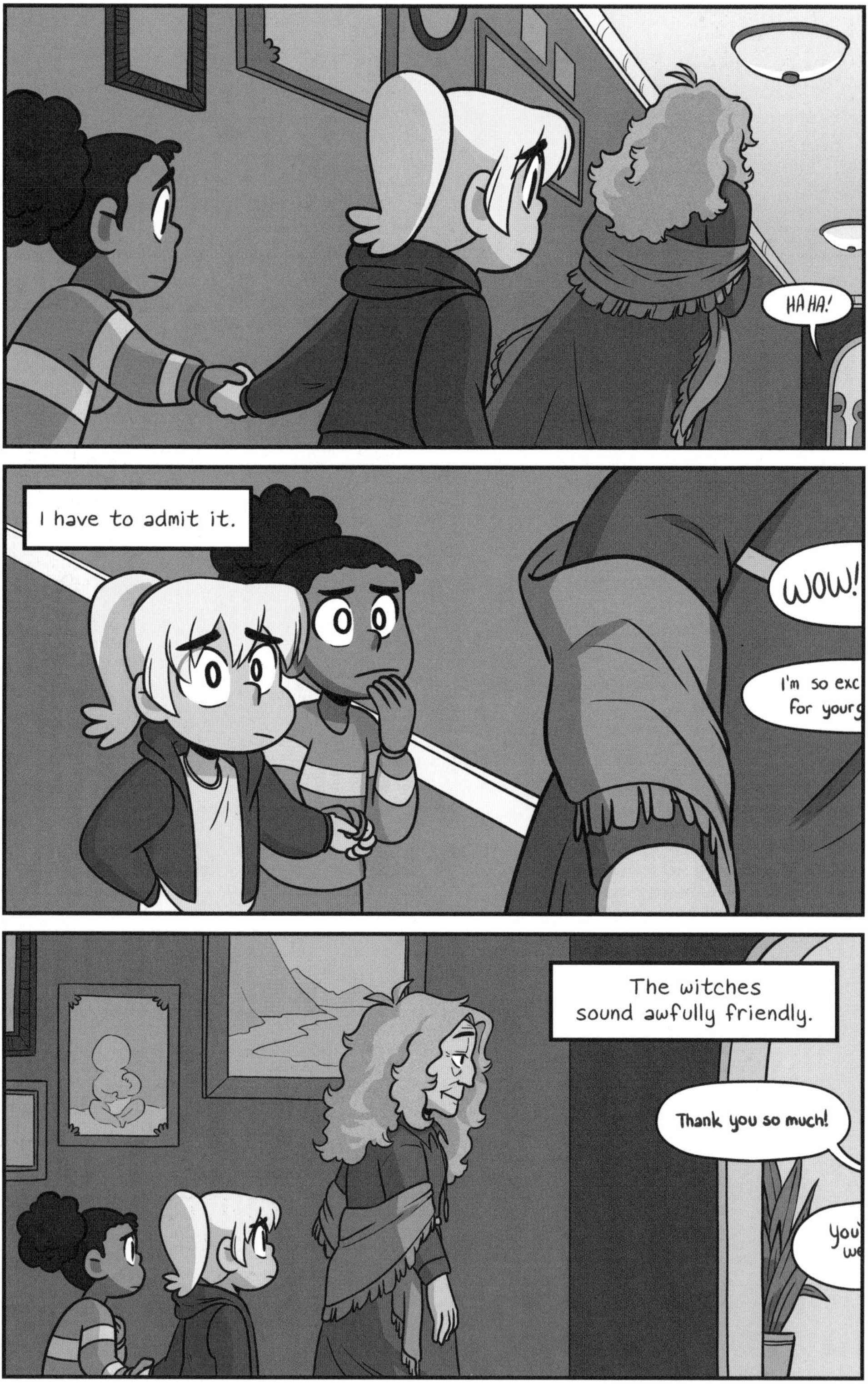

HA HA!
I have to admit it.
WOW!
The witches sound awfully friendly.
Thank you so much!

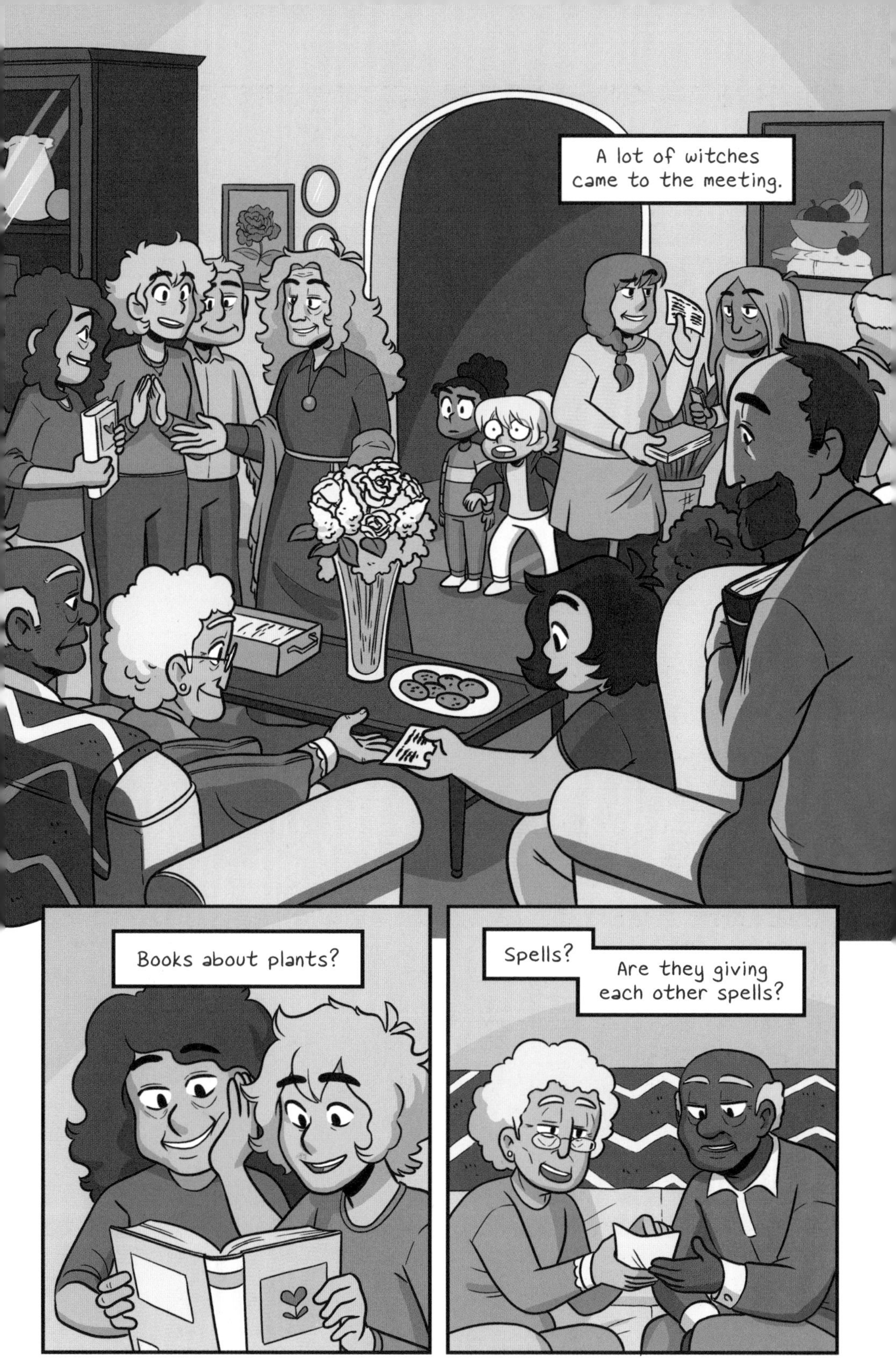
A lot of witches came to the meeting.
Books about plants?
Spells?
Are they giving each other spells?

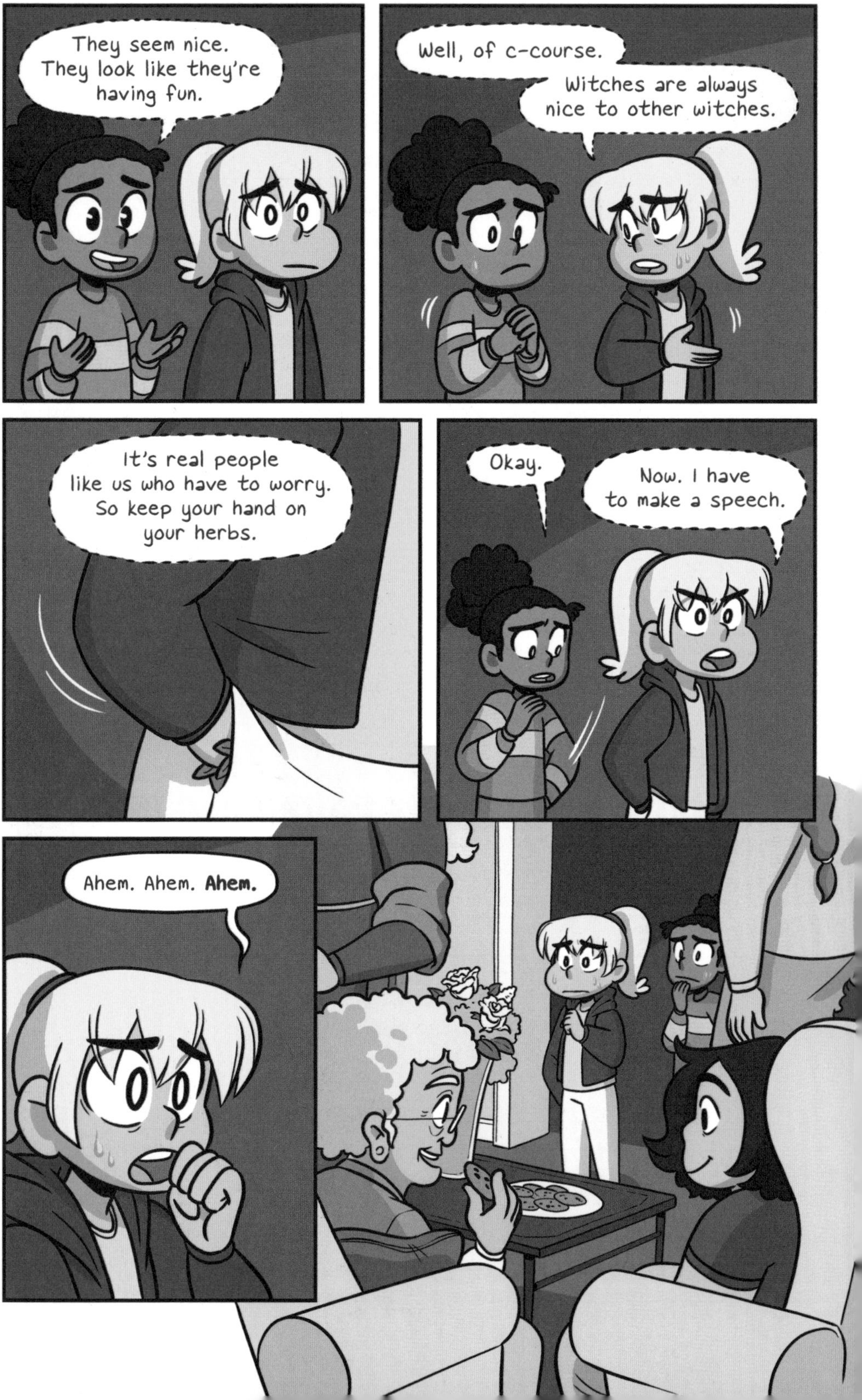
They seem nice. They look like they're having fun.
Well, of c-course.
Witches are always nice to other witches.
It's real people like us who have to worry. So keep your hand on your herbs.
Okay.
Now. I have to make a speech.
Ahem. Ahem. **Ahem.**

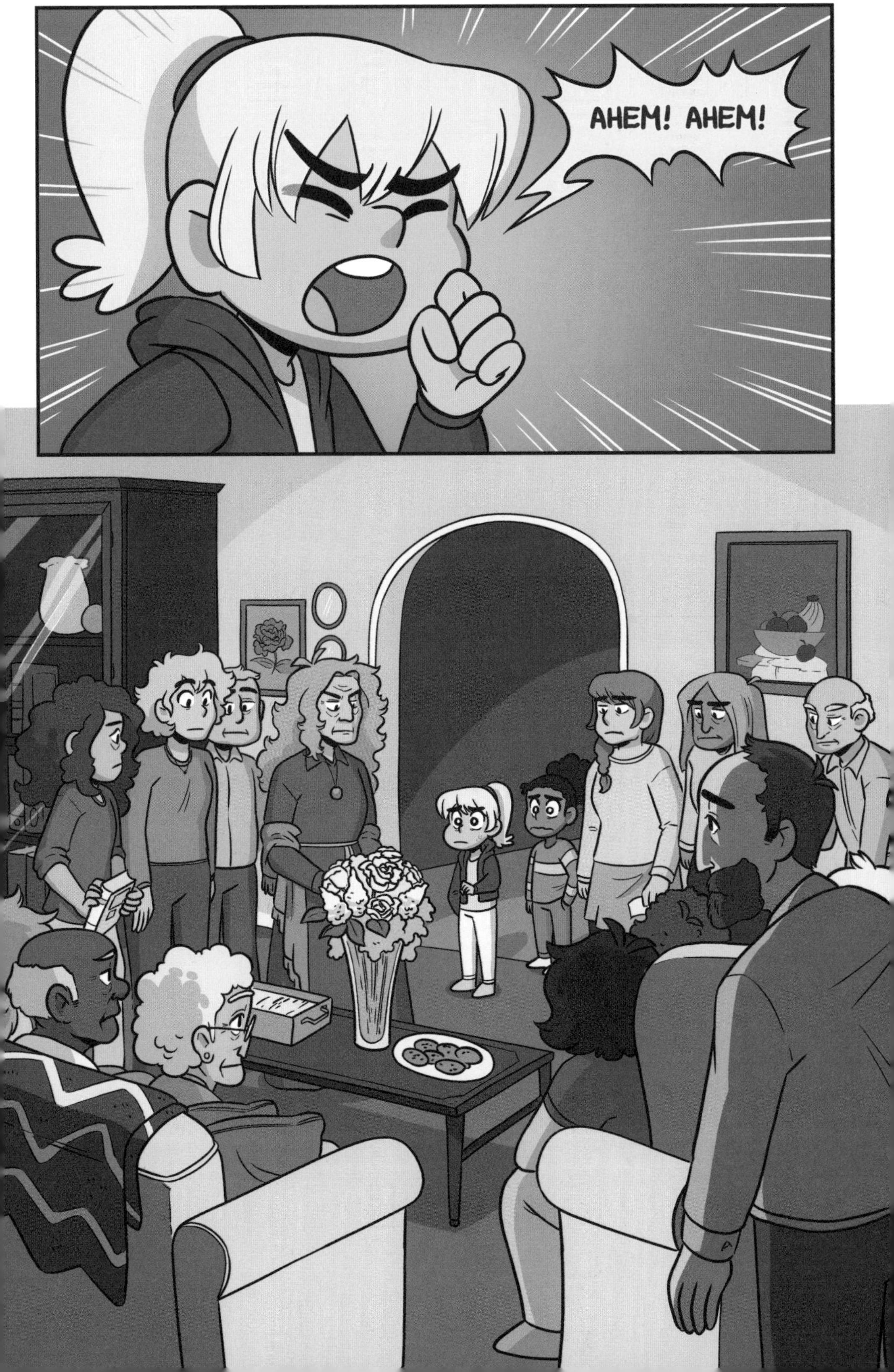
AHEM! AHEM!

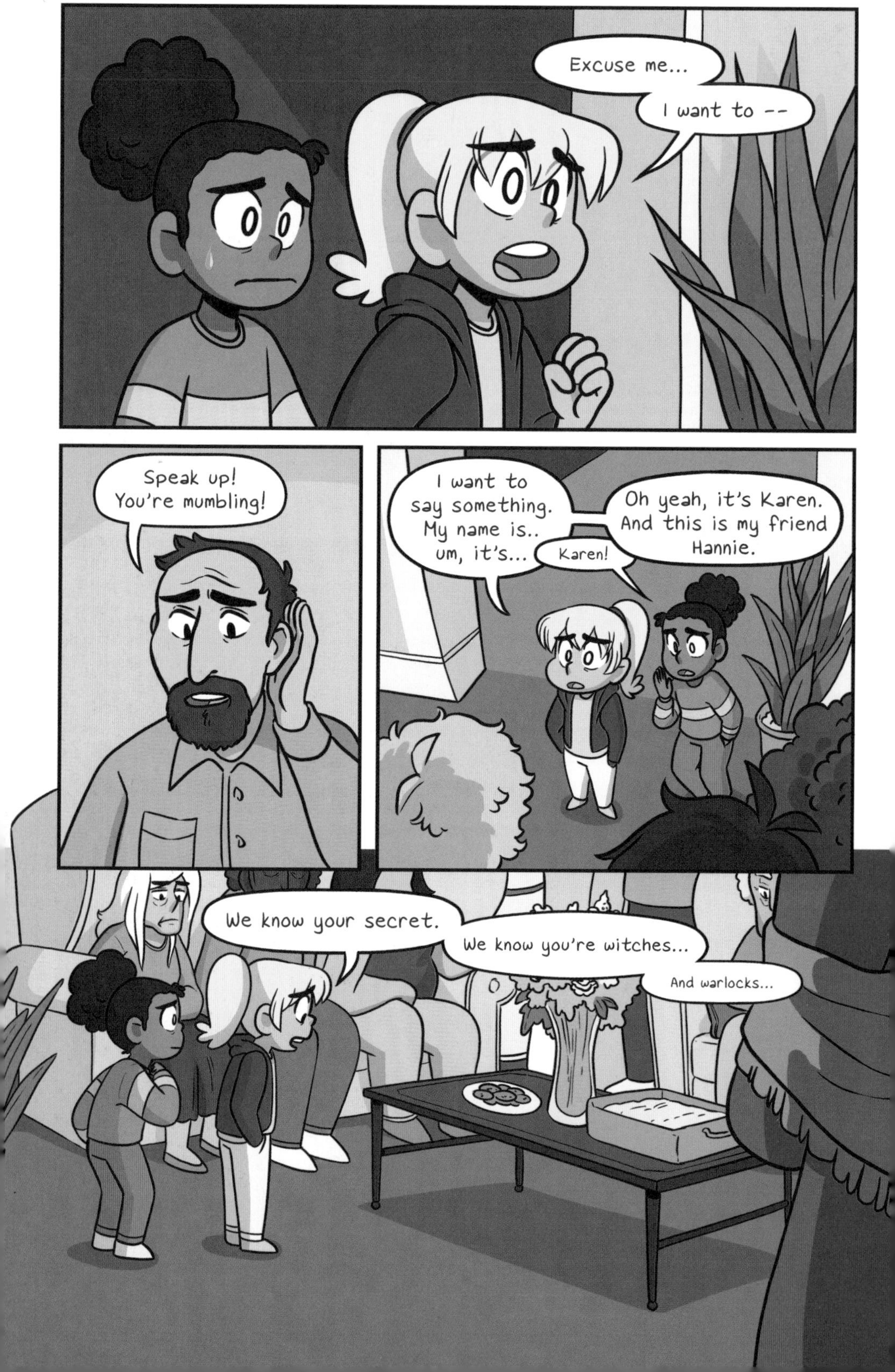
Excuse me...
I want to --
Speak up! You're mumbling!
I want to say something. My name is.. um, it's...
Karen!
Oh yeah, it's Karen. And this is my friend Hannie.
We know your secret.
We know you're witches...
And warlocks...

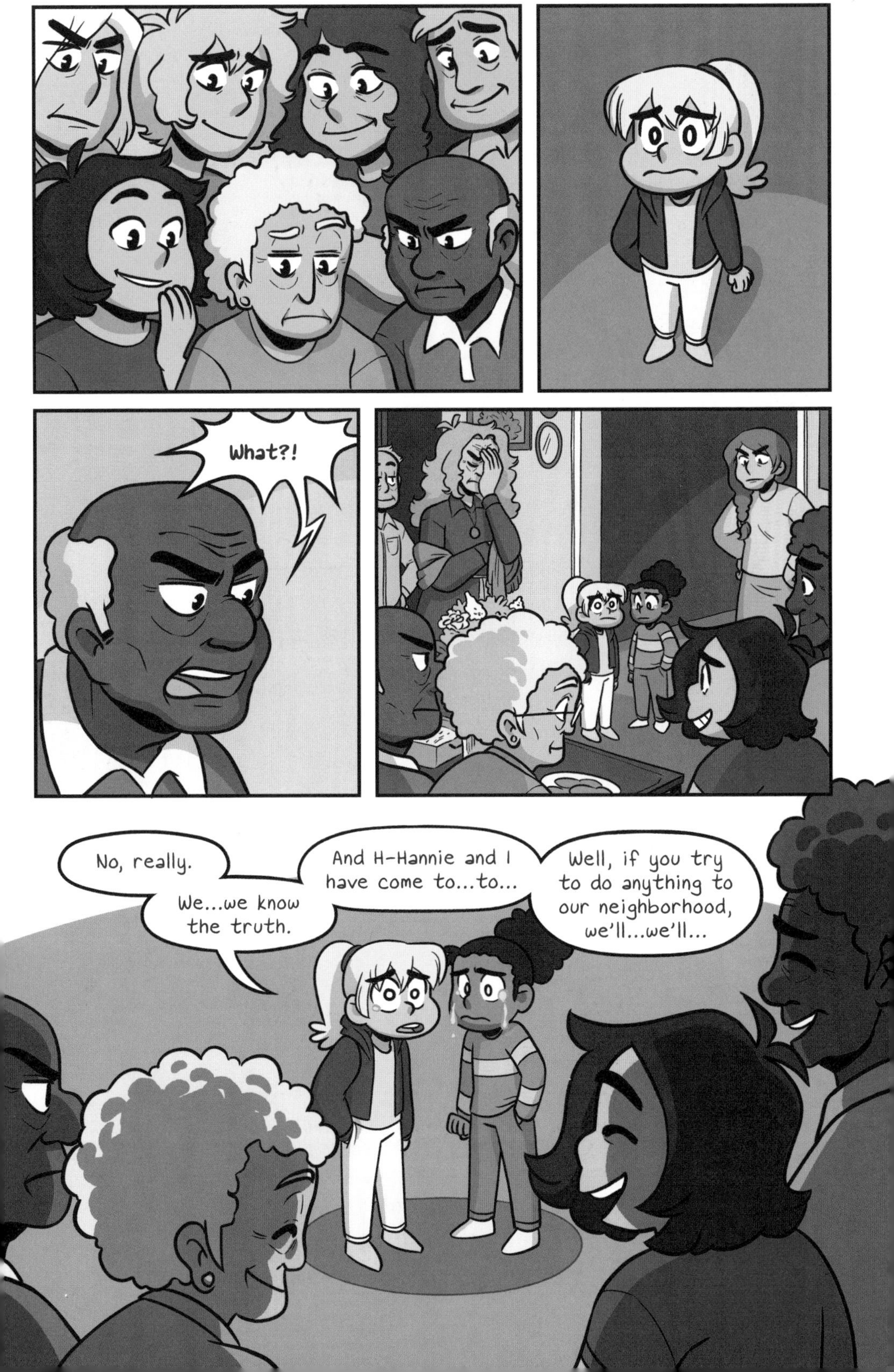
What?!
No, really.
We...we know the truth.
And H-Hannie and I have come to...to...
Well, if you try to do anything to our neighborhood, we'll...we'll...

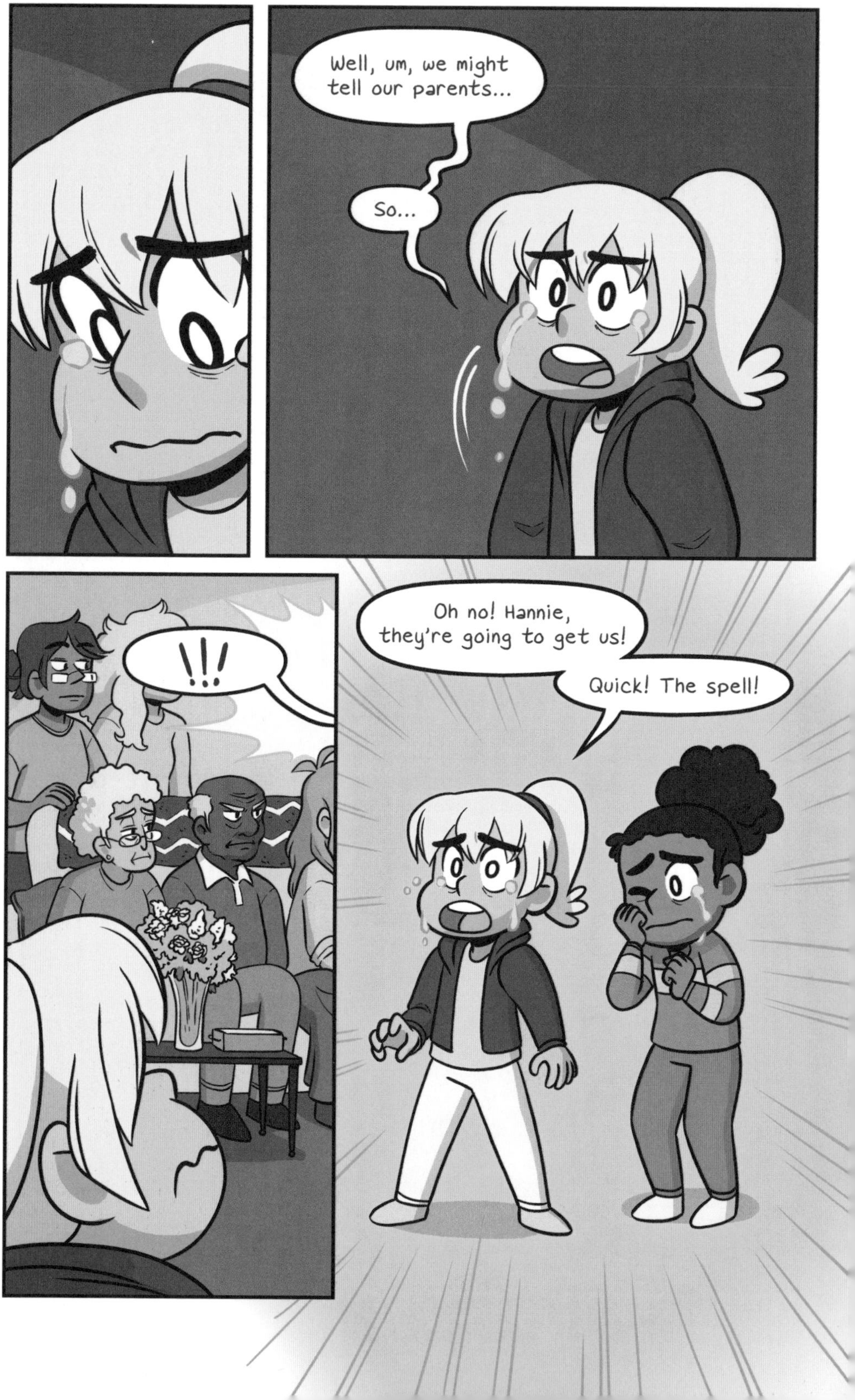
Well, um, we might tell our parents...
So...
!!!
Oh no! Hannie, they're going to get us!
Quick! The spell!

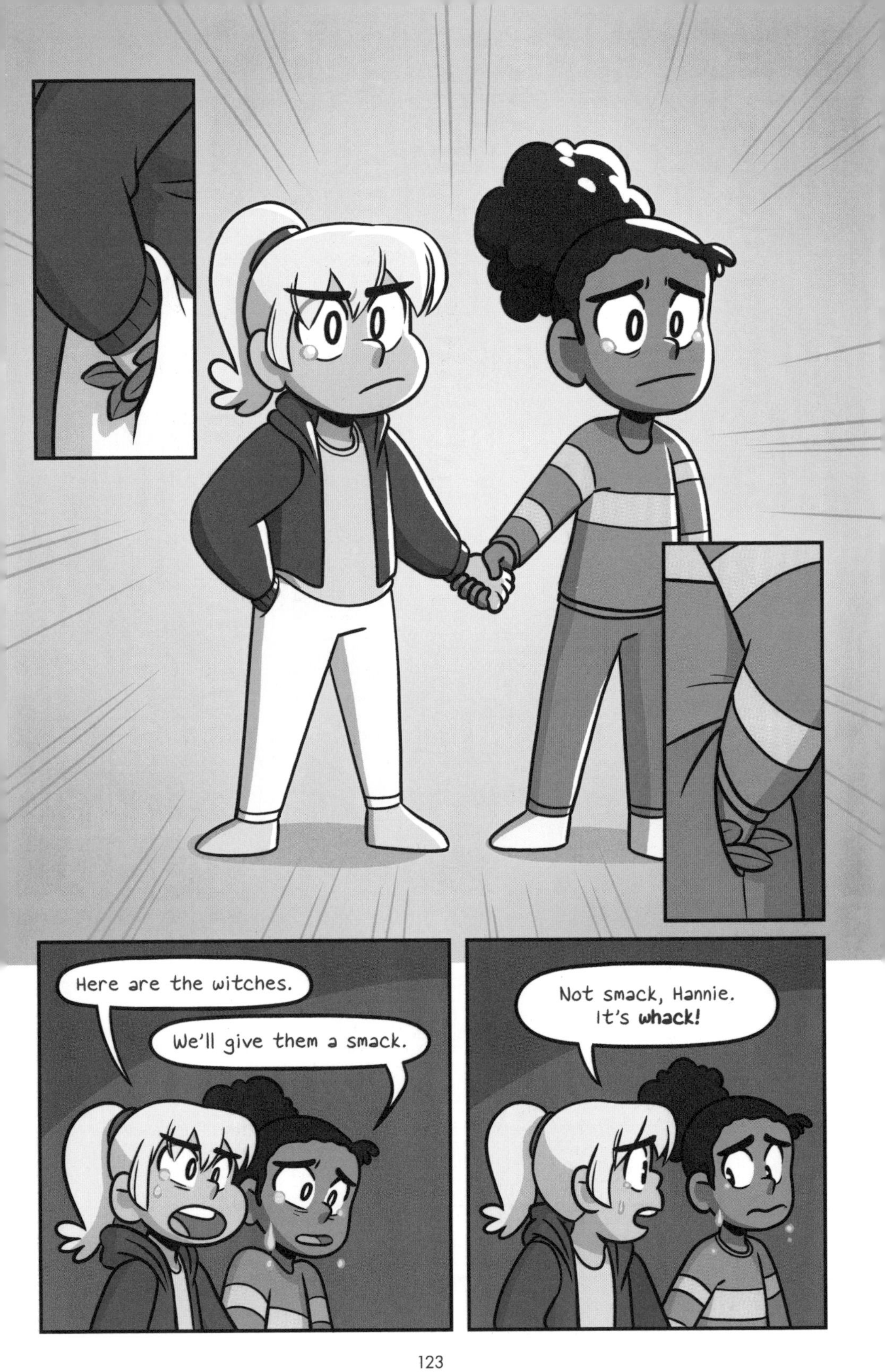
Here are the witches.
We'll give them a smack.
Not smack, Hannie.
It's **whack!**

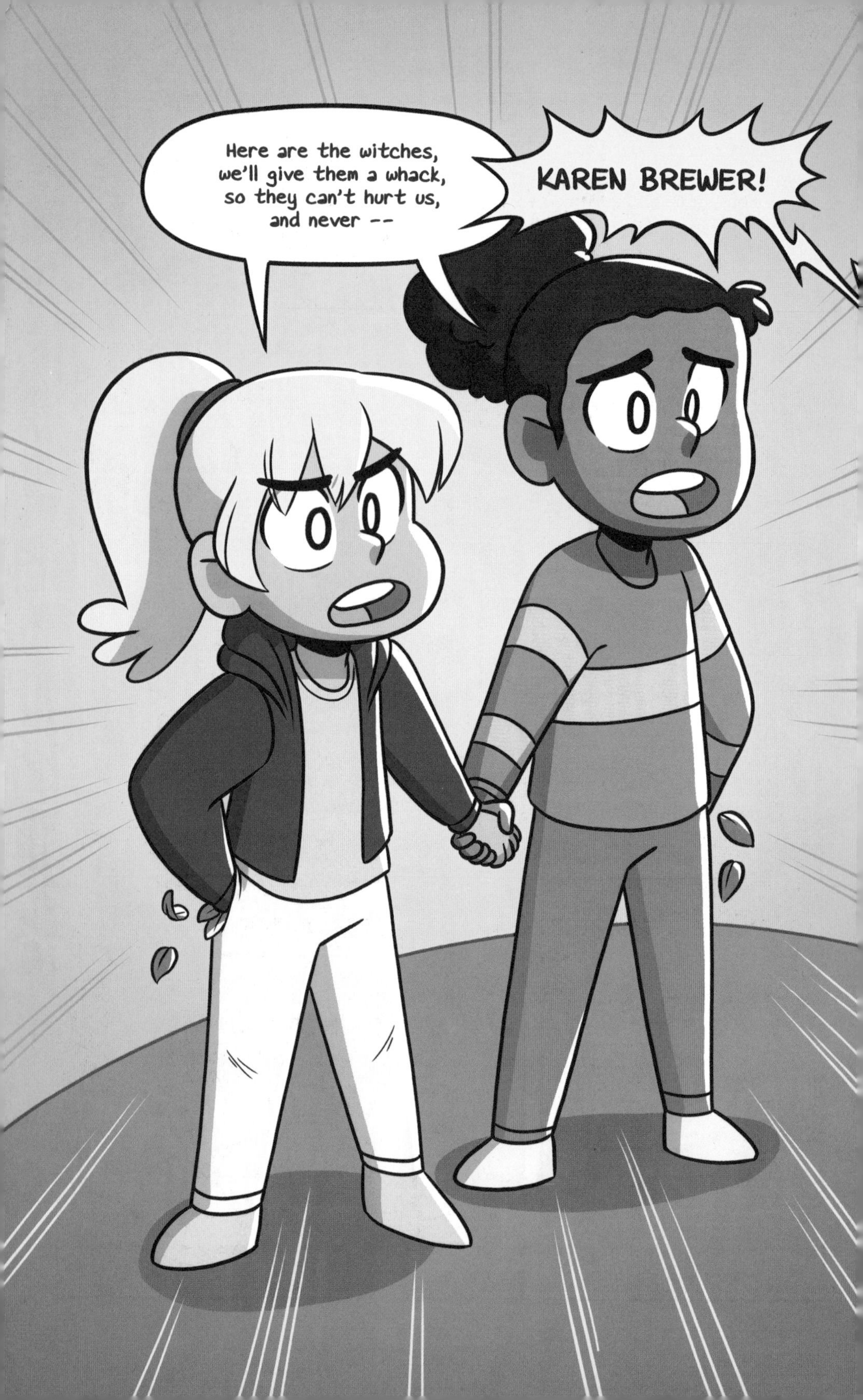
Here are the witches, we'll give them a whack, so they can't hurt us, and never --
KAREN BREWER!

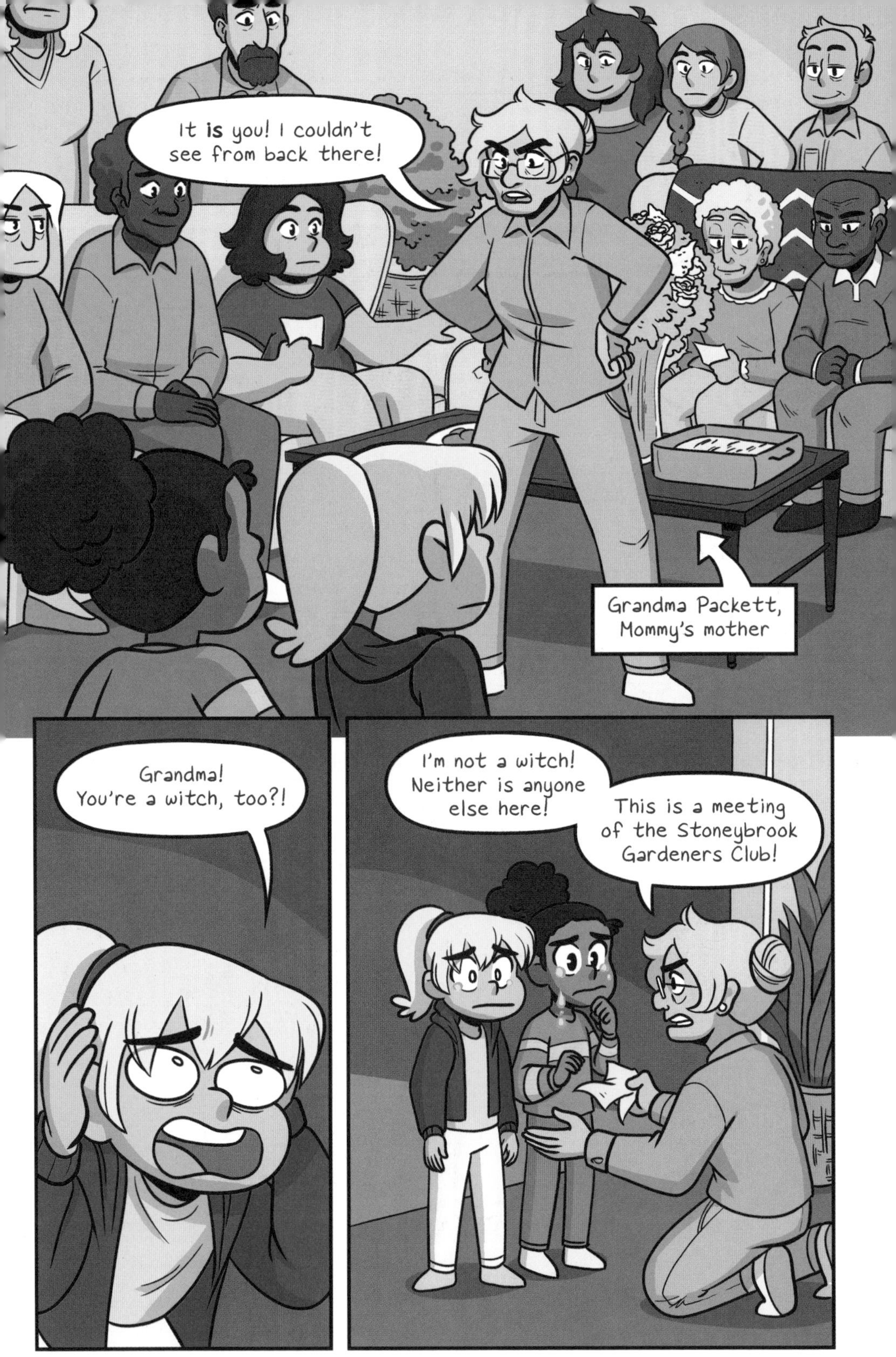
It is you! I couldn't see from back there!
Grandma Packett, Mommy's mother
Grandma! You're a witch, too?!
I'm not a witch! Neither is anyone else here!
This is a meeting of the Stoneybrook Gardeners Club!

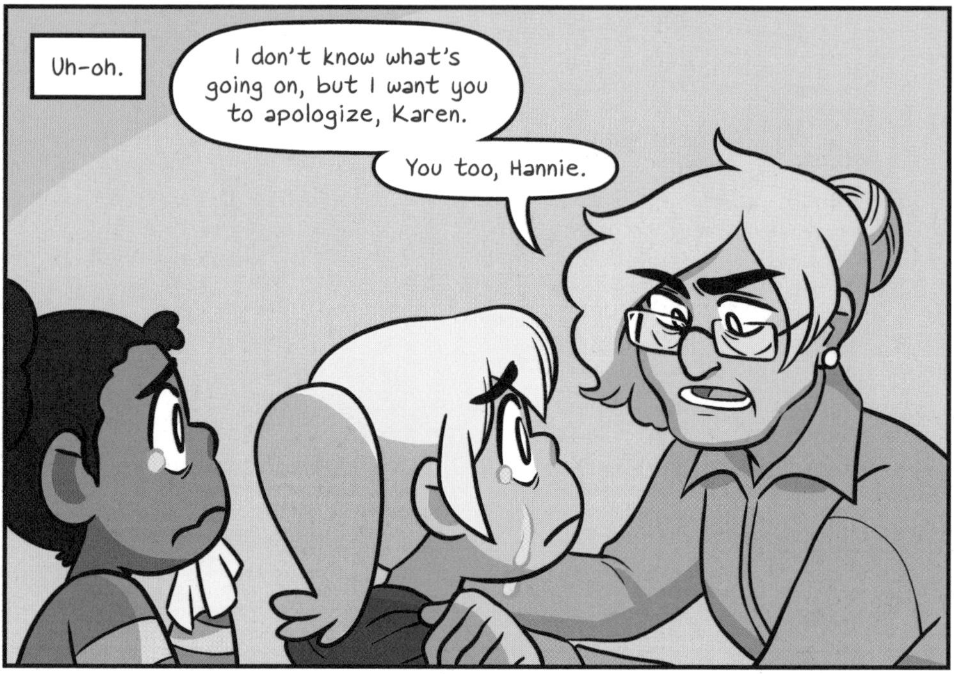
Uh-oh.
I don't know what's going on, but I want you to apologize, Karen.
You too, Hannie.

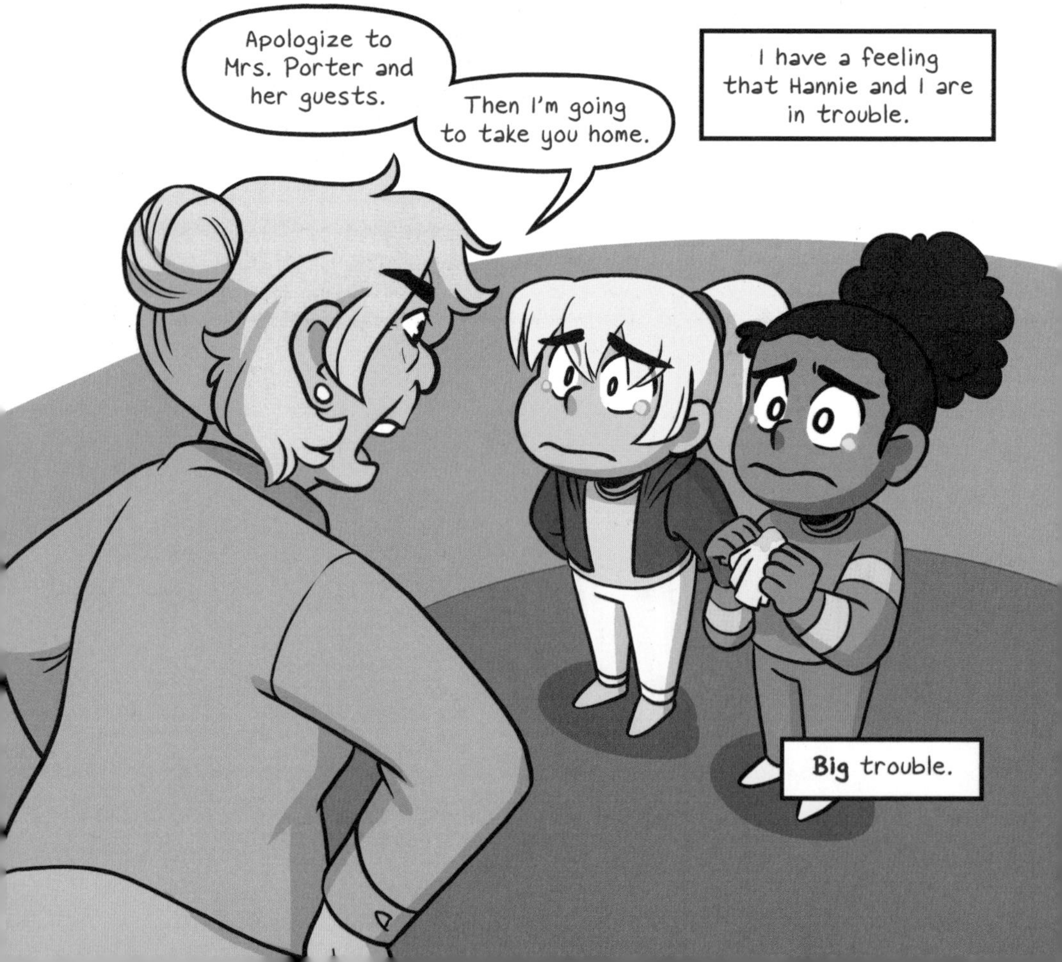
Apologize to Mrs. Porter and her guests.
Then I'm going to take you home.
I have a feeling that Hannie and I are in trouble.
Big trouble.

CHAPTER 10

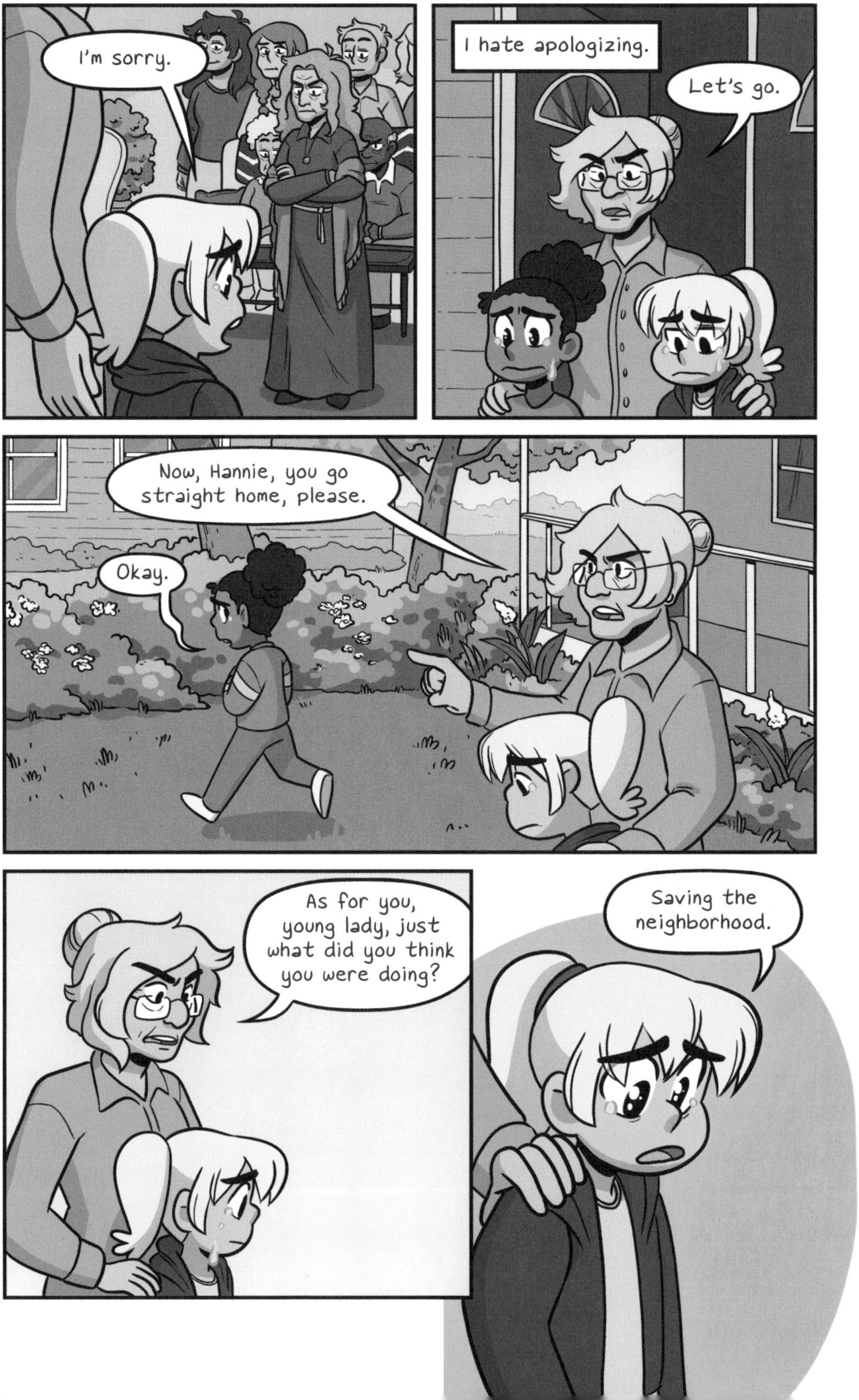
I'm sorry.
I hate apologizing.
Let's go.
Now, Hannie, you go straight home, please.
Okay.
As for you, young lady, just what did you think you were doing?
Saving the neighborhood.

KNOCK KNOCK

Hello? Watson? Elizabeth?

Mother Packett?

Let me tell you what your daughter has just done.

Hello, Mrs. the World.

Hee Ma!!

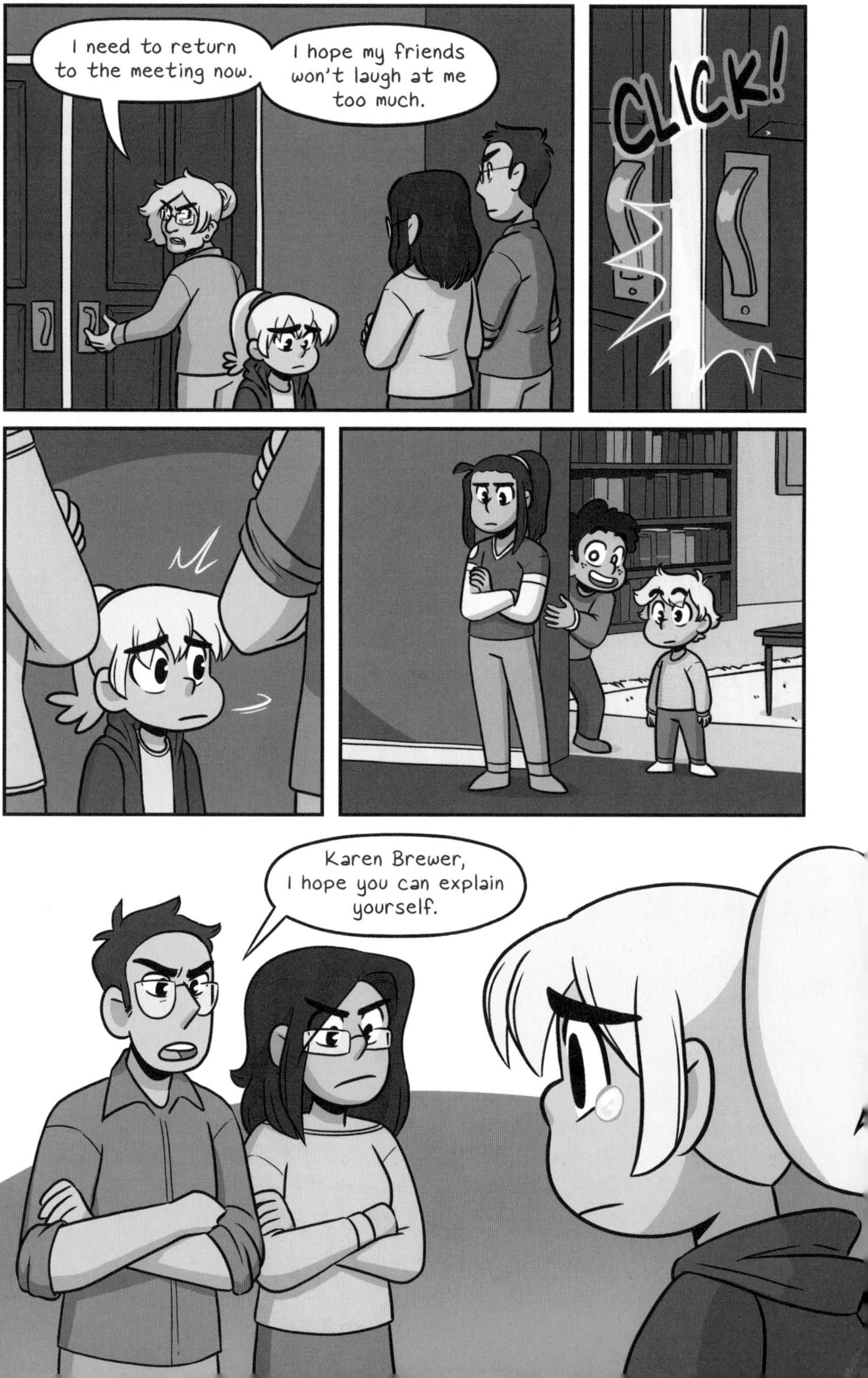
I need to return to the meeting now.
I hope my friends won't laugh at me too much.
CLICK!
Karen Brewer, I hope you can explain yourself.

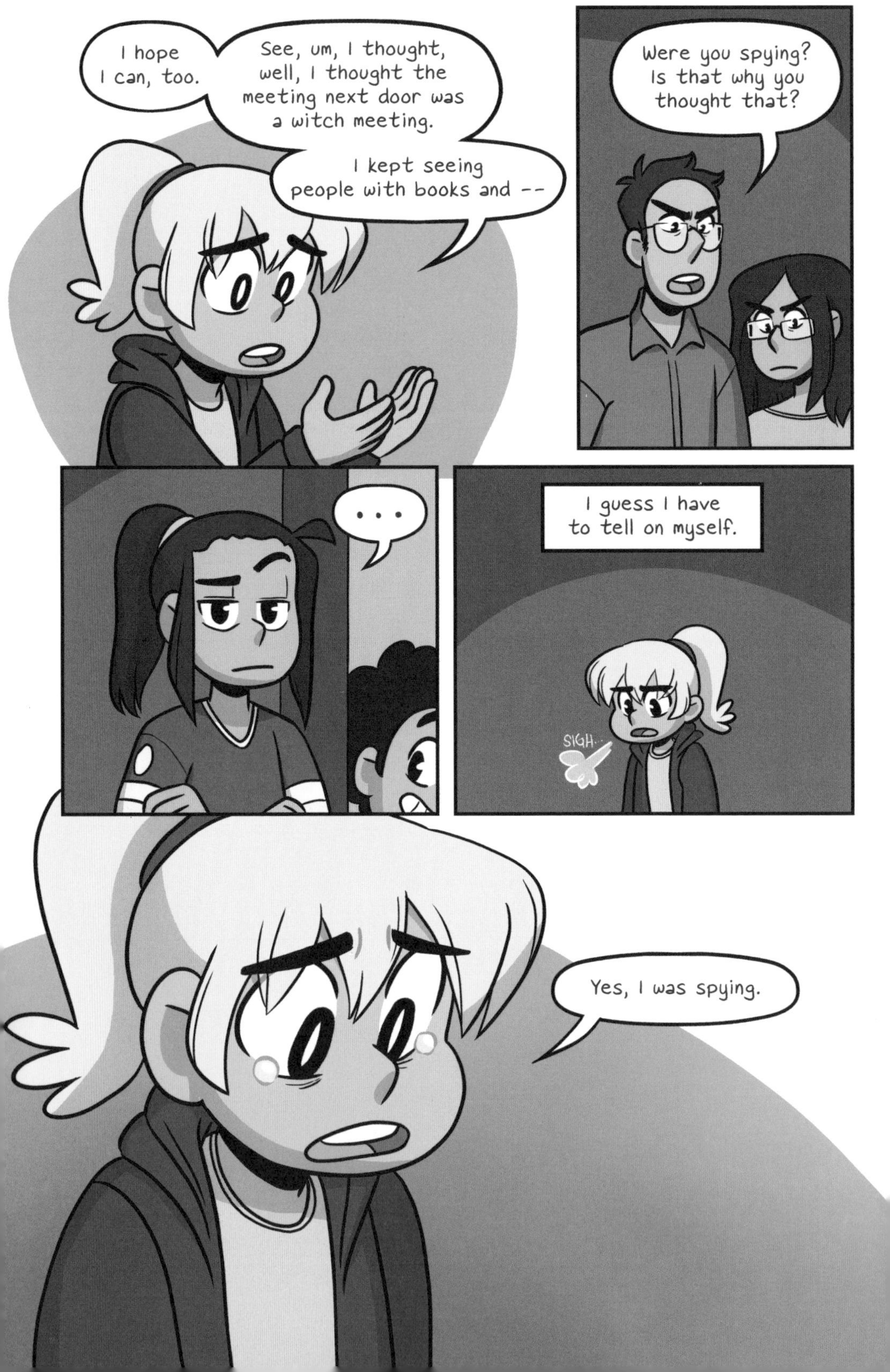
I hope I can, too.
See, um, I thought, well, I thought the meeting next door was a witch meeting.
I kept seeing people with books and --
Were you spying? Is that why you thought that?
. . .
I guess I have to tell on myself.
SIGH...
Yes, I was spying.

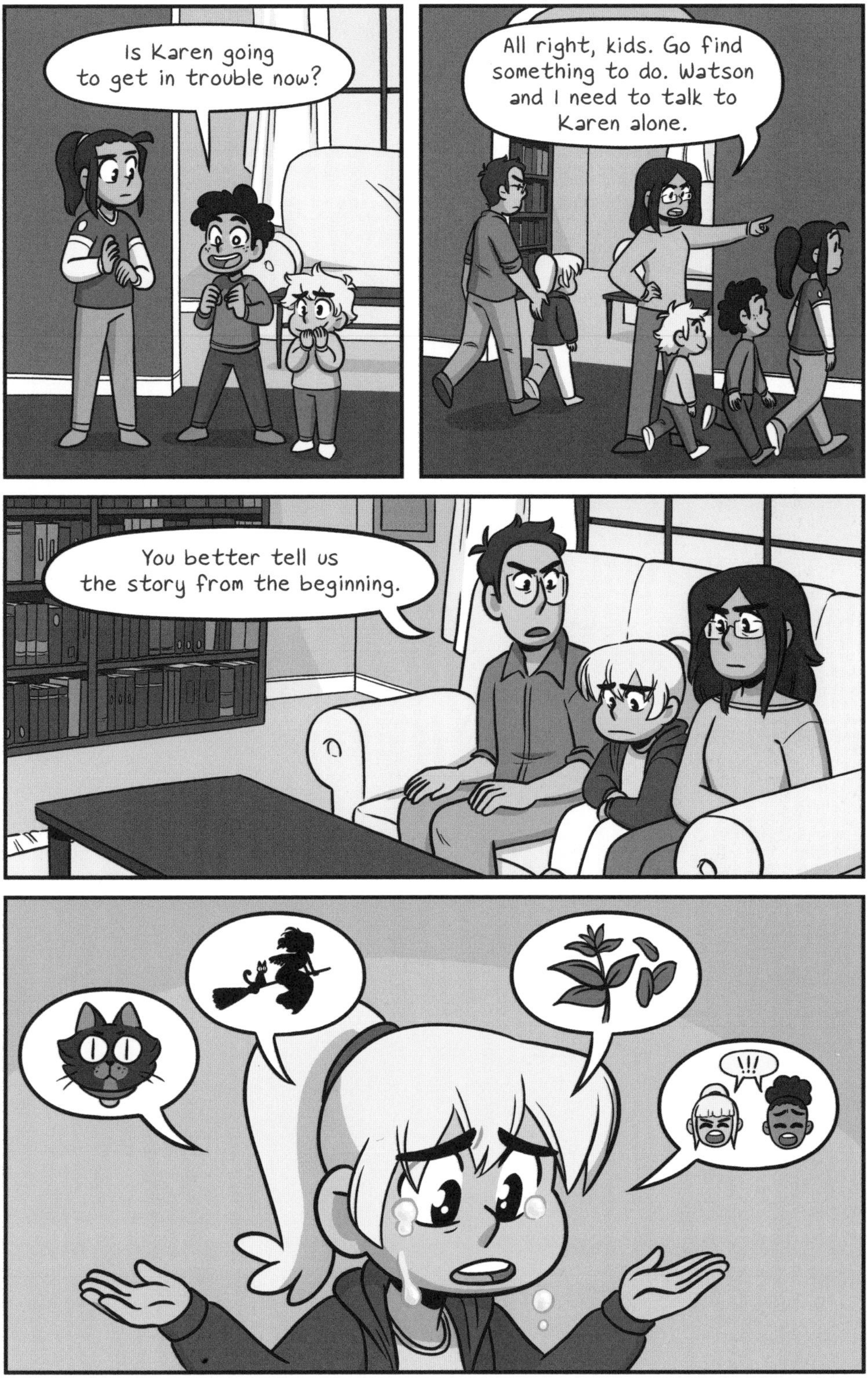
Is Karen going to get in trouble now?
All right, kids. Go find something to do. Watson and I need to talk to Karen alone.
You better tell us the story from the beginning.
!!!

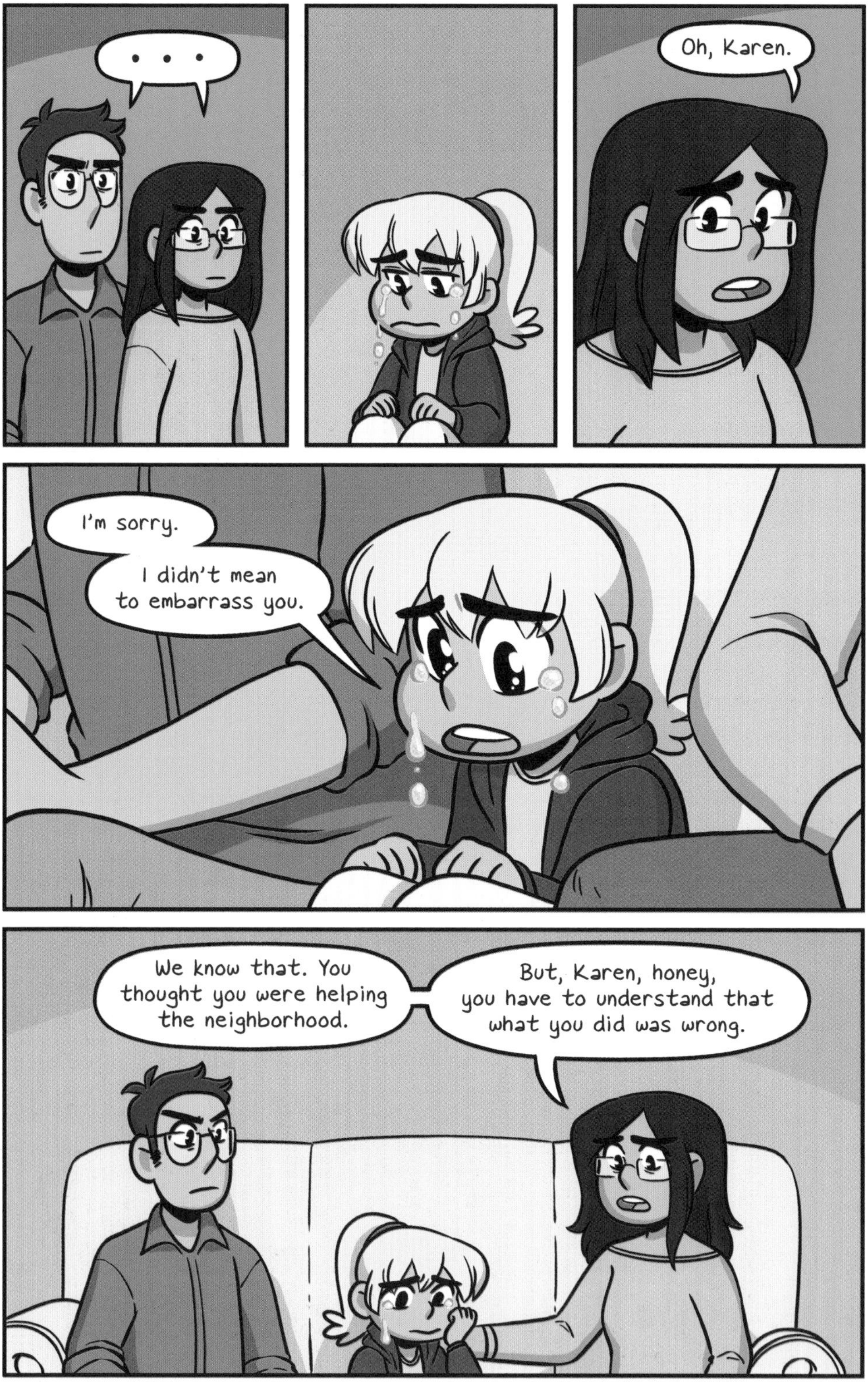
. . .
Oh, Karen.
I'm sorry.
I didn't mean to embarrass you.
We know that. You thought you were helping the neighborhood.
But, Karen, honey, you have to understand that what you did was wrong.

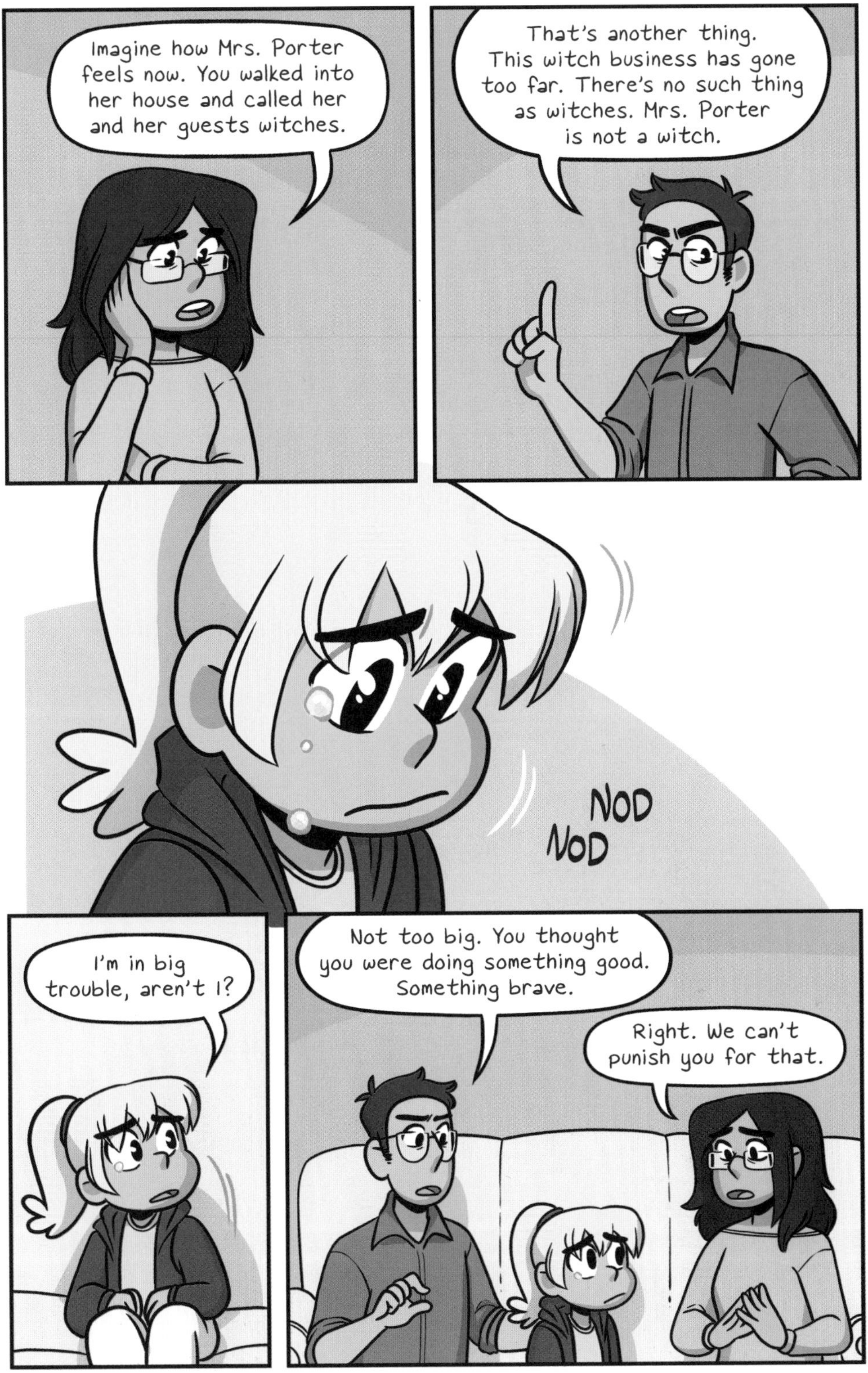
Imagine how Mrs. Porter feels now. You walked into her house and called her and her guests witches.
That's another thing. This witch business has gone too far. There's no such thing as witches. Mrs. Porter is not a witch.
NOD
NOD
I'm in big trouble, aren't I?
Not too big. You thought you were doing something good. Something brave.
Right. We can't punish you for that.

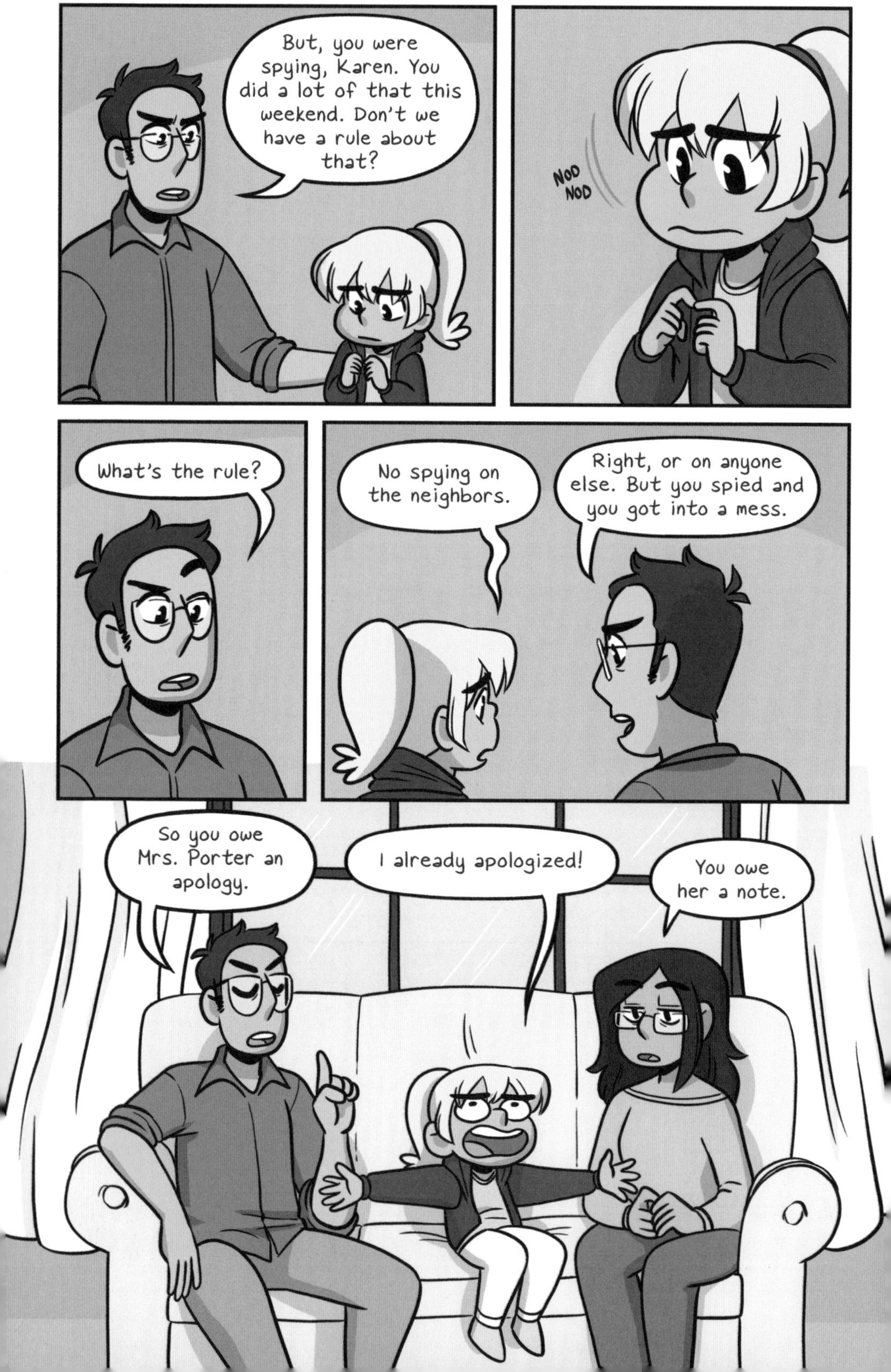
But, you were spying, Karen. You did a lot of that this weekend. Don't we have a rule about that?
NOD NOD
What's the rule?
No spying on the neighbors.
Right, or on anyone else. But you spied and you got into a mess.
So you owe Mrs. Porter an apology.
I already apologized!
You owe her a note.

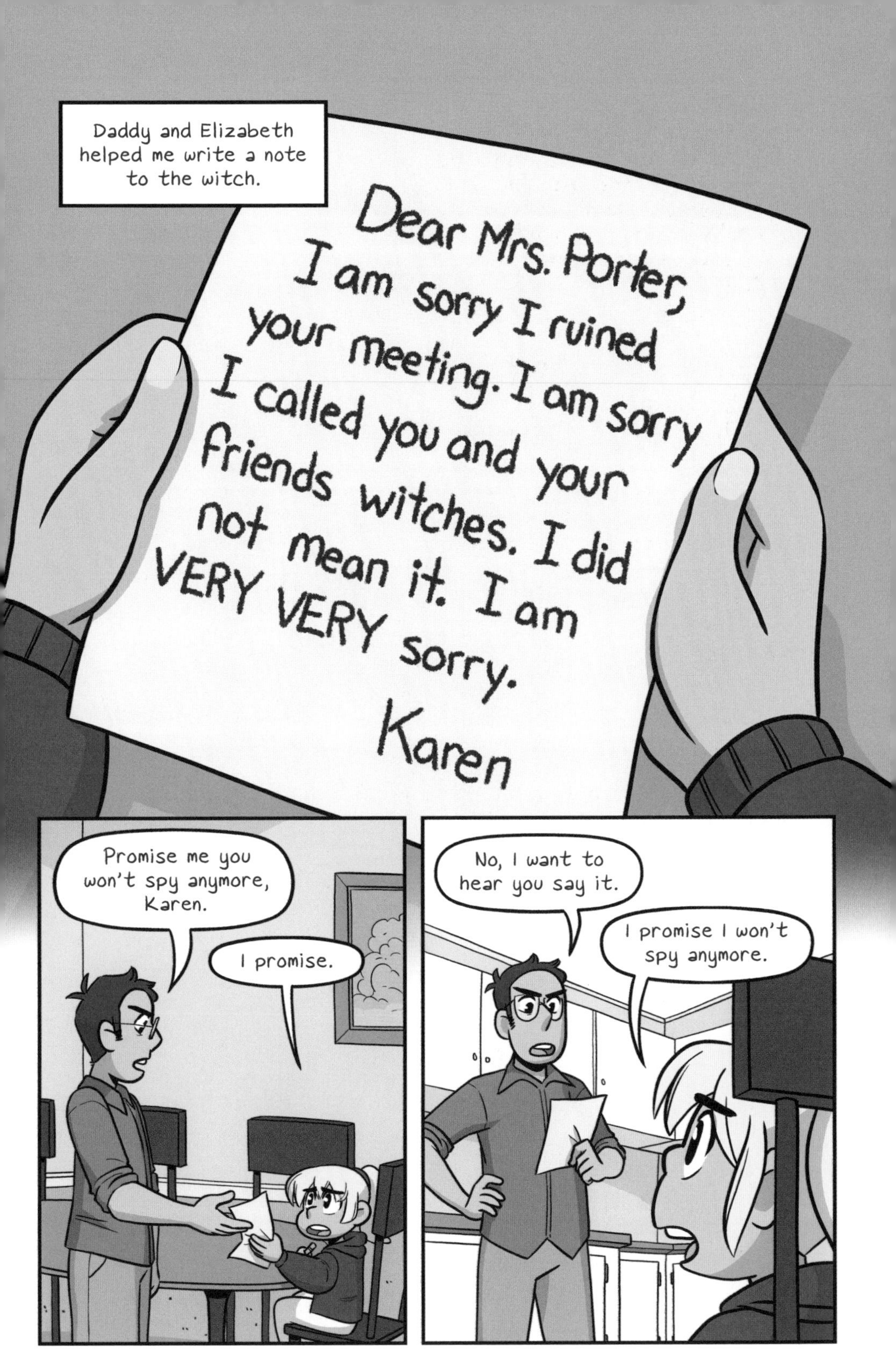

Daddy and Elizabeth helped me write a note to the witch.
Dear Mrs. Porter,
I am sorry I ruined your meeting. I am sorry I called you and your friends witches. I did not mean it. I am VERY VERY sorry.
Karen
Promise me you won't spy anymore, Karen.
I promise.
No, I want to hear you say it.
I promise I won't spy anymore.

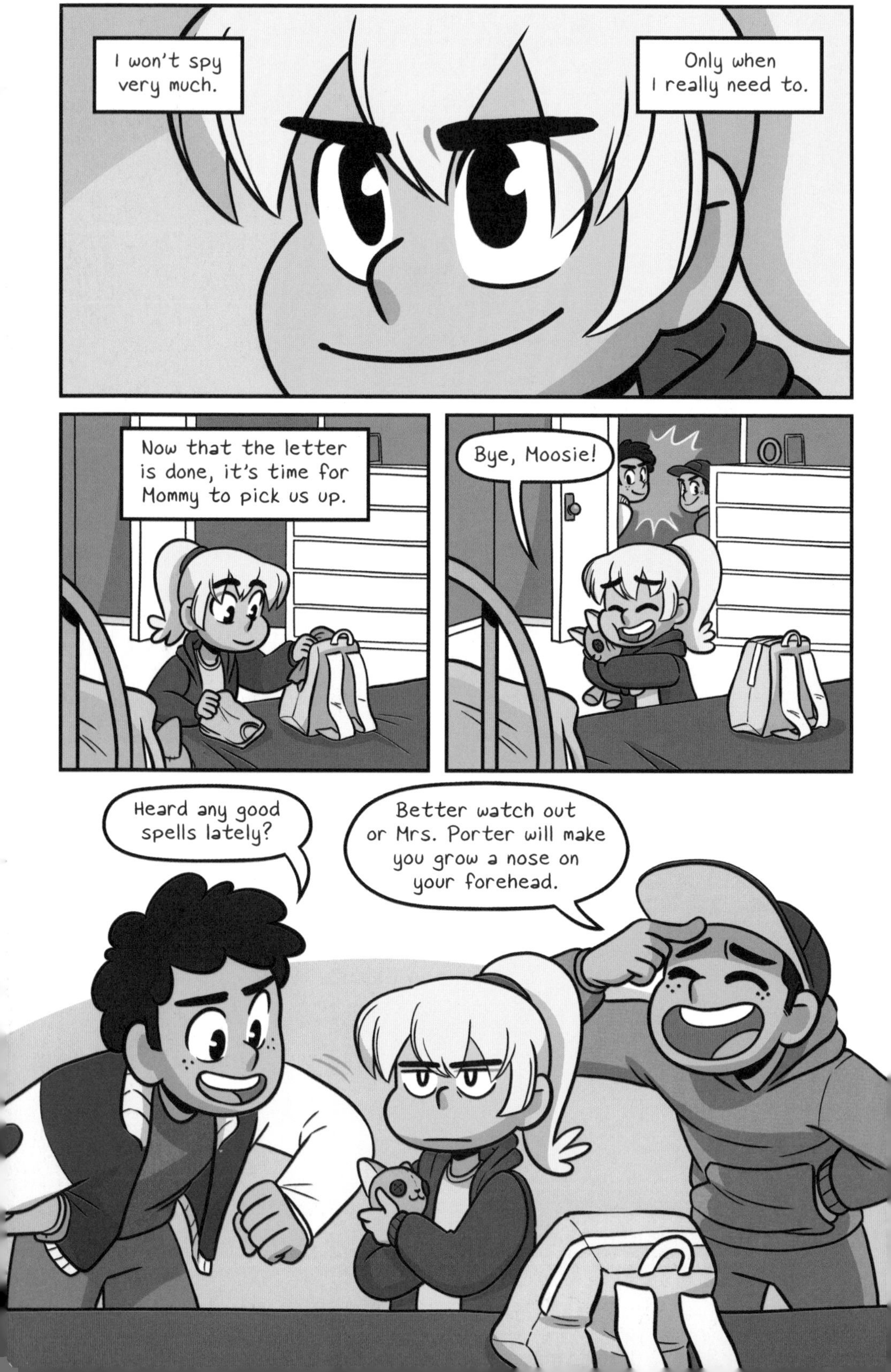
I won't spy very much.
Only when I really need to.
Now that the letter is done, it's time for Mommy to pick us up.
Bye, Moosie!
Heard any good spells lately?
Better watch out or Mrs. Porter will make you grow a nose on your forehead.

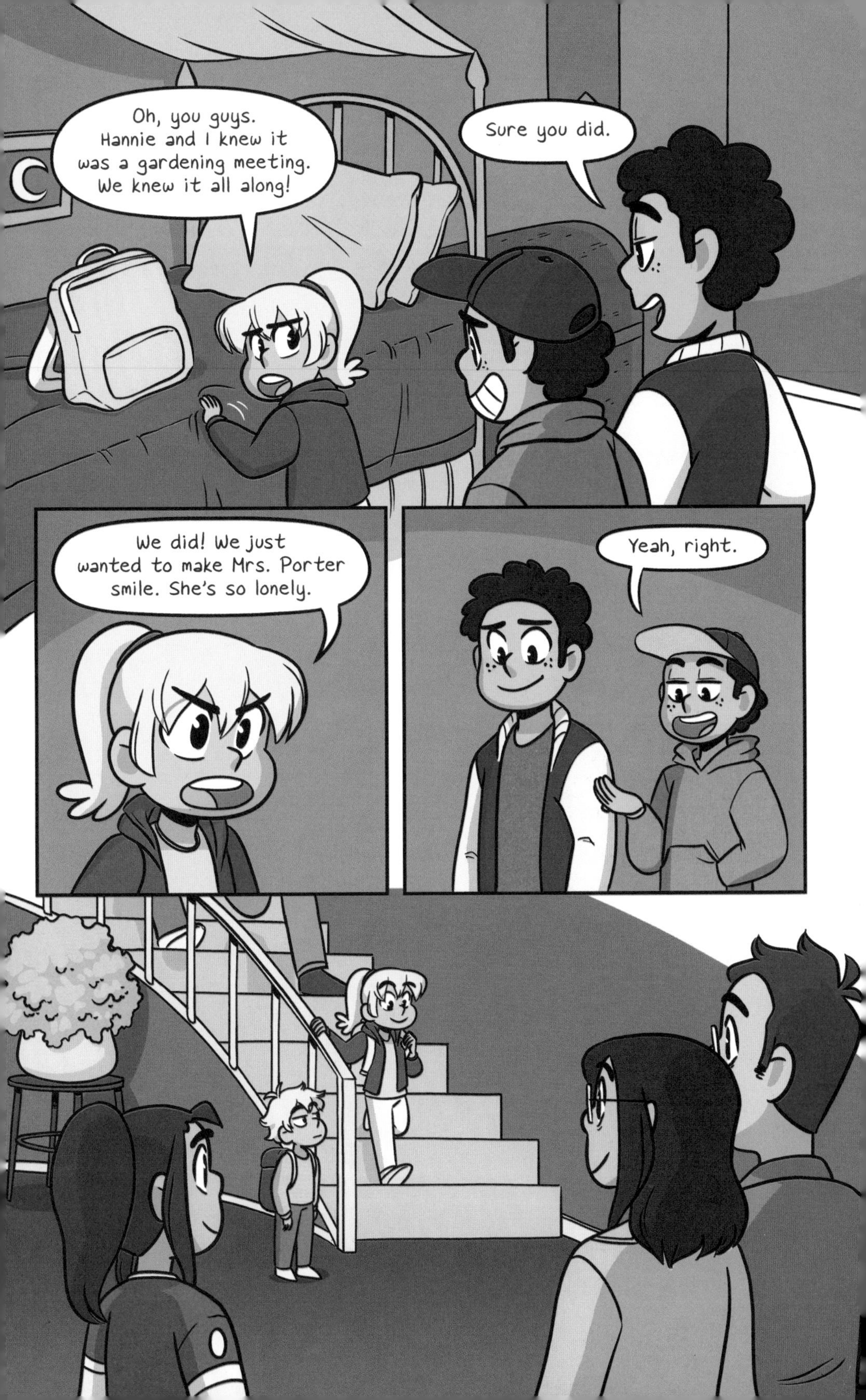
Oh, you guys. Hannie and I knew it was a gardening meeting. We knew it all along!
Sure you did.
We did! We just wanted to make Mrs. Porter smile. She's so lonely.
Yeah, right.

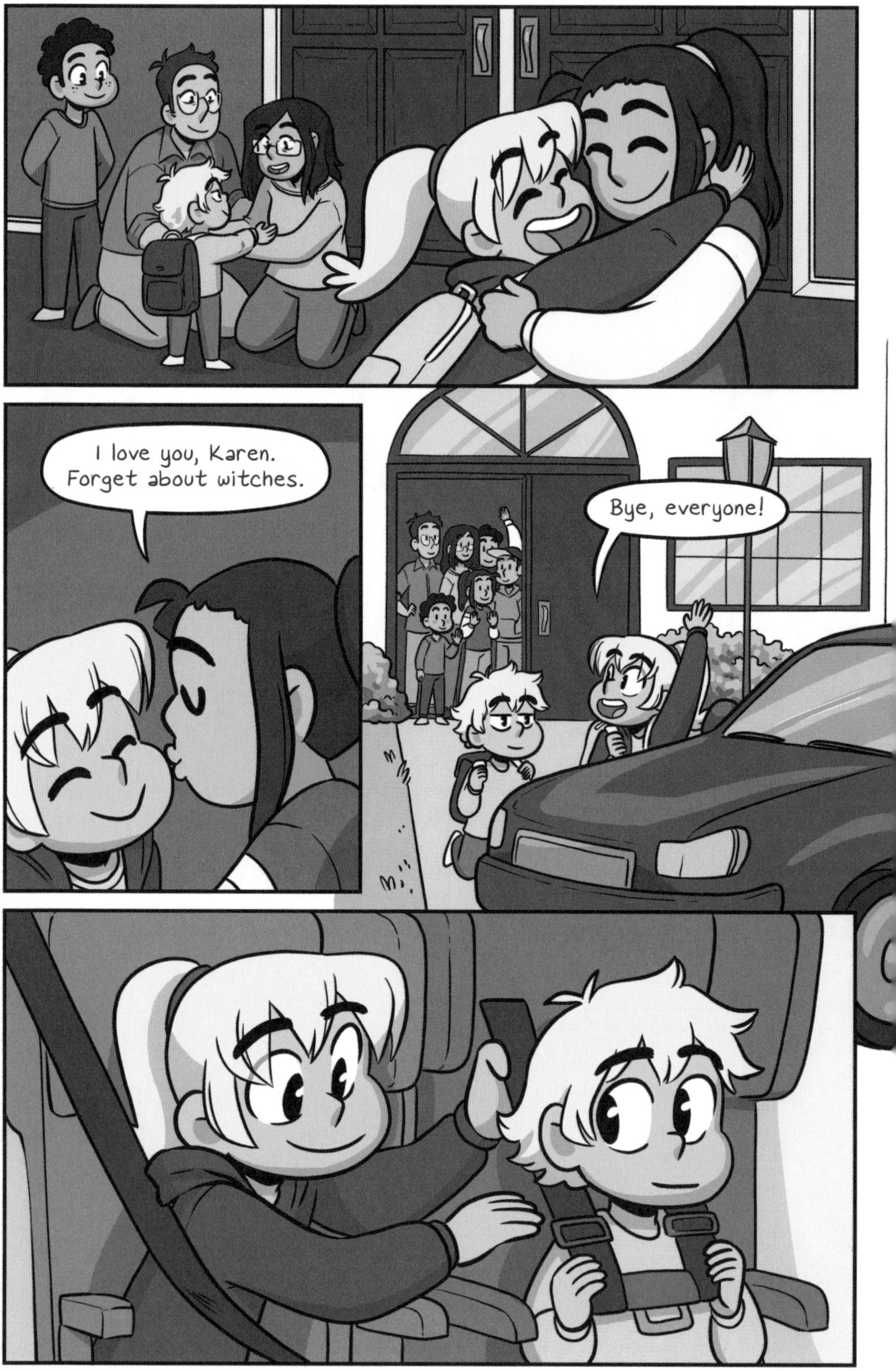
I love you, Karen.
Forget about witches.
Bye, everyone!

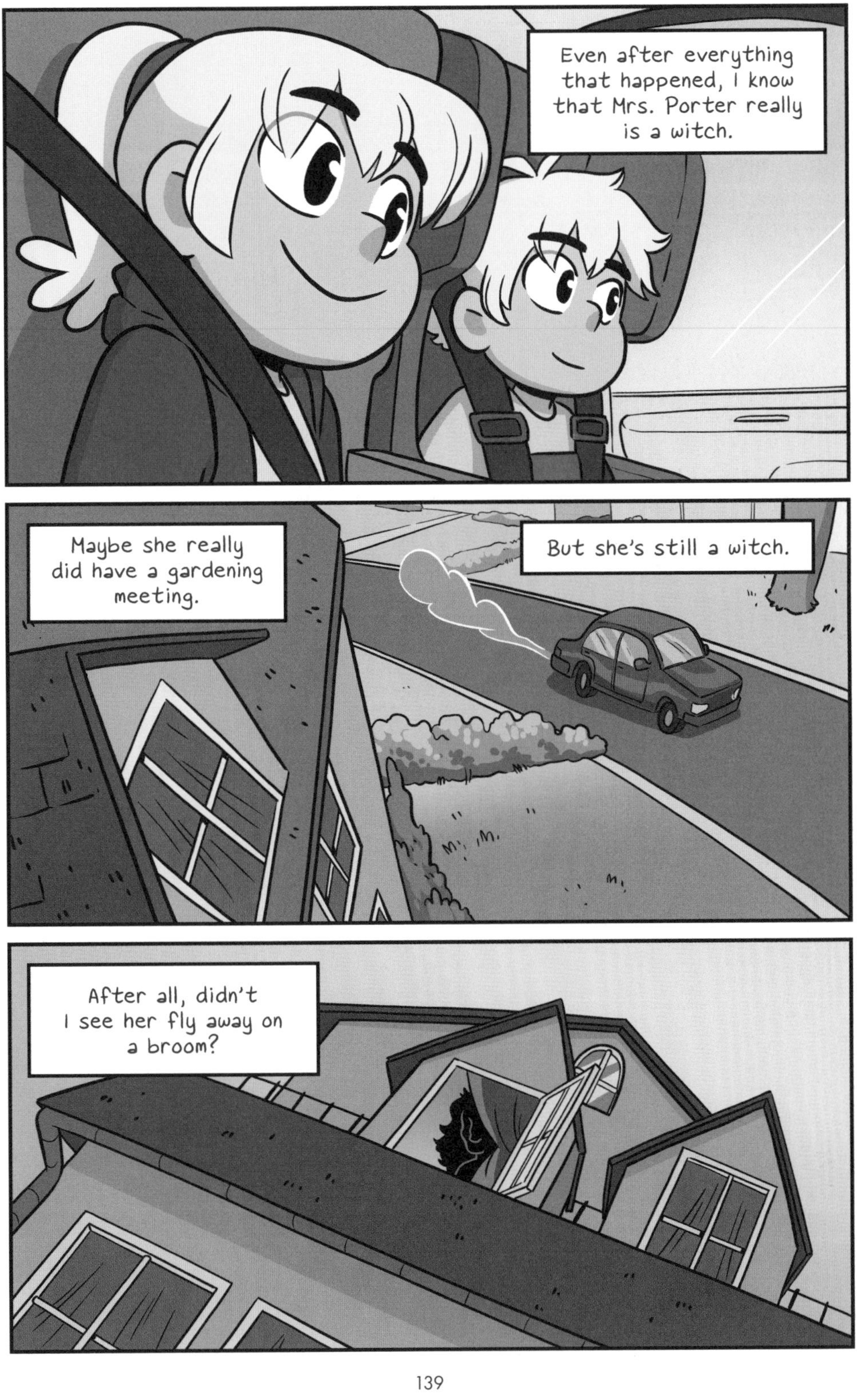
Even after everything that happened, I know that Mrs. Porter really is a witch.
Maybe she really did have a gardening meeting.
But she's still a witch.
After all, didn't I see her fly away on a broom?

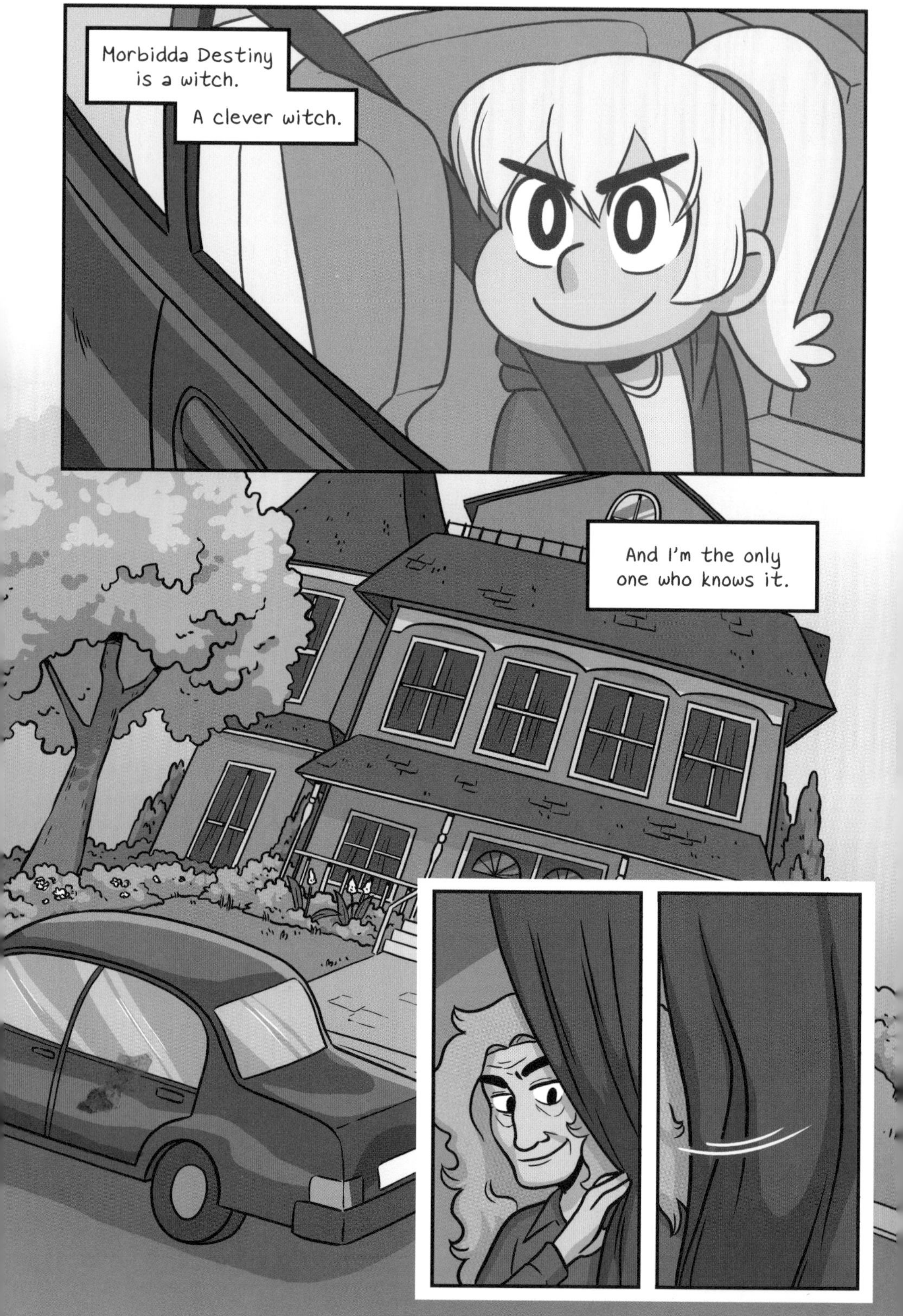
Morbidda Destiny
is a witch.
A clever witch.
And I'm the only
one who knows it.

ANN M. MARTIN'S The Baby-sitters Club is one of the most popular series in the history of publishing — with more than 176 million books in print worldwide — and inspired a generation of young readers. Her novels include *Belle Teal, A Corner of the Universe* (a Newbery Honor book), *Here Today, A Dog's Life,* and *On Christmas Eve,* as well as the much-loved collaborations, *P.S. Longer Letter Later* and *Snail Mail No More,* with Paula Danziger, and *The Doll People* and *The Meanest Doll in the World,* written with Laura Godwin and illustrated by Brian Selznick. She lives in upstate New York.

KATY FARINA is a comics artist and illustrator based in Los Angeles. She's currently a background painter on *She-Ra and the Princesses of Power* at DreamWorks TV. In the past, she's done work for BOOM! Studios, Oni Press, and Z2 Comics. Visit her online at katyfarina.com.

DON'T MISS THE BABY-SITTERS CLUB GRAPHIC NOVELS!

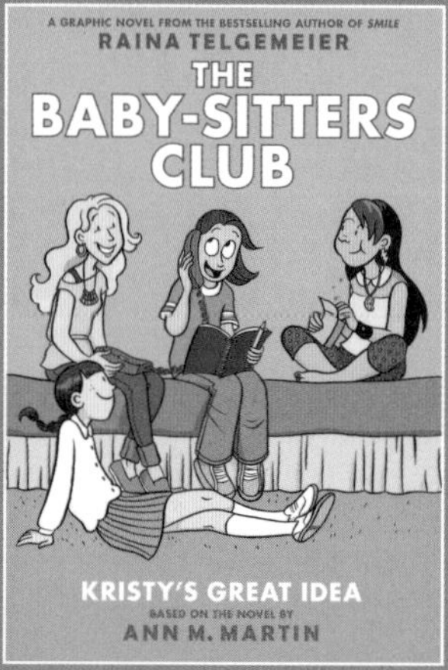
A GRAPHIC NOVEL FROM THE BESTSELLING AUTHOR OF SMILE
RAINA TELGEMEIER
THE BABY-SITTERS CLUB
KRISTY'S GREAT IDEA
BASED ON THE NOVEL BY
ANN M. MARTIN

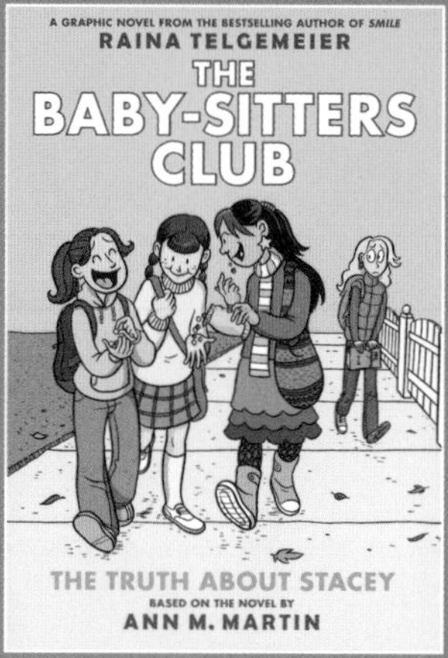
A GRAPHIC NOVEL FROM THE BESTSELLING AUTHOR OF SMILE
RAINA TELGEMEIER
THE BABY-SITTERS CLUB
THE TRUTH ABOUT STACEY
BASED ON THE NOVEL BY
ANN M. MARTIN

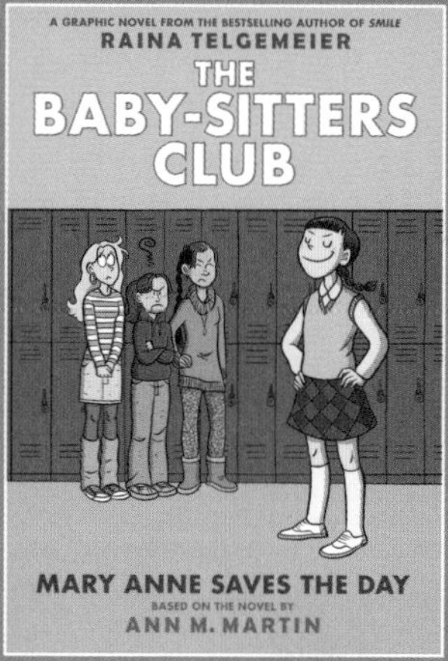
A GRAPHIC NOVEL FROM THE BESTSELLING AUTHOR OF SMILE
RAINA TELGEMEIER
THE BABY-SITTERS CLUB
MARY ANNE SAVES THE DAY
BASED ON THE NOVEL BY
ANN M. MARTIN

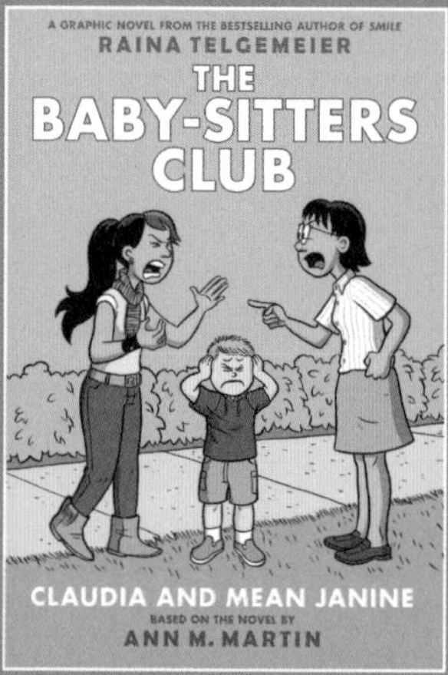
A GRAPHIC NOVEL FROM THE BESTSELLING AUTHOR OF SMILE
RAINA TELGEMEIER
THE BABY-SITTERS CLUB
CLAUDIA AND MEAN JANINE
BASED ON THE NOVEL BY
ANN M. MARTIN

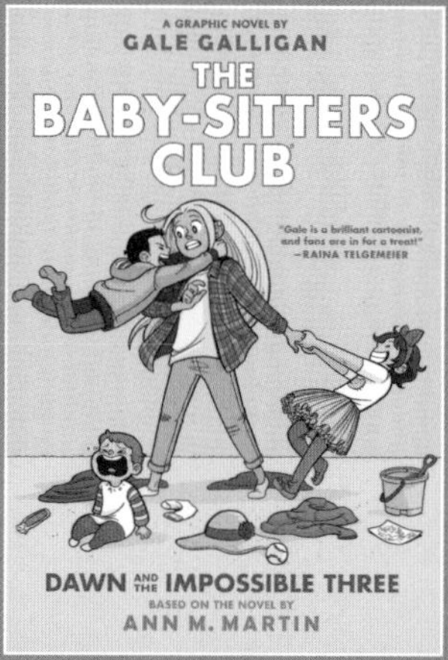
A GRAPHIC NOVEL BY
GALE GALLIGAN
THE BABY-SITTERS CLUB
"Gale is a brilliant cartoonist, and fans are in for a treat!"
—RAINA TELGEMEIER
DAWN AND THE IMPOSSIBLE THREE
BASED ON THE NOVEL BY
ANN M. MARTIN

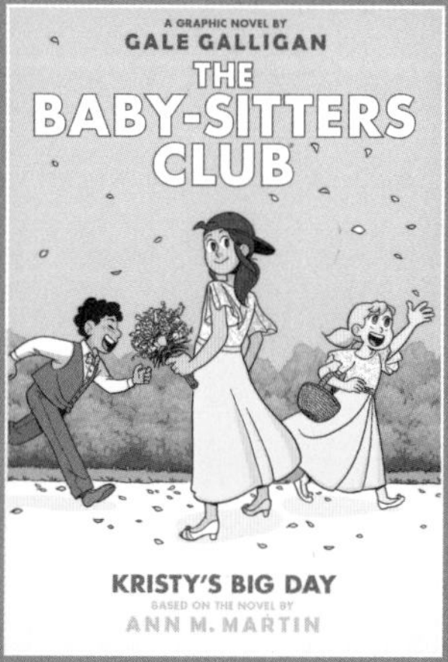
A GRAPHIC NOVEL BY
GALE GALLIGAN
THE BABY-SITTERS CLUB
KRISTY'S BIG DAY
BASED ON THE NOVEL BY
ANN M. MARTIN

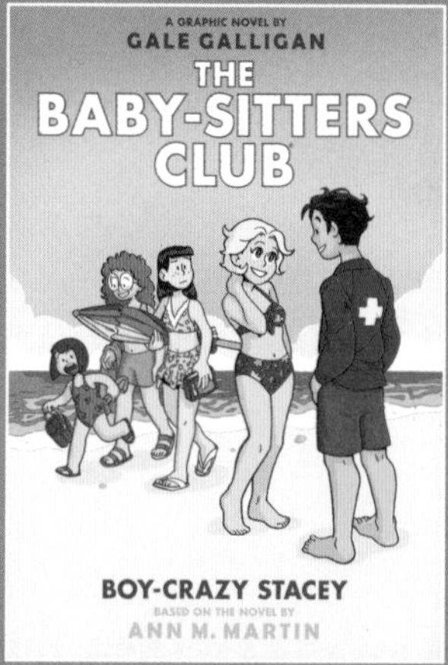
A GRAPHIC NOVEL BY
GALE GALLIGAN
THE BABY-SITTERS CLUB
BOY-CRAZY STACEY
BASED ON THE NOVEL BY
ANN M. MARTIN

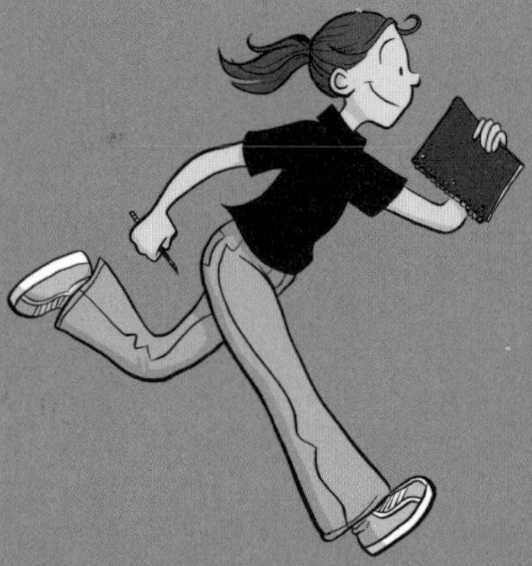